DAPHNE

BY THE SAME AUTHOR

If The Spirit Moves You
Wish I May
My Mother's Wedding Dress

DAPHNE

A NOVEL

JUSTINE PICARDIE

BLOOMSBURY

Published by Bloomsbury USA, New York

Every reasonable effort has been made to trace the copyright holders of material reproduced in this book, but if any have been inadvertently overlooked the publishers would be glad to hear from them.

All papers used by Bloomsbury USA are natural, recyclable products made from wood grown in well-managed forests. The manufacturing processes conform to the environmental regulations of the country of origin.

LIBRARY OF CONGRESS CATALOGING-IN-PUBLICATION DATA

Picardie, Justine.
Daphne / Justine Picardie.—1st U.S. ed.
p. cm.
ISBN-13: 978-1-59691-341-7 (hardcover)
ISBN-10: 1-59691-341-X (hardcover)
ISBN-13: 978-1-59691-340-0 (pbk.)
ISBN-10: 1-59691-340-1 (pbk.)

1. Du Maurier, Daphne, Dame, 1907–1989–Fiction. 2. Women authors, English–20th century–Fiction. 3. Biography–Research–Fiction. 4. Symington, John Alexander–Fiction. 5. Brontë family–Manuscripts–Fiction. 6. Forgery of manuscripts–Fiction. I. Title.

PR6116.I33D37 2008
823'.92–dc22
2008014694

First U.S. Edition 2008

1 3 5 7 9 10 8 6 4 2

Typeset by Hewer Text UK Ltd., Edinburgh
Printed in the United States of America by Quebecor World Fairfield

For my father, Michael Picardie

'We can never go back again, that much is certain. The past is still too close to us. The things we have tried to forget and put behind us would stir again, and that sense of fear, of furtive unrest, struggling at length to blind unreasoning panic – now mercifully stilled, thank God – might in some manner unforeseen become a living companion, as it had been before.'

Daphne du Maurier, *Rebecca*

'Menabilly was one of these houses, in which layers of time seemed to have worn thin in places, so that the past now and then showed through. There were rooms in which a lot seemed to have been going on before you entered them, and would probably do so again once you, the intruder, had left . . . There, even at midday, one sometimes had the distinct impression of being watched. In winter, I always tried to spend as little time as possible getting ready for bed, although the watchers were in no sense malevolent; they were just *there*.'

Oriel Malet, *Daphne du Maurier: Letters from Menabilly*

'It is impossible, with the Brontës, as with many other writers, to say when fiction ceases and fact begins, or how often the imagination will project an imaginary image upon a living personality . . .'

Daphne du Maurier, 'Second Thoughts on Branwell', Brontë Society Transactions

CHAPTER ONE

Menabilly, Cornwall, July 1957

To begin. Where to begin? To begin at the beginning, wherever that might be. Daphne woke, too early, just before dawn, when the sky had not yet come alight, but was as dark-grey as the Cornish sea. The beginning of another day; another day, how to bear another day? She heard the rats running behind the walls and in the attics; she felt the weight of last night's dreams upon her chest; the nightmares hung over her, heavier than the sky.

Daphne considered, for a moment, the idea of staying in bed, pulling the covers over her head, taking another sleeping pill, and another; letting the white roses on the faded wallpaper blur into a mist. But she made herself sit up, get out of bed, put on her clothes. There was a crisis, and she must face it. She must be brave.

She looked at herself, briefly, in the mirror of her dressing table, and shuddered, very slightly. The woman who looked back at her was still beautiful at fifty; but Daphne feared what she might see in the looking glass, not of what she saw now –

that, she could bear, the fine lines and wrinkles, the slackening flesh and greying hair, the shadows under her eyes – but of what she glimpsed in her dreams. Rebecca, she dreamt she saw Rebecca gazing back at her, eyes narrowed, lips smiling, a ghost in the mirror, the story come to life; the other woman in the bedroom last night.

'Pull yourself together,' Daphne said to herself, just under her breath, and she turned to her dog, Mouse, a West Highland terrier that was by her side, always; her companion when the family were gone, when the house was empty, though not silent; Menabilly was never silent, there were voices that whispered from its walls. 'The worst is over,' she murmured, like a prayer; for today could not be worse than yesterday, when she left Tommy in the nursing home in London. And the day before yesterday, today could not be more terrible than that; though its scenes kept spooling through her head, over and over again, she could not rid herself of what she saw then, when she arrived at the nursing home, having been summoned there from Menabilly.

'Sir Frederick is unwell,' his secretary had said to Daphne on the telephone, 'it seems to be his tummy playing up, and his nerves.' Her voice was blandly reassuring, so perhaps Tommy had managed to hide the worst from her, and from the rest of his staff at Buckingham Palace; he was such a stickler for protocol, for maintaining a polished and immaculate façade.

But when Daphne arrived at the nursing home, an expensively discreet redbrick Victorian townhouse just off Harley Street, she could not control her own anxiety, it seeped in with her, like the traffic fumes, creeping through the mahogany doors and up the dark burgundy carpeted stairs. A nurse directed her to Tommy's room on the top floor, and as Daphne climbed the stairs, her blood pulsed so loudly in her ears that she thought everyone would hear her, even though the thick carpets deadened her footsteps. She paused on the highest landing, and looked out of the window overlooking the mean backyards of Marylebone; all of them too small, thought Daphne, as she glanced down, to support those tall, proud-looking houses that rose up from the pavements; surely their foundations could not be sufficiently substantial to keep everything standing? Surely it would not take much to bring all of it crashing down? She forced herself away from the window, trying to look purposeful, steadfast, though she felt dizzy as she went up the final flight of stairs and into Tommy's room. The floor seemed to be tilting, it was like stepping on to a boat; nothing was stable or firm beneath her, as she walked over to the hospital bed. 'Tommy,' she said to the body lying there, and as he opened his eyes, they filled with tears, her husband was weeping, he would not stop, and his hands were shaking, like her voice. She asked him if he could explain what was wrong, and he did not answer, until at last he whispered, 'I cannot ready myself . . .' She did not understand what he meant, and then he said, 'I can't go on, I can't do this, I'd be better off dead . . .'

As he spoke, tears trickled down his face; this man who Daphne had never before seen cry, Lieutenant General Sir Frederick Browning, Treasurer to the Duke of Edinburgh, but the titles seemed to mean nothing. It was her husband, Tommy, yet he was almost unrecognisable; suddenly become pitiful and weak and shrunken, his hair lank, his face like yellowing parchment against the starched white sheets. She sat with him for a little while, but he did not stop weeping, and eventually, she went to find a doctor, to ask him to explain what was wrong. The doctor was a young man, not the chap in charge, but he seemed confident enough. 'Your husband has suffered a very serious mental breakdown,' he said to Daphne, and she nodded, as if she was a woman strong enough to hear such news without crumpling, but her head was spinning again; no, not spinning, it was compressed, as if there were too much pressure within it, as if the outside and the inside were misaligned. She tried to follow what the doctor was telling her; it was something to do with nervous exhaustion, the after-effects of Tommy's army career in two world wars, and the pressure of his responsibility for the Royal Family, and he'd been drinking far too much, and must stop. His liver was damaged, but the main problem was . . . the problem was . . . How was she to deal with this problem?

Of course, the doctor didn't know everything, and nor did Daphne, not then in the stuffy, airless rooms of the nursing home, not until she got back to the flat, Tommy's flat; his London lair, even though Daphne paid for it, just like she paid for everything. The telephone started ringing as soon as she put the key in the front door, as if it had been waiting for her, as if someone was watching and waiting, waiting for her arrival: an ambush, of sorts. It took her a minute or two to get the key to turn in the lock, but the telephone carried on ringing, insistent, shrill, and so Daphne picked it up as soon as she'd got into the hall, without even switching the lamp on, caught unawares in the twilight. 'Hello?' she said, not wanting to give her name, not knowing which title to use here on this unfamiliar territory.

'Is that Lady Browning?' said a woman's voice.

Daphne said yes, though she felt uncertain as she spoke, as if this woman might accuse her of being an impostor, an intruder in Tommy's flat. The voice sounded familiar, but it was somehow surprising to hear the woman speak out loud, as if she were a character in one of Daphne's books, suddenly brought to life, yet disembodied at the end of a phone line. Daphne recognised the woman's name, though she didn't really know her, not properly; they'd met once at the ballet, in Covent Garden, a year or so ago, when she had been a blurred face from Tommy's London life. But Daphne sensed some danger, even then, after that single encounter, for in her mind she'd christened her the Snow Queen, like one of the ballerinas they watched on the stage that evening; irresistibly beautiful and bewitching to those under her spell, yet cold at heart, turning everything to ice around her. Not that Daphne said this to Tommy at the time, nor to anyone else, it would have sounded so childish, though the woman made her feel like a child, albeit a suspicious one, and she'd marked her down as one to watch, for she knew her kind.

The woman's tone was clipped, rather patronising, a little like her mother when she had been angry with her for reasons that Daphne, as a child, did not fully understand. 'We've reached a crisis,' she said to Daphne on the telephone, 'a breaking point.' Those were her words, and as she said them, they stuck in Daphne's head, and she wanted to say, 'you've broken everything, it's your fault,' but she stayed silent, and tried to concentrate on what the woman was saying, on her relentless stream of words. 'We need to talk,' the woman said, but she was doing all the talking, she was having an affair with Tommy, they were lovers, she said the words out loud. 'We are lovers,' she said, 'and we have been lovers for well over a year. I love him, you must understand this, I've left my husband for Tommy, this is not a passing fling.'

Daphne put her hand to her mouth to choke a sob, and felt her throat constrict. 'I must tell you,' the woman went on, her voice low and urgent, 'that it's clear to me that Tommy's increasing anxiety – his intolerable anxiety – is largely due to the stress of keeping our relationship a secret from you, of leading a double life. And that's also why he's drinking too much: it's his way of trying to cope with you.'

At first, Daphne was shocked, almost too shocked to breathe, she was holding her breath, as if she'd slipped into a pool of icy water. And then a hot flood of rage came pumping through her veins, her heart was thudding, and she wanted to say, 'How dare you, how dare you say these things to me, how dare you talk of yourself as my husband's lover?' But she couldn't lash out at this woman, this interloper that had invaded her life. Daphne didn't want the Snow Queen's voice in Tommy's flat, nor in her head; she didn't want any sort of prolonged conversation, it was too humiliating, she couldn't allow herself to rage at this woman, or to plead or be abject.

'What truly matters now,' she said to the woman, keeping her voice smooth, mouthing the lies, joining in with their duplicity, making it hers, as well, 'is Tommy. We both know that he's terribly ill, and somehow we must rise to the occasion, the two of us together, we must rise above our embarrassment and discomfort, for his sake.'

'You've been very sensible,' said the woman, at the end of the telephone call. But Daphne did not feel sensible. She felt . . . she felt she did not know where to begin.

Afterwards, she thought about ringing her daughters, and confiding in them. But what, exactly, was she to say to them? They were both still so young, Tessa an army wife at nineteen, and now her hands were full with two babies, and Flavia was also just a newly-wed, married to another soldier, a captain in the Coldstream Guards; and it wasn't fair to expect the girls to deal with problems that were not of their own making. Daphne glanced over to her daughters' wedding photographs on the sideboard, she and Tommy looking like proud parents, such a charming couple, everyone said. But it was all a sham, because he was already betraying her when he stood beside her in the church while Flavia and Alistair were saying their wedding vows this time last year, and yet she was so foolishly oblivious then, blind to Tommy's treachery; she suspected nothing as he smiled at her, all the while a traitor to their own wedding vows.

And now the entire family was supposed to be gathering for a party at Menabilly in less than a fortnight's time, that was the hell of it, to celebrate her and Tommy's twenty-fifth wedding anniversary. The invitations had already been sent out, everyone was expected: Tessa and her husband Peter and their children; Flavia and Alistair, and Daphne's beloved youngest son, her only son, her boy Kits, home from Eton. And Daphne's mother, of course, and her two sisters, and her cousins, the Llewelyn Davies – the entire clan were invited to Menabilly. But Daphne knew she must find the strength to tell all of them that there was to be no party, and an acceptable excuse must be found, as well, for she could not tell them the truth; the truth was too terrible to be told.

The phone calls to the girls would have to wait until tomorrow, though; she was too exhausted to speak, let alone come up with reasonable explanations. She drew the dusty curtains in the flat, ran a bath and sat in the tepid water, allowing herself to cry, turning on the taps to hide the sound of her sobbing, and then she let the dirty water drain away, and she felt drained as well, and empty, there was nothing left, she didn't want to feel anything, she couldn't bear the feeling to come back again. She dried herself on one of the threadbare towels, wondering why the flat was so comfortless; and was it part of the problem, her fault, another of her faults, for she'd not been constant, she failed to be a good wife at Tommy's side; and was that why he sought comfort elsewhere? She started shivering, her legs trembling, the numbness ebbing away; so she swallowed two sleeping pills, to blot everything out, to be shrouded in blessed nothingness, just for a few hours.

And then in the morning, she took a taxi back to the nursing home through the dusty London streets, beneath an opaque city sky, stretched tight like the skin of a drum, enclosing everyone within it, sealing them in, so that there could be no escape for any of them. 'We are all in this together,' she whispered to herself, as she went into the nursing home, yet she did not want to be seen there, she did not want to see anyone, so she hurried out of the taxi, head down, furtive, like a woman with a guilty secret.

It would be so much easier to turn a corner and vanish into the city, but she forced herself up the stairs again, and through the door into Tommy's room, closing it quietly behind her. There he lay, like yesterday, dishevelled and unkempt, as if he had left his impeccably dressed public self back in Buckingham Palace, abandoning it as easily as a snake sheds its skin. She sat on a chair by his bed, and reached for his left hand, held it in both of hers, so that she could feel his wedding ring as she spoke, keeping her own hands from shaking, keeping her voice gentle and calm against the muffled, churning background of the London traffic on the other side of the locked window.

'I had a phone call last night,' said Daphne, 'and now I know everything about the affair, more or less.'

Tommy looked at her, saying nothing, but his eyes widened in fear, and she said, 'Don't worry, darling, I don't want a divorce, and I hope that you don't, either. We just need to straighten things out between us, don't we?'

And still he was silent, so she kept spooning out banalities, in a soothing voice she barely recognised as her own. 'We've had to lead such separate lives,' she said to him, 'almost from the beginning, haven't we? There was your army career, right from the start, and all those long years when you were posted abroad during the war, you doing your duty, and me writing away all the while, keeping the home fires burning, and then you got your grand job at Buckingham Palace, which was such an honour, darling, I know that, I truly do, and I'm so proud of you, I've always been proud. But that's kept you in London during the week, and you know I can't work there, it's too noisy and busy for me to think straight, I have to be in Cornwall to write, I must be in Menabilly, or the books will dry up, and so will the money. But we've been so happy together, and we can be happy again.'

He sighed, and then coughed, a small, dry, pathetic little cough. 'I love you, my darling,' she said to Tommy, even though she loathed him at that moment.

'I love you too,' he said, but he whimpered the words as he wept; and she felt nothing but contempt for him then, for he sounded like a little boy, not a man; he'd lost the commanding authority she had fallen in love with, her handsome major in the Grenadier Guards, a quarter of a century ago. She did not refer to their physical relationship, or its decline in the last decade; they did not talk about that; they never had done. She was fifty, and he was ten years older; she assumed that these things happened, this slow fading away of desire, this dwindling of the flesh. Boy Browning: that was his nickname in the regiment when she first met him in 1932, and it stuck, even as his boyish good looks aged; and now she was following in his footsteps, youth shrinking behind them, everything withering away.

Daphne could not bear to stay another night in London knowing that she was sleeping in the bed where her husband had been with his lover, her head on the same pillows, tangled in the same sheets; knowing that this place contained their words of endearment, their secrets, so she'd already crammed her things into a suitcase and taken it with her to the nursing home. She wondered if she should feel guilty about abandoning Tommy alone in his room on the top floor; and what would the doctors think of her, leaving her husband in London? 'Sir Frederick will need complete bed rest here for at least another week,' the young doctor said, taking her to one side as soon as she arrived. And she knew then that she would go mad if she stayed there with her husband;

she would end up a wreck like him, locked up in that suffocating attic, with just a square of sky glimpsed through the window.

'I'm going to have to go home to sort everything out, darling,' she said to her husband, trying to keep her voice bright. 'I'm cancelling the wedding anniversary party, so you don't need to worry about that, you just concentrate on having a jolly good rest here, and catch up on your sleep.' She despised herself for sounding like a mother talking to a child; but she could not help herself, she could not help him, everything was twisted and distorted out of shape.

'Where are my boys?' he said to her; and that was all he could say, a grown man asking for his teddy bears, the boys, he called them, the tattered teddies he'd kept since childhood, that had travelled in his case to and from London and Menabilly for years, and before then, around the world with him, while he fought wars and led regiments of men; a steely-eyed general upon whom a nation depended, yet who himself relied on the comfort of a baby's soft toys. 'You must find my boys,' he said. 'I need to have them here with me.'

'I'm not sure where they are, darling,' she said. 'When did you see them last?' And he starting crying again and shook his head, unable to speak. They stared at each other mutely for a few seconds, and then she fled from the room, and went straight to Paddington Station. It seemed the only thing to do, to take the train back down to Cornwall, to make the long journey home.

And so here she was, alone again; not that she would ever be entirely alone in Menabilly; not here, with all the voices murmuring, soft yet insistent, asking her to listen . . .

'I'm not listening,' said Daphne, and went downstairs to let the dog out in the garden. The sun was just rising, but not yet visible in the flushed pink sky above the tall trees that surrounded Menabilly. She decided, suddenly, to walk down through the woods to the beach; to keep moving, she must keep moving. 'What is past is also future,' she muttered to herself, but she was not quite sure what this meant, though she believed it to be true when she wrote it late last night in a letter to Tommy. She did not know whether she would send the letter; she did not know the right thing to say to him; she feared that words had failed her, had failed them. Would they ever find the right words for each other again? It was as if they had somehow drifted into speaking in two different dialects, with no translator; and yet, right up until this crisis, they were still pretending to understand each other, they picked up on the occasional familiar word or phrase; they nodded and smiled, they were always apparently civilised.

As for Rebecca, the shape-shifting mistress of dissembling and pretence . . . 'I know you're here,' said Daphne, quietly. 'What do you have to say for yourself now?'

The woods were all shadows, tangled and overgrown, slippery with mud and moss, scented with a sweet decay, even in the high summer, but Daphne was sure-footed, she walked this path so often, Rebecca's path from the house to the sea. She passed the corpse of Tommy's old boat, *Ygdrasil*, that he sailed on their wedding day to the little church just along the estuary at Lanteglos, slipping through the rippling, silvery water, and afterwards they'd spent their honeymoon aboard it, hidden away in Frenchman's Creek, the waves lapping at them like a secret caress, only the birds as witnesses to their kisses, and the crescent of a new moon. But now the boat lay abandoned on dry land, rotting into a ghost ship, choked with ivy, tendrils of rhododendrons reaching out to it, threatening to submerge it for good; the trees encroaching on it, as always at Menabilly, their roots like dead men's fingers, ready to advance and recapture their lost ground. They sighed in the wind, the leaves rustling in warning around Daphne, as if she were the intruder, here in her own kingdom, as she followed the ribbon of her path through the woods, until she reached the beach, where the trees must make way for the waves.

The tide was low this morning, the ancient shipwreck visible, a century-old skeleton half covered in sand, its funeral wreath of rotting seaweed draped about it still; and there was something almost obscene about its nakedness, its humiliation, revealed for all to see; the seagulls swooping over it with their mocking cries. But there was no sign of Rebecca, that sly girl, whom time did not fade. 'Where are you?' called Daphne, and her voice was caught by the wind and echoed against the rocks. 'You, you, you . . .' murmured the echo.

Daphne picked up a stone and threw it, and another one, and another. They cracked against the shingle, like gunshots, and she thought of Tommy's revolver, back at the house, she must hide it before he came home to Menabilly, it wasn't safe for him to have a gun, or his bows and arrows, which stood ready in sharp serried rows by the front door. He was at breaking point, something might snap, irrevocably, the act would be over, the veneer cracked; and in a blind rage, he could shoot her, like Maxim killed Rebecca, in the sinister little cottage on the beach. But Rebecca wouldn't die, even now, twenty-one years after Daphne first wrote her into existence; except then Daphne imagined herself as the second Mrs de Winter, shy and young and inexperienced, obsessed and possessed by Rebecca, haunted by the ghost of her glamorous predecessor. And slowly, slowly, the pattern turned in on itself, like a kaleidoscope, until Daphne was Rebecca, and her husband was ready to kill her, and replace her with a younger woman, but a clever one, no innocent anonymous girl, this time; for Daphne must face the implacable Snow Queen, who put a sliver of icy glass into Tommy's eye, as well as his heart, so that he could no longer see straight, he was cold to everything he once loved: a doomed and frozen de Winter.

'Stop it,' said Daphne, out loud, shocked at how fast these thoughts had risen and consumed her, like the tide on the turn, and the dog looked at her, surprised. 'Get a grip,' she whispered; she must get a grip; she could not let herself *be* gripped by the wild ideas that twisted and coiled within and without her; by these irrational thoughts of plots. There were no plots. 'This is it,' she said to herself, 'there is nothing more than this.' She was a fifty-year-old woman, walking on the beach, not long before her silver wedding anniversary, with a family gathering to postpone, lists to make and dates to check. Her husband was having an affair, but this could be dealt with, it was a messy episode in the ordinary muddle of life; the marriage would recover, just as it did after Daphne's affairs, not that poor Tommy necessarily knew about them all those years ago though perhaps he guessed, except surely not about Gertie, Tommy could not begin to comprehend such a thing. But Gertie was dead and gone; disappeared from the world of the living in a way that Rebecca was not.

Not Rebecca. She was not Rebecca. She wrote Rebecca, and she could write her off. She killed Rebecca, after all; she made her die, chose the manner of her ending, and if Rebecca rose again, why, she was nothing without Daphne; for she was Daphne's creation.

She whistled for the dog, turned her back on the waves and the melancholy wreck, avoided looking at Rebecca's cottage, empty now, and walked homewards. It was a mistake to come down to the sea so early, it was not part of her routine; she should still be fast asleep, the routine must be resumed, the routes, she and Tommy called them, the safe routes by which their lives were mapped and secure. She needed a bath and breakfast and then work, she must concentrate on another book, nothing to do with Rebecca, this would be the way to recovery, this was the only way forward, step by step, moment by moment, until lunch and an afternoon walk with the dog, as usual, to clear her head, and more writing, she had letters to send, and dinner and reading and bed, and so on, and on and on, inching to safety, away from the abyss, until everything became clearer again

Tod was awake by the time Daphne returned to the house, pottering around the kitchen, making breakfast. She looked at Daphne but did not question her; they knew each other too well for that, for Tod had been with Daphne for nearly forty years, on and off, more often than not, first as Daphne's governess in childhood, and then as governess to Daphne's own children, and now at seventy, she was still part of the household, though installed in a little flat of her own at the end of a long passage on the other side of the house. Tommy did not like her; he called her Mrs Danvers, after Rebecca's macabre housekeeper, which was absurd, of course, for there was nothing unnerving about Tod, just as there was nothing inherently murderous about Tommy, and though she was devoted to Daphne, it was not at all the same as Mrs Danvers' obsessive love for Rebecca.

What was clear, thought Daphne, as she looked at the familiar figure of Tod – rounded and comfortable, more like Mrs Tiggywinkle than Mrs Danvers – was that something would have to be done, if Tommy was to give up the London flat and the London job and the London woman, and live full-time at Menabilly, as Daphne suspected might be necessary in order to save their marriage. But he was often irritable and angry with Tod, and her feelings would be hurt, as had happened before now, like that uneasy Sunday lunch, not long ago, when Tod said that her throat hurt and asked Daphne for a remedy, and Tommy snapped, 'just cut it'. It would be impossible for the three of them to live together here, and yet Daphne felt responsible for Tod, who would be lonely if she was dismissed from Menabilly.

And then it came upon her again, the dread, with its choking sensation familiar from her recurring nightmares, not those of Rebecca in the mirror, but the other dreams, of the high tide, when Daphne was in the dark water, trying to keep afloat, but it was overwhelming, and she knew that she might drown. She must not panic: if the panic became too strong, she would be sucked under, dragged down to the depths; she must remember to breathe, though her throat was closing up.

'My dear,' said Tod, 'you look so peaky. You must eat something, you need your strength at a time like this.'

Daphne wanted to cry – it was easier to be alone, not to hear the kindness in her old governess's voice – but she would not break down in front of Tod; not after witnessing Tommy's terrible gulping tears in the nursing home, his face contorted, looking like a nightmarish gargoyle version of himself; Boy Browning turned into a weeping old man. She cleared her throat and told Tod that she was going to have some tea, and then she would be writing in her garden hut, as usual.

'Very sensible,' said Tod. 'Settle yourself into a routine, again. Best get on with your work.'

As Daphne walked across the roughly mown lawns in front of the house, she tried to gather her thoughts, her strength; she needed her strength, like Tod said. She could not run away from here. This was it; this was the task ahead of her, to . . . to do what, exactly? To return to her work, when her marriage was not working? She opened the door of her writing hut, breathing in its familiar smell of dust and wood and paraffin fumes from the old heater that warmed it in winter. Scattered across the desk were the untidy sheaves of notes and books she'd abandoned before rushing to London, to Tommy . . . was there any point in trying to pick up the pieces of what she had left here? What was she thinking, before the unthinkable happened? Daphne looked at the opened books – the Shakespeare Head edition of the Brontës; four volumes of their letters and juvenilia, filled with her pencilled marks in the margins – and it seemed to her as if it had been years since she had leafed through the pages, even though she recognised some of her notes as those she scrawled just a few days ago, along with the beginnings of a letter to the editor of these books, a Mr Symington. And then there was that name she'd written in capital letters on the front of her latest notepad. 'Branwell Brontë . . .' Daphne spoke his name out loud. 'Branwell?' she said again, but there was no answer, just the creaking of the floorboards as she walked across to her desk.

Why Branwell Brontë? Why try to write a biography of him now? It was risky, of course – he was a notoriously hopeless case, famous only for his failures – yet could she simply cast him aside; could she abandon the research she had already begun on him? Perhaps Tod was right, it would be good for her to get on with the book; Branwell might even be a lifeline. Yet the thought of Branwell in the water with her was not much help; he would be drowning, drunk already, or stupefied with opium, a dead weight dragging her down into the darkness, into the depths, the two of them tangled together, their limbs embraced . . . And really, what was the point of submerging herself with Branwell, or attempting to rescue him, when she had so many immediate problems to face? There were the conversations with Tommy to be had, and with his doctors; and she must find excuses for Kits to explain his father's stay in the nursing home, though perhaps the girls were old enough to understand the truth now, they'd seen enough of his drinking already, and the bouts of depression and melancholy which had led to his family nickname: Moper. ('Don't call me that,' he'd often said, but Daphne simply laughed. 'That laugh,' he said, 'the famous du Maurier laugh . . .')

Yet despite all the obstacles, despite everything, Daphne knew that to give up the book might be worse than continuing; for she couldn't bear the thought of being without it, of the emptiness and sense of futility that would engulf her otherwise; she must have some sense of purpose, a steady framework within which her mounting anxiety might be contained. If words had failed her with Tommy, then she must somehow grope her way into putting other sentences together, piecing them into paragraphs, into pages, however slowly; reminding herself that she was still a writer, even if she was a failure in every other part of her life.

And she was almost sure that Branwell was her subject. She had been preoccupied by him, ever since her pilgrimage to Yorkshire last winter when she visited the Brontë Parsonage in Haworth and walked through the austere stone house where the Brontës lived, and died, in the shadow of the graveyard; Branwell the first to go at thirty-one, the failure of the family, haunted by his sense that he had achieved nothing great nor good in his life, by the spectre of his unwritten masterpieces, his unpublished novels, his unfinished paintings; tormented by the knowledge of unfulfilled promise, of hope turned to ashes, to dust.

Daphne sat in front of her typewriter, keeping her eyes down, well away from the view of the sea, away from the wreck, away from the depths. 'Stay away from the water,' she said to herself, 'keep your eyes on the page.' And she tried to force her writing brain into action, making it tick over, clicking, forming connections; but would it misfire? The nagging anxiety could not be kept at bay; no, it was in the bay, along with the shipwreck. She glanced over at her notebook from the trip to Haworth, when she'd spent hours in the library of the Brontë Parsonage, reading fragments of diaries and letters, and the childhood stories of Angria, willing herself back in time; and then when the stone walls became too oppressive, she'd gone outside, following the path up across the moors, trying to walk herself into *Wuthering Heights*.

Closing her eyes against the sunlight, Daphne pictured a pen moving across a page; Branwell's hand, writing his Angrian chronicles, feverish and furious, shut away in an airless room on a sultry afternoon, when the thunder and the rain was pent up behind the clouds, and he was waiting, waiting to escape out into the world. Or was there no escape from the imaginary world that he conceived for himself and his sisters, the fantastical landscape they called 'the infernal world'? Was there no better place to be than there, amidst the Angrian wars and conquests, or the romances and tragedies of Gondal?

'Gondal,' she whispered, aloud, speaking the word that she'd already seized upon for herself, for Gondal was what she called her own, most private make-believes and secrets and fictions; Gondal was an island that she had already explored, if not yet conquered . . .

Daphne imagined reaching out and taking Branwell's pen from him and writing him into life on the page; the red-headed boy who burnt out in that infernal world, reincarnated in her brilliant book, her best yet; to match the best of Charlotte and Emily's work, to match Branwell, too, for in proving him to be a lost genius, she would also prove herself.

And then she heard it again, the mocking laughter, just behind her, or was it inside her? Was it a magpie's laugh or a seagull's cry or a call of the curlew, wheeling and soaring in the sky? Where was it coming from?

Daphne remembered a game she played as a child with her sisters and their friends in the garden at Cannon Hall; the other girls called it 'Grandmother's Footsteps' but Daphne christened it 'Old Witch'. She had to stand at the end of the garden, with her back turned to the rest, and one by one they crept closer to her. Every few minutes she spun around, suddenly, to try to see them moving, and if she caught one of them out, that girl would have to go back and begin again. But there was always one who moved silently and pounced while your back was still turned. Now, the rear of Daphne's neck prickled as she waited for a hand to tap her on the shoulder or to feel another's breath in her ear, but she would not turn round, she must not look behind her, she could never go back again.

Menabilly,
Par,
Cornwall

9th July 1957

Dear Mr Symington,
Forgive me for writing to you today
without a proper introduction. We have never met, but I
am a great admirer of yours, having spent many hours
absorbed in studying your magnificent Shakespeare Head
edition of the collected works of the Brontës that you
edited alongside your late colleague, Mr Wise. I am a keen
member of the Brontë Society, and have been so for many
years, though I never had the opportunity of meeting Mr
Wise, who I understand was a former president of the
Society back in the 1920s. I joined the Brontë Society as a
girl, some years previously to Mr Wise's tenure when Sir
William Robertson Nicoll was still president, following the
encouragement of my governess, who shared with me a
passion for the Brontës. Indeed, my first novel, 'The Loving
Spirit', took its title from a line from my favourite of Emily
Brontë's poems, 'Self-Interrogation'.

However, it is not as a novelist that I write to you today,
but as an amateur researcher, hoping to seek your advice,
for I am aware, of course, of your status as a leading Brontë
scholar, particularly regarding the enigmatic Branwell.

I am fascinated by the facsimiles of the Angrian
manuscripts that you reproduced in the Shakespeare Head
edition, and have laboured to decipher the minute

handwriting in which they were written by Branwell and Charlotte. For an amateur like myself, it is of course difficult to distinguish between the handwriting of the four Brontë children, which seems remarkably alike to an inexpert eye. But I am much struck by the vast amount of Branwell's work that has never been published and has been dismissed as worthless, without even being transcribed. Indeed, the more I read and think about Branwell, the more certain I am that a myth has grown up around him that has obscured his true worth, by which I mean, the stories of his debauchery have been used to discredit him. It seems to me that because his sisters are so loved and admired, it has somehow become necessary to despise their poor, belittled brother.

I have been in touch with Mrs Weir, the former secretary of the Brontë Society, who told me that you possessed many of Branwell's manuscripts – that you were, in fact, the leading collector of his work – but it is possible that I misunderstood her, and that these manuscripts are all in the Brontë Parsonage Museum in Haworth, or the Brotherton Collection at Leeds University. I know that you were formerly curator and librarian at both of these venerable institutions, and are therefore possessed of a unique expertise, hence my approach to you. I would be very grateful if you could tell me how to locate the whereabouts of Branwell's manuscripts, and also your opinion of his talents as a writer.

In short, I am fascinated by Branwell, and cannot understand why modern academic research has ignored or misrepresented him. I am quite certain that Emily's Heathcliff was developed from Branwell's fictional alter ego,

Northangerland, as was Charlotte's Mr Rochester, and that the Brontë sisters exchanged ideas and manuscripts with their brother far more frequently than is generally supposed. Hence my eagerness to know whether you think this a theory worth pursuing,

Yours sincerely,

Daphne du maurier

CHAPTER TWO

Newlay Grove,
Horsforth,
Leeds
Telephone: 2615 Horsforth

11th July 1957

Dear Miss du Maurier,

It was an unexpected pleasure to receive
your letter, and to learn of your interest in Branwell Brontë.
As you so rightly say, he has been very unfairly treated by
Brontë scholars and commentators, from Mrs Gaskell
onwards; indeed, my task in restoring his reputation has been
a lonely one, which has set me apart from others in the field
of scholarship, though my singular knowledge of Branwell's
manuscripts has been rewarding, of course.

I am taking the liberty of enclosing two exceedingly rare
books from my library, both of them from my privately printed
limited editions of Branwell's writings. The first is a nicely
bound copy of 'And The Weary Are At Rest', a story of
Alexander Percy, otherwise known as the buccaneering

Northangerland, a swashbuckling hero who you may already be familiar with from the Brontë children's chronicles of Angria, though this particular adventure was written when Branwell was a young man. Only fifty copies of this edition were printed in 1924, in a literary collaboration I undertook with my former colleague at the Brontë Society, Mr Clement Shorter. The second item, 'The Leyland Manuscripts', was produced by myself in equally small quantities the following year, and is a collection of my complete transcription of Branwell's letters to a close friend, a sculptor named Joseph Leyland. The original documents were held in the library that I assembled for Sir Edward (later Lord) Brotherton, at that time housed in Roundhay Hall, his mansion in Leeds where I had the pleasure to work. As you doubtless know, Sir Edward served as president of the Brontë Society from 1927 until his death in 1930.

I believe you will find both of these volumes to be of interest, and should you wish to keep them, perhaps you could be so kind as to forward me a cheque for £4?

I take it that you have a complete set of the Shakespeare Head edition? I am most grateful for your kind remarks about my work as editor of these Brontë volumes. I laboured over this great task for many years, and latterly without much help from Mr Wise, it must be said, when he was in the fog and mist surrounding the alleged exposure of his supposed forgeries in other fields. This was over two decades ago, of course, and at the time it would have been inappropriate for me to offer any comment on such murky matters. Nor would I wish to apportion blame or judgement now. However, between ourselves – and I know I can count *on your complete discretion on keeping this secret – I very much doubt the genuineness of the various signatures of Charlotte and Emily Brontë which appear on many of the earlier manuscripts. How can we therefore be sure that it was Emily, and not Branwell, who wrote such marvellous poems?*

Mr Symington paused, crossed out the final sentence of his letter, and then tutted to himself as his fountain pen dripped ink on to the already blotted paper. He bent his head closer to the page to examine his words, squinting through his spectacles in the shadows, and sighed. It was noon, but the summer's day did not intrude into Mr Symington's study; the blinds were drawn against the sunshine, as he always instructed, to protect the contents of his bookshelves from the damaging light. Mr Symington himself looked as pale as the papery leaves of the manuscripts that he had just retrieved from within hidden boxes and files; he looked as if he did not often venture outside.

He was almost certain that he had locked the door of his study behind him, as was his custom, and put the key in his pocket, along with all the others, but then, suddenly, he felt anxious that he was mistaken, and stood up again, to check that the door was securely fastened, though he had already done so several times this morning. 'You cannot be too careful these days,' he muttered to himself, as he always did when locking his study, as if the words provided an extra protection, along with his regular checks on the door. The house was silent around him, aside from the buzzing of a dying fly at the closed window. His wife Beatrice was running errands (what did she do with herself on these outings, he wondered; where did she go?) and their days of employing three full-time servants were long gone. Beatrice must be content with a weekly char, and though she had been grumbling, Symington feared that even that expense was far too much for him.

He threaded his way back through the piles of books that formed ramparts around his desk – a big, mahogany bureau that dominated the study – and reread the letter that had arrived this morning, to which he was attempting to reply. It was a most unexpected letter to receive, amidst the usual bills and circulars, from a lady novelist, Daphne du Maurier. Symington had never read any of her books, though he vaguely remembered seeing a play of hers in Leeds after the war; Beatrice had persuaded him that they should go, because she was a fan of du Maurier's. And what was the name of the leading lady? Symington pushed his thumbs into his temples hard, as if he might squeeze the answer out of his head, and then he smiled in triumph; Gertrude Lawrence, that was it and the play was called *September Tide*. He couldn't recall the details of the plot, nor the titles of du Maurier's other work, aside from the one that was turned into a film, the famous one, *Rebecca*; though Beatrice had a stack of the books somewhere in the house – romantic novelettes, he believed them to be, inconsequential and far more appropriate for his wife than himself. But even so, he was flattered to receive the letter; for the author was famous, and remarkably well connected, Symington realised, after looking up several references to her and her family in his well-thumbed copy of *Who's Who*. He felt some pleasure in the discovery that Daphne was the daughter of Sir Gerald du Maurier, who played Captain Hook and Mr Darling in J. M. Barrie's first production of *Peter Pan*, and granddaughter of George du Maurier, the author of *Trilby*, a novel that Symington enjoyed, many years ago, when he was still a young man. For some reason, these facts coalesced in his mind to evoke a curiously compelling picture of her as a winged creature, a beautiful butterfly, perhaps, like those he had collected as a boy, netting and etherising them, before pinning them in a series of wooden cases that he still possessed, stacked in dusty piles in the attic.

Symington also imagined that Daphne du Maurier must be very rich. Somewhere in his extensive, boxed collection of magazines he vaguely remembered an article about her, that he'd put away for Beatrice, describing her reclusive life in a remote mansion in Cornwall by the sea – the setting for *Rebecca*, which was Beatrice's favourite – and her marriage to a renowned military man, knighted after the war, and subsequently appointed to some high-up job at Buckingham Palace. Symington filed these things away in his head – he tried to be orderly, after his years as a librarian – but instead of putting Daphne du Maurier in her place, they made him feel uncertain. He would have preferred to be dismissive of this woman – why did she assume he had any time to spare her, when he had his own research to continue, and his own literary ambitions to fulfil? Yet he could not suppress his eagerness to know more about her unexpected interest in Branwell Brontë, and perhaps to sell her a few of his manuscripts. Though probably not . . . he reached out to touch the fragile pages he had withdrawn from his files this morning.

Why should he trust her with these most precious of possessions? What if she were to mistreat them, or disregard them? She was likely to be as misguided and neglectful as everyone else who coveted his manuscripts, and all the others who must be kept at bay.

Symington glanced over his file of household accounts that sat to the left of his desk blotter; neatly notated by him, as always, in small columns, everything added up, except it didn't add up, the house was eating up money, and so did Beatrice, what did she spend all the money on? He closed his eyes tightly and sighed, and when he opened them, the room swam around him for a moment, before settling down in the dusty half-light. There was nothing for it; he would have to part with some of his papers to this Daphne du Maurier, but not many, not quite yet.

Symington picked up his pen again, and let it hover over the figure of four pounds that he proposed as payment for the two books. He had already taken several minutes to fix on this price; he did not wish to appear greedy or grasping – he could not bear a repetition of earlier transactions, which became unpleasant in ways he did not like to recall – but neither was he prepared to donate the books to her. He had other copies, of course; of the fifty original copies of each edition, he had placed only fifteen for sale with a firm of antiquarian book dealers, soon after their publication, keeping the rest for himself. But even so, it pained him to see any of Branwell's writings scattered from his house, instead of remaining safely at home, in his meticulous care.

Another drop of ink fell on to the page; Symington blotted it, and paused for a while. He did not want to stop writing: he had matters he would like to share with Daphne, who seemed surprisingly knowledgeable, as well as gratifyingly deferential in her tone to him; and it had been a long time since he could bask in such respect. But he knew he must choose his words carefully, he must not give too much away, for there was always a price to be paid. He wondered how much she already knew about his co-editor on the Shakespeare Head edition; did she know about the scandals concerning Wise? Mrs Weir was discreet, of course, and it had all been hushed up and brushed under the carpet at the time, but even so, there were whispers of gossip over the years. And if she had heard the rumours of Wise's activities as a forger of first editions and signatures, and a thief of manuscripts, then Symington felt it would be necessary to place some distance between himself and his former colleague, even though Wise had died twenty years ago; for Symington did not want to be tainted by association; not again.

He wiped his pen nib clean, and wrote, 'I doubt if anyone, at this time, could unravel the whole mystery of the Brontë manuscripts. I spent many years trying . . .' Symington hesitated, considering whether to add, 'and failing', but decided against it. 'As I am sure you aware, this is a most sensitive matter,' he continued, 'but of course, when someone signed Branwell's manuscripts with a forgery of Charlotte's signature, and in other instances, with Emily's, it was in the knowledge that the Brontë sisters' signed manuscripts would fetch far more money than their brother's, who has been sadly neglected by the literary establishment for over a century now. Fortunately, I have managed to preserve several of Branwell's original manuscripts in my own private collection, where they have remained safe from tampering. And I can assure you, they reveal his work to be of the highest standard.'

Symington stopped, and crossed out these last sentences. It sounded as if he was writing a reference for Branwell, for his miserable job as a railway clerk. No, this would not do, it would not do at all. He crumpled up the second page of the letter, and decided that he should end instead with his previous comment that no one would be able to solve the mystery of the Brontë manuscripts. That might make a more tantalising opening for Daphne; a veiled challenge to entice her to continue the correspondence. He signed his name with a flourish, underlined the signature, and blotted the page, again. Then Symington put down his pen, and started tapping his teeth with his fingernails, as if in a private code. This was a new beginning, he thought to himself. This was a very good beginning indeed.

CHAPTER THREE

Hampstead, January

I am trying. I am very trying. I must try harder. I am trying, though not yet succeeding, to write a proposal for what is supposed to be my PhD thesis on the Brontës' imaginary worlds of childhood, with particular reference to Branwell's influence on Emily and Charlotte. Or perhaps not, perhaps this idea is entirely misconceived, and I should start all over again with a different approach. 'Maybe you're trying too hard?' remarks my husband as he puts his head through my study door just now, and finds me hunched over my computer, looking miserable.

It's easy for him to say that I'm trying too hard. These things come more easily to him. He is an effortlessly successful English lecturer; though he would not approve of that description. He would say, ' "Effortlessly" is a cliché. Nothing is effortless.' And I suppose it must be an effort, being married to me.

Oh stop it, do stop this whining and self-pitying. I hate that in myself. That's why my mind keeps straying to Daphne du

Maurier instead of Branwell Brontë, that's what I like about her: her lack of self-pity, her remorseless, pitiless view of the world. You can see it in Emily Brontë, too. Nearly everyone is horrible to everyone else in *Wuthering Heights*. That's just the way it is, like the weather.

I wish I could find a way of incorporating Daphne into my thesis, because it was she who got me interested in Branwell in the first place. After I'd devoured all her novels as a teenager, I then read her biography of him, one of her lesser-known books, with a wonderfully gothic title: *The Infernal World of Branwell Brontë*. But I've already heard my tutor's views on this idea. 'Daphne du Maurier?' he said to me at our most recent meeting, wrinkling his nose as if the mere mention of her name brought a bad smell into the room. 'Surely she is far too minor a figure in twentieth-century publishing to deserve very much academic attention? Popular, of course, but certainly not distinguished by any great literary merit. And given that she is such an unoriginal writer, I doubt whether you could argue the case for her to be included within an original piece of research. *Rebecca* is simply a shallow, melodramatic rehash of *Jane Eyre*, and therefore less deserving of celebration than of accusations of plagiarism . . .'

My husband is equally damning, except I don't think Paul has ever read *Rebecca*, and he won't read it now, he is far too busy finishing a paper on Henry James. Don't get me wrong: I really admire James, of course I do. But I've never stayed up all night finishing any of his novels, apart from *The Turn of the Screw*, and Paul says, 'that's James at his most unashamedly populist', as if in fact I should be ashamed to find this particular story quite so absorbing. I've never obsessed about a possible sequel to *The Golden Bowl*, which is Paul's favourite novel, as it happens; and I'm always obsessing about the aftermath of *Rebecca*. What became of Mrs Danvers? Did she die in the flames that consumed Manderley? And was it actually Mrs Danvers that set the house alight in the first place? Could it have been the ghost of Rebecca – who was shot by her husband and then sent to a watery grave in a boat called *Je Reviens*, from where she returned to dry land, rising from the dead, filled with fiery vengeance?

Sometimes, it seems inconceivable that I am married to my husband, that Paul chose me, rather than anyone else, as if I must have invented it. But I didn't. The wedding was less than six months ago, a very quiet affair in the local registry office at the end of last summer, and I felt so happy that day, but dazed, as well. It was just the two of us – he said he didn't want anyone else there, that I was all he needed – and so our witnesses were strangers, an elderly couple that were sitting on a bench outside the registry office when we arrived. I wore a white cotton summer dress and dove-grey ballet slippers, and carried a small bunch of rose buds, tied with a forget-me-not blue ribbon that had belonged to my mother. Afterwards, on our way out of the registry office, we passed another, much bigger wedding party, and I heard one of the guests say, 'What a shy-looking young bride she is . . .' I blushed, because it's true, I was shy, and I wonder if I also looked childish beside Paul, who was so much more confident than me. I was still a student when we met – not his student, I hasten to add, he'd never do anything as clichéd as that, but I was his friend's lodger. I was in my final year at Cambridge, and Paul was (still is) an academic in London. Anyway, we met at Paul's friend's house, just over a year ago. I was living there, in the attic room at the very top of the house, and Paul came to stay for a week or so in December, while he was doing some research at the University Library, into the correspondence of Henry James.

And we got talking – not about Daphne du Maurier, I'd learnt by then to keep my mouth shut on the subject at Cambridge, where she was generally seen as irrelevant to the study of English literature – but about other stuff. I was alone in the kitchen when Paul got back from the library, and the house was empty, because my landlord, Harry, had already gone away for a few days. Paul hadn't appeared to take much notice of me when we first met the evening before, but now he glanced over as I filled the kettle to make us both a cup of tea.

'I don't suppose you know anything about George du Maurier?' he said, raising an eyebrow, quizzically.

'Actually, I do,' I said, which was true, because George was Daphne's grandfather, and I'd read everything she'd written about him, though I didn't say that to Paul. 'He was a fascinating character – an artist and illustrator who started writing novels very late in life, and had a transatlantic bestseller with *Trilby*, which I always thought must have been hard for Henry James, who was one of his closest friends, but not nearly as commercially successful as George.'

'Full marks!' said Paul, though I wasn't sure if he was being ironic or not. 'Most people make the mistake of seeing him only as Daphne du Maurier's grandfather, which simply cheapens him and his literary circle. So, guess what I've just come across in the University Library?' He didn't wait for an answer, but I knew he wanted me to listen, which is something I'm good at. 'I've unearthed a couple of rather intriguing letters written by Henry James, that offer some insight into his relationship with George du Maurier. James also happened to be friends with J. M. Barrie, who of course wrote *Peter Pan* for some of George's grandchildren, the five Llewelyn Davies boys. Barrie became the boys' guardian after they were orphaned, as you may already know?'

I nodded, and Paul went on. 'Well, the first letter I read today was one that Henry James sent to various newspapers at the time of J. M. Barrie's divorce proceedings in 1909, asking the editors to keep the matter private. Here, take a look at it.' He pulled a photocopy of the letter out of his briefcase, and came to stand next to me, close enough for me to be able to smell the faint scent of lime on his skin. 'Look,' he said, his finger tracing a sentence in the letter, 'James said they owed this discretion to Barrie, "as a mark of respect and gratitude to a writer of genius". George du Maurier was dead by then, but my theory is that James's real reason for protecting Barrie from unwelcome publicity might have been because of Barrie's involvement with George's daughter, Sylvia, and her sons. Which is why the second letter I've been looking at today is also interesting. Here, let me show you.' He bent down to his briefcase again and his hair was long enough to fall over his face, in thick, unruly curls. 'James wrote this the following year, to George du Maurier's widow, Emma, just after Sylvia died of cancer, and see here, he says "she leaves us an image of such extraordinary loveliness, nobleness and charm".'

I didn't think this was much of a theory, to be honest – the letters didn't necessarily prove anything, and it all seemed rather obscure and convoluted to me, I wasn't sure what he was getting at, exactly. But Paul was really excited about the letters, and so I carried on listening, while he told me that he was trying to work out whether Henry James believed that J. M. Barrie had been in love with Sylvia, as well as her five boys. And then we talked about whether Barrie had been a corrupting force, or an innocent, and from there we got on to *The Turn of the Screw*, and whether its ghosts were supposed to be real, or the projections of a neurotic woman. Paul was for the neurosis, I thought there was something to be said for the supernatural, but I didn't argue the point too vehemently. I wanted to agree with him, because I liked the way it made him smile at me, I liked his smile, and I wanted him to like me. Which might seem a bit pathetic – but I couldn't help it, he seemed so grown-up and sophisticated, with such breadth of knowledge, because I was only twenty, and he was twice my age, and very handsome, dark-haired and dark-eyed and sort of craggy looking, with lines etched on his face that I took as a mark of suffering. And yes, I confess, when I looked at him, I thought of Heathcliff and Mr Rochester and Maxim de Winter . . . and how could I not, when I had been waiting for them to step out of the pages of the books I loved; when I knew them so well, read them inside out and into myself?

It happened very quickly. We'd been talking for an hour or so, and then we went out for a walk, because he needed some fresh air after spending so long in the library, and we kept walking and talking, down West Road and then circling back again, past Newnham and on into the gothic grounds of Selwyn College, and he said it felt like walking into another century, being there, looking up at the mullion windows, all darkened now, and the castellated towers that rose up out of the clutch of the ivy. 'And you,' he said, 'you look like the heroine of a nineteenth-century novel, with your beautifully serious face and your grave, grey eyes. So do you have a suitably romantic story to tell?'

'Not very,' I said, 'though I suppose it's quite Victorian, being an orphan. My father died when I was very young, just before my fourth birthday, I barely remember him, and then my mother died, a month after I started in my first year at Cambridge, and I don't have any brothers or sisters.'

'That makes two of us,' said Paul, and then he kissed me. It was the most astonishing thing that had ever happened to me. He took my face in his hands, very gently at first, and kissed me in the twilight of the college gardens, in the long shadow of the chapel, on a frosty winter evening, close to the turning of the year. No one else was around: it was the holidays, the other students had all gone home for Christmas by then, but I was staying on in Cambridge. I didn't have anywhere else to go, which was fine by me, I liked it there. And I adored Paul, I loved him kissing me, the way he pulled me towards him; he seemed so much more expert at it than the boys I'd kissed before, not that there were very many of them, no more than two or three; two, in fact, to be honest, and one of them was so drunk he could have been kissing the floor.

We ended up spending that New Year's Eve together, a night which might have meant nothing to another girl, but it meant everything to me. 'You've never done this before?' he said to me, in the darkness, in my bed, in the empty house, sounding amazed; and my voice was trembling when I said, 'This is the first time . . .'

I told him I loved him that night – I could not stop myself – as soon as he started making love to me, as if he was somehow creating me as he did so, as if he was making me, so that I felt my limbs, my body, come to life as he ran his hands over me, wordlessly, his lips just touching my skin. His first wife had left him, and he was lonely, I could tell that he was lonely, because he was so hungry for me; he couldn't bear the sudden emptiness around him after she'd gone, and the sense of failure, and then I came along, and he saw me as something fresh and unspoilt. Paul said that to me, he said, 'You are my virgin territory.' He felt like a blessing to me – a miracle, appearing out of nowhere; and maybe that feeling swept us along too quickly, a joyous, impulsive urgency, though it didn't last long after our wedding day, it couldn't, not when the dark failure of his divorce was lurking in the corner, ready to spring out at us again, and I was no longer his virgin: he had conquered me. Of course, all his friends were disapproving, you could tell they thought he'd ended up with me on the rebound: a sweet young student, a blank page, no threat to his equanimity, but no real match for him, either, nothing but an easy salve to his wounded feelings after Rachel abandoned him and ran away to a new job at an American university, leaving him and everything else behind.

Maybe his friends were right. But here we are, married now, in his house in Hampstead, not far from the rented flat where I grew up on the other side of the high street, in Frognal. Yes, he's got a whole house, handsome redbrick Victorian, on a quiet road that leads straight to the heath; though it's not paid for out of an academic's salary, this was his father's house, and he left it to Paul in his will, ten years ago. That's one of the things we've got in common, Paul and me: our parents are dead, though his lived a little longer than mine, long enough to see him into adulthood. But we share some of that same feeling of weightlessness, of being adrift, though I suspect I have drifted further and faster than he has, carried out of my depth. He felt lost, of course, after Rachel left him, but he has the anchorage of his job, which he is very good at, and the house, and me. And I know I should be grateful, I should feel like the luckiest girl in the world, chosen by a handsome, intelligent man, the first man who ever told me that I was beautiful, who brought me to live in his house, this lovely, gracious house, filled with books and comfortable chairs in which to curl up and read. The light streams in through big, generous windows, and is reflected on polished wooden floors, and in the garden there are espaliered apple trees, and scented creamy roses that Paul's mother planted, en-twined with evergreen clematis and a climbing jasmine that smothers the brick walls, even now, in the depths of winter.

But sometimes I feel like a lodger again, as if I am just staying here until Rachel comes home to reclaim what belongs to her; cleaning her house, keeping it pristine and fresh for her; camping out in her bedroom, sleeping on her white linen sheets, beneath her feather duvet; borrowing her husband, who might already be missing her, or maybe he's just beginning to get bored of me. I have very few belongings of my own in this house, just my books, a pitiful collection, when compared to Paul's library, and my clothes, huddled like refugees in a corner of Rachel's empty mahogany wardrobe. And my face in her wardrobe mirror is washed-out and pale, and my fair hair turned into a colourless reflection, a curtain that shadows my eyes.

I'm not quite sure why I seem to be spending more and more time alone here, looking after the house, wiping and washing and ironing, just like I used to do for my landlord when I was a student, earning some money to supplement my grant. I don't think Paul notices all the cleaning I do when he is at work (though he might notice if I stopped doing it), but he is encouraging me to concentrate on my PhD. 'You're a very clever girl,' he says. 'You got a Cambridge scholarship, and a First in your finals, and funding for your PhD – so don't let it go to waste, don't fritter your time away like this . . .'

But I wonder, sometimes, if he says all this in order to make himself feel better about having married me; to make me seem more grown-up, less of a pointless appendage, an embarrassment in the eyes of his friends (and himself? Maybe that, too . . .) We hardly ever saw his friends before we got married – I was still at college during term-time, and in the Easter holidays, I stayed in Cambridge to revise for my finals. And then we went away for three weeks in the summer, to a rented cottage in the Cotswolds, just the two of us. It was idyllic, like a honeymoon before the wedding, with long, languorous days in the garden, and night after night entwined in bed together, when he said I made him feel young again. But afterwards, in September, he went back to work, and back to his previous life, too, seeing several of the friends he'd lost touch with after he and Rachel had split up. At first we saw them together, in the pub around the corner from his office at the university but I always felt uneasy with them, tongue-tied and gauche, while they traded jokes and told stories about people that I didn't know, and episodes in the lives they'd shared long before I came along.

I suppose that was when Paul began to see me differently; it was as literal a change as that, when his eyes narrowed slightly after one of those uncomfortable evenings in the pub, and he tilted his head to one side, and stared at me, appraisingly. 'How about getting a haircut?' he said. 'You look like a schoolgirl auditioning to play Alice in Wonderland, with your hair brushed straight down your back like that.' So I went to the hairdressers, hoping for a transformation, but not really wanting a radical crop, and the stylist just trimmed a couple of inches off, saying, 'You've got beautiful long glossy hair, you should enjoy it, at your age, while you're still young enough.' Paul didn't comment on it; I'm not sure he even noticed, he seemed quite preoccupied with work by then, and as the weeks passed, I realised that he was seeing his friends by himself, straight from the office, before coming home later in the evenings. I didn't mind that – I didn't particularly like his friends; they seemed so pleased with themselves, and competitive, like the contestants in a radio quiz, all eager to get the first word in, and score points over one another.

But what I do mind is that there's this niggling tension between us now, even when we're alone together, that wasn't there before; or at least, I don't think it was there until I finally admitted to him that I was just as interested in Daphne du Maurier as the Brontës. 'Oh God, not her again,' he said, when I told him this a few weeks ago, after he'd discovered me in my study rereading *Rebecca*, instead of getting on with my thesis. 'Why is it that adult women have this obsession with Daphne du Maurier? I can just about understand why an immature teenage girl might be fixated on her, but surely it's time to grow out of her? I can't believe that you would be as *predictable* as that.'

He sounded dismissive, but furious, as well, and I couldn't understand what I'd done to make him so angry; his outburst was illogical, and completely disproportionate. 'This is absurd,' I said. 'I happen to think du Maurier is an intriguing writer, and to dismiss her seems to me to be a kind of knee-jerk intellectual snobbery.'

'Better to be an intellectual snob than a dimwit,' he said, and then went downstairs and turned the television on, while I slipped out for a walk in the dark wintry evening, which wasn't very satisfactory as a protest, because he fell asleep on the sofa and didn't even realise that I'd gone.

Still, I want to make everything right between us again, but it keeps going wrong. I can't seem to find the right thing to say to him, or the right way to touch him, so I wait for him to reach out to me, which happens less frequently than before, so that sometimes when I'm with him I feel like I'm shrinking and disappearing, blurring at the edges into a nobody; though when I'm alone, and away from this house, I feel more myself again.

And now I have this odd sense that there's an unspoken secret that stands between us; a secret, which shouldn't be a secret, that has something to do with what he sees as my obsession with Daphne du Maurier. But at the same time, it's hard to stop thinking about Daphne, because Paul's house is just across the road from where she lived in Hampstead, when she was growing up as a child in Cannon Hall, one of the grandest mansions in London. I don't understand why Paul isn't as fascinated as I am; in fact, his antipathy seems downright perverse to me, given his interest in Henry James and J. M. Barrie and so on. After all, this is the very same house that Barrie used to visit every week; Daphne writes about it in one of her memoirs; she'd call him 'Uncle Jim', and play games pretending to be Peter Pan, while one or the other of her sisters was Wendy, and her aunt Sylvia's boys might be there, too, the Lost Boys, playing hide and seek with their younger cousins.

I can see into what used to be her back garden from my study on the top floor; I can see into it now, when the leaves are all fallen from the trees, and the bare branches look like a dark lattice against the sky, and the earth is black and sodden, with just a few snowdrops in the ground. But if I close my eyes, it's easy to imagine the du Maurier family are still there, Daphne and her two sisters, Angela and Jeanne; three girls, invisible yet very close, calling out to one another at the end of a summer's day, when the light is slanting, soft and golden, and the roses are in full flower. It's the most wonderful place, a secret garden that is hidden from the street by a circle of very high brick walls, and built into the side of the wall, at the point furthest away from the house, is the old Hampstead lock-up, a tiny prison cell with barred slit windows. But there's nothing confined about the garden – it's an acre or so of terraced greenery, south-facing, with a view over the whole of London – and it was once even more rambling, before the vegetable patch and tennis court beneath the parapets were sold off to provide a building plot for a multimillionaire. Cannon Hall itself is as beautiful as its garden: a graceful Georgian house, amongst the biggest in Hampstead; elegantly symmetrical in design, tall sash windows filling it with sunshine, I imagine, and a grand sweeping staircase, though I have never been inside, only examined it from my vantage point, my attic eyrie.

Now it's owned by someone very rich in the City, a man one never sees; not at all like Daphne's father, Gerald du Maurier, who was a well-known actor-manager when he bought it in 1916, and a familiar figure in Hampstead, presumably. He'd spent his childhood just around the corner from here, first in Church Row, then in New Grove House, where his father, George du Maurier, wrote *Trilby*. Imagine! Daphne's grandfather might have walked along this road with Henry James, on their weekly expeditions to Hampstead Heath, before going home to tea; and it was during one of those companionable Sunday afternoons that George told Henry the outline of his idea for the story of *Trilby*, and Henry encouraged him to go ahead and write it as a novel, never dreaming that his friend would become immensely rich and famous.

I think Paul would prefer me to give up on the Brontës altogether, and write a PhD on George du Maurier and his relationship with Henry James: it would be sufficiently scholarly a topic for research, he says; even though George du Maurier is now dismissed as much more minor than James, he is not quite as minor in the literary canon as Daphne. 'He's almost certainly due for a comeback,' says Paul, 'and I could help you out on the Jamesian connection, of course . . .' Ridiculous, isn't it, these league tables? As if you can measure literary excellence with precise instruments; as if there were a science of writing, governed by equations that reveal immutable truths.

Me, I can't help myself. I'm still stuck on Daphne, lost in the fog. Have been for years, ever since I first read *Rebecca* when I was twelve, and devoured the rest of her books, terrifying myself with her short stories, wide-eyed and sleepless after 'Don't Look Now' and 'The Birds', which were probably far too scary for me at the time (I've been wary of magpies and crows and yellow-eyed seagulls ever since). It was the same when I started reading the Brontës about six months later. I was totally enthralled by them, and frightened, too, by Cathy's ghost with her bleeding wrists at the windows of *Wuthering Heights*, and the living wraith that is Mrs Rochester, slipping through the doors of her attic prison, carrying her candle, dreaming of burning the house to ashes; though Charlotte annoys me sometimes when she gets too priggish about religion, as if she is trying to dampen down her overpowering rage, and put out the fire within herself. I mean, can you actually remember the exact details of the ending of *Jane Eyre*? Everyone goes on about the madwoman in the attic and the reworking of gothic plots – Mr Rochester and his crazed first wife; conflagrations and blindings and revelations, all of which I love – and then they ignore the preachy Christianity in the final pages, with St John Rivers leaving England to be a missionary in India, as if anyone cares about him by then; all they want to know is that Jane has married Rochester, and they've had a baby, and look set to live happily ever after, for ever and ever, amen.

As for my own happy ever afters . . . Well, I'm beginning to wonder if I'm heading for a dead end, the point of no return, where stories unravel into unhappiness. That's what often happens in Daphne du Maurier narratives, the details of which are preoccupying me just as much as those of the Brontës. Because here I am, living across the road from Daphne's childhood home, not far from my own, in a part of London that has just as many ghosts as the Cornish coast or the Yorkshire moors; city ghosts that might rise up from between the cracks in the pavement, if the mist has blown in from the heath, where Wilkie Collins first saw his woman in white. The heath is London's moor, a place that can slip just beyond the reach of the rational mind, or at least it does if you are feeling alone, in the midst of this crowded city. And I do feel alone here, sometimes, when I walk along the streets at dusk, glancing into the lighted rooms, where families gather, and they have a whole life spilling out of them, shining bright against the winter gloom; though not all the houses are filled with life, there are several on this road with shuttered windows and drawn blinds, turned inward, away from the world. That's when I start thinking about Daphne du Maurier again, and it hasn't escaped me, the parallels between my life and the heroine of *Rebecca*, the orphan who marries an older man, moves into his house, and feels herself to be haunted by his first wife (and then there's the unsettling matter of *My Cousin Rachel*, which happens to be another of my favourite du Maurier novels, but I suppose I'm getting ahead of myself here).

Paul, of course, would be horrified if he caught me thinking like this. He believes in coincidence. I mean it – he really *believes* in coincidence, in the coincidental being evidence of the essential randomness of the world; he can't bear it if I see patterns in life, or echoes or mirroring, he sees that as magical thinking, as irrational foolishness, as the most insidious kind of intellectual laziness.

Even so, I think I've just stumbled across something interesting. Not here, not in this house: that would be too neat. But I'm hoping that I might be able to track down something that might, just might, constitute original material for my PhD: some of Daphne's old letters, written by her to a now-forgotten Brontë scholar called John Alexander Symington, when she was working on *The Infernal World of Branwell Brontë,* which is actually dedicated to Mr Symington. And I'm hoping I'll discover Symington's replies to her, as well. I have no idea if any of these letters have survived, but the correspondence must once have existed, because Daphne referred to it in several other of her letters to a close friend; letters that form part of the du Maurier Family Archive at Exeter University. Yes, there is such an archive, and I've been emailing a very nice librarian there, and she put me in touch with another librarian at Leeds University, and then *he* told me about Daphne's visits to Leeds in the 1950s, when she came to the university library to examine a special collection of Brontë manuscripts whilst researching her biography of Branwell.

Paul doesn't think this is particularly interesting. 'It's a cul-de-sac,' he said, when I tried to tell him about it last night, 'as moribund as du Maurier's book about Branwell. This can't possibly lead you anywhere.'

'But it could be relevant to my PhD,' I said.

'How do you know any of this is relevant,' he said, 'when you don't know what's in these letters, if indeed the letters are there to be found?'

'I don't know, but until I do, how can you be so sure it's irrelevant?' I said, suddenly furious with him. He didn't answer me, just walked out of the room, banging the door hard behind him. But whatever Paul says (or doesn't say), I'm still intrigued by Daphne's letters to Symington, and by his replies to her. What did they write to one another in their letters? What did they feel about each other? Were they united by a strange, shared passion for a dead writer, whom just about everyone else had forgotten, or consigned to the dust-heap of failure? Did they fall in love with each other, as well as with Branwell? No one knows, and maybe no one cares, except for the librarian at Leeds University, who told me that Mr Symington was himself a librarian at the university, and at the Brontë Parsonage Museum in Haworth. OK, I'm sorry, there are a lot of librarians in this story, and libraries as well (which maybe doesn't bode so well for originality). People are often dismissive of librarians and libraries – as if the words are synonymous with boredom or timidity. But isn't that where the best stories are kept? Hidden away on the library bookshelves, lost and forgotten, waiting, waiting, until someone like me comes along, and wants to borrow them.

CHAPTER FOUR

Menabilly, July 1957

Daphne always cherished her isolation at Menabilly, indeed, fell in love with the house for its remoteness from the first time she saw it, as a trespasser, nearly thirty years ago, when it had been derelict and uninhabited, the trees coming close to colonising its abandoned rooms, the rampant ivy strangling everything, creeping into the roof, slithering through the cracked windowpanes. Now, Menabilly was restored, brought to life again by Daphne's love and a great deal of her money; which was as it should be, she thought, given that her fortune was made by *Rebecca*, a story inspired by Menabilly; no, more than that, she felt, a story that *belonged* to Menabilly as much as it did to her. All of it was made safe, except for a crumbling, uninhabited wing where none but Daphne dared venture, for its rooms were the most shadowy of places, with no electricity to bring light to dark corners, though this part of the house seemed to possess an occasional crackling humming of its own, on a frequency that only she could hear.

She also took care to preserve Menabilly's secrecy, along with its walls, this house that could not be seen from the road or the sea, its grey stones hidden by the contours of the land and a shroud of impenetrable forest. It was the closest place she could find to a desert island, she told her cousin, Peter Llewelyn Davies, when she moved into Menabilly at the end of 1943. 'But you will adore this house, as I do,' she wrote to Peter. 'You must come to stay, though I'm hoping the bats and rats and ghosts will keep all other visitors away.'

She was true to her word, and kept Menabilly as an island; peaceful in her solitude; the very opposite of her father, who could not bear to be without a great gang of friends and family around him, and who could only tolerate silence when his audience held their breath during a brief, dramatic pause in the theatre, waiting for him, and the action, to move on, until its foregone conclusion, the cheers and thunderous applause . . .

Yet for the last few days, she had been chafing at the seclusion, longing for a message from the outside world; specifically, for the arrival of a reply to her letter to Mr Symington.

This morning, at last, the postman made his slow way up the long, curved drive from the West Lodge, and Daphne was waiting at the front door, having seen the red van from her bedroom window. Much to her relief, the delivery was of a brown paper parcel with a Yorkshire postmark, addressed to her in spidery black capital letters, and as she opened the package, pulling at the knotted string and examining the musty-smelling contents, Daphne experienced a moment of pure pleasure, such that she had not felt for a very long time. For not only did the parcel contain a rare copy of one of Branwell's stories, as well as a privately printed volume of his letters to a friend, Joseph Leyland, Mr Symington had also enclosed a very intriguing handwritten letter, partially obscured by inkblots and heavily crossed out sentences, yet hinting that there might be a mystery associated with Branwell's manuscripts. Daphne scanned the letter rapidly, still standing in the hallway, then went to her chair in the library, where she reread it, several times over, until she could make sense of Mr Symington's elaborate circumlocutions.

And yes, he was guarded, his language as fenced and hedged as the Menabilly estate, forcing Daphne to read between the lines, and those crossings-out and obscuring inkblots were as infuriating as they were intriguing. But even so, Symington's letter suggested that he suspected there had been some previous deception concerning the Brontë manuscripts. If this were true, then she might be on the trail of a most remarkable literary scandal, and the very idea of this was thrilling to her now. Symington did not say who was responsible for the forgeries, though Daphne wondered whether he might have been hinting that his former colleague, T. J. Wise, was the culprit? Why else would Symington have referred to what he called 'the fog and mist' that surrounded Wise? It seemed unlikely – after all, Wise was a widely admired president of the Brontë Society – and Daphne wondered if there was another element to the story; perhaps Symington had some hidden feud with Wise?

But the important thing was that he had replied to her letter in the most tantalising of ways, and as she reread his words, holding them in her hands, an anticipatory sensation seemed to tingle in her fingertips. Symington asked her to keep the information a secret, not that he had given her any hard facts or provable information, not yet . . . But part of Daphne's pleasure was triggered by that request, for he had chosen her to share his secret, and in doing so, perhaps he was extending a tacit invitation to share more with him? She would become his confidante, she was almost certain of that; and there was something intensely exciting to her about the prospect of this being conducted in a manner both intimate – for Symington's handwritten letter seemed to bring him very close to her; she could sense his presence between the lines – and yet also at a safe distance. Daphne was less sure, however, about whether she could reciprocate in kind; she preferred keeping her own secrets, for now, in the safety and security of Menabilly.

As for Branwell himself: well, Daphne wanted to be entirely alone with him, so she took his books with her to the writing hut, telling Tod not to disturb her, she would not be needing lunch, and settled down at her desk there to read his volume of letters. The door to the hut was closed behind her, but the window was open, letting in the soft scent of honeysuckle and the temptations of a clear blue sky. Yet as Daphne worked her way though the volume of letters, it seemed to her as if they summoned up a cloud that was obscuring the sunlight; not constantly, but little mackerel clouds, gathering together and then scurrying apart; and with this came a troubling undercurrent of anxiety, mixed in with her excitement.

The letters appeared to corroborate the story told in Mrs Gaskell's biography, *The Life of Charlotte Brontë*, suggesting that Branwell's downfall was precipitated by his dismissal, in July

1845, from his position in the Robinson family household at Thorp Green Hall in Yorkshire as tutor to their son, Edmund. Daphne's childhood copy of Mrs Gaskell's book lay open on the desk, covered with her pencilled notes and asterisks, though as she reread it, alongside Branwell's letters, she found herself wishing that his youngest sister, Anne, had provided some form of substantiating evidence. After all, Anne had also been working for the same family as a governess to the Robinsons' two daughters, and left her job just before Branwell's abrupt departure. Mrs Gaskell believed that Branwell was disgraced because of the discovery of his scandalous affair with Mrs Robinson, who was not only married, but fifteen years older than her son's tutor; and certainly, that was the impression Branwell himself gave in his letters to Leyland. But what did Anne believe to be the truth of the matter? And anyway, whispered a small voice in Daphne's head, what gave her the right to uncover the truth over a century afterwards? Who was she to rummage through the indignities of someone else's life, when she protected the fragile dignities of her own?

Still, she could not stop reading, she felt a kind of compulsion to continue, despite a faint nausea that rose in her throat and an odd feeling of weakness, as the day wore on. There was something exhausting about having Branwell so close at hand, his words in her hands, as she turned the pages. For as much as Branwell declared himself to be thwarted in love, his despairing frustration as a writer came spilling out of these letters in equal measure, or thus it seemed to Daphne. His voice, which remained cloaked in the pages of his childhood Angrian legends, was far clearer in the letters; so much so that she began to hear it in her head, drowning out her own thoughts, drowning out her thoughts of Tommy, and his silent presence in the nursing home. Branwell appeared to have no such need of silence; his was an anguished voice, sometimes plaintive, sometimes excitable, that demanded her attention, demanding not to be forgotten. Daphne made copious notes as she read, copying out quotes that seemed particularly relevant, trying to make sense of the tumbled unhappiness, the choked ambition and panicky self-importance. And amidst the confusion of his life, as told in these letters, Daphne began to trace his story, though gaping holes remained within it.

Most intriguing of all, she thought, was the letter that Branwell wrote to his friend Leyland in September 1845, declaring, with a mixture of pride and melancholy, that he had 'devoted my hours of time snatched from downright illness, to the composition of a three-volume <u>Novel</u> – one volume of which is completed – and along with the two forthcoming ones has been really the result of half-a-dozen by-past years of thoughts about, and experience in, this crooked path of Life.' Yet by the following spring, the promised novel remained incomplete, as far as Daphne could tell from the letters, while Branwell was still professing himself to be broken-hearted over Mrs Robinson.

She copied out a sentence from one of his letters, half-hoping that her act of writing Branwell's words might summon up his ghost for her, here in the little hut. 'Literary exertion would seem a resource,' he wrote in May 1846, and Daphne whispered his words out loud, 'but the depression attendant on it, and the almost hopelessness of bursting through the barriers of literary circles, and getting a hearing among publishers, makes me disheartened and indifferent; for

I cannot write what would be thrown, unread, into a library fire.' He made no mention of his sisters' first venture into publishing, which presumably coincided with his letter that month, when their poems were printed, at their own expense, under the names Currer, Ellis and Acton Bell. It was not clear whether he even knew about their book; or did he prefer to pretend not to know, wondered Daphne, given that he had not been asked to contribute to it by his sisters, who were formerly his collaborators and closest friends?

There were so many unanswered questions; indeed, the letters seemed to add to them, rather than provide her with the answers she sought. Only two copies were sold of the Brontë sisters' book of poetry, so where could the others be? And did Branwell actually send a manuscript of his novel to his sisters' publishers, or indeed, to any publisher? Had his novel been rejected, or was it simply never finished? Certainly, if his letters to Leyland were any indication, Branwell appeared more preoccupied by the fact that Mrs Robinson, who had been widowed on 26 May 1846, did not (would not, could not?) marry him, even after a suitable period of mourning.

Daphne kept reading the letters as the afternoon wore on, not stopping for her usual walk down to the beach, or out to the headland; and as she continued, it seemed to her that she was in the middle of a mystery with an unknown ending, rather than moving towards the outcome of a story that she already knew. Branwell informed his friend Leyland that Mrs Robinson had been prevented, under the terms of her husband's will, from remarrying: 'she is left quite powerless'. And then the story became even more dramatic: Branwell claimed to have received a letter from 'a medical gentleman' who had attended Mr Robinson in his last illness, and subsequently witnessed Mrs Robinson's terrible decline. 'When he mentioned my name – she stared at him and fainted. When she recovered she in turn dwelt on her inextinguishable love for me – her horror at having been the first to delude me into wretchedness, and her agony at having been the cause of the death of her husband who, in his last hours, bitterly repented of his treatment of her. Her sensitive mind was totally wrecked. She wandered into talking of entering a nunnery: and the Doctor fairly debars me from hope in the future.'

As Daphne read this letter, and those that followed, she was puzzled by Branwell, and by his endless querulous complaints, but she also found herself wondering if the entire episode with Mrs Robinson was an invention on his part. Somehow, the story didn't ring true to Daphne – the cruel terms of the husband's will, the judicious intervention of the doctor, the talk of nunneries – could these be the twists of a plot lifted out of Branwell's Angrian tales; a gothic adventure for a Byronic hero like Northangerland, rather than a lonely parson's son? But if Branwell's story was real, then it revealed him to be hopelessly weak, intent only on using the end of his affair with Mrs Robinson as a reason for his lack of success as a writer. Perhaps what was most perplexing of all, thought Daphne, was Branwell's apparent assumption that by marrying Mrs Robinson he would share her inheritance, and therefore be able to live at leisure, rather than earn a living. Was it unfair of her, she wondered, for this to remind her of Tommy? After all, he had always worked hard, though of course her income was far greater than his army wages, or his salary from Buckingham Palace, and so it was her money that kept him in the style to which he had become accustomed, her books that paid for his boats and his hand-tailored suits, and was it her money that had underpinned his affair? No, she must stop thinking like this, it was too tormenting, it could serve no purpose, she must make herself purposeful again . . .

She swallowed, and tried to concentrate on Branwell's words; but it was impossible to suppress a small sense of exasperation, for while Branwell wallowed in self-pity in his letters to Leyland, his sisters wrote their masterpieces. As to whether Branwell knew about these novels, published secretly under pseudonyms like their poetry, his letters made no mention of this, though Daphne underlined a line in one of his rambling missives to Leyland: 'I know only that it is time for me to be something when I am nothing.'

His hopes were to be extinguished. In June 1848, when *Jane Eyre* was already a resounding success, he wrote to Leyland again in a panic, hoping that his old friend might help him fend off his persistent creditors, including the landlord of an inn, who was demanding payment of an outstanding bill. 'I am RUINED. I have had five months of such utter sleeplessness, violent cough and frightful agony of mind . . . Excuse this scrawl. Long have I resolved to write to you a letter of five or six pages, but intolerable mental wretchedness and corporeal weakness have utterly prevented me.' Three months later, Branwell was dead.

But had he left his promised novel behind him? Daphne turned to the second book that Symington had sent, feeling a surge of hope as she examined it. She traced the forefinger of her right hand over the gold embossed typeface on the front cover. 'And The Weary Are At Rest' . . . it seemed a resonant title, given that this was a posthumous publication, though Daphne doubted that Branwell was at rest; his voice that emerged from the books was far too capricious for that. This one looked impressive – very handsomely bound in black leather – but if she was to be entirely honest with herself, the story seemed fragmentary and muddled in places.

Yet there was much that was intriguing within it, in particular Branwell's hero, his Angrian alter ego, Alexander Percy, the Earl of Northangerland, who embarked on an illicit love affair with a married woman, Maria Thurston of Dark-wall Hall. And surely Darkwall had something of *Wuthering Heights* about it? For a moment, Daphne's heart leapt, wondering if this story could perhaps have been an early outline of the later novel, and Maria and Percy the forerunners of Cathy and Heathcliff? Branwell told Leyland that he was working on his novel in September 1845, when Emily might have already been working on *Wuthering Heights*, for as far as Daphne could tell, Emily's book was finished the following summer. But could her ideas have overlapped or mingled with those of her brother? Branwell's plot was uncertain – almost non-existent at times – and his story seemed to have no linear narrative, no rational beginning or middle or end; nothing was resolved within it, but instead left scattered and random, yet even so, Daphne could not read it without being reminded again of *Wuthering Heights*, with Heathcliff clearly prefigured by Branwell's Northangerland. And as Daphne neared the end of 'And The Weary Are At Rest', she also found herself comparing it with Branwell's story of his affair with Mrs Robinson; for all of these tales seemed tangled together, in a sprawling,

imaginative legend that was a continuation of Northangerland's role in the childhood landscape of Angria.

It was twilight by the time Daphne finished reading the
books, the rooks no longer circling above the trees, dusk
mingling with the shadowy woods, and her exhilarating delight of the morning had dissipated with the setting sun,
fading with the copper and crimson pathway that trembled
and then vanished across the sea. Branwell's life was too
gloomy for unadulterated celebration, too frustrated, and
frustrating, and it heightened the familiar sense of foreboding
that often descended upon Daphne as night fell in Menabilly,
though she told herself that she embraced the darkness, that it
was as fruitful as the light. But even so, she had a strange sense
of being wedded to Branwell: they were in this together, in
the shadowlands, for better, for worse. She vowed, in some
unspoken way, that she would try to do her best by him – to
show that he had a hand in *Wuthering Heights* – and perhaps
reveal that he was more sinned against than sinning, for there
was the intriguing matter of the forged signatures on Branwell's manuscripts that she should pursue. But she knew, also,
that she must see him clearly; that this was the only way
forward, for she must tell the truth, or hope that it would find
a way of being told.

Daphne rose from her desk and left the hut, feeling stiff,
walking slowly across the garden to the house, knowing that
she should begin to make arrangements to return to London,
to visit Tommy at the nursing home, and then bring him
home to convalesce, at last, as soon as the doctors said he was
fit to travel. There were bats flying above her head, and an owl
that swooped, white-winged, towards the trees, but the moon

was obscured by the clouds, and she could not see the stars, they all remained hidden.

Rebecca was quiet, also, as she had been throughout the day, pushed aside by Branwell; but Daphne sensed her, resentful and ignored, in the darkness at the edge of the woods, a vague outline against the rustling leaves and the pale, beseeching branches of the beech trees. 'Don't sulk,' said Daphne, quietly. Rebecca would have to wait, and so would Branwell, put aside for a little while; though what would they make of each other, should their paths ever cross, in the forested estates of Menabilly? Daphne laughed, and then felt, suddenly, a flash of elation. There need be no more evasion or invention. Tommy must be persuaded to understand the truth about their marriage, about its past, as well as its present tribulations. And from that, the future would at last become clear.

Menabilly,
Par,
Cornwall

20th July 1957

Dear Mr Symington,

Thank you very much indeed for your most interesting letter, and for sending me the two books. I am delighted to have been given the opportunity to add them to my library, and I enclose a cheque for £4, as requested.

As you can imagine, I have been studying them closely. Several things puzzle me. 'And The Weary Are At Rest' seems somewhat disjointed, and though it is generally held to have been written in the autumn of 1845, after Branwell returned from Thorp Green, several parts of it appear to me akin to earlier fragments of the youthful Angrian tales. I should very much value your opinion on this matter, as you have laboured longer on the juvenile works of the Brontës than anyone else, and I therefore believe your judgement to be the most worthwhile and authoritative, amongst the living, at any rate (but if only the dead could speak, to guide us through this mystery . . .)

Frankly, it seems to me that other Brontë scholars appear to be so besotted with Charlotte and Emily that it suits them to believe that Branwell never wrote anything worthwhile, yet when one carefully examines the lesser known stories and poems in the Shakespeare Head volume of Misc. Works, several that are attributed to Emily seem very much like Branwell's in style and content. There would, of course, be a scream of protest if one were to dare to suggest such a thing! But I wonder if Emily and Branwell worked more closely with one another than is generally recognised, particularly in the years from 1837 to 1839, when they spent a great deal of time alone at home together, while Charlotte and Anne were living away from Haworth? Certainly, there appears to be an overlap in the characters and plots that they invented for Gondal and Angria, and perhaps in later stories and poems, as well.

As for your intriguing references to forged signatures appearing on Branwell's manuscripts: naturally, I will treat what you tell me as being confidential, and you can count on my discretion, I assure you. But my mind has been running over this, and I wonder if you might tell me more about the manuscripts that were tampered with? Presumably, it would have been profitable to dispose of the juvenile Brontë manuscripts for a good price to wealthy private collectors in the US, especially if they bore the signatures of Charlotte or Emily?

It is presumptuous of me to ask you so many questions, I know, but you are the only person that I can share this with. I wonder if you would consider selling me any more of the books or manuscripts that you possess in your fine Brontë library? I live so far away from Haworth that I cannot make the journey there as often as I wish, and commitments at home keep me here, so I am forced to rely on borrowing Brontë literature from the London Library.

Incidentally, have you ever met the widow of the late Clement Shorter? She married again, and lives down in Cornwall, where she is now a Mrs Long. I called on her earlier this year, to ask if she had any Brontë letters or manuscripts still in her possession. But she was most evasive, and gave neither a firm yes nor a no. I wonder if she has any treasures hidden in an attic. The manuscript of *Wuthering Heights* is bound to be produced one of these days, and imagine what it might reveal!

Excuse this long letter. I do look forward to hearing from you again soon,

Yours sincerely,

Daphne du Maurier

CHAPTER FIVE

Newlay Grove, July 1957

Beatrice had gone out to visit a friend in Leeds for lunch and
would not return until the evening. 'It's as quiet as the grave
in this house,' she said just before she left, looking accusingly
at her husband. She did not call him Alex, his familiar
boyhood name; these days, no one ever did, he realised,
not even himself, except in his signature, and only then on
occasional private letters, such as the one he wrote to Daphne
du Maurier. If he addressed himself – which he did, from time
to time, silently, in his study, it was as Symington. 'Press on,
Symington, press on,' he told himself, half-encouraging, half-
scolding.

Beatrice seemed annoyed with him today, as she was
yesterday, not only because of the extra housework that
she must do in the absence of sufficient servants, along with
the other cost-cutting measures imposed by Symington, but
perhaps because he avoided discussing with her his letters
from Daphne du Maurier; at least, in no more detail than their
original, brief conversation, when he told her the novelist had

written to him concerning Branwell Brontë. When the second letter arrived from Cornwall this morning, Beatrice looked questioningly at him, having seen the postmark on the envelope, but Symington simply tucked it into his pocket, where it remained until he was in the safety of his locked study.

She's sharp, this one, thought Mr Symington, rereading Daphne's letter again; for she appeared to have picked up on something that he took rather longer to realise all those years ago: that the story he sent her was incomplete. But what she might not yet know was that it was never more than a series of bits and pieces, inexpertly fitted together first by Branwell himself, in a futile attempt to form an entire novel, and then reassembled, without much more success, by Symington and Wise, and their colleague (Wise's friend, Symington's enemy) Mr Clement Shorter.

And she was asking the right questions, too; not only enquiring as to whether she might buy more manuscripts, but also making discreet moves to draw him out on the subject of Shorter. 'Incidentally,' she'd written in her final paragraph, but Symington knew that nothing in her letter was incidental and that Daphne must be very serious indeed to have tracked down Shorter's widow. Not that the woman would give anything away about the mysteries concerning her former husband and the Brontë manuscripts . . . why, the old rogue died in 1926, only a couple of years or so after he had introduced Symington to the great Wise.

Symington poured himself a large glass of whisky from the bottle he kept hidden from Beatrice in a locked desk drawer, and tried to navigate a way through the facts that he must explain to Daphne. 'The facts, stick to the facts,' he muttered to himself. But it was so hard to know the exact truth of the matter. He wrote down a phrase in his notebook in capital letters. WHERE THE TRUTH LIES. It looked like a title for a book, he thought, and not a bad one at that. 'Press on, Symington,' he repeated to himself, taking a sheet of his headed paper, the address printed in a neat black font. 'Get on with the task in hand.'

Dear Miss du Maurier

   Thank you for your letter, and the cheque, which arrived today. I must say, it is an unexpected delight to discover that another writer is now taking so close an interest in Branwell after all these years of his neglect. I feel certain that we would have much to discuss, were we to meet.

 You are quite right about the poems attributed to Emily being by Branwell, and I did get a great protest some thirty years ago when I dared to say so.

He underlined 'great protest', and paused, uncertain for a moment, trying to remember where and when, exactly, this episode had taken place, and over which poems the arguments raged; but he could not remember the details, they slipped away from him, though the memory still felt raw to him, the recollection of being unjustly attacked and hounded and denounced. He swallowed a little more whisky, and gripped his pen tighter.

Forgive me if this information is already familiar to you, but perhaps I might provide some background to the Brontë manuscripts in my possession, and those elsewhere, as well? As you may already know, Mr Clement Shorter, like Mr T. J. Wise, was a faithful member of the Brontë Society. Indeed, when the Brontë Museum was opened in Haworth, in the closing years of the last century, its collection consisted largely of Brontë relics and manuscripts lent to the Society by Mr Shorter and Mr Wise.

Now, you might well ask, how did these gentlemen come across such precious treasures? Mr Wise was an astonishingly fervent and dedicated bibliophile – the owner of one of the most valuable collections of literary manuscripts and books in the country, which he left, after his death in 1937, to the British Museum, where it still resides, in the Library. He had the most uncommon flair for hunting down the rarest of original manuscripts by Byron, Shelley, Wordsworth, Browning, and many more – and in 1895, it was at his behest, and his expense, that Mr Shorter (a journalist and the editor of the Illustrated London News, but an avid book collector at heart, like Mr Wise) travelled to Ireland to the home of Arthur Bell Nicholls, one-time curate of Haworth, and formerly Charlotte Brontë's husband, for a few happy months, until her untimely death in 1855.

Mr Shorter discovered Charlotte's widower at a moment when Mr Nicholls was prepared to talk, not only about his former wife and their life together, but also about the possibility of selling a large number of Brontë manuscripts and letters, which he had preserved for so many years, including their extraordinary childhood tales of Angria and Gondal, those little books written in a microscopic hand, as if for Lilliput. Mr Shorter bought the entire haul for four hundred pounds on behalf of Mr Wise; Mr Shorter retained the copyright of the material for future publication, though the ownership of the manuscripts themselves stayed with Mr Wise. As you can imagine, this treasure trove was already priceless, though we must be thankful that Mr Shorter rescued it, before Mr Nicholls consigned it to the flames of his fireplace, which I believe had been his original intention. That, at any rate, was the story Mr Shorter told me.

Mr Wise retained some of these precious manuscripts, but not all of them, particularly not those belonging to Branwell, in whom he had no great interest, unfortunately. Some were sold soon afterwards – many were scattered to collectors across America, where Charlotte was already widely admired, unlike her unhappy brother. In the years to come, I purchased a number of Brontë manuscripts on my own behalf from Mr Wise to add to my treasured collection, and others for the late Lord Brotherton, the esteemed Lord Mayor of Leeds and MP for Wakefield, who had employed me in 1923 as librarian to his private collection (which came to be known, under my stewardship, as the Bodleian of the North).

Sadly, these friends of mine died many years ago: Mr Shorter in 1926, soon after we had worked together on the two volumes of Branwell material, the story and letters that I enclosed with my last letter. Then my great patron, Lord Brotherton, died in 1930, bequeathing his collection to Leeds University, on the understanding that I was to care for it as librarian, and Mr Wise, as I have already mentioned, passed away in 1937. So I have struggled on alone, and my task has *been a particularly arduous one, especially when it comes to restoring Branwell's reputation to the wider world. Sometimes, it feels as if I, too, have been adrift in Angria . . .*

As you may know, I am now approaching retirement, and although my researches and writing activities will continue, of course – for I could never fully retire from a lifetime of passionate commitment to uncovering the real truth about Branwell Brontë – the time has come to begin disposing of certain parts of my library, into the best possible hands. Should you wish to acquire further items, perhaps you might let me know where your interest lies?

Symington decided this was a good place to end his letter, for the time being. He was struck, as before, by the power of his phrasing; but even so, he felt suddenly very tired. He thought, briefly, of his five sons – all of them grown men now – and how he had admonished them to keep quiet when they were boys while he was working, working, working, for Lord Brotherton and Wise and Shorter, working for Branwell, also. Did any of them understand how hard it had been for him? His first wife, the boys' mother, had died in 1927, three days after their twelfth wedding anniversary. Poor Elsie – Elsie Fitzgerald Flower, the daughter of a Pocklington butcher – though Symington still remembered how betrayed he had felt by her when she passed on and left him with five motherless children. Elsie had called him Alex, not like Beatrice, who called him nothing, now.

It had not always been this way. Beatrice arrived at his house as a servant, soon after Elsie's death, to work for him as a housekeeper and nanny. She knew what it was to be bereaved – her first husband had died two years previously – and it seemed natural that they should come together; indeed, they were married in June 1928, less than a year after Elsie's death, which caused some tongues to wag in Newlay Grove.

But their lives were sweet, for a time, thought Symington, for all her sourness now. He was earning a handsome salary from Lord Brotherton, who was generous, as well as rich, and also making a good deal of extra income, buying and selling books and manuscripts as a private dealer, following on in his father's footsteps in the trade, though without his father's shop-front, nothing as vulgar as that, Symington knew how to be discreet. There was money, then, for a cook and a maid and a gardener, even a chauffeur to drive them about in their big car; there was a manicured lawn tennis court in the back garden, and a great aviary full of exotic birds, much prized by Symington, their feathered plumage bright in the gloom of the cage. And he owned a handsome holiday house by the seaside in Filey, close enough to visit for weekends; and another house acquired next door in the Grove, a smaller one, but necessary to contain Symington's expanding library and collections of birds' eggs and fossils and stamps, and much else besides. Oh, and there were garden parties at Lord Brotherton's mansion, invitations to tea there, and expeditions to Haworth; more and more of those, after Symington and his employer (no, not his employer, his patron) joined the Brontë Society in 1923. Those were the good years, when doors opened wide to him, when everything seemed possible. He became librarian and curator for the Brontë Parsonage

Museum, as well as shouldering his responsibilities for Lord Brotherton, and was also an assiduous editor for Shorter and Wise: he did all their hard work for them, and generously let them share the credit.

But no good deed goes unpunished. That was what his mother had said to him, and she was right. Was that why she left him so little in her will, when she died a decade ago? Just the defunct lead type and blocks from her father's printing press? Was she still trying to make some sort of point? Symington reached for his bottle of whisky to pour himself another glass, and found, to his surprise, that it was already empty. 'Press on, Symington,' he said to himself. 'Better press on.'

He closed his eyes and considered, briefly, what it might be to drink a little ink, now that the whisky was finished. There was ink in his blood, after all: his father a book dealer, his mother the daughter of a printer, it was his inheritance. Symington imagined sipping the ink, blue-black, and words filling his mouth as he swallowed it, poetry slipping out between his lips, wonderful sonnets, issuing as easily as a song. But his mouth was dry, like his hands, like the yellowing, faded manuscripts on his desk. He felt suddenly angry with all of them: with Elsie and his sons, who cared nothing for Branwell; with Beatrice, who thought only of herself; with Brotherton and Wise and Shorter, who grabbed all the glory; with his enemies at the Brontë Society and at Leeds University, who treated him disgracefully; and most of all, with Branwell himself. He considered picking up his magnifying glass, yet again, and examining Branwell's impossible, illegible writing; but he knew that nothing would have changed, that

Branwell remained elusive, mocking, enraging. There was a time, soon after the manuscripts first came into his hands, when he believed Branwell would emerge out of the pages that had been hidden away for so long; a papery-white ghost, exhumed from the darkness, yet with a clear voice, grateful to be rescued by Symington, happy to step out of his coffin and into the light. But Branwell was obstinate, ungrateful, perversely incomprehensible . . . and he gave nothing away, thought Symington. He gave nothing.

CHAPTER SIX

Hampstead, 15 January

When I woke this morning, Paul was already gone, and his side of the bed was cold, like the T-shirt he left beside me, discarded after he slept in it. The heavy velvet curtains were still drawn, as if he didn't want to wake me, though it probably wasn't yet light when he got up; he always leaves early for work, to avoid the rush hour, and to avoid me, perhaps. He doesn't need an alarm clock, though there is a clock on the little table on his side of the bed, an old wind-up one that ticks, very quietly, and sometimes I wake in the night and hear it ticking, and I wonder if it was Rachel's clock, and if it is waiting for her, marking time, while she bides her time, while she plans her return.

The walls of the bedroom are red – a dark red, not a colour that I'd ever choose, it's too reminiscent of the nightmarish red room that Jane Eyre was locked up in as a child; and the curtains are even darker than the walls, an inky blue-black. Sometimes I imagine saying to Paul, 'Let's redecorate the bedroom, let's paint over everything, please, let's begin again . . .' But it never seems to be quite the right time to say those words. In the last month, there's been so much silence between us when we're together, that it makes me even more awkward, because I wonder if I'm to blame for the silences, if I'm not much good at conversation. And that's when Paul starts talking about Henry James again, to fill in the gaps, I suppose, but it just makes me switch off, even though I know I should be interested, because he's so clever – Paul, I mean, though obviously James is a genius, as Paul keeps reminding me. I must say, there's nothing like being lectured on Henry James by one's husband to put you off both of them.

Anyway, I felt a bit abandoned this morning, lying in the big, Victorian mahogany bed like a child whose parents have disappeared, but also as if I had lost something else, something important, it was slipping through my head and disappearing into those blood-red walls, and I would never get it back again. I don't know what the thing was – that was part of the frustration, of knowing that I was forgetting it already; like I was forgetting myself.

So it wasn't just my husband that slipped away in the grey dawn, and maybe the feeling of losing him isn't the real issue, because to be honest, sometimes I wonder if I ever really had him, or if it was just borrowed time. Which is how I feel about my father, but when I tried to talk to Paul about this last night, he looked impatient. 'You're imagining things,' he said. 'You'd be better off focusing on your PhD, don't you think?'

We were lying in bed at the time, not touching each other, and I was shocked at the fury I felt when he spoke, like the red of the walls was seeping into me, staining me inside like a dye.

'You know what I think?' I said. 'I think it would be good if I could talk to you about Rachel. It's like she's a forbidden subject, and it's getting in the way of us talking – she's coming between us, even though you never mention her name.'

He didn't say anything, but a muscle in his cheek twitched slightly, and his mouth tightened.

'Well?' I said.

'Well what?'

'Tell me about Rachel.'

'I don't want to talk to you about . . . her,' he said, and as he paused, just for a heartbeat before saying 'her', I could see that it was hard for him to even speak her name to me. 'It feels . . . it would feel . . . inappropriate.'

'In what way, inappropriate?'

'Disloyal,' he said. 'Treacherous . . . I don't know.'

'Those are peculiar words to use,' I said. 'What do you mean exactly? That in talking about your ex-wife to me, you'd be betraying her?'

'That's not what I meant,' he said, keeping his eyes away from mine, apparently examining his nails, though his hand was curled almost into a fist. 'I just think she's irrelevant to our relationship.'

'How can she be irrelevant?' I said. 'She lived here, for God's sake. You slept with her in this bed. She's everywhere around us.'

He looked at me, briefly, as if startled by my outburst. 'What do you want me to do about it? What do you want to ask me?'

I was stuffed full of questions, of course – why did he and Rachel split up, did he still love her, did he love her more than me? – but now that he'd given me the chance to ask them, I didn't know where to start, they were choked inside my throat, where I always rammed them down. 'When did the two of you move into this house?' I said, even though I knew the answer.

'About ten years ago,' he said, with a small sigh. 'As you know, it was after my father died. My mother was already dead by then, and Dad had been living here by himself for quite a while.'

'So did the two of you redecorate the house together? Did you make it your own?'

'Yes, but slowly,' he said. 'You can't rush these things . . .'

He closed his eyes, and rolled away from me, facing the wall. Within a minute or so, I could tell from his breathing that he was almost asleep, which seemed astonishing, when I was more wide awake than before. 'Paul?' I said, but he didn't answer. I touched his back with my fingertips, writing my name on his skin, but he just sighed again.

This morning was the worst in a week of bad mornings; I can taste them in my mouth, dull and metallic, like a chemical, or a virus; the very opposite of how I'd felt a year ago, when I'd wake up early and Paul's arms were wrapped around me, and he'd say, 'Hello, sweetheart,' and trace my face with his fingertips, 'you're like a petal,' he'd say, and start kissing me, as if he couldn't get enough of me, wanting more and more.

I lay there for a few minutes, thinking about all of this, and then I couldn't stand being in that claustrophobic bedroom, so I got up, had a quick cup of tea, and decided to go for a walk on the heath to clear my head before I started working. It was about half past nine by then, but the kind of dull January day that never seems to get properly light; when everything is shrouded. No one else was out on the heath, apart from a couple of dog walkers going in the opposite direction, and a tramp sitting on a park bench, drinking a can of beer in the drizzle. I wasn't thinking about where I was going — just walking, wondering how it could possibly be so dark when the trees were still leafless, but the sky was like a deep shadow over everything — and I ended up on one of the muddy paths that snake through the woodland beyond Kenwood. It's not my favourite bit of the heath — it can feel dank on a rainy winter's day — so I tend to avoid it, though I used to meander around these woods as a teenager, in my gloomiest adolescent moods, half imagining that if I found the right path, a secret, magical one, Hampstead might lead into Haworth and Wuthering Heights. Suddenly, something ran across the ground just in front of me, a big rat, its tail flicking behind it as it scuttled into the undergrowth, and I stopped in my tracks, because I didn't know where I was, I'd completely lost my bearings.

I started walking faster, almost running away from that sinister rat, and it seemed like I was going around in a circle, but there were railings on both sides of the path, and no gate out again. I passed a fallen tree that I thought I'd already seen a couple of times that morning, and I heard something in the distance, the sound of a child's voice, calling out, and then crying, a thin, faraway wail. But the woods weren't thinning, it was like being in a tunnel, and I couldn't find a path that would lead me on to the open ground.

Eventually, there was a clearing and I recognised where I was, and felt foolish and relieved all at once, and set off back home again. Just before I turned into our road, I stopped for a few seconds outside Cannon Hall, and peered in through the locked gates, into the courtyard in front of the house. There was no sign of life inside – the blinds were drawn, and it looked closed up for the winter – and I imagined the owner was away on the other side of the world, escaped to blue skies and sunlight. But I felt like I was going nowhere, my head not cleared at all by the walk, but dull and clogged and fogged up; the opposite of yesterday, when I'd been so excited at the thought of tracking down those missing letters between Daphne and Symington, and discovering something new.

It's my own fault that the rest of the morning went badly. When I got back, I picked up the newspaper that was lying on the table in the hallway, where Paul must have left it, unread, after it had been delivered earlier. I went downstairs to the kitchen, thinking that I would just flick through the pages quickly while eating some toast. But as I opened it, I was as startled as when I saw the rat. There was a piece about Rachel – a centre spread, impossible to miss, with a big photograph – because it turns out she's got a new book of poetry coming out. And I read the article, several times, knowing that I would not be interrupted, knowing I was alone in the house. It's all about how Rachel is the most talented poet of her generation, as brilliant as she is beautiful, and an esteemed academic, as well, according to the newspaper: 'an inspiring teacher to her students', and a great loss to British academia when she took a job at an American university.

She looks extraordinary in the photograph, not that I can see her properly, she's turning away from the camera, and her face is partly hidden by her dark hair, and in shadow, but still, she's mysterious and elegant and very grown-up. Well, of course she looks grown-up: she's Paul's age. They were a striking couple, it says in the piece, and all their friends were surprised when their marriage ended; no one was sure why, exactly, given that they'd appeared to be such a perfect match.

It's the first time that I've come across a picture of Rachel, which is odd, really, because her image is stamped all over this house: in the antique mirror in the hallway that would have reflected her face every time she came in or went out; in the the strong colours that she chose for the walls, the red bedroom, a lilac bathroom, the yellow kitchen – a Van Gogh sunflower yellow that I'm certain was nothing to do with Paul. Maybe that's why I chose to have my study in the attic – it's white, and feels somehow free of Rachel, as if it had been a spare room when she lived here, and of little consequence to her.

Anyway, I sat at the kitchen table – her table, scrubbed pine, with a pale lime-wash finish; or maybe I'm imagining it was hers, it could have belonged to Paul's parents, I suppose – and studied the picture of Rachel, so closely that the contours of her face were etched into my mind, even when I closed my eyes for a moment. And when I opened my eyes again, and looked around me, at Rachel's cookery books on the shelf, which still contained her buttery fingerprints, propped against a jar full of shells and stones that she must have gathered with Paul from a beach, I felt I had to prove myself to her, as well as Paul, and the only way I could imagine doing so was to discover the letters between Symington and du Maurier, and use them as a basis for an outstanding dissertation. I imagined rescuing Daphne from the misunderstandings of insensitive critics that had obscured her true worth; I imagined making people realise that she was a great writer, as well as a popular one; I imagined being interviewed in the same newspaper as Rachel, and my photograph being taken, and Paul telling me how proud he was of me. And Rachel would see me, too, and be impressed and intrigued. She might not think me beautiful, but she would want to know more about me, just as I do about her.

I'm aware that it's ridiculous, of course, this idea that the newspapers would get hold of a minor piece of academic research, but even so, I was swept away by the fantasy, imagining my dissertation turning into a book to rival Rachel's; and I actually came up with its title, I think it's a really good one, 'Self-Interrogation', after Emily Brontë's poem, which inspired du Maurier's first novel.

So I got up to go to my study, determined to write another email to the librarian in Leeds, to get on with locating the correspondence between Symington and du Maurier. But halfway up the stairs, I began to feel stupid. I mean, really stupid, and not just about the foolish fantasy of public recognition, but also as if I could no longer think clearly, with the same fogged feeling as earlier. It was impossible, this idea of tracing the links between du Maurier and the Brontës, as impossible as making my marriage work, as improbable as making Paul think that Daphne was worthy of interest; as if the two were somehow linked, and his contempt for her writing was also indicative of what he felt about me.

At that moment – the instant I felt a physical sense of my own inadequacies – I stumbled on one of the steps, and my feet were slipping, my socks skating over the wooden stairs, and I went bumping down, banging my head before I could break my fall. For a few seconds I was dizzy, literally unbalanced, and I wanted to cry, to call for someone to come and pick me up off the floor. Actually, the person I really wanted was my mother – for her to be there, so that I could bury my face against her shoulder, like I did when I was a little girl. And even though she was dead, the memory of her seemed more real to me than Paul.

'What am I doing here?' I whispered. There was no answer, of course, just the almost imperceptible hum of the house, and I couldn't understand why I was in this place – not just crumpled at the bottom of the stairs – but also how I had come to be here, married to a man who no longer appears sure that he wants me. That sounds old-fashioned, doesn't it? I mean, why don't I seize the initiative in our relationship, and make it clear what I want? But it feels like we're both frozen, unable to move towards one another in bed at night, yet pretending that nothing is wrong. And when he does reach out to me, it's as if he is compelled by a desire that he no longer trusts, as if he is swept up by it for a while – and sweeps me along with him – and then afterwards, he seems desolate, like a man washed up by the tide in a place where he does not belong, does not even recognise. And we don't discuss it; just as we don't talk about why Rachel left him.

I stood up, carefully, because my legs still felt shaky, and murmured to myself what my mother used to say when I'd fallen over, 'Don't worry, nothing's broken.' I took a few steps along the hall, just to check that I hadn't sprained an ankle, which I hadn't, and then I caught sight of my face in the mirror, and for a few seconds, it was like seeing a girl in a dream, and not knowing if she were me, as if I was watching myself, rather than *being* myself. But at least it was my reflection; a bit pale, but indisputably there. Which was a relief, because I was beginning to wonder if I'd imagined everything, if I imagined myself here in this house, and if I looked into the mirror – Rachel's mirror, of smoky Venetian glass – there'd be no one there. I reached out, and touched the glass, tapped the reflection with my fingertips, because I didn't want to think what I had been thinking; that I was becoming disembodied, like a whispering ghost who has forgotten what it means to be alive, or maybe she never was alive, just a ghost of other people's lost hopes and desires.

The thought seemed like a horrible one – maudlin and neurotic, and yet I'd let it out, I'd released it into the house, where it might hide, or breed. I turned away from the mirror, and took a few deep breaths, like I used to do before the beginning of a race at school. I was always good at running – not the best, but a reasonably fast sprinter – and I knew that I needed to steady myself again, to stop panicking.

I suppose it was then that I began to realise that I had let myself get too isolated here, that I was talking to myself too much in my head, becoming disconnected from everyone else, and losing touch with reality. Not that I've ever been surrounded by lots of friends, but I'm not a completely solitary creature. I got a scholarship to a private girls' school in Hampstead, just a mile or so down the hill towards Swiss

Cottage. Most of the other girls lived in very different homes from mine. Even if their parents were divorced (and quite a lot of them were), they were part of big, sprawling families, with siblings and cousins and uncles and aunts and step-parents. Their houses were full of people, in a way that my mother's flat could never be: she was an only child, like my father, and all four of my grandparents were dead before I was even born. I had one great-aunt, who lived in Chelsea with a caged canary, and she died when I was about ten. Other than that – well, I know it seems implausible, but there were no relatives in my life. My mother was in her early forties when I was born, and my father was fifteen years older than her; I was an unexpected baby, much cherished, but a surprise, never-theless. 'I'd almost given up hoping,' my mother told me, 'and then there you were, my miracle daughter.'

If she wondered why I so seldom brought friends home to the flat, she never asked me. She was very tactful in that way; never probed too much, and as a consequence, I tended not to ask her questions about herself, either. We were happy together, adhering to a gentle routine, which I preferred to keep separate from my friends by the time I was a teenager. I wasn't ashamed of my mother, or the flat we lived in, but she was so different from the other mothers; older than them, less fashionably dressed, and the flat reflected that, with furniture that had been there since I was born, the walls covered in bookshelves, and a little portable television in the corner that was a fraction of the size of those in the other girls' living rooms. So my friends assumed that I'd want to go to their houses, to watch TV and sprawl on the sofa and eat takeaway pizza;

which I often did on Friday and Saturday evenings, though I was happy to stay in with my mother during the week, when we read, or played Scrabble, or listened to *The Archers* (my mother's favourite, which I pretended to find boring, though she knew I was as addicted to it as she was).

I had several friends at school, none of them Queen Bees, the Alpha females with their long blonde hair and mocking laughs; we tended to stay on the sidelines, not unaware of the daily theatrics of teenage dramas, but not part of them, either. We weren't complete geeks – we listened to pop music, read magazines – but there was something about us that made us invisible to boys. 'Don't worry,' one of my friends' mothers said to me. 'When you're older, men will begin to notice you, and they'll realise that you're beautiful, and so will you.' This seemed unlikely to me at the time, but at least I had the comfort of knowing that I was good at passing exams, and that this might be my escape route.

Except I didn't really know where I wanted to escape. I had a romantic idea of going to Europe, to write a novel, but my teachers encouraged me to read English at university, because they said it would be 'a good grounding', a phrase that reminded me as much of punishment as encouragement. But I was a good girl, who accepted the need for a good grounding; and when I got into Cambridge, I knew it would make my mother happy, because she'd studied English there and remembered it with affection. She had just retired by then, and once I'd started at college, it was as if she decided that I was in a safe place, and she allowed herself to leave me, very quietly, in death, as in life. She died in her sleep, the doctor told me. It was in the early hours of a Monday morning; and I'd spoken to her on the phone just a little while previously, as we always did on Sunday evening, it was part of the new routine we'd established since I'd started at Cambridge.

'Are you feeling OK?' I said to her, towards the end of the phone call, because she sounded tired, and her voice was slightly slower than usual.

'I'm fine,' she said, 'don't worry. I've just got a little headache.'

It was a brain haemorrhage, the doctor told me. She was in bed asleep, he said, so she wouldn't have felt anything. But I couldn't help wondering if he just told me that, to make me feel better, which it didn't. I imagined her brain filling with blood, and her lying there, awake, but unable to move or speak; silenced, in that silent flat . . .

Afterwards, my tutor at Cambridge said to me, 'If ever you need to talk about it, come and see me, OK?' I nodded, but I wasn't sure what the 'it' was; it was too enormous to be reduced to such a small word, or any words at all, so talking wasn't really an option. My mother was dead, and I was alone in the world, which was an embarrassment and an inconvenience to others, as well as cataclysmic to me. I dealt with this situation by not dealing with it; so that the awfulness of 'it' was put away in a box, leaving me to get on with each day, though getting on meant staying put in the place that my mother believed would be safe for me. If anyone asked how I was coping, I'd say, 'I'm taking each day as it comes.' And eventually, they stopped asking, and those days turned into weeks, and months, and now it's three years since my mother died, and here I am . . .

'I am here,' I just typed into my laptop in the attic. 'Is anybody there?' I thought about sending it as an email to everyone in my address book: my old tutor, my current one, my scattered school friends, and so on. Actually, 'and so on' is a euphemism. My computer address book is pitifully sparse, because I've lost touch with most of the girls I knew at school, apart from one who's teaching English in Prague, and none of them are living in the area where we grew up.

As for the people I knew at university: well, there were no proper boyfriends, no lovers, not until that astonishing night when I first slept with Paul. But I did have two close friends, both of them studious, bookish girls like me, and about the time I got married, one of them, Jess, moved to America, on a scholarship to an Ivy League college, and the other, Sarah, went back home to Edinburgh, to do teacher training. I could ring them or email them or write, I know, and sometimes I do, but less and less, because neither of them was convinced that I was doing the right thing in marrying Paul; both of them said, in the gentlest of ways, that they thought it was far too soon, that I should have waited. 'I understand why you want to get married,' Jess said to me, 'and I also understand why it might seem you need to get married – to feel safe, to have a home, all those things that other people might take for granted. But why don't you see how it goes with Paul, before actually marrying him?'

'I love him,' I said, as if that were as simple as that. And I did think it was simple at the time, but it's only now that I've realised that loving someone isn't enough; that it's not enough to make everything safe and secure.

I haven't said this to Jess; I haven't really told her or Sarah anything about what's been going wrong with Paul. It's not that I used to tell them everything – I never talked to them about my mother's death, I didn't talk about that to anyone – but our conversations about books have melted away, along with those consoling Cambridge afternoons of tea and biscuits in front of a flickering gas fire, and walks along the river, feeding the ducks, and talking about the impossibility of understanding the footnotes to *The Waste Land*, or whether Emily Brontë's childhood fantasy of Gondal could be traced in *Wuthering Heights*. When we were students, it seemed like the time we spent together would go on for ever; but of course, there was an ending, there had to be, when our finals were over, and we left to make way for a new batch of girls, who would move into the college rooms we had once occupied.

And maybe I've forgotten how to sustain friendship; maybe I live too much in my head. That was what my mother said to me just a few days before she died. 'Don't forget to talk to other people, darling,' she said. Which was odd, coming from such a quiet woman, a librarian, as it happens, who was accustomed to silence, who found it peaceful, rather than oppressive.

Perhaps that's why I became even more attached to *Rebecca* after my mother died; it was familiar, at the same time as remaining insoluble. I loved the book as a teenager, loved its promise of escape, its wild Cornish landscape that seemed a million miles away from London, and yet somehow within my reach. But now I reread it for clues, trying to see if there was anything I missed, just as the second Mrs de Winter tries to read her husband's face, trying to make sense of everything. Which is hopeless, of course; the novel is supposed to be mysterious, to leave one wanting to know more. One thing I'm certain of, though: 'the lovely and unusual name' which belongs to the nameless narrator before she becomes Mrs de Winter must be Daphne du Maurier.

Anyway, I've decided to make far more of an effort with Paul, and I'll start by persuading him to come home for dinner tonight, instead of working late. I'm not going to consult Rachel's cookery books – I'm not going to look at them ever again, they make me feel like an interloper – but I'll make roast chicken, like my mother used to do for the two of us on Sunday evenings. She always added lots of lemon juice, and bay-leaves and thyme from the garden, and in the winter she baked apple crumble as well, and we'd talk about the books that I was reading, about *The Wolves of Willoughby Chase* and *Wuthering Heights*; and I shivered at the thought of Cathy's ghost, tapping at the window, crying 'Let me in, let me in'; but I was safe, I knew I was safe inside with my mother.

I'm not quite sure what Paul and I will talk about – he clearly doesn't like it when I ask him what's keeping him so much at work these days, and I can't mention Daphne, either; I can't say anything about her to him ever again, because last time I did was disastrous, he said I was turning into a weird kind of du Maurier stalker, that I was losing touch with reality, as well as with him. I don't think that's true – he's the one that is spending more time away from this house, not me. But I don't want to argue with him again, I can't bear it when people shout at each other, and anyway, no one hears what's being said, it's just an angry sound.

But I also know that silence doesn't seem to help. 'Silence is your default setting,' Paul said to me last week, 'occasionally punctuated with a sharp burst of static electricity, and maybe you don't know how enraging that can be.' So I've vowed to try to find the right words for him, to make it clear that I'm not living only in my head; for if the outlines of our life together have become blurred and indistinct (if, indeed, they ever clearly existed), then I must find a way to fill them in, to make them real again.

CHAPTER SEVEN

Menabilly, August 1957

Daphne stood at her bedroom window as the sun was sinking in the sky, looking down to the drive that circled in front of the house, and she felt rigid, like a sentry, like Mrs Danvers . . . No, not like Mrs Danvers, she told herself. She was Lady Browning, a loving and dutiful wife, waiting for her husband to return home again.

Tommy was on his way back to Menabilly after three weeks in the nursing home, after tranquillisers and electric shocks and God knows what else, her husband was being delivered back to her this evening, like a parcel. No, not a parcel, what was she thinking of? 'He will need a great deal of your support and affection,' the doctor told Daphne on the telephone two days ago, when he rang to explain that Tommy was now well enough to leave the nursing home, and spend the rest of the summer convalescing in Menabilly. 'No stress, obviously, no over-excitement, absolutely no alcohol. Just keep everything very quiet and peaceful for him.'

It was inconceivable to Daphne that she could drive Tommy all the way from London (she rarely drove anywhere these days, not even to Fowey), and the train seemed too lacking in privacy, as did a hired driver. It wasn't fair to ask either of her daughters to take responsibility for such a long journey, but she didn't trust anyone outside the family, so in the end, she decided to ask her cousin Peter, who had been at Eton with Tommy, and served alongside him in the First World War. She telephoned Peter at the publishing company he ran with his younger brother Nico and he agreed, readily, and didn't ask for any further explanation than Daphne had already offered: that Tommy was suffering from nervous exhaustion, hence the stay in the private nursing home and the cancellation of the silver wedding anniversary party.

She made sure that Menabilly was looking at its best for Tommy's arrival: vases of roses in the Long Room and the entrance hall, and everything swept and scrubbed clean and polished, just as he liked it. Then she changed out of her usual nondescript trousers into a blue chiffon dress, dabbed perfume at her wrists and throat, and applied her make-up with unusual care, gazing into her dressing-table mirror at her pale, anxious face, powdering over its shadows and uncertainties. But would she meet Tommy's high standards? Would he find her lacking?

When Daphne saw Peter's car turn into the drive, just after half past seven in the evening, she took a sharp intake of breath, and smoothed her hands across her hair, then ran downstairs to the front door, so that she would be standing there, a smile on her face, ready to welcome Tommy. She'd got Tod out of the way with various errands, and the maids had left for the day, which meant that Tommy could slip in without a fuss.

'Darling,' she said, as he got out of the car, 'how lovely to see you again, and you're looking so much better.' In fact, she was shocked by his appearance, for although he was immaculately dressed in a suit and tie and polished brogues, his face was a powdery grey, like dirty chalk, and rather than his usual confident stride, he seemed to shuffle towards her.

'Good drive?' she said, patting him awkwardly on the arm.

Tommy shrugged, and gestured towards Peter. 'Ask your cousin,' he said. 'I had my eyes closed for most of the journey.'

'It was terribly kind of you,' she said, turning to Peter and kissing him on the cheek. For a moment she felt as if she were watching all of three of them, jerking like marionettes, as if she were back up again in her vantage point at the bedroom window, at one remove from this stiff little scene by the front door. 'I suppose both of you men are longing for a . . . for a cup of tea.'

Tommy grimaced, while Peter raised one eyebrow at her almost imperceptibly. 'You're sounding more and more like my mother,' said Tommy. 'What we all need is a stiff drink.' He stumped into the house, leaving the front door open behind him, and as Daphne looked at Peter, she wondered if he could see the flush that she felt rising from her neck, across her face.

'I take it a drink isn't yet in order?' said Peter.

'Not yet,' she said. 'Just hang on for a bit . . .'

By the time she found Tommy in the dining room, he had already poured himself a large glass of whisky. 'Darling,' she said, 'the doctors are very keen that you don't—'

'Damn the doctors,' he said. 'They've been torturing me for nearly a month. You have no idea, Daphne, the horror of it all . . .' His voice broke, and he put his hand over his eyes, turning his face away from hers.

'I'm so sorry,' she said.

'I see you kept well clear,' he said, 'as usual . . .'

'I didn't think it would help you, having me around, when you needed to rest.'

'Rest?' he hissed at her. 'Is that your definition of rest? A thousand volts of electricity shot into your head?'

She heard Peter cough outside in the hall, and said to Tommy, 'Shall we go and sit in the Long Room, where we can be more comfortable?'

'I don't want to sit anywhere,' said Tommy. 'I'm deadbeat. I'll finish my drink and take myself to bed.'

'Would you like some cocoa brought up to you?'

'By Mrs Danvers?' he said. 'With a sleeping pill on the side, to keep me quiet?'

Daphne was shocked by the bitterness in his voice, by the look in his grey eyes. 'Let's not argue, darling,' she said. 'I just want you to feel comfortable here.'

'Do you?' he said. 'I'd have thought you'd be more comfortable without me, cluttering up the house.'

'I love you,' she said. 'I love you being here . . .'

'Don't lie to me, Daphne,' he said. 'It doesn't become you.' Then he turned from her and left the room, and she heard his footsteps on the stairs, slow and unsteady, stopping on the landing, and then going painfully upwards, along the corridor to his room, where she had made sure to leave his teddy bears on the bed; his welcome party . . .

She stood in the dining room for a few moments, trying to calm her breathing, then followed him upstairs and knocked on his door, gently. There was no answer, so she called out his name, and when he still did not reply, she turned the handle. It was locked. 'Tommy?' she said, more loudly.

'I'm trying to go to sleep,' he said, sounding muffled. 'Can't a man get some sleep around here?'

Daphne went downstairs in search of Peter, feeling as if all three of them were playing some half-forgotten childhood variation of hide and seek, the rules of which she did not fully understand. She called out his name, hurrying from room to room downstairs, and found him eventually in the last place she'd thought to look, the nursery on the ground floor at the front of the house. 'It hasn't changed in here since my first visit,' he said. 'Still the same old pictures on the walls.'

He was standing by the drawings of 'Peter Pan' that Daphne had hung in the nursery, soon after moving into Menabilly. 'It's looking a bit shabby, isn't it, after fifteen years?' she said, suddenly noticing that the green and pink rose-print wall-paper had faded in places, like the matching curtains. 'This was the first room I decorated in the house – I wanted it to look cosy for the children, because they were a bit dubious about coming to live here, they called it the rat palace. I remember choosing this wallpaper, and getting the drawings of your namesake framed, and the ones of Daddy as the ghastly Hook.'

'Gerald was always terrifying,' said Peter, tilting his head to look at the sepia photographs of an early production of *Peter Pan*. 'That diabolical smile, and the appalling courtesy of his gestures, as he poured the poison into Peter's glass. And then he'd reappear as Mr Darling, and one had to remind oneself that he was neither Captain Hook nor Darling, that it was simply Uncle Gerald. Not that being Gerald was ever simple . . .'

He looked over at her, and smiled his half-crooked smile that she loved, and raised his eyebrow again. 'Well?' he said. 'When are you going to tell me what's going on? Tommy barely said a word to me today. The last time I saw him like this was forty years ago, when we were both shell-shocked recruits, and refusing to talk about the horrors of the trenches. But at least then we could mumble to one another about the cricket.'

'You were so young,' she said. 'Not much older than Kits, and straight out of Eton into the war . . . That's what I've been reminding myself for the last few weeks, while Tommy was in the nursing home: that things could be far worse, that at least there's not a war on.'

'True,' said Peter, 'but that doesn't explain what's wrong with Tommy.'

'I don't think I can explain,' she said. 'Not yet, anyway. It's a frightful mess. And I'm so sorry to drag you down here, it's ghastly for you.'

'Not as ghastly as it is for you,' he said. 'How long has this been going on?'

'The stupid thing is, I don't know. I really thought that he was fine until this sudden collapse last month. But I suppose we hadn't been seeing enough of each other, and I'd somehow lost track of things. And now he's in such a bad way with this depression that he just can't seem to shake off.'

Peter was silent for a few seconds, and then he said, 'Do you remember what Jim Barrie wrote about our uncle Guy, after he'd been killed in the Great War? "He had lots of stern stuff in him, and yet always the mournful smile of one who could pretend that life was gay but knew it wasn't." That rather reminds me of Tommy, and the rest of us, don't you think?'

She sighed, remembering how noble Guy had seemed to her when she was still a little girl and he came to the house in his officer's uniform, the medals glinting on his khaki chest, and she was too shy to speak to him, just stood and stared, until her mother told her to stop being so rude. But she couldn't help it, and she'd felt the same awe in the presence of Peter's older brother George, even when he bent down to kiss her goodbye. Poor George, dying in action in Flanders just a week after Guy, when he was only twenty-one, and the rest of his life should have been ahead of him. 'Uncle Guy was such a hero,' she said to Peter, 'and Daddy always said that George took after him. My father was broken-hearted after they died – that awful week, Daddy crying, not trying to hide his tears from me, but telling us that we must always be proud of Guy and George. That's the thing about having heroes in the family – they make everyone else look tawdry, these days.'

'I'm not so sure about that,' said Peter, 'I don't think Tommy is tawdry, do you?'

'He's certainly stopped smiling, whether mournfully or not,' she said, sidestepping Peter's question. 'I can't even recall the last time I saw him smile.'

'I know the feeling,' said Peter, 'but we struggle on, don't we?'

Daphne thought he was talking about his wife, Margaret, who was a bit of a moaner, and she'd not wanted to pry, so she simply slipped her arm through his, and said, 'Let's go and forage for some supper.' Tod had left a green salad and cold roast beef in the larder, which they ate by candlelight in the dining room; and then they took their glasses of wine into the Long Room, and when Daphne went to turn on the electric lamps, Peter said, 'Leave it, the darkness is so lovely here . . .' So she lit the candles by the fireplace, and they sat in peaceable silence for a little while.

'Uncle Jim never saw this place, did he?' said Peter, eventually.

'No, he died before I leased it,' she said, 'but if only he had, he'd have loved Menabilly.'

'You know he used to come to Fowey on holiday? And perhaps he came walking along the coastal path, and stumbled across Menabilly, just like you did.'

'I wish I'd asked him,' said Daphne.

'We all wish we'd asked him more questions,' said Peter. 'But isn't that the du Maurier way? Not to ask, just to watch, and smile . . .'

Daphne stood up, to go over to the piano, and as she passed Peter, she reached out and brushed a finger against his lips, as soft and quick as a moth's wing. He closed his eyes, and leaned his head back against the armchair. The windows were open, the curtains not drawn, and the cool night air was in the room. Daphne shivered a little, and then she played 'Clair de Lune', very softly, and the wreaths of their cigarette smoke rose and twisted together towards the ceiling.

Peter left early the next morning, before Daphne came downstairs for breakfast. He slipped a note under her bedroom door, but by the time she woke and read it, he was gone. 'Dearest D,' he had written. 'I wish you courage in all that lies ahead. Excuse my hasty departure, but deadlines loom at the office, and I also imagine that you and Tommy need some quiet time to catch up with one another . . .'

In fact, the house was filled with people from that afternoon onwards. Tessa arrived first, with her husband and children, all squashed into a car with a large quantity of luggage; and then Flavia and her husband, and Kits came soon afterwards, on the train. 'How lovely,' said Daphne, at teatime, passing around slices of cherry cake, 'to have all of us here together again . . .'

And in the days that followed, Daphne tried to lose herself in the rhythms of family life, to give in to its ebb and flow. But she could not stop herself feeling anxious, for Tommy was always on edge – on the edge of tears, of anger, of irritation, of frustration – and he did not like being disturbed by Tessa's children, his little granddaughter, Marie Therese, who was two and a half, and the baby, Paul, who was only sixteen months.

Daphne did her best to get the children out of the house as much as possible, down to the beach to paddle in the rock pools. But the weather was thundery – sudden and violent downpours, which sent everyone scuttling back into the house – and Daphne felt oppressed by the lowering skies, the clouds the colour of bruises, though she smiled, always, and was charming, she tried very hard to be charming. She made no mention in Tommy's presence of their silver wedding anniversary last month, nor the cancelled party; no mention, either, of his time in the nursing home. Daphne did her best to explain to Flavia and Tessa about what happened, but she could not bring herself to use the words 'mental illness' or 'breakdown', so she repeated the same phrase to both of them, which was 'nervous exhaustion', and she was also careful to avoid any reference to the Snow Queen; she was trying not to think about that woman, not here, not in Menabilly . . .

As for Kits: he was still too young, just sixteen, and despite his veneer of sophistication that he'd picked up at Eton, she cherished his bright-eyed innocence, his undimmed optimism and capacity to see the best in everything, and everyone. He reminded her of Peter's younger brother, Nico, who seemed somehow unscathed by the death of both his parents; and of course, he was just young enough to have avoided serving in the First World War. Was it their experiences in the trenches, she wondered, that had left Tommy and Peter with a streak of melancholy? Tommy was brave, there was no doubt about it, he had won a DSO for courage at the age of nineteen, but he still woke at night, crying out, indistinct sounds, and in the morning, when she asked him if he had been dreaming, he said, 'It's always the same nightmares, the bodies in the mud, and the rats, and the noise of men screaming . . .' But maybe it wasn't only the war that was to blame, maybe it was the du Maurier melancholy that descended upon Peter, as it did Daphne; and perhaps this was what had infected Tommy; perhaps it was Daphne who brought it upon him, though their son had so far escaped.

Sometimes, she looked at Tommy, and wondered if it was his double who had come home to Menabilly, a brooding, stooping, saturnine twin; while the real Tommy was still walking around in London, gay and charming, with a confident smile on his face, and the upright stance of a successful soldier. And if so, must she keep her own dark double locked out of Menabilly, the angry, vengeful woman who knew she was wronged? Was it Rebecca's voice, or hers, that wanted to spit insults at Tommy, that longed to taunt him and mock his weaknesses? But it was a voice that she made certain to keep silent, and she vowed that she would not complain, so when anyone enquired about Tommy's health – for something was clearly wrong, he was drained and white-faced and shaky – she answered in brave little lies, explaining that he was suffering from exhaustion, and his blood was going too slowly through his system, he needed pills to thin his blood. She said this so often that she began to believe it: the blood was not reaching his brain, hence his collapse.

And Daphne wondered if her blood was too thick, if her brain was starved, like Tommy's, for there were moments when she could not think straight; she felt literally unbalanced, and slept only fitfully. A week after Tommy came home to Menabilly, when the house was filled with other people's uneasy dreams, and the air inside too heavy to breathe, she decided to try to sleep outside in the garden, on an old lilo and moth-eaten blanket, dragged out from the cobwebby summer house. At first, she kept her eyes wide open, looking up at the midnight sky as the clouds gave way to infinite stars, and she told herself it was too beautiful to sleep, but she must have dozed, at last, for she heard a woman's voice whispering beside her, and then with a start realised she was awake, not dreaming, certain that someone else was there. At that moment, Daphne thought the voice was telling her something important, speaking to her through a tear in the veil between this world and another, secret one; but she could not grasp the words, they disappeared into the darkness as soon as they were spoken. She tried to cry out, distressed, but no sound came from her mouth, and there was silence all around, even in the woods, everything stilled and quietened, no wind to rustle the leaves, no living creatures in the undergrowth. And in that silence, a terrible dread had risen up and taken hold of her, and she ran back to the house, heart pounding, panic in her veins, leaving the makeshift bed behind her, fearing that if she stayed, she would be beckoned to a place from which there was no return.

Now, in the daylight hours, there were voices all around her; not only those of her family, but a ceaseless monologue of her own, looping and spiralling inside her head. A little of it was about Branwell Brontë – when she could snatch an hour or two to work in her writing hut, she was attempting to understand the chronology of Angrian history, which was more circular than linear, with endless digressions – though she was often distracted, and found herself repeating her wedding vows, not out loud, but running through them in her mind, over and over again. 'For richer, for poorer, in sickness and in health . . .' Tommy was sick, that much was certain, but she worried that he was sick with longing for someone else, for the Snow Queen.

One rainy afternoon, she sat in an armchair with Marie Therese on her lap, and read to her from a childhood collection of Hans Christian Andersen fairy tales – the same book she'd read to Tessa and Flavia, and that her mother had read to her in the nursery. This frightened Daphne as a child, in a way that she had never forgotten, for her mother pretended to be the Snow Queen, and her face looked icily hard and blank, as if her true self had been revealed in the telling of the story, revealing what Daphne suspected, that her mother did not love her . . . And even now, after all those years had passed – so quickly that time seemed to have circled in on itself – when Daphne came to the tale of the Snow Queen, she had to blink hard to stop herself from crying. Close to the end, Marie Therese was nearly asleep, but Daphne kept reading aloud, very quietly, about how the little girl, Gerda, travelled far away to find her dearest friend, Kay – a boy as close to her as a brother – and at last she found him, sitting alone in the Snow Queen's palace, motionless and chilled to the bone. Gerda wept hot tears over him, and they dissolved his frozen heart, so that eventually, he began to cry, and a speck of glass came out of his eye; he could see clearly again, and the spell was broken. But Daphne could not cry, would not shed tears, not in front of Tommy, not in front of anyone. She felt that if she started weeping, then she would not stop, the tears would turn into a sea, and she would drown in them.

Daphne closed her eyes, while her granddaughter dozed against her shoulder, and let her thoughts drift to her father, whose bouts of weeping were inexplicable to her when she was younger. 'Life may be pleasant when you're young, but it's not so much fun when you come to fifty,' he used to say, and no one knew what brought on such sudden melancholy; it might have been prompted by little more than a sudden downpour of rain or a cold wind from the east; or maybe it was the memory of his brother Guy, or his sister, Sylvia, lying in their graves, leaving Gerald behind them.

Was there something of her father in Tommy? He drank too much, like Gerald did, and suffered from similarly unpredictable bouts of depression. 'The horrors,' Gerald called them, when he would stand with hands over his eyes, trembling, until the worst of it had passed. Tommy was handsome, too, like Gerald – six foot tall, and as debonair and beautifully turned out as a matinee idol – and still attractive to women, there was no doubt about it. Daphne knew about her father's affairs – they all did, his three daughters, and his wife, too, and everyone who had anything to do with the London theatre world – but she laughed about it then, when she was a teenager, poked fun at 'Daddy's stable', some of whom, like Gertie Lawrence, were only a few years older than she was. And most of the time, apart from a very occasional outburst, her mother seemed able to accept this arrangement, rarely acknowledging Gerald's liaisons with Gertie and all the rest of those pretty young actresses, though now Daphne found it hard to understand this; how had she been so uncomplaining? Surely it must have been enraging for Muriel, not only as Gerald's wife, but also as an ageing actress, to know herself betrayed by him with girls less than half her age? But she had often complained about Daphne (the middle daughter, caught between parents, her father's favourite child). And then later, her father was furious with her, too, when she was old enough to have boyfriends, interrogating her when she came home at night, accusing her of behaving improperly, as if she was somehow betraying him. He stood guard on the landing at Cannon Hall; she could remember him still, staring out of the window, waiting for her, turned into a night-time monster, his features distorted with rage. 'Did you let him kiss you?' he'd hiss at her, as she came up the stairs. 'Where did you let him kiss you?'

It was all impossible, the past and the present, tangled into a terrible mess, and she could see no way of smoothing it out. Her mother was still alive, living just across the river from Fowey, at Ferryside, with Angela (the favourite daughter, thought Daphne, and then scolded herself for self-pity). Muriel was old now, and declining fast; watching the tides from her bedroom window, trapped and immobile in what had once been a place for carefree summers, the holiday house that Gerald had bought in the prime of their lives. She tried to imagine going over to Ferryside, telling her mother everything, asking for her advice about how to make her own marriage work, asking Muriel to share her secrets, too, but she knew this would never happen, it was inconceivable: some secrets were not made to be shared.

And when another letter arrived from Mr Symington, Daphne slipped it into her pocket, deciding to keep it private, hidden from everyone else. It was absurd, of course – this was not a love letter, but even so, Daphne did not want to discuss its contents, nor Mr Symington himself. She imagined what he might look like – he couldn't be much older than Tommy, given that he was still a youngish man in the 1920s, when he joined the Brontë Society, and took over as curator at the Brontë Parsonage. She had never seen a picture of Mr Symington, but was beginning to think of him as looking rather like her grandfather George, who died a decade before her birth, leaving his self-portraits behind him. She kept one hanging in the drawing room at Menabilly, and his face seemed as real to her as if she had actually known him in childhood, a handsome, bearded gentleman, blind in one eye, and fearful of losing his sight altogether, yet more noble and resolute-looking than Gerald, she thought; a man to admire, a novelist as well as an artist; and looking at his portrait again, she was overcome with powerful nostalgia, longing to go back to a past she never knew; longing to be with her grandfather, in a time before his grandchildren existed.

Daphne was tempted by the idea of sending a note to Symington suggesting that they meet. It would be a diversion from her days with Tommy, when everything felt brittle, ready to crack, unbearably tense, at times – yet she also worried about leaving Tommy, about not being by his side. She had hoped that the last few weeks would bring them closer together – that her loyalty and forgiveness would elicit some tenderness. But instead, he seemed to have withdrawn from her, as if in punishment, just like her father again whenever she'd been out at night with a boyfriend, though Gerald was less silent than Tommy; Tommy never shouted at her, bombarding her with hysterical accusations.

Sometimes, she wished that her husband would say more, accuse her, even, for at least then she would know what he knew about her. As it was, she wasn't sure if he was certain of anything, for she had never confessed to her own past infidelities; and he had never asked her outright. She imagined revealing, in a rush of emotion soon after discovering his affair with the Snow Queen, that she, too, had been unfaithful to him. But the story seemed impossible to tell; it was so shabby, so shaming. How, exactly, would she explain her behaviour to

Tommy? 'Darling, when we were staying with the Puxleys in Hertfordshire, while you were stationed nearby, I became involved with Christopher . . .' Well, it was impossible to say aloud; and it might do Tommy more harm than good, to rake over the past, for it had been, what, seventeen years ago? Her marriage was far more important, infinitely stronger, than any passing affair; and Christopher Puxley had ceased to matter to her long ago; though she felt more and more guilty about his wife, Paddy, her friend who she had betrayed, repeatedly, blinding herself to the consequences. She was just as selfish as her father, though now she was being punished, now her infidelity had come back to haunt her . . .

Daphne considered writing a letter to Paddy, asking for her forgiveness all these years later; but when she sat down, and tried to do so, she found herself unable to give shape to her wretchedness; there was only one phrase in her mind, which was 'I am rotten to the core'. And Daphne did feel rotten inside; she wondered if she would be punished, like Rebecca, with uterine cancer, for she was as twisted as Rebecca, unforgivably disloyal and treacherous and malformed, and not only in her betrayal of Paddy. Who could blame Tommy if he felt as murderous as Maxim de Winter, if he was to say of her, as Maxim said of Rebecca, 'She was not even normal?' He would have every right to say such a thing, if he ever discovered the real truth about her relationship with Gertie; he would be disgusted, horrified . . .

Not that Daphne was certain as to what that truth might be, for it seemed dream-like, both in recollection and at the time, a fantastical improbability, a fantasy, perhaps; though sometimes, in the night, when she woke from dreaming of

Gertie, feeling her hands still upon her, it felt more real than anything around her, closer than Tommy, who lay sleeping in his bedroom across the hall. She could never tell Tommy about those dreams, of course; she could not tell anyone what Gertie had meant to her, or explain why she had been so obsessed by this woman, one of her father's mistresses of all people, the last of Gerald's actress lovers.

None of it made sense when she tried to untangle what had happened, or why, for it was Gertie who became sick, not Daphne, Gertie who died of a malignant tumour, five years ago, when she was only fifty-four. And in the dark, as Daphne lay awake while the rest of the household was sleeping, she feared the death was in some way her doing, a repeat of her actions in killing off Rebecca and Rachel in the novels, as if that were the only solution to the knot they were all in; as if Gertie was another of the mysteriously threatening women who must be exorcised from Menabilly to preserve its peace and sanctity.

'Except you can't get rid of us, can you?' whispered Rebecca's voice in her head, just as Daphne was drifting towards sleep, at last, in the slowly whitening hour before dawn.

When she heard the voice, Daphne wondered if she might be going mad, and yet she could not rid herself of the suspicion that she was to blame for Gertie's death. And her self-accusations did not dissipate with the daylight, for there was no escaping the fact that she wrote *My Cousin Rachel* during the period she was spending most time with Gertie, and then Gertie died just after the book came out.

As for Tommy: what did he make of her misery over Gertie's death? He knew they were friends, of course, but nothing more; though perhaps Tommy guessed something when Daphne went off on holiday with Gertie to Florida, halfway through writing *My Cousin Rachel*. Afterwards, Gertie sent a letter to Menabilly, enclosing a photograph she'd taken of Daphne lying in bed, naked apart from a crumpled sheet, and on the back, she'd written, 'Darling, when can I borrow you from your husband again?' And it was so stupid, so reckless, but she'd left the photograph on the dining room table while they were eating breakfast, and Tommy picked it up and looked at it, before Daphne could stop him; falling silent when he read Gertie's inscription, and though he had said nothing, a muscle in his cheek had twitched, and he'd walked out of the room, closing the door behind him. At first, Daphne wanted to say to him, 'It's harmless, there's nothing to it,' but then she worried that this would make things worse; that it was better to say nothing, and perhaps that was when the distance between the two of them became so damaging.

Now, six years later, she was beginning to see that she must try to explain things to him, as a way of making amends; except it was hard to find an opportunity to talk. They were rarely alone in a room together – Kits darted in and out, arranging impromptu games of cricket and croquet, and Tod was always on hand, proffering cups of tea, while Tessa chased after her children and organised the meals, and Flavia sat with Tommy, making soothing small talk. At night, as always, Tommy went to his own bedroom, and though this was partly a relief to Daphne, she was also aware that he was avoiding her; barely able to look at her, let alone initiate a conversation.

Eventually, over two weeks after Tommy's return to Menabilly, she made certain that no one else would be with them on an afternoon stroll, as the rest of the family had gone off to Fowey to watch the summer sailing regatta. The sky was clear, for once, and a light breeze came off the sea, rippling through the trees, so that the leaves seemed to shiver and dance. Daphne took Tommy's hand as they walked slowly across the lawns, towards the view of the headland that they both loved, telling him that she needed to be honest with him. 'I've been going over and over this in my head,' she said, 'and I want you to know that the thing with Gertie was to do with my feelings about my father, not you, do you see?'

But if he saw, he gave no sign of it, just kept looking straight ahead. 'It's terribly important that you understand this, darling,' she said, trying not to falter, 'even though it was ages ago, because it might make sense to you now. I think it was a kind of nervous breakdown, going on inside myself, when I was in a terrible muddle . . .'

She paused, giving him time to answer, or ask questions, but he was just walking blindly forward, slipping his hand out of her clasp, so there was nothing for it but for her to go on, too. 'Because Gertie was so like Gerald, you see, all that gaiety and wit and charm, but with a sadness in the eyes, which was probably why they fell for each other, and they were both like Peter Pan, the kind of people who couldn't really grow old. And I adored her, like I adored Daddy, I couldn't help myself, though I'm not trying to make excuses . . . It was just a silly obsession, and it's gone now, you must see that?'

But it was no good, she couldn't get it straight in her head, and she couldn't make Tommy understand, and why should he, when Daphne couldn't understand it herself? No wonder, then, that he still said nothing, as he came to a sudden halt, though his hands were shaking, like an old man's, and his eyes were fixed on the ground; he would not look at Daphne, nor out towards the headland. 'Darling, shall we go on walking a little further, down to the beach?' she said to him, unable to bear the silence, and he just shook his head.

Since then, they had not walked anywhere together; their routine had not yet resumed, those rambles to the sea through Happy Valley, past the azaleas and rhododendrons, the dog padding at their heels. And though the days were warm, Tommy still seemed frozen, still bound to the Snow Queen, setting himself apart from Daphne, barricaded behind an icy silence. Daphne imagined his affair dragging on, as hers had done with Puxley, the betrayed wife knowing about the infidelity, yet unable to stop it, everything poisonous and rotten, when, like a tumour, it should be cut out, cleanly removed with a surgeon's knife. But nothing was clean or clear now; everything seemed unresolved, uncertain, unending. If this were one of her books, Daphne knew she would bring matters to a head, there would be an escalation of tension, and finally, a bold conclusion; except there was nothing to conclude here, this marriage must go on and on; and she must find a way to endure.

Menabilly,
Par,
Cornwall

5th September 1957

Dear Mr Symington,

Forgive my delay in replying to your last letter, but I have been inundated with visitors, and trying to do my duty as a wife, mother, and grandmother! But I haven't forgotten about Branwell, or your kind offer to sell me some of your library. And I would, indeed, be very interested in this proposal, because as you may have guessed, I do have a tentative idea of writing a book about Branwell.

I was wondering if you might perhaps be able to meet with me in London later this month? Perhaps I could take you to lunch somewhere in Bloomsbury? I am planning to spend a week or two there, working in the Reading Room of the British Museum, and transcribing as much of the manuscripts as is possible in that time. One of the many mysteries that are occupying my thoughts at present is that of Emily's poetry. I have been looking at the various editions, and note that the manuscripts were sourced from scattered sheets of paper that had been sold to American collectors, and others from Charlotte's widower, Arthur Bell Nicholls. But I can see no proof that each of these manuscripts was definitively Emily's work, rather than her brother's. What is really needed, I suppose, is a completely unbiased authority on handwriting that could distinguish between the various members of the Brontë family, without any preconceived opinion.

Of course, I would need to get together enough fresh material on Branwell to make a new book worthwhile. And there are so many questions that I should have to answer in my researches. Why, for example, was he never sent to school? I suspect that he suffered from petit mal, the almost imperceptible form of epilepsy, but I have absolutely no evidence for this, as yet. Who were his close friends, and what was the influence of freemasonry on his life, given his attendance at the local Masonic lodge? I should dearly like to know the details of his time with the Robinson family at Thorp Green; after all, he was there for two years – and Anne for even longer – and yet all we are ever told is the bare rumours of the disgrace accompanying Branwell's dismissal.

Now, I must stop all these musings, and get this letter off to the post. I look forward to hearing from you, and perhaps even meeting you in the near future. Looking at my diary, I see that I would be free to meet you the week after next, if that would suit you.

Yours sincerely,

Daphne du Maurier

CHAPTER EIGHT

Newlay Grove, October 1957

The days were shorter now, and Symington was short of breath, he coughed as he unlocked his storerooms or searched through his books, returning to old hiding places, rustling amidst his files. The letters from Daphne du Maurier had sent him back to his manuscripts, but he knew he should not have gone back, that nothing had changed.

'She will learn . . .' he muttered to himself, for Branwell could not be rescued from the maze of incomplete manuscripts, scattered and mutilated by Shorter and Wise; yes, Wise too, it was not only Shorter who had betrayed Branwell and Symington. The pair of them, Shorter and Wise, had profited from Branwell's losses, and as it was Wise who was the expert in forgery, surely it was Wise who had forged first Charlotte's and then Emily's signatures on Branwell's manuscripts, and sold them to rich yet gullible collectors; thinking nothing of it, for he thought nothing of Branwell, nor much of anyone other than himself, the Grand Panjandrum, who had fooled everyone, for such a long time.

Symington knew that Daphne hoped she would discover something extraordinary; he guessed that she dreamt of proving, at the very least, that Branwell had a hand in *Wuthering Heights*, as well as writing many of the poems attributed to Emily. Good luck to her, he thought, but only briefly; for he did not wish her well, he did not want her to succeed with Branwell where he had so far failed.

He had not replied to her last letter, which arrived weeks ago; she asked too many questions, and anyway, if anyone was to write a book on Branwell Brontë, it should be himself, not a romantic lady novelist, who knew nothing of scholarly research. And he had time on his hands to write, for Beatrice was rarely at home, but always attending some committee meeting or other, the British Legion, the Women's Voluntary Service, the St John's Ambulance Brigade. 'You'll have to look after yourself,' she said to him, before she sailed from the house, felt hat pinned firmly to her head, brown shoes polished and grey serge coat buttoned up to the collar.

So the slow mornings passed by, and no one called for Symington, only for Beatrice, who was indomitable, un-crushed, and Symington sometimes wondered if he was shrinking, dwindling like the daylight hours. He wished that he had not told Daphne his suspicions about the forged signatures on Branwell's manuscripts in an early rush of enthusiasm, but guessed, also, that she would not be able to proceed any further in her investigations, for Wise was dead, and Symington would keep his mouth shut from now on. That way, she would never know about that strange conversation he had with Wise not long before the old man died, when Symington had told him of his troubles and the lawyers' letters, and Wise had said, 'Well, they're on to both of us now, though we did it for the best, didn't we?'

But why rake over the past? Instead, Symington decided he would rearrange his collections, he would reconsider his cataloguing systems; he must do this, before he could embark on any further research for his book about Branwell, the masterpiece that was waiting for him to breathe air into it, waiting to be brought alive. The book in his mind was perfect, but his cataloguing systems were not, and they demanded his immediate attention.

Which meant he was very busy indeed; he was faced with a deadline of immense proportions, and this is what he told his son, when Douglas telephoned one afternoon, wanting to bring the child, Symington's grandson, for tea. The other boys had moved far away – Donald gone all the way to New Zealand – and Symington couldn't say he greatly missed them, though he felt angry and aggrieved when he thought of his sons, complained to Beatrice that they were insufficiently grateful for all he had done for them. But Douglas went to work for the family bookshop, until it was sold after the war, and now he was a bookbinder in York, so he should understand that there was important literary work to be done, that work must come before pleasure.

'So when shall I bring my little boy for tea?' said Douglas.

'You must talk to your stepmother about that,' said Symington. 'She is in charge of our social arrangements.'

Beatrice wanted to take charge in other ways, too; she'd told him that he must finally dispose of his collection of newspapers and magazines, pamphlets and theatre programmes – thousands and thousands of them, stored in wooden packing cases and cardboard cartons, filling up the boys' old bedrooms. 'It has been hard to find a buyer,' he said to Beatrice.

'Of course it has,' she said, 'no one would want a load of ancient newspapers. Just burn them in the back garden.'

'Beatrice,' he said, the blood rushing to his face, though he tried to speak slowly and clearly, to make her understand the importance of what he was telling her, 'you cannot possibly ask me to do such a thing. This collection is essential for my Brontë bibliography. I must work my way through all of it, in order to ascertain what new material may have come to light. Surely you can understand that?'

'Then why tell me you're trying to sell it?' she said, exasperated. 'You can't have it both ways.'

'You leave me no option,' he said. 'You force me into a corner, instead of supporting my work.'

'Oh, I support you,' she said, her dark eyes narrowing, her jaw more fixed than ever, 'I have always done that.'

Now, there was an uneasy, silent truce between the two of them. Beatrice stopped cleaning his study, and the dust was thickening there, slowly encroaching from the corners of the room, steadily gaining ground. Symington had managed to drag a few of his packing cases out of the bedrooms and into the cellar, but then his back seized up and it was too painful for him to move any more heavy loads. If he winced in front of Beatrice while trying to bend over to pick something up, she turned away, her face expressionless. And at night, she slept on the other side of their big mahogany bed, leaving as much space as possible between the two of them. Symington lay there, dozing fitfully, dreaming of stained and crumpled manuscripts, and he tried to smooth them out, but as his hand moved across the yellowing pages, they crumbled beneath him, turning into dust, and his mouth felt full of dust, and so did his throat, and his eyes.

Sometimes, very early in the morning, just before it was light, he went downstairs to his study, and examined the signatures on his Brontë manuscripts, hoping that he would see everything more clearly. Symington was certain now that Wise had attributed many of Branwell's early Angrian stories to Charlotte, and several of Branwell's poems to Emily, perhaps more; but how was he to prove this to the world, when he could not do so before? And why did he not ask Wise to confess to his forgeries, before he died? Why had he not pressed him for more details, instead of simply staying quiet in that final encounter with Wise? And Symington had gone on defending him, for years and years, his former mentor, and the source of so much of his own collection of manuscripts; as if, in defending Wise, he was also defending himself and his library. Yet in his darkest, most panic-stricken moments – when everyone else was sleeping, and his heart pounded so loudly that he felt a rushing in his ears – Symington feared that his own career had ended with Wise's death and disgrace. He could not find another job after his dismissal as librarian from Leeds University in 1938 when his enemies had conducted a mockery of a trial against him; a private tribunal, they called it, but it was an unjust inquisition. And that wasn't the only injustice, no, there were more, for they had locked him out of the very library that he had established for Lord Brotherton, and that Brotherton had bequeathed to the university, when in truth, it would have been in safer hands with Symington.

At least he had been able to ensure that some of the most precious items of the Brotherton Collection were secure in his house, where they remained, hidden away from the dirty fingers of careless students and fumbling academics, along with those manuscripts he kept safe from the bungling amateurs at the Brontë Society and the Parsonage Museum. Of course, he had been forced to sell some of his collection to an acquisitive American university a decade ago; and very handsomely they had paid, too, agreeing to his asking price of $10,000, which kept Beatrice from grumbling, at least for a time. And the Americans took him seriously – which was, in part, why he had decided to sell to them, for they were very respectful, those representatives from Rutgers University.

Even so, Symington's stomach lurched whenever he thought of Branwell's 'History of Angria' that had gone across the ocean to New Jersey, one of Branwell's most minutely written manuscripts, nine pages of microscopic, indecipherable text. It had defeated Symington for twenty years, remaining almost entirely incomprehensible, despite the hundreds of hours he devoted to it, poring over it with his magnifying glass, ruining his eyes. And it was for that reason, perhaps, that he let it go to America; suddenly feeling that he wanted to be free of it, to abandon Angria, but instead of fleeing it, he banished it as far away as possible from himself, as if it were an island that could be set adrift.

But now Symington did not feel liberated, but bereft and thwarted. For long before Daphne came along, with her own literary ambitions, he'd hoped to prove that Branwell was the author of much of *Wuthering Heights*; yet he had not even been able to prove that the manuscripts of Branwell's best poems were sold off by Wise, with Emily's signature forged upon them, or that Wise had copied Charlotte's signature on to Branwell's Angrian manuscripts, in order to fetch a better price for them.

As for the handwritten notebook of Emily's poems he'd borrowed from that pompous ass, Sir Alfred Law (a man who called himself a collector, using his considerable fortune to snap up Brontë manuscripts, outbidding Symington whenever he could), well, Symington had kept it safe for nearly quarter of a century, to serve as a true comparison with Branwell's writing. No one could possibly accuse him of stealing the notebook of poems – he had simply taken it on loan from Law's collection, to get it copied as a facsimile for the Shakespeare Head edition, and then Law had died in 1939, and to whom, exactly, was Symington supposed to return the notebook, after that?

Since then, other collectors had searched for Emily's notebook for so long, and bewailed its loss so loudly, that Symington could not possibly admit to having it now. And there were further complications, too. If he was to make his case for Branwell, he would need money to pay for scientific analysis of ink and paper, to establish when and how the signatures were faked, and just suppose he did find the funds, somehow, and the investigations proved beyond any doubt that Wise forged Charlotte and Emily's signature on Branwell's papers, then where would that leave Symington? He would be labelled as the owner of a library acquired from a forger and a cheat: Wise's collaborator, when all was said and done. And this would not do, this would not do at all.

So, thought Symington, round and round in circles, there was no escape, no way out of this hard place; he was locked up with his remaining manuscripts, in a limbo of his own making, along with the papery ghosts, and the shadows in the corners of the room.

CHAPTER NINE

Hampstead, February

I had never realised until recently what a colossal number of pieces of paper are stored, most of them untouched for years at a time, in archives and libraries around the country: millions and millions of sheets, some of them indexed, some of them not, just boxed up without being catalogued, abandoned like ancient, yellowing bones in the catacombs beneath a city.

I suppose I should have known this before, as the daughter of librarians, and actually, one of the very few memories I have of my father is going with him to where he worked, to the Reading Room of the British Museum, and him showing me what must have been a card index. I'd never seen so many pieces of paper, there were far too many to count, and anyway, I didn't know what a card index was, I just remember him saying, 'look, these are the As.' Then he wrote out the alphabet for me on a piece of paper, 'A is for apple', and so on, which I didn't understand, because A didn't look like an apple, it looked like one of the step-ladders in the Reading

Room that my father climbed up to reach the highest shelves. When I tried to follow him, he said, 'You're too small to go up the ladder', and it somehow stayed in my head, the ladder, not the apple. He must have died soon afterwards, and so it was my mother who taught me the alphabet, just by reading to me every evening, me sitting by her side, looking at the pictures, until one day the words and the pictures seemed to merge into one; she was showing me a picture of Peter Pan, and then she pointed at his name on the page, and I could read it, I could see that it was the boy who could fly in the picture, and the feeling I had was like flying, it was like a swoop inside me.

I was thinking about that when I fell asleep last night, and about my parents, and what they would make of me now, carefully picking my way through the catacombs, searching for documents relating to the almost entirely forgotten Mr J. A. Symington. It would all be second nature to them, but it still seems astonishing to me, to discover that there are thousands of pages that have passed through Symington's hands, once you start looking, and I have been looking, trying to follow the faint trail that is left in library catalogues and archives. I've sent dozens of emails to various librarians, and phoned several of them to pester them, and they've all been helpful with suggestions about where his letters might be stored. Some of Symington's papers seem to have ended up in New Jersey, at Rutgers University, but as far as I can tell, that acquisition dates back to the late 1940s, which was almost certainly before his correspondence began with Daphne du Maurier. Then a couple of days ago, I found a reference to another cache of papers, tucked away in the far reaches of a West Yorkshire municipal archive, donated by Symington's widow soon after his death. No detailed catalogue exists for this bequest, aside from a note that it contained a collection of his printing blocks (over 3000 of them), a huge quantity of apparently random newspapers and magazines from the 1920s and '30s, and what was simply referred to as 'various correspondence'. So it was obvious that I had to catch a train to Yorkshire and search through the archive myself.

And it seemed extraordinary that no one else should care; that no one else has thought to look, that I was going there alone. But none of that mattered, really, because it was like setting off on an adventure when I left the house this morning at the same time as Paul, and it was good to feel that I had a purpose, that it wasn't just him on his way to work as we stepped into the lift at Hampstead tube station together, going down underground. It was already busy, and I was pushed up close to him on the Northern Line carriage, and he took my hand, then brushed his lips against mine as I got off before him at King's Cross. 'Good luck,' he whispered into my ear, and smiled.

He wouldn't have smiled if I had told him I was looking for Daphne du Maurier's letters, but I hadn't gone into that much detail, I'd just said that I was spending the day at a West Yorkshire archive, and I had a hunch it might yield some original research for my PhD. 'Very romantic,' he'd said, 'though romantic with a capital "R", hopefully, if your quest yields some interesting Brontë material . . .' But I knew what I was looking for in the archives, and it had Daphne du Maurier's name on it.

Not that any of the Symington collection was properly indexed, so it was hard to know where to start. There was no explanation for the printing blocks, no documentation to give clues as to why they had formed part of the collection; but there they were, in a packing case, along with a load of ancient periodicals, *Picture Post*, the *Radio Times*, and magazines I'd never heard of, like *John Bull*. A lot of the collection was tied up in brown paper and string, dusty and faded and mouldering, as if no one had touched it since Mr Symington's death, as if no one had been interested to discover what lay inside. The frustrating thing was that I didn't have time to go through all of Symington's files of correspondence – there were hundreds and hundreds of pages – and the journey had already taken most of the morning, first the train to Leeds, then a slow bus to a suburb in the north of the city, and then a fifteen-minute walk to this redbrick civic building that housed a section of the local archives. There was only one other researcher inside, an elderly man researching his family genealogy, or so I guessed from his whispered questions to the solitary archivist, their faces solemn beneath the fluorescent light, their voices hushed, as if we were in a church rather than a windowless room that felt like it hadn't been aired since it was built in the 1950s. Why, precisely, Symington's widow had decided that his correspondence should be deposited here, I have no idea; though I can see it made slightly more sense that it had stayed in Yorkshire, unlike other parts of his collection of manuscripts and rare books, which appear to have been sold to the university library in New Jersey while he was still alive.

But what matters is that Symington kept Daphne's letters to him, and the local archives preserved them, and I found them – or maybe they found me . . . It was the address that leapt out at me from the vast jumble of files – *her* address, typed on her typewriter: Menabilly, Par, Cornwall. I wanted to call out to someone, 'Look, over here, just see what I've found!' but instead, I made a small yelping noise as I flicked through the pages of her letters. There was something so astonishing about their physical existence: the pattern of the ink on the yellowing paper, and the shape of the words themselves on the page, in her irregular typescript that sometimes slopes downwards, instead of keeping to a straight line. I thought of saying that to the archivist, when I was asking him if I could make photocopies of the letters, but then I thought that might seem a bit obsessive, rather than professional, so I just showed him my postgraduate card from London University, and he nodded, and gave me a form to fill in.

Even the photocopies of the letters seemed precious, and it felt like a privilege to be taking them away with me on the slow train back to London. I was wide awake, reading them over and over again, while the other passengers began to doze, lulled by the rocking carriage and the fug inside, as the rain ran down the windows. By the time I got home, Paul was already asleep in bed, so there was no one to talk to about my discovery, but that was just as well, because I couldn't have told him that I'd unearthed the du Maurier letters, he would have been too angry, and the day would have been spoilt by his disapproval, so I hugged the secret all to myself.

Of course, I don't have Symington's replies to Daphne; but the thrill of possession hasn't yet gone; I can't stop looking at her letters, can't bear to put them away in a drawer, even though it's really late, and I should be sleeping next to Paul. So now I've got them on my desk, right beside my computer, and I know it sounds childish, but I still feel excited just seeing her address. These pages were written in the house that became Rebecca's Manderley; they came from inside the walls that I have imagined so many times – slipping into Menabilly, exploring its rooms in my head – which is why her letters seem almost like a series of clues or a kind of key into a closed and hidden place that Daphne called her house of secrets.

Not that she says anything so explicit to Mr Symington. Her first letter is brisk and to the point, but with sufficient detail to make it clear that she'd already done quite a lot of Brontë research, and therefore had some basis for her belief that Branwell was talented. But it's curious going through these letters, trying to map Daphne's thought processes, because of course I've already read her Branwell biography, the unwritten book that was taking shape in her head during the correspondence with Symington; a book which explores, amongst other things, what Branwell might, or might not, have written, as well as the blurred borderline between his fantasies and the reality of his short life.

Anyway, the letters continue for about a month – and you can tell from reading them that Symington has responded enthusiastically to Daphne's approach, has even sold her some rare books and papers from his Brontë library. And then the flurry of correspondence appears to stop until the beginning of 1959, a year and a half since it first began in the summer of 1957.

Oddly, in her last of these early letters to Symington, Daphne tells him that she has to go to London for a week or so, and perhaps they might arrange a time to see each other there. That's when it all goes quiet, which makes me wonder what, exactly, happened next, in that long, extended silence?

Did they meet? Did they fall in love, and then out of love, did they quarrel or did they become disillusioned with one another? Somehow, this silence of theirs feels oddly reassuring; to me, that is. It makes me feel less alone, knowing that there are gaps in their lives, as well as their letters; spaces that I might fill, if only I could find a way into them.

CHAPTER TEN

Menabilly, October 1957

Daphne was not writing, she did not want to write; she did not want to think, she did not want to think about what was happening to her. She whispered instructions to herself, so quietly that no one else could hear: 'You need a good shake,' she murmured, but this did not help, for she was already shaking, like Tommy. 'Get a grip,' she said, but it was no good, she was already gripped, body and soul, and it was all out of her control, she could not break free. If only she knew what was behind the vice she was fixed in, it would be easier; perhaps it was her own vices, she thought, perhaps it was these that held her in their grip, so tightly that she couldn't breathe.

In her more lucid moments, she feared she was going mad, driven mad by Branwell, as much as by Tommy, by knowing and not knowing; by not knowing enough. And it was this that made her curse herself, for believing that Branwell could rescue her from Rebecca, that he was powerful enough to push Rebecca aside, but now she saw that he was as bad as

Rebecca, that the two of them would consume her; for they should never have been exhumed from the crypt.

At other times, the worst times, she suspected conspiracies all around her; and if they were not real, then someone must have slipped a sliver of ice into her eyes, so that she could not see straight, she could not see things as they truly were. Or maybe she could see the truth, when no one else was able to see straight; perhaps she was the only person who really saw through everything, even though she could not unravel the words in Branwell's manuscripts, those impossible manuscripts, that were ruining her eyes, along with everything else.

The troubles started on her trip to London, for a fortnight in September. Tommy had refused to go back for any further appointments at the nursing home. 'You'll not force me into that torture chamber ever again,' he said to Daphne when she suggested that he consult the doctors there before attempting to return to work. But after four weeks of convalescence at Menabilly, he was judged well enough by the local doctor in Fowey to resume his duties at Buckingham Palace, though Daphne wasn't convinced by Tommy's apparent show of good health. True, he was less grey-faced than when he had first arrived home, and he no longer wept and had cut down on his drinking. But after the children and grandchildren left Menabilly, his silence in Daphne's presence did not abate, and she wondered if he had convinced the doctor to let him go back to work as a ruse to resume his relationship with the Snow Queen. Daphne was almost certain that he still spoke to her on the telephone, whenever she was safely out of the way in her writing hut; though she could not bear to confront him with this suspicion, it seemed too humiliating, too reminiscent of her father's displays of jealousy towards her. Instead, when the time came, she travelled back to the flat with Tommy to settle him in; those were the words she used to describe what was happening, but she knew that he knew that she wanted to keep an eye (both eyes) on him.

The journey from Cornwall was almost silent, the two of them sitting opposite one another in a stuffy first-class compartment; Tommy hidden behind a newspaper fortress, Daphne staring out of the window, as the train trundled through woodland and moors, where the leaves were beginning to fall, and the bracken was fading. After the train crossed the bridge at Plymouth, high over the River Tamar, Daphne felt her heart sink, dragged down by the sense that she was leaving her own country, losing her safe haven. She knew the journey so well, but dreaded it in this direction, even her favourite part of it, when the railway line snaked along the edge of the Devon coastline, seeming to hover almost above the waves. 'Darling, do look,' she said to Tommy as they skirted the wide estuary at Dawlish, where the low tide had left a flotilla of boats grounded on the mud flats.

Tommy put down *The Times* for a moment, and said, 'Faintly depressing on a grey day, isn't it? Endless vistas of mud from here to the horizon . . .'

'I think it's always beautiful,' said Daphne.

'Do you?' he said. 'Maybe I've just seen this view too often, trailing up and down from London, week after week, for all these years.' He picked up the paper again, lifting it so that his face was obscured, and Daphne suppressed a sigh, swallowing it back inside her. She wanted to say to him, 'I've been doing this journey, too, for the last thirty years,' but she knew it was pointless to remind him of that, and anyway, it was to be expected that she felt differently from Tommy; they were, after all, such separate entities.

By the time the train had shunted into Paddington, the silence between them seemed to have gained a sound of its own; a kind of rasping tension, like the noise of someone grinding their teeth in their sleep at night. They queued for a taxi at the station, and then both sat hunched in their own corners of the back seat, Tommy gripping the handles of his suitcase, his knuckles whitened, his hands shaking slightly. Was it the vibrations of the engine, Daphne wondered, that made his hands tremble, or was it still the after-effects of the treatment at the nursing home? She reached out, suddenly overcome with pity for her husband, and put her right hand over his. 'It's like shell shock, isn't it?' she said to Tommy.

'What is?' he said.

'What we've been through, this summer. It's as if we've both got battle fatigue, and now we must rest up and recover . . .'

But there was no rest to be had in London; there was no peace to be found there, only gloomy despondency. Daphne could not write in the dreary Chelsea flat, with its faint smell of gas that permeated everything, and its dismal view of sooty chimney pots and blank walls and the occasional diseased pigeon perched on the windowsill, limping on deformed and twisted claws. It was impossible, she could not breathe there, surrounded by the traffic and the grey-faced crowds, the redbrick canyons bearing down on her, no open space except for that bit of dusty scrub in Sloane Square, all of it choked and obscured in the thick fog of a million strangers' thoughts.

She could only concentrate at home in Menabilly, in the silence, her island, her Gondal, away from the city's babble of meaningless talk; it was sending her crazy, being away from her safe house and her hut in the garden and the path to the sea, away from her routine, from her routes, from everything that kept her sane . . . Apart from Rebecca; Rebecca was part of Menabilly, and not safe at all, but at least she was a familiar danger, and Daphne had tactics to keep her at bay, or in the bay, if need be, alongside the shipwreck, that was the way to steer clear of her; let the sea submerge her, though she was uncovered at low tide, and there was nothing that one could do to avoid her then, but at least one could be prepared for those occasions.

Finally, Daphne gave up trying to write in the confined little flat, and decided to get on with her research in the Reading Room of the British Museum, for T. J. Wise's collection of Brontë manuscripts was held there, along with other rare letters and books that she needed to consult. She would work there all day, she decided, and perhaps meet up with Peter for lunch, as his office was just across the road from the museum entrance in Great Russell Street.

So why did she not ring Peter that day? Why, just after Tommy left for work in the morning, did she ring the Snow Queen instead? She had not planned the conversation, but suddenly found herself flicking through Tommy's address book by the telephone, and then dialling the number, half hoping that no one would answer. But there was an answer, and when Daphne heard the other woman's voice, saying, 'Hello?' she had to force herself to speak, to fill the questioning silence. What, then, should she say to the Snow Queen? Daphne wanted to ruffle her, to make her feel as disturbed as she was, to make the ice melt, to make this woman real, instead of a looming figure in Daphne's imagination. She wanted to be cruel, to reduce the woman to tears. But she found herself saying something else, something she had not expected. 'I'm in London, as you may already know,' she said, 'And I thought it might be a good idea if we were to meet.' She did not give the other woman time to disagree, but kept talking, quickly, suggesting that they meet later that day, in the forecourt outside the British Museum.

And though the Snow Queen's voice had remained cool on the end of the telephone, she agreed to the meeting, rather to Daphne's surprise. But it was hopeless, of course, she was as difficult to read as the Brontë manuscripts inside the museum: she gave nothing away, this woman, and Daphne had to struggle not to stare at her, as they sat on a bench together, side by side like a couple on a first date, or lovers on a secret assignation. The Snow Queen was as composed and graceful as a ballet dancer, or one of Gerald's leading ladies. Nothing seemed to make her falter or stumble, and she was unmoved by the sight of the tears that welled up in Daphne's eyes, or at least, she pretended not to notice, just smoothed back her blonde chignon, and her cold blue gaze remained steady. Daphne felt inelegant beside her, and badly dressed, her trousers too mannish, her shirt too shapeless, a hat jammed over her hair; entirely unsophisticated next to the Snow Queen's perfectly tailored beige silk dress and expensive cashmere coat. And Daphne's fingers were stained with black ink, her nails were broken and bitten, unlike the Snow

Queen's, which were painted a shimmering pastel pink, though they should have been blood red talons.

It was as if she had suddenly been turned back into the hapless, nameless second Mrs de Winter, Daphne de Winter, inept and inexperienced when faced with her rival. But her rival was alive, indisputably real this time, not dead like Rebecca, though the Snow Queen had something of Rebecca about her, she was beautiful and could never be defeated, and her voice was steady and her stare unwavering when she told Daphne that she would not promise to stop seeing Tommy.

'I love him,' she said to Daphne, 'and he loves me, you must realise that.' Daphne wanted to tell her that a Snow Queen can know nothing of love, only of destruction, but she remained silent, just looked away.

The woman continued talking. 'I've given up my husband for Tommy,' she said, 'and don't you think it's time to be realistic about your own marriage? From what Tommy tells me, it sounds like there have been irresolvable problems between the two of you for years, since the war. And it's not as if you've been faithful to him, have you? You can't claim to occupy the moral high ground.' Daphne did not answer her, she could think of nothing to say, it was all too futile for words, and after a few minutes, the woman stood up, smoothed down her skirt, and said, 'We're not getting anywhere like this, are we? I think it would be better if you didn't try to get in touch with me again, unless you've got something useful to discuss.'

Daphne was too distracted to say goodbye, because by then she'd begun to notice them, in the corners of her eyes, the figures in the lengthening afternoon shadows of the British

Museum, several of them amidst the stone columns of the portico, though it was hard to be certain, as they slipped between the unknowing passers-by. She was sure they were watching her, or was it the Snow Queen they were spying on? No, that couldn't be right, because after the Snow Queen walked away, her sharp grey heels tapping on the flagstones, the watchers had remained beside the colonnade. There were too many of them to be private detectives, she thought, and anyway, surely Tommy would not set detectives on her trail? He was the one with the secrets, after all; for Gertie was dead, and she had nothing left to hide from him . . .

She felt panicky when she went back into the museum, unable to concentrate either on her encounter with the Snow Queen or her study of Branwell's manuscripts; she stared at his faded handwriting, but it made no sense, none of it made any sense, the pages might as well have been covered with ancient Egyptian hieroglyphics, like the papyrus relics displayed alongside the mummified bodies in a gallery nearby; and when she turned to her notebook, she had nothing to write, the pages remained blank, like blind, unseeing eyes. There were other eyes, though, that were watching her. Inside the Reading Room, she was safe, she had to be, they would not dare to follow her in there, but outside, they were waiting, she sensed them, though she did not understand what they wanted from her.

Daphne stayed in the Reading Room until closing time, when one of the librarians, a young man, came over to her and said, apologetically, that it was necessary for him to take the Brontë manuscripts back from her, but would she like him to reserve them for her tomorrow morning? She gazed at him, aghast, and he looked concerned, asking if he could do anything to help, and she just shook her head, then rushed out, head down, trying not to meet anyone's eyes. She'd bought a return ticket from Sloane Square underground station that morning, having planned to take the tube home again, from Russell Square, so as not to have to sit on the bus as it stopped and started through the interminable traffic, but when she walked out of the museum gates, she set off in a different direction, not thinking straight, knowing only that she needed to shake off the figures who were still following her. There was a tall man in a tweed suit and a trilby hat; he was the leader, she thought; the others followed his hat through the crowded streets, the hat was a signal to them. The men were getting closer, gaining on her, and she started to run, stumbling past office workers on their way home, and they looked at her, startled, but no one helped, no one could help her, and she feared going underground, someone might push her beneath a train, disposing of her as easily as a piece of tissue paper. So she hailed a passing taxi, and asked the driver to take her to Buckingham Palace. He looked at her through the open car window, half-smiling, and then she feared that he was part of this conspiracy that she did not understand. She pulled back from the taxi, horrified, and the driver called after her, but she did not stop, she was running faster now, and jumped on to a bus, it didn't matter where it was going, as long as it took her away from this place.

At Piccadilly Circus she got her bearings, and caught another bus to throw them off the scent, and then slipped on to a different one at Hyde Park Corner, and finally, she reached Sloane Square, and was almost certain that no one was following her down the King's Road, as she hurried back to the flat.

The main entrance hall to the block smelt of rubber, as always, but there was something else in the air; an almost imperceptible scent of the Snow Queen's perfume, or was it even more poisonous than that? She held her breath, and dashed into the lift, the iron gates clattering behind her; and by the time she got out, Daphne felt choked of oxygen, as if some invisible presence in the lift had wrapped its fingers around her throat to suffocate her. Tommy was already there when she unlocked the front door, and he looked at her strangely. 'What on earth is the matter, old girl?' he said. And she caught sight of herself in the hall mirror, ashen-faced and sweating. She wanted to tell him everything – about the meeting with the Snow Queen, about the people who had been following her, about the menacing ringleader in his trilby hat – but then she was struck by a terrible thought. What if Tommy was in on the plot? Could he have been brainwashed, just as he'd been deluded by the Snow Queen, so that he could no longer see straight? Could that have been the reason for his breakdown? Not the slow moving of his blood, but water washing into his brain, a rising tide, swallowing everything he held dear?

After that terrible day, Daphne came home to Menabilly. She would be safer here, in the house hidden from the outside world, invisible, even, from the sea. She must be very cautious, very careful, she now realised. It was dangerous to let one's guard down to strangers, dangerous to even allow their letters into the house. She would not reply to Mr Symington's letters, nor to anyone else's, except those from her children (but what if they had been got at? No, surely not . . . though how could she be certain?). Tod could be trusted, at least, but the doors must be locked at night, the rusting wrought iron gates kept closed at the West Lodge, and the second set of gates must be shut, as well, closer to the house. They might come through the woods, if she was not careful; you couldn't be too careful, these days. She must speak to the farmer about renewing the barbed wire around the boundaries of the estate; she would retreat, yet also be prepared against attack. Menabilly had withstood siege in the Civil War, as a Royalist stronghold. Let it be a stronghold again, thought Daphne, as she checked and re-checked that the front door was bolted; as she walked the passageways at night, like a restless ghost, like Rebecca, too swiftly for anyone to catch her; fighting sleep, until the dawn came, and she lay down at last.

CHAPTER ELEVEN

Newlay Grove, November 1957

Symington felt old, declining as the year drew to its close. He was tired, and his bones ached, and his head hurt, as did his eyes. Everything was blurred around him, his spectacles no longer worked, he could not read, even the legible words in Branwell's manuscripts swam away from him, the letters dissolving into watery confusion.

He was so tired, he longed to close his eyes and sleep his way through the afternoons, but Beatrice would disapprove, and it didn't matter if she was out of the house, she somehow sensed if he had been in their bedroom while she was gone; she said he creased the sheets that she had smoothed and tucked in so carefully first thing in the morning.

Today, he considered stretching out on the floor of his study, but it was too dusty, too hard, and he worried that even if he managed to lower himself to the ground, he would be too stiff to get up again, his joints betraying him; he might petrify and fossilise there, and Beatrice would not care, she came into his study so seldom these days, she might not find him until it was too late.

Everything was silent now, the house shrouded and quiet, and the outside world seemed to have receded and disappeared in the winter fogs and perpetual rain clouds. There was no word from Daphne du Maurier, not even a brief acknowledgement of Symington's previous letter. Not that he had said much in the letter to her, it had been just a note, telling her that he had been unable to provide precise answers to her last set of questions, but that he was rereading his notes and files, in the hope of revealing some new information. Which was, in fact, entirely truthful, though he did not tell her that his investigations concerned the wrongful attribution to Emily of an unfinished poem by Branwell. The poem, as it happened, was one of Symington's favourites, and he found himself quoting it out loud, knowing that no one would ever hear him.

> The Heart which cannot know another
> Which owns no lover friend or brother
> In whom those names without reply
> Unechoed and unheeded die.

Symington was surprised by the sound of his own voice, declaiming the lines, confident and strong, but he also realised, not for the first time, that he remained unsure of what, exactly, Branwell was suggesting in his poem. He knew that Wise had bound the manuscript in green morocco leather, as part of a slim volume sold to a wealthy American collector, Mr Bonnell, who had no interest in Branwell, but was happy to accept this fragment as being by Emily, once her forged signature was added to it. He knew, also, that the poem was written on the back of a letter drafted by Branwell in the summer of 1835, to the secretary of the Royal Academy, when Branwell was coming up to his eighteenth birthday, and hoping to come to London to study art. He knew that Branwell never went to the Academy; indeed, that his only trip to London, planned in the expectation of an interview at the Royal Academy, was alleged to have ended in disgrace, drunk in a Holborn tavern, after wandering the streets, if, indeed, Branwell ever actually made it to the capital city at all; which remained unproven, like many other episodes in the life of the Brontës. Symington knew all these things, from his studies at the Brontë Parsonage, which inherited, amongst other treasures from the Bonnell collection, the green morocco volume of poetry, the same volume that Symington had brought home with him while he was working there in order to examine it in more detail.

The green morocco volume was still in his study – for safekeeping – but Symington worried that he would die before making sense of the poem, for even though it was written in a clearly legible hand, unlike Branwell's Angrian histories and manuscripts, it was nevertheless as opaque in meaning as it had been when he first read it at the Parsonage, over a quarter of a century ago.

'The Heart which cannot know another,' muttered Symington, again. 'Which owns no lover friend or brother . . .' As was so often the case with Branwell, the composition was fragmentary, inconclusive and spattered with misspellings and grammatical quirks; but he liked the sound of the words, their rhythm and pace, which gave them purposefulness. And though the meaning had proved elusive, there must be a *purpose* to the poem; it was simply a matter of finding it. 'Press on, Symington,' he urged himself. 'Press on . . .'

He closed his eyes, and tried to remember a time when his heart had echoed with thoughts of another, another who was not Branwell. And into his mind floated the memory of the last time he had felt prosperous; back in 1948, it must have been, he sold a stack of manuscripts to Rutgers University, and one of their professors travelled all the way to Leeds to see him. Beatrice had cooked them roast beef and Yorkshire pudding for lunch, and then Symington took him to his library annexe in the house next door, and the American had been impressed, the look on his face was unmistakeable, when he saw the book cases stacked to the ceiling with treasures. 'This is an Aladdin's Cave,' said the professor, 'it is quite extraordinary . . .'

Afterwards, Symington had shown Beatrice the cheque for $10,000, and she put her arms around him and said, 'Oh Alex!', and he waltzed her about the room, and she threw her head back and laughed. It was a winter of fuel cuts and fog, he remembered that, but the house seemed full of light that evening . . . and the next day, he bought tickets for them to go to the theatre, for Beatrice's birthday treat. What was it they had seen? Of course – and Symington slapped his hand on the desk as the memory surfaced – it was the play by Daphne du Maurier.

He stood up, suddenly struck by an idea, and went over to a packing case, and rifled through its contents. It was in here somewhere, he knew it was, and after several minutes of scrabbling, he found it – the programme for *September Tide*, November 1948, starring Miss Gertrude Lawrence; he had not been mistaken.

Could this possibly be a clue to the purpose in Branwell's words? Was this the hidden message of the poem, after all these years, that he should swallow his pride, and relinquish solitude, if he was to avoid following in Branwell's wake, unheeded, sinking into oblivion? Symington felt a surge of energy and excitement, and a sense of awakening, of adventure, even. He understood the poem at last: it was a call to arms, not an admission of defeat; a message of hope, rather than despair or submission. He must write again to Daphne. They would be comrades in their endeavours.

Symington picked up his pen, and then realised that he was smiling; but not only smiling, he was making an unfamiliar wheezing noise; no, not wheezing, he was laughing, he heard the sound of his own laughter, for the first time in years . . .

12th November 1957

Dear Miss du Maurier,

I do hope that your Brontë research is progressing satisfactorily, as the nights draw in. I expect you have also been kept very busy with your family; my wife Beatrice certainly has her hands full at the moment.

I, too, have been much preoccupied, though with domestic matters of another kind, relating back to the Brontës' life at the Parsonage, and those stories that they wrote in between peeling potatoes and so forth. Not that Branwell was likely to have been involved in culinary activities, though one never knows!

But forgive me for my whimsical approach. In fact, I have been engaged in very serious investigations, and I feel certain that you would be interested to know more about the precise information that I have uncovered.

One more afterthought, before I get this letter off to the post box. While sorting and re-ordering my files, I came across this old theatre programme of the touring production of your play, 'September Tide'. I happened to see the play when it came to Leeds in 1948, as my wife was a fan both of yours and your leading lady, Gertrude Lawrence. It brought back memories of a most enjoyable evening, despite a very thick pea-soup fog that surrounded the *theatre! I enclose the programme, which I thought might amuse you.*

I look forward to hearing from you,
Yours sincerely,

J. Alex Symington.

CHAPTER TWELVE

Hampstead, 14 February

Something very odd happened today. I haven't got it quite straight in my head. I went to the British Museum Reading Room – the old one, where Daphne would have done her original research – because I wanted to look around there, even though the Brontë manuscripts she studied are now in the newer British Library building on the Euston Road. I suppose it was a bit of romantic whimsy on my part, and not just to do with Daphne; I also liked the idea of going there because it was where my parents met. It's one of the very rare stories my mother told me about my father – that it took him a month of seeing her there every day, before he had the courage to say a word to her. Not that they were allowed to talk inside the Reading Room – silence prevailed, of course – but he managed to say hello to her outside, in the courtyard at the front of the museum, and in the following weeks, they progressed to sitting on a bench together, and then having tea around the corner, and eventually (her word, not mine), they were married.

She had just started working in the Reading Room when they met; my father was already a librarian there, and he'd been working at the museum for many years, a solitary man, more at home with books than people. At least, I imagine he was, but my mother never really talked about their life together, and there was something about her silence that made it impossible for me to ask her to tell me more. He died the week before my fourth birthday – I don't know exactly how or why, she just said he was ill, he had a weak heart, and then he died, and for some reason, I didn't feel able to ask her for further details – and I can't remember much about him, just that day he took me to the library, and a trip to the theatre, and the feel of his rough tweed jacket against my cheeks when he carried me in from the cold.

My father was a writer, as well as a librarian, I know that, but I don't have any of his books, I don't even know if they were published; I think not, because I've never found any record of them, and I've searched for a very long time. All I have are half a dozen small black leather-bound notebooks, filled with his tiny, indecipherable handwriting, which I found tucked away in my mother's desk, after she died. I was clearing everything out before giving up the lease; not that there was much to clear in a little two-bedroom attic flat. Still, I'd felt lucky to live there, at the very top of a big old Hampstead house called Bay Tree Lodge, which my father had already rented before he met my mother. 'We live on the servants' floor,' my mother used to say, with a small smile curving her lips; but I thought it was by far the best place to be, high above the streets.

As far as I know, my father had always earned his living as a librarian, like my mother, though she said his heart wasn't in the job, but in his writing. And this worried me as a child, in the years after his death, when I thought about him. I imagined his heart as having been weakened and then separated from his body, and somehow contained within the dusty leather covers of an old book, and the dust wasn't good for his heart, it was clogging everything up, slowing his heart down, and then one day it stopped, and he was dead. As for the book that had contained his heart . . . well, I wasn't sure what had become of it, but I knew it was lost to me.

Anyway, although all of this is odd, it is not the odd thing that happened today. It's Valentine's Day, which Paul ignored, because he says it's a load of commercialised rubbish, but then he looked embarrassed when I gave him a card before he went to work this morning; a card I'd made myself, with a red heart on the front, shaped out of rose petals from the back garden, that I'd pressed and dried last summer, just after I'd moved here. That was something my mother taught me to do – to put flowers between sheets of white tissue paper, and then into the leaves of the heaviest book we could find, which was her copy of the Shorter Oxford English Dictionary, the one I still use it now. I'd wanted to find a romantic quote from Henry James to write inside the card, but nothing seemed quite right, so in the end, I just wrote, 'I love you', and when Paul read it, he said, 'You're such a sweet girl . . . And too young to know the meaning of heartbreak, aren't you?'

So there I was, sitting in the Reading Room today, trying to write an outline of my dissertation, but wondering what Paul was trying to tell me, and not getting anywhere. Then I started thinking about broken hearts, and I wished I'd told Paul that I *did* know something about them. I knew a little bit about my father and his heart, and also about heartbroken Branwell, who never got to fulfil his dream of coming here to the Reading Room; though in the end, the year before his death, he'd written a letter to his friend, Joseph Leyland, saying that he'd once thought it would be paradise to spend a week in the British Museum, but now he was so depressed, his eyes would roam over 'the most treasured volumes like the eyes of a dead cod fish'. Poor, lugubrious Branwell; if only he'd escaped from home . . .

I scribbled a reminder to myself, to check the references about whether Branwell had ever actually visited London. And then all of a sudden, out of the corner of my eye, I thought I saw Rachel at another desk, bending over a notebook, writing in it. It was hard to tell, with her smooth dark hair falling over her face, but the longer I stared at her, the more I wanted it to be her, which was not at all what I'd expected to feel. After a few minutes, she glanced up, as if she'd somehow sensed my gaze, pushing her hair away from her eyes, and she smiled at me, almost conspiratorially. I blushed, as if I had been caught out doing something wrong, though of course I hadn't. She didn't know me, she'd never met me, as I'd only started seeing Paul after she'd left him and gone to America. Half an hour later, when I got up to leave the Reading Room, she came after me, or maybe she just happened to be going at the same time, and as we went down the stone steps outside, she said, 'Do I know you? I'm so sorry if we've already been introduced – I'm good at remembering faces, but hopeless with names.'

Her voice was light, with a promise of laughter in it, and she smiled as she spoke. I wasn't sure what to say – I mean, I wasn't completely certain that it was Rachel – so I could hardly tell her that she didn't know me, but I knew her, because I was married to her ex-husband. So I just said that I thought I recognised her from a photograph in the newspaper, the one that accompanied the piece about her new book of poetry, and then I apologised for saying so, for being intrusive.

'That's OK,' she said, and she was close enough for me to smell her perfume, a kind of exotic, expensive scent of amber; and she wore an amber necklace, as well, heavy beads that shone against her golden skin. 'I never expect to be recognised anywhere, least of all here. I just like spending time in the Reading Room, when I'm working on a new poem. I think of all the other writers who have sat here, and I find it comforting.'

I told her that I was a fan of her writing – that I thought about it a lot, which is true, I've bought her latest book; though of course I didn't say that I keep it carefully hidden in the bottom drawer of my desk, and that I only read her poems when Paul isn't around. But maybe Rachel sensed that I was fascinated by her – because I am, of course; by everything about her, especially when I realised that she looked so like Paul that she could almost have been his sister – and perhaps she found it flattering, without needing to know much more about me, because it was all about her, that was what I tried to make clear when I talked about how much I liked her new book. 'The poems have lodged themselves inside my head, ever since I read them,' I said, 'they're really haunting.'

'That's so good to hear,' she said, 'and it's a very well-timed bit of encouragement. I'm in London for a few days, to see my publisher about another book.'

'Do you think you'll come back to live here again?' I said, trying to keep my voice as light as hers. 'The piece in the newspaper mentioned that you were working at an American university?'

'Well, I'm beginning to miss London,' she said, 'and the fellowship at Rutgers was never supposed to be a permanent one.'

'Rutgers?' I said. 'I was just doing some research into someone whose collection of manuscripts ended up there.' And I found myself telling her about Symington and Daphne du Maurier; the story came spilling out for the first time, and she listened to it all, and it was easy to tell her the details, in a way that it would not have been with Paul, partly because she was good at listening, and also because she said that she was a du Maurier admirer, had been for years.

When she said that – that she was a fan of Daphne – I felt my cheeks flush, and I said, 'You too?' But I stopped myself saying anything else, even though I was burning to know more. Why did I not tell her about Paul? Well, I was embarrassed, I suppose, because I didn't know how to, not at the beginning, and then after I'd told her about Symington, it was much too late to add, 'Oh, and by the way, guess who we have in common?' Also, I had the strangest feeling that we might be allies after all, because we both like Daphne, despite Paul's disapproval; and I wanted Rachel to like me, too; there was something about her that made me wish we could be friends, a kind of warmth and intelligence in her eyes, though I could imagine her being fierce as well; the sort of woman you'd prefer to have on your side, rather than your enemy. Which sounds so childish, doesn't it? But I realised, as we talked – not for very long, only ten minutes or so – that I haven't ever been able to speak like that to Paul. At the end, she said, 'Oh God, is that the time? I'm going to be horribly late for a meeting – I must get a move on.' So there was no awkwardness about her asking my name – it just didn't come up, and then she was in such a rush to go, and flashed another quick smile at me, and said, 'Good luck with Daphne' from over her shoulder as she started running towards the street, which was impressive, given that she was wearing patent black leather boots with very high heels. Fuck-me boots, I thought to myself, and then I felt faintly ashamed, but also a twinge of discontent as I looked down at my own shoes, a pair of scuffed grey canvas sneakers with pink laces that suddenly seemed childish.

It was only afterwards, when I got back home, that I started to worry about meeting Rachel. It's not just that I didn't tell her the truth about myself – but the fact that we came across each other at all is making me feel uneasy. I mean, it seems too much of a coincidence, doesn't it? Of course, Paul would say that there's no such thing as too much of a coincidence – that that's the point about the coincidental; it is simply a haphazard event in a random universe. He might also say to me, as he often does, 'Don't read so much into things.' Which is a bit rich, coming from a man who spends his working life reading books, picking them apart, and ferreting meaning out of them.

But I can't talk to Paul about it, and there isn't anyone else to tell, either, which seems really weird; I mean, I must be freakish to have ended up as solitary as this. And, also, if I'm honest, I'm starting to feel anxious that I somehow imagined the whole thing, especially as Rachel is the name of a du

Maurier character; the central pivot to the entire plot of *My Cousin Rachel*, which also hinges on whether the narrator in the novel is actually unhinged. But surely this couldn't be possible, me imagining the entire encounter, because I don't feel delusional in other ways. And the physical details were so clear: Rachel's black silk shirt and her narrow jeans and the gleam of her glamorous boots; her dark red lipstick, the same colour she'd chosen for the bedroom walls; her nail varnish, which was even darker, almost black; and her eyes, which are grey-green, like Paul's, cat's eyes, I thought, as I looked at them. Or is that part of the problem of being delusional? That the details of the delusions feel completely real and true?

OK, I've got to stop thinking like this, or I'll drive myself crazy. I happened to meet a woman called Rachel in the Reading Room of the British Museum. She happened to be my husband's ex-wife. She also happened to be interested in Daphne du Maurier, like me, like thousands and thousands of other people . . . That's all. These things happen in a big city: sometimes the universe chimes, very quietly. That's what my tutor once said to me, at college, when we were discussing the role of coincidence in Victorian novels. I'd not really understood what he was suggesting then, but now, it seems like a wonderfully helpful phrase. Anyway, it's not as big a coincidence as in *Jane Eyre*, when Jane discovers that the strangers with whom she has sought refuge are, in fact, her cousins. It's simply one of those occasional happenings in an ordinary life; a marker amidst the random chaos of the everyday, a small yet helpful sign on a map that might provide a clue to where I am going to, as well as where I have come from.

That's what I was telling myself just now, anyway. And then I went upstairs to run a bath, before Paul arrived home from work (and where the hell is he? It's getting really late . . .) I undressed, and decided to light an expensive-looking candle that I found last night when I was tidying one of the cupboards in the spare bedroom. I suppose I was imagining a romantic scene, with me lying naked in the water, in the gentle glow of candlelight, when Paul came into the room to find me. But a few seconds after putting a match to the candle, as the wax was softening, I suddenly recognised the fragrance that was beginning to rise from the flame. It was the scent of amber, Rachel's perfume. It was her candle that I was burning in the room.

CHAPTER THIRTEEN

Menabilly, November 1957

'This is Lady Browning,' said Daphne, when the Buckingham Palace telephone operator finally answered her call. 'Shall I try to put you through to Sir Frederick?' said the man's voice, sounding faintly puzzled. 'It's nearly midnight, Lady Browning, so I would imagine he's left his office for the evening.'

'I'm sure you're right,' said Daphne, trying to keep her voice calm and authoritative, though she felt like weeping with panic and anxiety. 'The thing is, there's an emergency, and I need to speak to someone in charge, and it's terribly urgent.'

'Wait one moment,' said the operator, and the line seemed to go dead for a few seconds, but then there were faint clicks, and Daphne gasped, wondering if somebody was eavesdropping on the call.

'Hello?' she said. 'Hello, is anyone there?'

She drummed her fingers on the table in the hall, and glanced behind her, very quickly, but it was impossible to tell what might surround her, at the edges of the dark corridors and blind corners, beyond the small pool of electric light in which she was standing.

At last, another voice came on the line. 'Lady Browning?' he said. 'This is the night duty officer. Is there anything I can do to help?'

'You must listen to me very carefully,' she said, taking a deep breath, attempting to steady herself. 'There is a plot against the Royal Family – a life-threatening plot, that you must take seriously. It is my duty to warn you, and your duty to act upon my warning.'

'Can you give me some more details?' said the man, his voice still smooth.

'The details of the plot?' she said.

'Yes, that would be helpful.'

As he spoke, she felt herself lose the thread of her thoughts, they were unwinding and tangling inside her, and the details of the plot were obscured, even though they had been so vividly clear in her mind a little while ago.

'Lady Browning?' he said. 'I'm not quite clear whether you *are* Lady Browning?'

'I'm so sorry,' she said, after a long pause. 'I'm not sure, I'm a little confused . . . I must go now.' She put the telephone down without saying goodbye. It was as if she had once known the answer to the man's question, but the precise outline of the plot was now gone and forgotten, the same feeling that consumed her when she woke in the early hours of the previous morning, after a recurring nightmare, in which she knew she had been expected to do something important, something involving a meeting, and money, and specific figures, not the watching figures from that nightmarish day at the British Museum, but numbers, arithmetic, like the sums she did in her red accounts book at the end of every week at Menabilly, adding up everything she had spent. Afterwards, she woke with a sense of being spent, of everything slipping away from her, of being mistaken and confused and utterly forsaken.

She did not discuss the telephone call with Tommy; she wasn't even sure if the Palace had mentioned it to him. Perhaps he chose to stay silent on the subject, hoping it would pass over, preferring not to talk about the details of the evening, given that he had not returned home that night, or so Daphne suspected, for after that terrible, shaming phone call to the Palace, she'd tried to reach him on the telephone, ringing his Chelsea number repeatedly, every half an hour, then every five minutes, until finally, at four o'clock in the morning, she took a double dose of sleeping pills, to stop herself doing what she wanted to do, which was to dial the number of the Snow Queen's flat.

The next day, she was exhausted, with a sinking sense of humiliation, yet at the same time she felt a strange chemical feeling of adrenalin pumping through her veins that kept her pacing up and down, unable to settle at her desk, unable to write or read or do anything other than circle the house. She rang the doctor in Fowey, and asked him to come and visit her at home. 'I can't leave the house,' she said to him on the phone.

'Can't you get a taxi to the surgery?' he said.

'No, you don't understand me,' she said. 'I cannot leave Menabilly.'

He arrived in the early afternoon after the morning surgery was finished, and she told him that she couldn't think straight, because she couldn't sleep. 'It's not good for you to be alone in this empty house,' the doctor said to her, 'letting your worries prey on you, no wonder you can't sleep.'

She nodded her head, and forced herself to smile at him, so as not to arouse his suspicions. 'You're quite right,' she said. 'But my son is back at boarding school, and our housekeeper – well, of course you know about Tod, she's over at Ferryside, helping Angela with my mother, who's not too good at the moment. So we're all at sixes and sevens for the time being, as they say . . . I just need a good night's sleep, and then all will be well again.'

He took her pulse, and prescribed her some new sleeping pills, and an iron tonic for her nerves. After he'd gone, she took the dog for a walk, hoping to be soothed by the wild anemones in the woods, and the deserted, wind-scoured beach. But then a heavy curtain of rain swept in from the west, submerging the pale winter light, and the seagulls dived and shrieked, their beaks as sharp as knives, as if they might turn on her and pluck out her eyes, and she thought, 'There can be no more desolate place than this.' She trudged back up Rebecca's path to Menabilly, feeling the rain running down her face, like tears. That night, she ate sardines on toast, and drank a glass of wine that tasted too vinegary to finish. She went to bed early, having taken two of the new pills, and dozed, fitfully, between inexplicable yet dreary anxieties about the train timetable from Par to Paddington, and diversions and delays on the line. Eventually, she fell into a deeper sleep just as the birds started singing outside the bedroom window, and dreamt that she was setting off for London from Fowey harbour, determined to sail there in a boat, Tommy's boat, but when she was out at sea, the boat started filling with water, and however fast she tried to bail out, it was not fast enough to keep afloat, and she knew she was scuppered and done for.

There was the same, odd chemical feeling in her bloodstream the following morning, and yet, despite her agitation, she forced herself to try to come to a rational judgement about her best course of action. When she felt the fear of a plot seeding itself in her mind again, and her thoughts running wild like the hydrangeas outside, she knew she must go back to London. She must do what the doctor told her, to get away from the silence of the empty house, and spend a little time with Tommy, and see Peter, who would understand what she meant if she were to talk to him about the darkness that seemed part of their inheritance, the vein of unhappiness that ran through the family's bloodline. Not that she would necessarily say these things to him, but the thought that she could, if need be, was a comforting one.

When she arrived in London that evening, Tommy seemed surprised, but not unfriendly. 'What a lot of rushing up and down you're doing,' he said, as he opened the door to the flat. 'I got your telegram, saying you were on your way from Cornwall today, but I must say, isn't all this travelling a bit much for you? We should buy shares in the railway . . .' He looked at her, quizzically, and she wished he would put his arms around her, like he did in the old days, before they had started shrinking away from each other. But at least he was calm, back to his usual measured manner, with none of the shakiness of the summer, nor did he seem angry with her, and she wondered if her suspicions about the Snow Queen were unfounded, because after all, he was here in the flat, with no sign of another woman. Perhaps the worst was over . . .

And although being back in London was maddening, at least it was in a different way, in a more familiar, manageable form this time. Of course, she still felt swamped by the crowds, as always, but she did not believe herself to be pursued through them by a faceless man in a trilby hat. What continued to worry her, however, was that even if she could now recognise her paranoia as being irrational – which she did, except when she was in the throes of it – she could not predict when it might descend upon her again.

So she decided that the only remedy was to concentrate on Branwell Brontë, to keep hold of him, even when she was most distracted, to write her way out of the mess that she was in, by turning Branwell's chaotic life into a beautifully composed biography. She rang her publisher, Victor Gollancz, to arrange a date to talk to him about her idea for the book. 'I'd like to see him as soon as possible,' she said to Victor's secretary, 'tomorrow, preferably, as it's rather urgent.' Once that appointment was safely in her diary, she telephoned Peter, to ask him to meet her for lunch that day at the Café Royal.

'Is everything all right?' he said, after they had ordered a bottle of wine, and she realised that she was tapping her foot, very fast, beneath the table.

'Of course,' she said. 'Why do you ask?

'It just seems slightly out of character,' he said, 'you being in London, instead of Menabilly. Though I'm delighted you're here, naturally.'

'I needed a change of scenery,' she said. 'I was getting a bit jittery at home, and anyway, there's a tremendous amount of work that I have to get on with at the British Museum.' She started telling him about the Brontë manuscripts, and about all the misunderstandings that surrounded Branwell, though as she tried to explain her research, Daphne felt anxious that Peter wouldn't understand what she was saying, that she wasn't making her ideas clear. 'Do I sound like a lunatic?' she said.

'Not at all,' he said. 'It sounds to me like you've got under Branwell's skin. Or has he got under yours?' She laughed, but then Peter suddenly looked more serious, and said, 'Go carefully, Daphne, don't lose yourself in Angria or Gondal.'

'Don't worry, I'll leave a trail of breadcrumbs behind me, to find my way back.'

'And where are you coming back to?'

'To Tommy, of course,' she said, feeling a sob rising in her throat, and biting her lip, hard, to stop herself from crying.

He reached his hand out to her, and said, 'You are very loyal to him.'

'Am I? I'm not sure Tommy would agree with you.'

'How is Tommy?'

'Back at work, and apparently coping with the pressure, though under strict doctor's orders not to overdo it. A little less silent than when you saw him last, and looking himself again, but still not tremendously talkative . . .'

'And into the silence steps Branwell?'

'Yes,' she said, 'though he's apt to go quiet on me, too.'

The next day, she lunched with Victor Gollancz, and he readily agreed to her proposal for a biography of Branwell. 'The story of the Brontë family always seems to me to be at least as dramatic as their novels,' he said.

'I warn you, it's going to be a very serious, scholarly affair,' she said. 'I want to do something really worthwhile.'

'Everything you write is worthwhile.'

'If only the critics agreed with you,' she said, trying to keep her voice steady.

'Who cares about them? You're the best-selling author in the country.'

'I care,' she said. 'And I'm hoping that this will be the book that finally proves me.'

'But you've already proved yourself, time and time again, to millions of readers.'

'It doesn't feel like that,' she said. 'I'm feeling somewhat of a failure. And Victor, I do fret when you advertise me as a best-selling author, it puts the critics off, because nowadays it's something to be ashamed of, don't you think?'

Victor looked at her, and laughed, as if she had just made a joke; and so she smiled back at him, though she worried that her right eye was twitching. It was hard to concentrate on what he was saying about the book trade, but she forced herself to do so, and then the conversation became a little easier, when she asked him if he knew anything about T. J. Wise, and the rumours surrounding his forgeries. Victor said he had come across some of Wise's faked first editions of

Browning poetry, and there were stories that Wise had torn pages out of rare books at the British Museum, and then sold them in discreetly conducted deals to private collectors. Victor had never heard of Mr Symington, however, though he remarked to Daphne that any of Wise's former colleagues might perhaps be considered as unreliable, potentially untrustworthy. And Daphne rushed to defend Symington, determined that he should not be judged as harshly or unfairly as Branwell had been, and she felt an unexpected sense of protectiveness about both of them, almost as if any hostility expressed toward Symington or Branwell was also a challenge to herself.

'Don't forget,' she said to Victor, 'Symington has been open with me from the start – he's the one who suggested that Charlotte and Emily's signatures could have been forged on Branwell's manuscripts.'

'Perhaps,' said Victor, 'or might that not be a double-bluff? Because if it was Symington who was responsible for the forgeries in the first place – or if not him, then Wise, with Symington's full knowledge – he could be trying to put you off the scent.'

'That sounds like a rather overly complicated conspiracy theory,' Daphne said, and Victor smiled, saying, 'My dear, you're the expert on literary conspiracies and fictional plots – the consummate mistress of them all – so I have no doubt in your ability to find your way through this one.'

She laughed, which was what he wanted, but that night, Victor's words niggled at her, like whining mosquitoes. Why, exactly, did he mention plots to her? Was he sending her the subtlest of messages? And if so, what was the message?

'You're looking tired,' said Tommy to her, over breakfast the following morning. 'Why not try and have a break from working?'

'I need to have a break from not working,' she said. But the trouble was, every time she sat down at her desk to read through her notes from the British Museum, or to sketch out an early plan for the form her book might take, she found herself returning to her meeting with the Snow Queen, reliving it, reworking their dialogue. She wondered whether their conversation could have taken a different direction; whether she might have been more forceful with the Snow Queen, and proved herself to be as implacable as her adversary.

Still, she kept trying, kept to a routine of mornings reading manuscripts at the British Museum and afternoons at her desk in the flat, and then dinner with Tommy, and sometimes Flavia and her husband, who were living nearby. Occasionally, Daphne realised that she was talking aloud to herself, which didn't matter when she was alone, but she often wasn't alone, she was on a bus or in the Reading Room, and people were staring at her. So she told herself to concentrate harder, to strain every sinew and nerve in her body, to keep on top of things. The strategy seemed to be working, until a letter arrived from Mr Symington, forwarded to the London flat by Tod, and as Daphne opened it, and the theatre programme slithered out on to the table, with Gertie's name on it in big, bold letters, she was suddenly consumed with panic. Tommy wasn't there at the time, thank God, but if he had been, what would have happened then?

Daphne skimmed Symington's letter, with its odd little reference to *September Tide*, and then threw it into the dustbin in the kitchen, along with the theatre programme. She went out of the room, but it was no good, she couldn't leave the letter or the programme in the bin; what if Tommy noticed them there this evening, and suspected her of something? So she fished them out, and the envelope that they had arrived in, and cut all of it up into tiny slithers of paper. Then she put these into another, unmarked envelope and hurried downstairs to the street, and turned left, past the Chelsea Hospital Gardens, and down to the Embankment. She was about to dump it in a litterbin, but then she saw a man watching her from the other side of the road. So she kept hold of the envelope, and went to the parapet that separated the pavement from the river. She glanced over her shoulder, to see if the man was still staring at her, but he was pretending to look in the other direction, so she quickly threw the envelope into the Thames, and watched it float away with the tide, white and frail; but not sinking, why was it not sinking into the water? Daphne held her breath, leaning further over the parapet to see what was happening, and eventually the envelope disappeared, beneath Chelsea Bridge. She wondered if she should walk along there, just to check that it was gone, but then she noticed another man standing on the bridge, a man in a trilby hat, and so she strolled away, and only started running when she had crossed the road, and she ran all the way back to the flat.

Daphne said nothing to Tommy about the men at the Embankment, but she could feel them gaining ground again in her head; she knew she must be careful to keep ahead of them, and return to Menabilly. 'I can't keep track of you,' Tommy said to her, when she told him she was going back to Cornwall.

'Nor I you,' she said, but she kept her smile in place as she spoke the words, and patted his hand affectionately.

Could the watchers come to Menabilly? No, surely she was safe here, for the house remained hidden from view, from everyone, invisible from the road and the sea, even when the autumn leaves had fallen, for Menabilly was still protected by the impenetrable evergreens in the woods, the cypress pines and towering fir trees, the sharp bamboos and giant ferns thriving on the boggy ground between thickets of nettles and brambles, and everywhere the dense maze of tangled rhododendrons. The woods had protected Rebecca, for all these years, in her limbo-life; and perhaps Rebecca, too, would act as a kind of protection for Daphne, the gatekeeper to her secret world . . .

It was getting darker now, the nights were lengthening, and winter was upon Menabilly, irrevocable, those melancholy months that Daphne always feared. She must make a friend out of the darkness, she told herself, as another defence against the enemies that assailed her. She imagined Branwell in the midst of the long Yorkshire winters, writing by candlelight in the Parsonage, his face papery white against his fiery hair. Who, or what, had Branwell feared? Daphne did not know for certain, but sometimes she wondered if she might be at the beginning of a quest to rescue him from an abductor, like Gerda had been, the girl who freed her friend from the grip of the Snow Queen. Branwell had been similarly banished to the frozen wastes, distant from view, almost forgotten, deprived of everything that should have been his due.

But Gerda was young, and Daphne felt old. And Branwell was so remote, so far away, and how would she ever find him? Where was her map, and who would be her guide there? No, better to stay at home in Menabilly; let Branwell come to her here.

'Branwell,' she whispered in the darkness, in her writing hut. 'Branwell, speak to me . . .'

CHAPTER FOURTEEN

Newlay Grove, November 1957

No word from Daphne, still not a word, and Symington could feel the familiar leaden weight of disappointment. But he had work to do, as always, a rising tide of it that covered his desk and spread across the floor around him. 'I have my work cut out for me,' he said to himself, by way of encouragement, though it was hard not to feel oppressed. He was immersed in paperwork from 1930, unearthed when he was searching his files for several Brontë manuscripts; and though he did not find these particular manuscripts – there were so many boxes, so many hiding places – the letters that he came across instead were as absorbing as they were enraging, and he could not stop rereading them. All concerned the dreadful months that followed his dismissal from the Brontë Parsonage Museum, when he had been accused of stealing various manuscripts, drawings, letters and books, and had been hounded by the solicitors appointed by the Brontë Society, demanding that he return everything.

Symington had kept the carbon copies of his replies to the solicitors as well as their letters to him, and he felt breathless as he re-examined the correspondence, over and over again, his chest tightening, until it was almost too painful to move. So he stayed very still at his desk, the sheaf of papers in front of him, fanned out like a deck of cards; yet whichever way he shuffled them, he always held the losing hand. His door was locked – he did not want Beatrice to come bursting in, not that she showed any sign of doing so, she was still keeping her distance from him.

Beatrice knew nothing of this; she had no idea of his troubles then, of course, she never had. When he had been ordered to resign as curator and librarian at the Parsonage, Symington told Beatrice that it was because Lord Brotherton had asked him to make a choice between his work for the Brontë Society, or for the Brotherton Collection, as there were insufficient hours in the day for him to do both. And in fact, the story was a plausible one, for Symington had been increasingly overwhelmed by his responsibilities, by the enormous quantity of material to be acquired and archived and catalogued (not just the papers, but the Brontë relics too – the dog collars and lace handkerchiefs, the slippers and mittens – all of them as precious as if they had belonged to a family of saints, and been touched by the hand of God Himself). Not that Brotherton would have ever known the full exent of Symington's workload; nor asked him to give up his responsibilities at the Parsonage, for after all, Brotherton was a stalwart supporter of the Brontë Society, which ran the museum, and was also its president until shortly before his death.

And what a terrible loss that had been, leaving Symington defenceless against his enemies, who had moved in, like hyenas, a vicious pack of them, and no one had come to his aid, not even those who should have done, fellow Masons, who knew that he had been a loyal lodge-member for many years, like Brotherton. But it had meant nothing, in the end: freemasonry had done him no more good than it had done Branwell before him.

The accusations and legal letters had gone on for months, itemising everything he was supposed to have stolen, but Symington had remained robust in his written responses to the persecution, certain that he was right, and the Society wrong, for they were dullards who had no idea of how to care for such priceless treasures. It pained him, still, remembering that he had been forced to return several of Charlotte's letters and childhood writings, for these might have proved to be the key to unlocking Branwell's secrets, and not only that, they would have been indisputably safer with him as their guardian. Even so, some of the manuscripts remained in his safekeeping, despite those vultures at the Parsonage, who wanted to peck at the papers, tear them apart until all the life had gone from them.

Symington wished he could reassure himself that he had achieved some degree of triumph over his adversaries, but rereading the solicitors' letters left a bitter taste in his mouth; far too bitter to be washed away with whisky. What angered him – a rising anger that made his head pound, so that he could feel the rage throbbing, like blood – was that the Brontë Society had never recognised his talents and his skill. They had cut him off in his prime, when he should have been promoted instead, for he would have made an excellent president of the Society, as Wise had been, before Brotherton; and why Wise and not Symington? Symington knew himself to be every bit as industrious as Wise, and as talented a collector.

Worse than the anger, though, or the bitterness, were the moments of panic. Where, exactly, was each of the hidden manuscripts that he had kept safe for so many years? He would not use the word 'stolen', for he was not a thief, but a guardian, and a rightful one. But could a real thief have gained access to his collection? Surely not; his locks were secure, and he checked them over and over again. But that manuscript of Emily's poetry – the little notebook of her poems he borrowed from the Law collection – must now be worth a fortune, for as far as Symington knew, only one other of her notebooks of poetry had survived intact, and that was presented to the British Museum over twenty years ago. It was so hard to keep track of everything, for some of his collection had been stored at the smaller house in Newlay Grove, next door to his own, which Symington had rented in 1926 to accommodate his office and library, an assistant and a secretary. That had been such a good year, when everything had been expanding and growing, when Elsie was still alive, and treasures were all around him.

But he had been forced to give up his tenancy there, eighteen months ago, when the last of his money ran out, and the bank refused to increase his overdraft, and he'd had to move everything out of it, boxes and boxes filled with sheaves of papers that had overflowed into his study and the basement and the attic of the main house, much to Beatrice's annoyance. There had been no assistant to help him with reorganising his collection, no secretary, and it was overwhelming, he had not known where to begin.

And now, he must begin at the beginning again, he must put everything into order, before it was too late; he could not allow himself to be defeated. He must write to Daphne once more, and prove himself to her, for time was running out, he felt it, like Branwell had before him. He must prove himself, as Branwell never did; but in doing so, he would prove Branwell's worth; Branwell and him, they were inseparable; entwined together like vines, and surely something fruitful would come of this . . .

CHAPTER FIFTEEN

Hampstead, March

I knew that I shouldn't have gone into Paul's study today, but I told myself that I wasn't snooping, that I needed to check something in one of his reference books. And then when I was in the room, I couldn't help noticing that he'd left his laptop open on the desk, instead of taking it to work with him this morning, like he usually does. So I came up with a perfectly plausible excuse to look at it – an excuse that I could believe in, given that there was no one else in the house that needed to be convinced – which was that the Internet connection in my study was very slow, and it would be quicker to check the reference online on Paul's computer, rather than searching through his bookshelves.

I went over to his desk, which overlooks the back garden, and the laptop was already on, he hadn't shut it down last night, like he usually does, so it was impossible to avoid seeing what was already on the screen. Because there it was, just waiting to be read: a draft email to Rachel, dated from yesterday, though not yet sent, and beneath it some previous emails, as if he'd just pressed 'reply' to the last one that had arrived from her. I sat at his desk – how could I not? – and started scrolling down the screen, reading the emails in the reverse order that they'd written them to each other. I couldn't understand why he hadn't deleted the previous messages, and simply started a new one, but he hadn't – at least, not yet – so the entire correspondence was there, beginning with the draft of his most recent email.

Dear Rachel,
I hear that you may be returning to London in a few months' time, to return to your job in the English department for the start of the autumn term. If this is the case, then our professional paths will doubtless cross in due course, and we should probably talk before then . . .

Dear Paul,
Well, that was a remarkably quick turnaround, wasn't it? So much for your broken heart. It appears to have mended quickly, with the help of your new wife who is, by all accounts, half your age.
Good luck to both of you . . .
Rachel

Rachel. My divorce lawyer will be in touch with yours. Best wishes, Paul

Paul. Your problem is that you are jealous of me and my success as a poet. Don't worry, you won't be hearing from me again. Rachel

Rachel – if you have nothing more constructive than lies and denials
to add to this conversation, then I don't want to hear from you.
Paul

Dear Paul,
You appear to mistake female friendship for lesbianism: a
common trait in unreconstructed men, but an unworthy
response in you,
Rachel

Rachel,
I hardly think 'paranoia' is a truthful description of my feelings.
Did you really think I wouldn't notice your flirtation with her?
Give me some credit, please, for being able to interpret those covert
glances and remarks.
Paul

Dear Paul,
Your paranoia about my alleged betrayals of you has always
undermined our relationship – far more so that any physical
separation through work. You use the word 'fact' about my
alleged infidelities, but there are no facts, only your destructive
fantasies.
Rachel

Rachel,
If you still can't see why your move to Rutgers constitutes the latest
in a series of betrayals, then I'm not sure how I can be expected to
explain, yet again. We have talked and talked and talked about
this, and the endless arguments are wearing me down. Surely you
must understand by now that if I truly believed that your move to
America was simply for professional reasons, then of course I would
support it. But given the fact that you have used geographical

separation on previous occasions as a cover for your infidelities to me,
then I see no reason why you won't do the same in America.
Paul

Dear Paul
As partings go, that was as bad as it could be. I don't
understand why you have precipitated this crisis. Surely you
should support my opportunity to take the fellowship at
Rutgers? It's only for two years, and I will be coming back to
London in the holidays, which are, after all, as long as the
term times. Why do you seem intent on turning my
acceptance of a very good career move into a marital
separation?
With love, as always,
Rachel

It only took a few minutes to read the emails, and of course,
reading them should have changed everything, for wasn't
this reassuring proof that Paul didn't love Rachel, that he
didn't want her back again, and didn't regret marrying me?
It was almost as if he'd left his computer for me to find,
accidentally on purpose, as evidence that their marriage was
over.

But there was something strangely unsettling about seeing
the visual, concrete evidence of their relationship – the
undeleted letters on the screen – and whichever way I read
them, both forwards and backwards, I still felt as if I'd been
stung by the words on the computer, by those bitter little
sentences that loomed large in my mind, yet seemed too small
to chronicle the enormity of an unravelling marriage. Yes, I
knew that the emails were simply the shorthand account of

what had doubtless been months of convoluted arguments and tortured negotiations and prolonged misery. Even so, when all that emotion was reduced into this email correspondence, it seemed so mundane and petty and . . . and *childish*. Because they were supposed to be the grown-ups around here, weren't they?

As for that small yet deadly grenade contained within the correspondence, that Paul suspected Rachel of a flirtation with another woman, well, I didn't want that ticking away in my head. I didn't want to look at those emails ever again; I wanted to forget all about them. I told myself they were none of my business – but it was impossible, they rooted themselves inside me, like fungus spores in the dark.

I went straight upstairs to my own study, not stopping to look at anything of Rachel's in the house – not her mirror, not her candle, not her bed, not her bathroom – and I shut the door behind me, to keep the scent of Rachel out. As I switched on my computer, all I wanted was to concentrate on my work – my stuff, nothing to do with Rachel and Paul – and I started reading my PhD notes, determined to lose myself in these, and sweep everything else aside. But there was nothing of any real merit in the notes, just a jumble of disconnected ideas about the Brontës and du Maurier, and a title, 'Self-Interrogation', which I can't use, because Rachel has already used it as the title for one of her poems; she got there first, just like she did with my husband.

I wanted to hate Rachel, and her poem, to dismiss it as a clever-clever re-appropriation of the Emily Brontë poem that provided Daphne du Maurier with the title of *The Loving Spirit*. But then I reached into my bottom drawer for Rachel's book of poetry – which is a strange thing to do, isn't it, if you are intent on ignoring something, or someone? – and when I reread her 'Self-Interrogation', I was reminded, again, of how intriguing it is. She takes Brontë's seventh stanza as an epigraph for her poem ('Alas! The countless links are strong/ That bind us to our clay;/ The loving spirit lingers long,/And would not pass away!'). But then she does something quite different, because she seems to use the idea, suggested by Emily Dickinson, that one might read a poem backwards. No one knows if Dickinson was definitely referring to Emily Brontë as a poet whose lines could be reversed, but Rachel flips one of Brontë's phrases, so that it reads, 'long lingers spirit loving'. If I were still a student at Cambridge, I'd say Rachel's poem was about literary identity, and how elusive and slippery it can be, but now, I'm not so sure about trying to pin a writer down in that way, especially one apparently intent on not being captured.

Anyway, after I reread Rachel's poem, I got out my old copy of *The Loving Spirit*, and started flicking through it again, which I haven't done for years, because it's not my favourite of Daphne's books. And on the last, blank pages of this paperback edition, there are some of my handwritten notes, which must date back to my first year at Cambridge, when I was brooding over du Maurier, as usual, instead of getting on with writing an essay on someone more academically respectable. So what I scribbled was this:

Daphne wrote her debut novel – at twenty-two – during a winter at Ferryside, the house that her father had bought in Cornwall, overlooking the harbour at Fowey. Imaginative reworking of the history of a local boatbuilding family, beginning with the story of Jane Slade, a real woman, and the original matriarch of the family, transformed by Daphne into Janet Coombe, the fictional heroine of *The Loving Spirit*. Janet's passionate love for her son Joseph continues beyond death, and borders on an incestuous version of Cathy and Heathcliff's tempestuous union. Check: Is the real Jane Slade buried in the church where Daphne married her husband?

Seeing my note reminded me that actually, there's a lot of near-incest in du Maurier's work – like the love affair between the stepbrother and sister at the heart of her novel, *The Parasites*, which also has a faint echo of Cathy and Heathcliff. And then there are those sly, curious passages that she slips into her biography of her father, which is written almost like a novel, with Daphne as a character in it; the oddest of all – a clue, or a joke? – is her story of Gerald's engagement to Ethel Barrymore, several years before he met Daphne's mother, Muriel. I took down my copy of *Gerald* from the shelf, and turned to the page that I'd already marked with a pen ages ago, then put to one side, trying to forget about it. It's Daphne's description of Ethel, a pretty, nineteen-year-old actress, who 'looked elfin, and adorable, and never more than fourteen'. But instead of calling her Ethel, Daphne refers to her by her middle name – Daphne – a decision that creates a disconcertingly perverse effect. So there's a scene in Ireland, when Daphne-the-daughter writes about how Gerald begged Daphne-the-lover to marry him as soon as possible, 'but she was very wilful, and would not make up her mind, and asked if they couldn't be like brother and sister . . . Whereupon Gerald, dramatising the situation at once, threatened suicide, and, rushing down the Kerry beach, waded in water up to his neck, fully aware that Daphne was sobbing wildly, "Gerald, Gerald, come back!" '

If I were forging ahead with my PhD, I suppose I'd be piecing together these suggestive hints in her writing and turning them into a solid theory for my dissertation, but somehow, when I try, it all seems to unravel in my hands. For a start, I'm not sure if my speculations about her relationship with Gerald can be linked, in any meaningful way, with her research into the Brontës. But also, what right do I have to try to make connections between her books and her life? It's dangerous territory – like all those dated, sentimental Brontë biographies, spinning the myth about saintly Charlotte and spiritual Emily and bad Branwell and gentle Anne. Those kinds of books make me feel uncomfortable; it's the literary equivalent of catching butterflies, and then killing them, in order to pin them down and display them in a box. But what's odd is that I get the same uneasy sensation when I think about that weirdly unsatisfactory email exchange between Paul and Rachel, and also about Rachel's poem, and the less certain I am of the meaning of her 'Self-Interrogation' the more I want to understand it, yet the harder I try, the quicker it slips away. Which is, perhaps, the point: that what we read into things may not be the truth, or that the truth is not a solid and immutable substance. And that's the problem with the original Emily Brontë poem, though it's only a problem if you're looking for a definitive answer within it. It's about whether to live, or die, or at least I think it is – about loving life at the same time as longing for death. It's suicidal, and yet vividly alive – a dangerous poem, if you're feeling at all unbalanced.

As it happens, I was feeling a bit unbalanced after I'd been staring at my computer for several hours, trying to make sense of all this stuff. It's no wonder that my head started hurting, and everything was getting muddled up, Emily's poem and Rachel's poem; du Maurier's first novel and her biography of her father; Paul's accusations and Rachel's denials; all of it a stew of knowing and not knowing. I should have been sensible and gone out for a walk to get some fresh air, but it was raining – not much of an enticement for a stroll on the heath – so I opened the little door from my attic to the balcony. I don't go out there very often – it's less of a balcony, more of a ledge, really, and so high above the street that it makes me feel dizzy. But it seemed like a good idea, today, so I gave the door a shove – the wooden frame had warped and swollen this winter after all the rain – and there I was, looking into the gardens of Cannon Hall. It was like being on the prow of a boat – I felt slightly sea-sick – but I also realised that if I was just a little higher, if I climbed up on to the parapet itself, I might be able to see more, I might even be able to see into the windows of Cannon Hall, into the rooms where Gerald told Daphne that he loved her. And I actually started climbing – I reached out my hands to pull myself up, at the same time as finding a foothold in the crumbling brickwork – and then suddenly, I thought, what the hell are you doing? You could fall so easily, it's not safe. But even as I was thinking that, there was another voice inside my head that said, go on, don't be frightened, it will be amazing – you'll be able to see as far as you want, further than you've ever seen before. So I just stayed there, hovering, one foot still on the balcony, another halfway up the parapet, uncertain of whether to climb up or back down.

I don't know how long I was out there, but eventually I started shivering. I looked down and glimpsed a dark-haired woman turning the corner at the end of the street, and for a second, I thought it was Rachel. But I don't think it was actually her, I just wanted it to be her, like when my mother died, and in the months that followed, I'd see the back of her old beige raincoat, rounding a corner ahead of me, or her face behind a misted window on a bus, swooping past me when I was crossing the road.

And it was the thought of my mother – or her ghost – in that familiar old raincoat that made me feel somehow ashamed, but also more myself again.

I thought of how she'd taught me to cross the road – I could almost hear her voice saying, 'Look left, look right, look left again' – and how she always used to say to me, 'Take care, sweetheart' before I went to school in the morning. And she said it to me in our last conversation. 'Take care of yourself,' she said. 'I will,' I said, and afterwards, when she was dead, I was so sorry that I hadn't told her that I loved her before putting the phone down, that those should have been my last words to her. Now, when I remembered her again, I thought, well, the least I can do is keep my promise, instead of hanging over a parapet. 'I love you, Mum,' I whispered, and then I came back inside, closing the door behind me, but I didn't lock it; I didn't like the idea of being locked in.

I felt too shaky to go straight back to work, and too foolish, as well. I thought, God, I hope no one saw me up there on the balcony, behaving like a lunatic. What I needed, I told myself, was to do something comfortingly normal like make a cup of tea and rummage through the biscuit tin (my biscuit tin, not Rachel's). So I went downstairs to the kitchen, and ate two chocolate digestives while I was waiting for the kettle to boil, and then, just as the steam started coming out of the spout, I was struck by an idea. Well, not a whole, fully formed idea, exactly, just the beginnings of one . . . Daphne was using the Brontë poem as the starting point for her novel when she was almost exactly the same age as her cousin Michael Llewelyn Davies had been, when he drowned in a pool at Oxford, as an undergraduate. Also, she had turned fourteen less than a week before Michael's death, on a sunny May afternoon, and I wonder . . . what on earth went through her mind then?

By the time I'd made my tea, I was feeling quite excited, and I rushed back upstairs to my study to see whether Daphne had written anything about this in her autobiography. I've already read it loads of times, searching for clues – it's the most elliptical of memoirs, but it contains these tantalising snippets from her diary (a diary which is now locked in a bank vault, as she instructed in her will, not to be released until fifty years after her death). Anyway, as I flicked through the book, I already knew that she didn't refer to Michael's drowning, but I was almost certain that his death coincided with the period in her life when she felt her first sexual awakenings with her cousin Geoffrey. What I needed to double-check in her memoir was the timings – and there it was, on page 60 – the summer that she was fourteen she was on a family holiday with Geoffrey, her aunt Trixie's son. He was thirty-six, and old enough to be her father; indeed, was as close to her father as a brother. She kind of hints at an incestuous impulse, both with Geoffrey and her father; she says – and I've underlined this in the book – that her flirtation with Geoffrey was 'a reaching out for a relationship that was curiously akin to what I felt for D[addy], but which stirred me more, and was also exciting because I felt it to be wrong'.

So, I suppose there might be a link between sex and death in all of this. Michael drowned in the arms of another male undergraduate; Geoffrey and Daphne held hands together in secret, by the sea, hiding from her possessive father; and later on, in several of her most climactic fictional episodes, her heroines are engulfed by the waves – Rebecca, murdered by her husband for taking lovers; and the daughter in *Julius*, drowned by her father, whose incestuous desire for her is such that he would rather kill her than let her have sex with another man.

And then I suddenly remembered the girl in her short story, 'A Borderline Case' – at least, I thought I remembered it, but first I had to find the book it was in, which took me about ten minutes of frantic searching, while I got more and more agitated. Finally I discovered it, in a second-hand edition without a jacket that had fallen down behind my desk, but it was just as I remembered it, about a girl who travels to Ireland soon after the death of her father, and ends up making love with a man who turns out to be her real father, an ex-British army officer who lives on an island, and conducts clandestine operations for the IRA. 'Don't go, don't ever leave me!' she cries out to her father, just after they have made love;

as if in an echo of Daphne's words in her autobiography, when she described her panic, as a girl, when Gerald announced that he was going up on the roof of Cannon Hall during an air raid. 'I stretched out my arms and cried, "Don't go . . . don't go . . . Don't ever leave me."'

The trouble is, as an idea, it doesn't get me very far with a PhD on Daphne and the Brontës. And it certainly doesn't seem to be doing much for my own marriage. I mean, there's far more sex in Daphne's writing than there is in my life right now, not that I want the incestuous sort that lurks between the lines in her books, even if Paul is old enough to be my father. Admittedly, I don't have much in the way of experience to judge these things, but I don't think it can be normal to live like this. Paul slept in another bedroom last night – he says it's a temporary measure, because I've been so restless at night and keeping him awake, making him too exhausted to be able to cope with his job. So there we were, marooned in our separate beds, me alone in the room he had shared with Rachel, and him on the other side of the wall, back in the single bed he had slept in as a child.

And we're separated in our daytime lives, as well, because Paul seems intent on becoming hermetically sealed from me. I'm almost beginning to wonder when he'll start refusing to share the milk; it's as if he's frightened I'm going to infect him with something. Either that, or he finds me repellent, and most of the time, he avoids looking at me, but occasionally, I'll catch him staring at me, appalled, like he's seen a ghost.

When I start thinking about it, though, about what might happen if he tells me to leave, because he doesn't want to live with me, it's impossible – it's literally impossible, I've got nowhere else to go, nowhere to be; it would be like climbing out of the attic again, up on to the parapet . . . No, I'm not going to let myself go there again; no good can possibly come of that.

So. I'm trying not to think about the separate beds; or about those emails, which I can't talk to Paul about, because I can't admit to having read them. They'll have to be a secret, just like Rachel's book in my drawer, just like the secret of Daphne's relationship with Gerald. What was it that Paul said in his email? That he knew how to interpret Rachel's covert glances and remarks? But what if he was wrong? And maybe I'm misinterpreting Paul's current desire for solitude; maybe it's nothing to do with me, maybe he just needs some time to be alone?

This is why I've got to concentrate on my PhD instead. I'm hoping several solutions will present themselves, if I keep on working at it. Not that I'm entirely sure what 'it' is. But that, too, will probably come clear, one of these days. In the meantime, I've just reread Emily Brontë's diary entry, written on Branwell's twentieth birthday, when she was looking ahead in time, to four years hence, when she would be twenty-two, the same age as me. 'I wonder where we shall be and how we shall be and what kind of day it will be then let us hope for the best.'

CHAPTER SIXTEEN

Menabilly, December 1957

'Lady du Maurier is peaceful, but sinking further into a coma,' said the doctor to Daphne, just before she went into see her mother in the bedroom at Ferryside, his voice hushed yet still professional. Daphne nodded, to indicate that she understood what the doctor was telling her – that her mother was close to death – but as she walked into the room, she felt as if none of it was real, as if she had been propelled into a scene in someone else's book. She tried to concentrate on what the doctor had said to her, though his words seemed to float past her, past the frail old woman lying in bed, and then Daphne imagined her mother's body in the rising night-tide that lapped a few feet beneath the window, drifting and submerged by the waves, but not yet sinking, not quite yet.

She sat on the chair by the bed, and leant down, resting her face against her mother's cheek, and as she did so, Muriel turned and kissed Daphne, very gently, her eyes still closed, her lips as soft and papery as a moth's wings. Then she sighed, almost imperceptibly, seeming to move further away again, and Daphne told herself that her mother was at peace, not only because all of her suffering was nearly over, but also because there was a reconciliation between the two of them, after the undercurrent of hostility that had pulled them apart in the early years.

They had begun to make their peace a long time ago, after Gerald's death; but even so, Daphne wanted to believe that the kiss melted any remaining ice in both of their hearts. She wished she could lay her hands upon her mother's face, and smooth the years away, but instead she took her mother's hand, cradling it in hers, feeling the pulse still flickering, and though the doctor had warned her that this was the end, Daphne was comforted by the warmth of her touch, which seemed as if it would endure, even when Muriel's body turned cold.

Yet they were not together at the moment of Muriel's death; her mother slipped away when Daphne was not in the house, saving her final goodbye for Angela, who she always loved more. Although Daphne told herself not to see this as another rejection, she could not help but brood on it, and she wondered if the unexpected sharpness of her grief was as much for herself as her mother. After the funeral at a crematorium near Truro – a bleak affair, on a raw and melancholy afternoon, the last day of November – she and Angela and Jeanne caught the train to London, taking with them an urn of their mother's ashes, and scattered them beside their father's grave in Hampstead, close to the house where he had been born. Standing in the churchyard between her two sisters, surrounded by all the family graves, Daphne found herself wishing that she could stay there, a kind of quiet death wish, though it was not necessarily oblivion that she sought, but the beginning of another chapter, or a different story.

Daphne almost expected to see her father at her sisters' side, for surely he was as close as he could ever come to them now? 'Suppose that we were really dead, and didn't know it?' she said to her sisters, and they both looked at her, surprised, but didn't answer. When Gerald was still alive, he'd visited the graveyard often, on the anniversaries of his family's births and deaths, bringing spring flowers for his parents, and bulbs for his sister Sylvia, and a wreath with the Fusilier ribbon on it for his soldier brother, Guy; laying his offerings beside the headstones, and sitting there with the dead for a while, as if in a family reunion. Was this how he had felt then, the longing that Daphne felt now?

Poor Gerald, who died of cancer a week after his sixty-first birthday, on 11 April 1934, the dates carved on to his grave. She did not go to her father's funeral, for she could not bear to see the coffin lowered into the earth, knowing that his body would be trapped and rotting there in the dark, locked away and abandoned. Instead, she'd stayed behind at Cannon Hall, and then walked across the road to the heath, taking with her a cage of two white doves. At the top of a grassy rise, unseen by anyone, Daphne opened the cage, just as her father had done so often when he was still alive; he bought caged wild birds from an East End market, linnets and finches and thrushes, hundreds and hundreds of them over the years, and set them free in Hampstead, saying that birds should not be imprisoned, it was too cruel to keep them behind bars.

And she'd done the same thing as a child, releasing the pet doves she was given by her aunt Trixie for her fifth birthday, half-terrified that the birds would not choose freedom. She remembered a similar moment of fear when she went to the heath after her father's death, turning her head away after she unlocked the cage and put it on the ground, willing the doves to take flight, while she muttered the lines from her favourite poem by Emily Brontë, closing her eyes, as if in prayer. And as Daphne stood beside her father's grave now, she whispered the lines again, like an incantation.

> Alas! The countless links are strong
> That bind us to our clay;
> The loving spirit lingers long,
> And would not pass away!

Then she lifted her head up, hoping to see a sign, and there were birds in the sky, wheeling and soaring, and she wished that her father was free of the earth, at last, and her mother up there beside him.

But she suspected that they were still lingering here on the ground. Daphne imagined them gathering together after she and her sisters had gone home, a clan of du Maurier ghosts, congregated around the gravestones. The words on her cousin Michael's memorial were simple: 'An undergraduate who was drowned at Oxford while bathing 19 May 1921', but no one had known how to talk about his death, and what would his family of ghosts say about it now? Would they change the subject, in death as in life; would they do just as they had always done?

Not long after her cousin George had died in the war, Uncle Jim had taken her on a Sunday afternoon outing to the zoo with Nico, and they had stared at the lion's cage, but when Michael died, there was no question of going anywhere, Barrie had been inconsolable, and he had broken down; that's what her father had said, 'Jim broke down in the dressing room at the theatre, just after he'd heard the news, and I should have felt sorry for him, but I couldn't help hating him.' And that was that, her father said nothing more, and the funeral had taken place without Daphne, without comment. Daphne bought a little bunch of violets for Michael a few days after his burial, and left them for him by the newly dug grave, slipping away from the house, not telling anyone, but wondering if she was being watched, in the churchyard, wondering if Michael was there, laughing at her, in that gently mocking way of his.

She'd stayed in touch with the other Llewelyn Davies boys, of course, with Jack and Peter and Nico; and though handsome Jack was the cousin who Daphne admired most when she was a girl (swooning over him as a teenager, and tongue-tied as a child, when he would come to visit her, bringing sweets and balloons), and charming Nico the easiest to get along with at parties, she had always been closest to Peter. 'Family, that's the most important thing,' she said to him, when they met for a drink at the Café Royal, after Muriel's ashes had been scattered. She reached over and touched his hand, just for a moment, and as he smiled at her, with that grave, crooked smile, she thought to herself that perhaps she should have married him, not Tommy, that they would have understood one another so well.

'How did we come to be so grown-up?' she said. 'Peter Pan isn't supposed to grow old.'

He flinched as she spoke, and she said, 'Oh Peter, I'm so sorry, I know you hate it—'

'That terrible masterpiece,' he said, and raised his glass, as if in a mocking toast to his namesake.

'What's in a name?' she said.

'My God, what isn't?' he said. 'If that boy so fatally committed to an arrested development had only been dubbed George or Jack or Michael or Nico, what miseries might have been spared me?'

'But Michael suffered too, didn't he?' she said. 'When I was little, I overheard a conversation that I shouldn't have been listening to, between my nanny and yours. And your nanny said that Michael was having bad nightmares, of ghosts coming through the windows, but when I heard them talking, I knew the nannies were wrong. It wasn't ghosts that frightened Michael, it was Uncle Jim and Peter Pan.'

'Poor Michael,' he said. 'I remember his nightmares, and mine too, about winged creatures . . . You know, peple used to tell us that Barrie was our guardian angel, but now I look back on it, perhaps there was something of the angel of death about him. Maybe Michael knew something about him that we didn't.' He laughed, as if to take the sting out of his words, but Daphne made sure not to mention Peter Pan again in the conversation, knowing that the burden of Barrie's most famous creation weighed heavily on Peter, who as he grew older seemed increasingly oppressed by his ageless counter-part.

She was still preoccupied by this the next day, on the train going back to Cornwall with her sisters. 'Who said it first?' she muttered on the train, hardly knowing she was speaking aloud.

'Who said what?' said Jeanne, looking up from her newspaper.

' "To die will be an awfully big adventure",' said Daphne. 'I was just wondering who Barrie got it from?' Jeanne shrugged, and Angela's eyes were closed, her mouth twitching, as if she was dozing. 'I think it was Michael,' Daphne said, almost to herself, 'he always had a way with words. And Barrie was always quick to seize on them . . .' That's what Peter had said to her, years ago, that Barrie had taken his words out of his mouth, when he was a child, and those of his brothers, too, and woven them into the myth of Peter Pan.

'Daddy said he seized on all of us,' said Jeanne. 'Mind you, if it hadn't have been for Uncle Jim, we might never have been born.'

Daphne nodded, needing no reminder that her parents had first met and fallen in love in a production of a Barrie play, *The Admirable Crichton*. It was part of the family history, and so was Barrie, which was why he had always been Uncle Jim to her and her sisters, just as he was to her cousins; they had all grown up listening to his menacing fairy stories, for he understood how to frighten children, as well as entrance them.

And it was impossible to forget Barrie, even now, as the train gathered speed out of London. He came with her, just as he had been there in the Hampstead graveyard, hovering at the margins of the gathering of the ghosts. Could he fly, at last, that small, slight man, who had dreamt of Neverland? They had all been drawn into Jim's kingdom – all of them, even Angela, cast as Wendy when she was eighteen, and already knew the play off by heart, like Daphne and Jeanne, for they'd watched it every Christmas since they were little girls, knowing it was written for their cousins, and acting it out themselves in the nursery, sometimes for Uncle Jim to watch, longing for his applause.

Which is why, perhaps, Daphne could not rid herself of the idea that if her ghostly relations were scudding across the sky above her, they were attached by unseen wires, like the actors had been in Peter Pan; not yet free, and still bound in some way, not only to one another, but also to the material world.

Back in Menabilly, at last, she did not feel comforted by this thought, for it suggested that she would be earthbound, now and always, so that there could be no real prospect of escape. Christmas was coming, and another family gathering, which might bring with it a return of all of the tensions of the summer, Tommy drinking steadily, then becoming unsteady, and everyone pretending that nothing was wrong. Daphne considered, briefly, the whimsy of having Branwell as a distraction at Menabilly – not simply in her head, in an unwritten book (a book that might never be written, if she did not get a move on), but as a guest in the house; a disreputable yet intriguing figure to draw the attention away from Tommy.

And just for a little while, she smiled. Other people's families were generally more manageable than one's own; though Daphne occasionally longed for just an hour of Branwell's company, with a nostalgia as deep as if he had once been part of her past; as if he had been her own brother, or lover, or father, as deeply as she had once longed for Peter Pan, and all the other Lost Boys, when she had willed them to be real, not grease-painted actors; yet at the same time wishing them freedom, taking flight from the dusty wings of a theatre, and out towards the stars of a clear night sky.

Freedom: that was the thing, to be free, not endlessly caught up on a stage, tangled and tripping over the wires; and was that what Michael had sought, unleashed in the water, unlocked from the words? Perhaps that was the only way forward, to be free of everything, of everyone, maybe even to be free of Branwell . . . But could she cut herself loose, at last?

Menabilly,
Par,
Cornwall

10th January 1959

Dear Mr Symington,

I hope this New Year finds you well. I have had so much pleasure from the Brontë books that I purchased from you – is it over a year ago, already? – that I have been wondering if you have any other volumes or material that you have not yet disposed of which I might be able to add to my collection?

I am afraid it is still only a hobby for the winter evenings, as I have not yet been able to devote sufficient time to a properly worthwhile book about Branwell Brontë, and I know that it would be essential for me to make a trip to Yorkshire to devote myself to the research. I have not given up on this idea altogether, but domestic problems have intervened. Sadly, my mother passed away last winter. Since then, my husband's health has been indifferent, my son has just left school and is starting his first job, and meanwhile I have been working on a new collection of short stories, which proved to be a distraction from Branwell.

Nevertheless, I have not given up studying the Brontë manuscripts in your Shakespeare Head edition, nor those in the British Museum, though they place an appalling strain on the eyes!

I shall be very interested to hear how your own research is progressing.

With kindest regards,

Daphne du maurier

CHAPTER SEVENTEEN

Newlay Grove, January 1959

Quite unexpectedly, a letter had arrived for Mr Symington, from Daphne, after her long silence. She did not apologise for the protracted delay in replying to his last letter, which he had sent over a year before, and Symington considered giving her a taste of her own medicine, and leaving the letter unanswered. But as he reread the letter, several times, despite his previous feelings of annoyance and betrayal by Daphne – who had picked him up and then dropped him, as if he were nothing but a stray dog – he found himself beginning to warm to her again. Not that he wanted to be too encouraging to her; not after the year he'd had, with that long spell in hospital after he fell and broke his arm and dislocated his knee, trying to move a box of manuscripts from the attic down to his study.

The fall had been a shock – he spent several hours on the floor, unable to move, waiting for Beatrice to get home – but in a curious sense, it was also a relief. While he was in hospital, one of the doctors had diagnosed him as having 'a weak heart'; there was no remedy for it, apparently, other than calm and rest. Beatrice had been more sympathetic since then, aside from the occasional tart remark about being run off her feet while he sat there with his feet up; but she appeared to be mollified, also, by their tacit understanding that he would no longer be engaged in examining the contents of his boxes. His son Douglas had been summoned to the house, to pack everything away back into the attic, and afterwards, Symington felt almost liberated, as if Branwell had been locked up in the attic, as well, with no chance of escape, and no means of voicing his complaints.

Occasionally, Symington had a momentary pang of guilt, thinking of Branwell's fate in the attic, shut away from the gaze of the world, and sometimes he woke in the night, his heart pounding, certain that he heard shuffling footsteps in the corridor outside the bedroom, or a low moaning noise, or a lunatic's laughter, coming through the ceiling, or closer, getting closer, right at the door, while Beatrice slept on, peacefully. Symington was uncertain which would be more terrifying: Branwell's ghost, or living burglars, though in daylight, he consigned both to the realm of fanciful imagination, or, more likely, a symptom of indigestion, which is what Beatrice suggested, when he told her that he had been suffering from nightmares. 'Best to steer clear of cheese in the evening,' she told him, not unkindly, and sent him to bed with a cup of milky Ovaltine.

During his convalescence, Symington tried to avoid reading anything about the Brontës, and browsed through some of Beatrice's books, instead, including several by Daphne. He enjoyed *My Cousin Rachel*, though he was frustrated by its inconclusive ending, which did not confirm whether the beautiful Rachel was an evil murderess, intent on poisoning those who stood in her way, or the innocent victim of her cousin's paranoid delusions. Similarly, he found *Rebecca* far more absorbing than he had expected, and once he had started it, he did not want to stop, but there were elements of the novel that were as exasperating as they were intriguing. Why did the narrator not have a name? Presumably it was to make Rebecca seem more alive, more in control, from beyond the grave, than her living successor, but even so, thought Symington, wasn't this too contorted a device? And who had started the fire that burnt Manderley to the ground? Was Mrs Danvers the arsonist, or not? At least you knew where you were with *Jane Eyre* when the fire was clearly ignited by the first Mrs Rochester.

Symington would have liked to question Daphne on these matters, to ask her directly about her motives as a writer, and how she conceived those cunning plots and brooding characters. Where, he wondered, had Rachel and Rebecca sprung from? He could hear no echo of their voices in Daphne's measured letters to him. But much as he was drawn to the idea of engaging Daphne in a direct dialogue about her books – a dialogue that would have a certain romance to it, given its basis in his privileged position of access to her – he was also aware this would be impossible. For to do so would be an admission that he had read her books; and he was loath to let her know this, as it might shift the precarious balance of power between them, making her the expert, and him the amateur, rather than the other way round.

It was, perhaps, for similar reasons that Symington waited for over a fortnight before replying to Daphne's letter, and when he did so, he tried to confine himself to the briefest of notes. Yet he could not bring himself to be entirely discouraging; for if she was to commence her researches again, then he should be keeping an eye on her. As for her request to buy more material from his library, Symington was uncertain which was more pressing, his financial needs or his decision to keep Branwell safely locked away. Finally, after much deliberation, he chose one of the dullest books in his library, the collected works of the Reverend Patrick Brontë; let the father speak for the son . . .

Newlay Grove,
Horsforth,
Leeds
Telephone: 2615 Horsforth

29th January 1959

Dear Miss du Maurier,

Thank you for your letter. I was glad to hear that you have not abandoned Branwell altogether; though to be truthful, I do not think it would be worth your while to go to the trouble of making the long journey to Yorkshire, for there is little prospect of you finding a shred of new evidence about Branwell.

But if you are intent on making such a visit, I will gladly be available to help you in any way I can, as your discreet comrade in arms. Meanwhile, I am still searching through my files of manuscripts, but in the interim I enclose 'Brontëana: the Collected Works of the Rev. Patrick Brontë', edited by one of the founders of the Brontë Society, Mr J. Horsfall Turner. I trust you will find it of very great interest,

Yours sincerely,

J. Alex Symington.

CHAPTER EIGHTEEN

Hampstead, May

After the morning that I went into Paul's study and saw those emails on his laptop, I felt somehow compromised – as if I was the one with the guilty secret, not him. I was relieved that he didn't appear to realise that I'd read the emails, but I couldn't help worrying that he'd find out somehow, that I would give myself away. So I suppose I've been even more withdrawn from him than usual for the last few weeks, trying to immerse myself in work; though actually, it's not difficult to get absorbed, it's easier to escape into my research than anywhere else. I've been burrowing around the Internet, up half the night, night after night, searching through the catalogues of various remote outposts of library archives, following ancient trails of Daphne's letters – there are dozens to her publisher and editor and agent, for she was an assiduous correspondent – but I'd just about given up on finding Symington's letters to Daphne. Then a couple of days ago I came across a reference to the fact that she'd destroyed many of her private papers in a huge bonfire when she was forced to move out of Menabilly, after her lease came to an end in 1969, and as soon as I knew that, I started worrying that she'd burnt Symington's letters, along with loads of other stuff. After a sleepless night of obsessing about what might have been lost in that fire – and her reasons for starting it, given that it seemed eerily like the work of Mrs Danvers – I decided that I needed to stop going around in circles, or at least, to try to consider things from a different angle. Hence my train trip up to Yorkshire again, but this time to Haworth, which seemed like a good place to think about the mysterious Mr Symington.

That's where I went today – well, yesterday, because it's after midnight now, but I'm too excited to sleep – and the journey there was far more nostalgic than I'd expected, because I'd only ever done it once before, with my mother, when I was about thirteen. I'd just read *Wuthering Heights*, which I loved, and was halfway through *Jane Eyre*, and my mother suggested that we went to the Brontë Parsonage Museum, to see where the books had been written. She was good like that, my mother. She made it feel like an adventure, rather than an educational outing. That was her at her best – she could talk to me about the books, and somehow through the books. It kind of made up for the times when she was silent, except now I'm beginning to wish that I'd asked her what she was thinking, during all those long silences; because I'm sure she was thinking about something, and it was clamorous inside her head . . .

Anyway, the thing that surprised me about the Brontë house when I'd gone there as a child, still surprised me yesterday, because although I'd imagined the parsonage as being high up in the middle of the moors, miles away from anywhere, and as isolated as Wuthering Heights, in fact it turns out that the Brontës lived close to Keighley, a big, bustling Victorian town. I suppose it was Mrs Gaskell who really started the myth that they were completely cut off from the rest of the world – that's what my mother had said to me, on the bus ride to Haworth from Keighley station – though Charlotte also did her bit to suggest that they were in a remote wilderness; a landscape which existed more in her mind, I think, than it ever did in reality. But maybe she needed to imagine it that way?

The parsonage wasn't too crowded – I managed to arrive just as a minibus of Japanese tourists were leaving – and I pottered around the museum by myself, trying to stop thinking about my mother and where she might be now and whether she was with my father. It reminded me of when I had just started junior school, and our teacher talked to us about heaven – I'd imagined my father floating through the Reading Room at the British Museum, up above where my mother was still working as a librarian, higher and higher, up to the glass roof, and then through it, just fading through it, into the sky on the other side. It's hard not to think about death when you're in the Brontë parsonage, not just because of all the deaths in the family, but also because of the immediate view over the graveyard, those grey ranks of headstones, hundreds of them, pressing up against the garden walls, as if they were waiting to be let in; or maybe it's the other way round, maybe they were waiting for the occupants of the parsonage to join them in the graveyard.

Yet there's such an odd feeling of aliveness there, as well – as if the Brontë children had just put down their pens and papers, or come back from walking the dogs, as if they were just around the corner, a little way out of sight, laughing quietly at everyone else, hands over their mouths.

I spent a long time halfway up the stairs at the parsonage, gazing at Branwell's portrait of his three sisters, where he has painted himself out of the picture, turning his figure into a sort of pillar. Which is odd, in a way, given that he was the very opposite of being a pillar in the family, though I suppose his unstableness and alcoholism drew his sisters together, closing ranks against the outside world, as well as against Branwell. Perhaps that's what the picture suggests, Branwell locked away inside his solitary column, separated from the girls, even though he is right beside them.

Then I looked at Charlotte's dresses and jewellery in her bedroom, wondering how they could have survived for so long after her death, and I thought about my father, and how I had so little of him, just his notebooks that I couldn't read, and a small photograph album with a few blurred pictures of my parents' wedding (only of the two of them – their parents were dead by then, though I often wonder why no one else was in the picture?) and several more of me as a baby, with my father gazing at me worriedly, as if I were a very small wild animal that might bite if he came too close.

When I went into the other bedroom at the front of the parsonage, which Branwell periodically shared with his father, from his earliest years into adulthood, it was impossible not to think about how suffocating that must have been for a son who dreamt of escape, who spent his time drawing maps of faraway lands, planning battles and romances. No wonder poor Branwell went mad and drank himself into oblivion, cooped up in the parsonage, his only way out through painting pictures and telling stories of his alter ego, Northangerland, the swashbuckling earl with three wives and a talent for piracy, and a ship that takes him around the world. And in the end, Branwell found an exit from his father's bedroom only in death, in a coffin that carried him no more than a hundred yards through the garden gates and into the graveyard.

I looked at Branwell's sketches of Northangerland, all of them wildly romanticised versions of himself, now displayed in a back room that was said to be his studio; and it felt dark and airless in there, or was that my own, equally romanticised version of a more complicated truth? And I started to get frustrated, staring at the little books that were locked away in a glass cabinet in Branwell's studio, so that you could just see a couple of pages from the Brontës' childhood stories of Angria and Gondal, with those incredibly beautiful, intricate illustrations made with delicate mapping pens. Eventually, my eyes were aching from trying to read their microscopic handwriting through the glass, and I was beginning to fantasise about staging a smash and grab robbery, at which point I decided it was probably time to get out of there, and buy myself a cup of tea and a tuna sandwich, before catching the bus from Haworth back to Keighley train station.

But instead of ending up in one of several Brontë cafés on the village high street, I wandered into a second-hand bookshop and started browsing. I was looking for books on Branwell to add to my collection, but there was nothing new, and then I picked up one at random, which turned out to be a dusty biography of a former president of the Brontë Society, Sir William Robertson Nicoll, who died in 1923.

Inside, written on the frontispiece in barely visible copperplate, there was a date – Christmas 1925 – and an inscription, 'To J. A. Symington'.

I was so excited that I let out a small shriek, and the grey-haired man behind the counter looked up from his newspaper. 'Found something interesting?' he said.

'Well, it is to me,' I replied, and handed over the money for the book (an absolute bargain at £2.50).

'You're keen on Robertson Nicoll, are you?' said the bookseller, looking surprised.

I told him I'd never heard of Nicoll, or his biographer, a Mr T. H. Darlow, but it was Symington that I wanted to know more about. We ended up talking for a while – I explained that I was a student, and I was looking for research material for my dissertation – and eventually, the bookseller said 'It's your lucky day; I've taken a liking to you,' and he disappeared into the back room, before emerging, five minutes, later, with a cardboard folder and a wide triumphant smile. 'Here's your Mr Symington,' he said, and told me to take a look inside. And there they were: faded carbon copies of Symington's letters to Daphne du Maurier, and some of his other correspondence as well, that had been tucked inside a small box of his books, including the Nicoll biography, bought by the bookseller at a local auctioneer's in north Yorkshire.

'Thirty quid, and they're all yours,' he said. 'No one else is interested in Mr Symington. That folder has been in the shop for two or three years gathering dust – it's about time it found a good home.'

I wrote out a cheque and thanked him, feeling a bit dazed – I mean, it seemed so unlikely – and then realised that I'd just missed my train. But it didn't matter, nothing mattered, apart from the fact that I'd found Symington's letters, or rather that they had found me, just like Daphne's had done in Leeds. It was as if I'd had another sign – I'm not sure who from, but it meant something, like an acknowledgement that I was on the right track.

And the letters are even more interesting than I'd expected, as I discovered when I read through them all, several times over, on the slow train home. It's not just the correspondence with du Maurier that is so intriguing; there are also Symington's replies to a firm of solicitors acting on behalf of the Brontë Society, stapled to the original legal letters he'd received from them, which were written over the summer of 1930, just after he'd stopped working as curator and librarian at the Brontë Parsonage Museum. The solicitors were threatening to take action against Symington, and accusing him of stealing various manuscripts and relics from the museum: thirty-one items, including original Brontë letters and manuscripts, and a set of keys for the locked cases in the Parsonage library and museum.

Despite the seriousness of the allegations, the legal correspondence appears to have had no conclusion – at least not in the letters I bought – and I wonder if the Brontë Society eventually decided to give up pursuing Symington, and their lost manuscripts; perhaps they felt that a public court case would be too embarrassing, that these matters should be kept secret. Certainly, by the time Daphne started writing to Symington, twenty-seven years after this suppressed literary scandal, she had no idea of the cloud over his departure from the Parsonage, and he gives nothing away to her, though reading between the lines, you can sense that he's in a difficult position, because she starts asking him about the whereabouts of certain manuscripts, which she has been told by a Mrs Weir, a retired secretary to the Brontë Society, are most likely to be in Mr Symington's possession.

All of his letters to the solicitors were typewritten in 1930, and he also referred to having a secretary, but by 1957 he was writing his letters to Daphne by hand (luckily, his prose is mostly very legible). There is a printed letterhead, giving his address – Newlay Grove, Horsforth, Leeds – and a phone number: 2615 Horsforth. I had to restrain myself from ringing it when I got home, because Paul's got one of those old, black bakelite phones that had belonged to his parents – not that I know what the code for Horsforth would have been – but in the quiet of the house, when it seemed like the city was sleeping, and only the foxes were out, it felt almost as if I could reach across the years, as if Mr Symington might still be waiting for me in Newlay Grove, sitting by the telephone.

And there are so many questions I'd like to be able to ask him. Why, for example, was he prepared to give hints to Daphne about his suspicions concerning the forgery of Charlotte's signatures on many of Branwell's early manuscripts of the Angrian chronicles, without quite naming the culprit? He comes pretty close to accusing T. J. Wise, his co-editor on the Shakespeare Head edition of the Brontës' collected works, telling Daphne that he did almost all of the work on these volumes, because Wise was not only in ill health, but subsequently in what Symington describes as 'the fog and mist' surrounding the exposure of his forgeries in other fields. Still, it's not an explicit accusation.

A bit later on in the correspondence, he also told Daphne that she was right to suspect that some of the poems attributed to Emily were, in fact, by Branwell, 'and I did get a great protest some thirty years ago when I dared to say so'. Where, I wonder, did the protest take place? I've not been able to find reference to it, or to Symington's claims on behalf of Branwell, in any official Brontë scholarship or academic research. More letters follow in quick succession, with Symington selling Daphne some of his library, which I would dearly like to get my hands upon, including several privately printed volumes of Branwell's letters and stories.

And then his letters stop for over a year – in line with Daphne's. It is Daphne who goes silent first, without any explanation, after a series of apparently cordial letters, but Symington comes to an abrupt halt, also. Why didn't Daphne immediately follow up his leads about the forged signatures? I mean, surely she should have been able to discover more about what could have been – could still be, perhaps – one of the greatest literary scandals for decades?

But the odd thing is, instead of diving into that investigation, she stopped writing to Symington, and in 1958 she wrote a collection of short stories instead, which she called *The Breaking Point*. It's out of print now, but I've got a second-hand copy, and the stories appear to have nothing to do with Symington, or Branwell, or any of the Brontës. But even so, they're really intriguing, because this is the book she wrote when she broke off her correspondence to Symington, though her later letters suggest that she was still studying Branwell's manuscripts in 1958. And rereading the collection, it's as if her stories are a response to his, though her own life is woven into it all, as well . . . and death; there's so much death in this book.

It's a very sinister collection, about murder and paranoia and men in trilby hats, and the most macabre story is 'The Blue Lenses', which describes a woman who is recovering from an eye operation. When her bandages are removed, and icy blue lenses are fitted to her eyes by the surgeon, she feels no pain. But afterwards, to her shock, everyone around her appears to have an animal head. Her favourite nurse, Nurse Ansel, has a snake's head, which she first sees as a reflection in the mirror, its pointed barbed tongue swiftly thrusting and swiftly withdrawn, as its twisting neck comes into view over her shoulders, through the looking glass. Then her husband Jim appears with the head of a vulture, with a blood-tipped beak and a neck encased in flabby folds of flesh, and when she finally sees herself in the mirror, the eyes that stare back at her are doe's eyes, and her timid deer's head is meek, bowed as if ready for sacrifice.

You could use these stories, perhaps, as evidence of Daphne's distrust of the world around her, as well as her uncertainty of how to interpret what she saw. That's what Paul might say, I suppose, if he read the stories, not that he would, and I'm not going to ask him to. I couldn't bear to listen to him being dismissive about something that matters so much to me; which is maybe why all of this is still my own secret, that has nothing to do with my husband. But I keep thinking about the name Daphne chose for the husband in 'The Blue Lenses', Jim, which surely is an echo of Jim Barrie; and Barrie's wife was called Mary Ansell, which is too close to Nurse Ansel to be coincidental.

I've been making notes on this, and another story from *The Breaking Point*, which is called 'The Pool'. You don't have to be a genius to link this to her cousin Michael's drowning, which was rumoured to have been suicide, though the Coroner recorded a verdict of accidental death; and there's a suggestion that suicide is a possibility for the narrator in Daphne's story. She's a girl on the verge of adolescence, still allowed into a secret world unseen by adults, which can only be entered beneath the surface of a dark pool hidden within the woods in her grandparents' garden. I imagine this pool as being in the woods at Menabilly, and the girl as Daphne's younger self; though time becomes fluid within the story, shifting and liquid, like the beckoning water of the pool, where a series of ghosts return, passing through it into another world.

I'm not sure what, precisely, this has got to do with a PhD about Daphne and the Brontës; apart from the fact that she was writing these stories at the same time as doing her research into Branwell. I really need to talk it through with someone – and the only person I can imagine doing that with is Rachel. I've just got this feeling that she'd be able to make sense of it. The likelihood of such a conversation ever taking place is almost as remote as me being able to discuss any of this with my parents, but even so, when I read 'The Pool', they feel closer, like the shadows and phantoms in the woods, making their way back to the secret world.

When I was a student, I remember hearing a lecturer who said that writing is about negotiating with the dead – and maybe that's what reading is for me. I'm certainly not talking very much to the living. Paul says I'm too isolated; but then he seems to have isolated himself from me. I never imagined that marriage could be so lonely; before I met Paul, I thought that finding a husband was a way of never being alone again. Which just goes to show how imagination can fail you; or if not fail you, then lead you astray.

Was this what Daphne felt, when she decided to return to Branwell, after *The Breaking Point*? That she would be safer with historical facts; that these would guide her away from the slippery edges of the pool, towards solid ground? Not that Branwell was very solid; but perhaps she thought that she could believe in him, like Mr Symington; or maybe it's just me that needs to believe in all of them.

CHAPTER NINETEEN

Menabilly,
Par,
Cornwall

7th February 1959

Dear Mr Symington,
Your parcel and letter arrived this
morning, for which many thanks. You have been put to
some trouble in searching through your library, and you
have not told me the price of the Reverend Brontë's book. I
trust that the enclosed cheque for five guineas will cover
this.

I must admit, I am a little bewildered, as some years have
passed since the publication of your Shakespeare Head
edition, as to the actual whereabouts of many of the
manuscripts included in your excellent edition. I know that
T.J. Wise's collection is in the British Museum, and the
Bonnell collection was bequeathed to the Brontë Parsonage

in Haworth. The Brotherton Collection is, I presume, in the hands of Leeds University. But what, and where, is the Law collection? I have heard it mentioned, but its fate seems uncertain.

I would very much like to track down every one of Branwell's manuscripts, in this country and in America, and have them photostated and transcribed (at any rate, all those that were not transcribed in the Shakespeare Head edition). Do you think this might be possible? I suppose that photostats cost a mint of money, but it would nevertheless be a useful step forward. I see that most of Branwell's stories of Alexander Percy, alias Northangerland, have never been transcribed; and I wonder if a comprehensive account of this curious character might throw some light on the development of Branwell's own dual personality.

I have also been giving some thought to your suspicions that various of the early Angrian manuscripts bear a forged Charlotte Brontë signature on the title page. It would be very interesting to have an expert in handwriting and forgeries study these Angrian manuscripts, and finally pronounce on whether they were written by Charlotte or Branwell.

I do look forward to coming to Yorkshire some time in the not too distant future, and meeting you.

Yours sincerely,

Daphne felt a sense of relief when she finished typing her letter to Mr Symington, for at least she now had a plan with which to proceed. Doubtless it would be expensive to copy the manuscripts, but she was determined to go ahead, whatever the expense, for surely this would be the key to Branwell, that would finally open the locked doors that had kept him hidden for so long. What Daphne did not say to Symington, but had finally admitted to herself, was that she must find a way of bringing her research to a conclusion, for though she had tried to set Branwell aside for a time, she could not free herself of him. It was as she had thought at the start of her research – that they were wedded in some way, as inextricably linked as she was to Tommy, and there was no means of evading that. And if she did not tell his story, as she had already vowed to do, then it would haunt her; he would haunt her, sending her round and round in circles, until she was altogether lost, with no sense of how to find her way out again. So it seemed to her that each manuscript she found and decoded would be a candle in the darkness, and if she followed them, step by step, they would lead her to safety, at last.

It was twilight when she walked back across the lawns to the house – five o'clock, and the winter's evening stretched ahead of her, like the long shadows of the trees beyond her writing hut, the place where she planned to be buried. Daphne knew she should be relishing her solitude: Tommy was working in London, seeming more able to cope by himself there, and Tod was away, also, visiting friends, so the house was empty, after the two maids went home. She reminded herself then that being alone like this in Menabilly

– her safe house, her blessed refuge – was the closest she would ever come to bliss.

She lit a cigarette, and sat down at the piano in the Long Room, picking out a tune, her father's favourite, 'Clair de Lune'. Yet she could not settle, and paced the room, quietly, stealthily, almost certain that the veil between the living and the dead, the past and the present, had worn so thin in Menabilly that she might slip through whatever it was that divided them; or perhaps those others who inhabited the house, and her memory, could come forward to greet her; the others that she sensed, just ahead of her, or behind her, close enough to hear their quiet breathing.

The maids gossiped about ghosts from a faraway past, all the way back to the Civil War, when Menabilly was a Royalist stronghold. But Daphne imagined summoning up the spirits of those who were hanging on the walls, captured in framed family drawings by her grandfather, or in photographs, the same ones that had stood on the mantelpiece of Gerald's bedroom at Cannon Hall; a shrine to his family, grouped around a silver cross, and he had kissed each of the photographs every night, and muttered a little prayer to all of them, the dearly departed dead. The same photographs were now set along the mantelpiece of the Long Room in Menabilly, but at their centre was another picture, of Gerald in adulthood, a cigarette in his hand, his expression slightly mocking, his hair combed back from his face, his parting as sharp as a razorblade.

Daphne felt his eyes on her, even when her back was to him, and as she spun around to meet his gaze, she thought she saw him move, very slightly, behind the glass. One of his eyebrows was raised, and he seemed to look at her more intently, coolly, appraisingly, with a faint smile on his lips. She turned away from him again, but her neck was prickling.

And he was still watching her. 'I will always be watching over you,' he said to her, just before he died, but also long before that . . .

The day he saw her from the cliff, staring down at her, he was as silent then as he was now, though she knew that he could see her; that he could not take his eyes off her, that he saw everything.

Daphne closed her eyes, she did not want to see her father, she did not want to remember this, but she could not get away from him, from that summer's day, when his shadow fell across hers. It was the year she was fourteen, just after Michael died, and the family had gone on holiday to Thurlestone, and Geoffrey was there, with his second wife. Daphne was still a child, paddling and shrimping on the Devon beach, but then one day she glanced up, and Geoffrey was smiling at her, and her heart missed a beat. Why had she felt that way? Geoffrey was far closer in age to her father – thirty-six years old, an actor like his uncle, and he and Gerald were the greatest of friends; they looked so alike that they might have been brothers. But that smile had been the start of a secret between the two of them, Daphne and her cousin. As August progressed, so did their understanding, and she knew that no one else must know of it. After lunch, when everyone stretched out on the lawn like corpses under their rugs, Geoffrey would come and lie beside her, and take her hand in his, but no one could see them, the blankets hid everything; and at night, he would hold out his arms and dance with her at the Links hotel, singing along to the orchestra as it played 'Whispering', and the room spun around and around.

On the morning he left for London, he said to her, 'Come along and have a last look at the sea.' So she'd gone with him to the beach, just the two of them, hand in hand, though they did not speak, until suddenly he turned to her and said, 'I'm going to miss you terribly, Daph.' She nodded, but nothing more, she could not speak, Geoffrey was kissing her, his tongue pushing between her lips. Then at last he pulled away from her, looking up at the cliff, and as she followed his gaze, she saw her father standing there, staring down at them, as if he might jump, or swoop upon her like a bird of prey, and she felt a blush spread, livid, over her neck and face. 'There's Uncle Gerald, spying,' said Geoffrey, laughing a little, 'we'd better go, before he fetches a shotgun.'

Gerald had not accused her of anything afterwards, but from then on, something in his attitude to her changed. Geoffrey had been packed off on a lengthy theatre tour of America while her father had stayed at home in London, and there were moments when she felt his eyes upon her, for no particular reason, and she would blush, again. By the time she was fifteen or sixteen, Gerald used to take her out to lunch or dinner at least once a week, and they'd walk into a restaurant, hand in hand, all eyes upon them. 'We make a handsome couple,' he'd say, smiling benignly.

Daphne sighed, and sat down in the big armchair her father called 'Barrie's chair', the one that Uncle Jim had always chosen for his own particular seat on his visits to Cannon Hall, when she sat beside him, and he told her the secret adventures of Peter Pan, and she wished so hard that she had been born a boy, like her cousins. Oh, those boys, they were everything she wanted to be, though sometimes she confused that with wanting them.

'Don't grow up, my darling girl,' her father used to whisper to her; but she could not stop herself, she could not help letting him down. When she was twenty, Geoffrey had come to stay at Cannon Hall while his wife was in a nursing home, and at night, while everyone else was safely sleeping, he had kissed her in the drawing room, even more passionately than before. Daphne had kept her diary from the time, locked away in a secret drawer of her desk, and she went and got it for herself now, flicking through its pages, as she sank back into Barrie's chair. Were it not for the evidence of her own younger handwriting, she would find it hard to believe the carelessness of her behaviour with Geoffrey; and yet there was a strange clear-sightedness in her observations as well. It had seemed so natural to kiss Geoffrey, she'd written in her diary, immediately after their encounter in the drawing room, and he was so sweet and lovable, but it was also just like kissing Daddy. 'Perhaps this family is the same as the Borgias,' she wrote, 'a sort of incest . . .' And Daphne remembered the insouciance with which she described her theory to Geoffrey at the time, in between kisses. 'Daddy is Pope Alexander, you are Cesare and I'm Lucrezia,' she said, and he laughed, and said, 'Stop talking nonsense, you little fool, it doesn't become you . . .'

Poor Tommy, he'd been so honourable and good and true when he came sailing into Fowey harbour, looking for the girl who'd written his favourite book, *The Loving Spirit*, not realising the web of deceit she'd spun around her. He sent her a note, saying he'd known her cousins at Eton, and asked if he could take her out on his boat. She said yes, and they spent an afternoon together at sea, a fine bright April day, when the waves sprayed over them, and the cold, clean wind blew all muddied thoughts of Geoffrey and Gerald away. That evening, the wind had dropped just as the sun was disappearing, and they watched the sky fade to the palest pink, and then a pearl grey, and the sea was calm, the colour of the sky, and she felt she could do anything, with this man by her side, she felt filled with a sudden, wild joy.

In the following weeks, he returned often to visit her in Fowey, where she was staying alone in Ferryside, and it had been such a glorious courtship; it seemed like the sun shone whenever they were together, walking along the footpath from Boddinick to Pont, and then over the rickety footbridge, where the creek narrowed, and the swans glided to their nests. 'Let's not stop yet,' she said, wanting to go on walking with him, and they went up through the woods to Polruan, pausing at her favourite vantage points on the way, so that she could show him the views out across the silvery water. 'The most beautiful sight in the world,' she said to him, and he kissed her, saying, 'Almost as beautiful as you.' He fell in love with Fowey at the same time as falling in love with her, and she loved him all the more for that, telling him that when she first came here, and caught sight of Ferryside, and the estuary beyond, she'd remembered a line from a forgotten book, where a lover looks for the first time upon his chosen one, and declared, 'I for this, and this for me.' She met Tommy's eyes as she said the words, standing high above Fowey at St Catherine's Castle, and he repeated them back to her, catching hold of her hands as he did so.

He'd drive through the night to be with her, whenever he could get leave from his regiment, bringing her an armful of roses on the morning of her twenty-fifth birthday in May, and a bottle of champagne that they drank together in the garden at Ferryside, watching the great ships go out to sea from Fowey harbour, led by a sturdy pilot tug, as the dinghies and wooden yachts bobbed around in their wake. And they explored the little town, breathing in its smell of tar and rope and tidal water, and the coastline beyond it, walking out past St Catherine's Point to Coombe, where there was a hidden beach, a smugglers' cove, and the encircling cliffs were covered in ox-eye daisies, sea campion and blossoming primroses, that somehow clung to the crevices, and lapwings swooped down to the water's edge. Finally, she took him to her secret place, further west along the cliff from Coombe to the beach at Polridmouth, and then climbing over the gate by the solitary cottage, up the narrow path that led through the woods to Menabilly. The bluebells were out, their smoky scent mingling with the moss and the young bracken; their colour a challenge to the sky. When they reached the deserted house, she took him by the hand and led him to the window where you could see through tattered curtains into an abandoned room with dark panelled walls and a great fireplace, and a forgotten corkscrew lying upon an oak sideboard, and the solemn faces of family portraits staring down through their veils of cobwebs and cracked varnish. 'One day I'll live here,' she said to Tommy.

'One day, I'll live here with you,' he said, and pulled her down with him, into the long grass.

Where had they gone to, she wondered, as she gazed out of the same window now, out into the wintry darkness, to the place where she and Tommy had been wrapped in each other's arms, cocooned in a nest of grass and sunlight? Did the ghosts of those young lovers still look through the glass, from the garden, while she and Tommy grew older indoors? If she closed her eyes, and listened carefully, she could almost hear his voice. 'I don't want anything sleazy for us,' he said to her, between kisses, 'an affair would be too sordid, too meaningless, when you mean the world to me . . .'

So there was nothing for it but to be married. They were engaged by the middle of June, and married in July, a little more than three months after Tommy had first introduced himself. She wrote to tell her mother the news, preferring that Muriel should make the announcement to Gerald; he promptly burst into tears, but nevertheless her parents were present for the wedding, along with Geoffrey. It was early in the morning when they took the boat from Ferryside to Pont bridge, so as to catch the tide, and then they walked up the steep path, fringed by wild honeysuckle and ferns, to the church, which stood alone amidst the fields. Above the entrance, there was a sundial, and an inscription that Gerald read out – 'Watch and Pray, Time Haste's Away' – and then they'd gone inside, where Tommy was already waiting for her by the altar, handsome in his Major's uniform. Daphne wore a blue skirt and coat, for she had sworn she wanted a quiet wedding, nothing showy, just a handful of guests. But standing there, in the ancient church, where Jane Slade had been buried, in the dappled sunlight that shone through the stained-glass windows, beneath the wooden arches of the medieval roof, Daphne had known this to be as romantic as a traditional love story.

Why, then, had she undermined her marriage from the start by asking Geoffrey to be there, when even her sisters and Tommy's family were not? What on earth had possessed her to do such a devilish act? As Daphne glanced over at her wedding photographs on the piano – Tommy looking so proud, and strong, too, blithe and oblivious of what lay ahead – she felt suddenly overcome with guilt, filled with a terrible sense of disgust at herself, knowing that Geoffrey's presence had been the beginning of her betrayals and treachery, that there was no one to blame but herself, for she had invited him into the holiest of places, into Lanteglos church; she had let him stand there, beside Tommy, making everything dirty again. Yet the deceits had begun long before then, for in kissing Geoffrey, she knew her father to feel betrayed, and that, surely, was itself a betrayal of her mother? And had she not thought of her father as she kissed Geoffrey, had she not imagined what it might be to kiss Gerald, or was it more than her imagination, had she, in fact, been kissed by her father, when she was still a child, had he desired her, just as Geoffrey did?

No, she would not think of it, she could not think of it; it was impossible, an obscenity that should be banished back into the crevice where it came from. Daphne's hands were shaking as she returned to her desk in the corner of the room to lock the diary safely away, and she could not make the key turn in the drawer, it seemed to resist her fingers. 'You little fool,' she muttered to herself, but as she spoke, it seemed to be her mother's voice that she heard. She dropped the key and fell to her knees, scrabbling for it on the floor; but there was a rushing sound in her ears, and voices, she could hear her father calling her. She swallowed hard, and saw the key, glinting in the corner, and this time she forced herself to be more careful as she picked it up and locked the drawer. Then she poured herself a glass of brandy to steady her nerves.

But it was no good, she could still see her father's face, eyeing her up from his vantage point on the mantelpiece; she had to get away from where he could watch over her. So she did what she had always forbidden her children to do: unlocked the door at the end of the Long Room, between the inhabited part of Menabilly and its unlived-in wing, and stepped into the darkness, where the rooms were filled with dust and bats and ghosts, where nothing had changed since she first trespassed here. There was no electricity in this part of the house, but her eyes soon grew accustomed to the shadowy gloom, for the curtains were shredded and the shutters decaying, allowing the occasional shaft of moonlight to shine through the windows, like a path across the floor. Daphne could hear rustles, though always just around the corner; rats, probably, this wing was infested with them, but sometimes she thought she could hear a low laugh, or the light tread of footsteps other than her own.

None of this frightened her – she felt safer here, on familiar territory, as if she might be one of Menabilly's ghosts, a companion to the lady in blue, who was sometimes glimpsed looking out of a side window on the upper floor, though her face was always hidden; or the Cavalier whose skeleton was found entombed in a buttress wall over a hundred years ago; or Rebecca, how could she have forgotten Rebecca? She moved quickly, deft, like Rebecca; she was strong, like Rebecca, the mistress of this house, dancing in the moonlight in an empty room, a phantom waltzing alone in the dust.

And then, all at once, the shadows seemed to gather into shapes, and they were too much for her, her breath caught in her throat. 'Watch your step,' whispered a voice into her ear, and Daphne spun around, but there was no one, she could see nothing, and she started running, stumbling, back to the door into her part of the house. 'Your house?' said the whisperer. 'I don't think so. You are not the mistress here.'

CHAPTER TWENTY

Newlay Grove, May 1959.

Symington was in a quandary, finding himself apparently unable to move forward or go back. Daphne had made it clear, in a series of increasingly frequent letters over the last three months, that she was determined to find each of Branwell's manuscripts, and would not stop until she had done so. She asked for his help, and Symington found himself offering it, but he knew that he was cornered. Daphne wanted him to go to the Parsonage, to transcribe Branwell's manuscripts that were held there, and to arrange for them to be copied, and Symington agreed to this – she was offering to pay for his services, and he badly needed the money. But he was also painfully aware that he would not be welcomed at the Parsonage; indeed, would almost certainly be turned away, should he request an appointment there.

Meanwhile, her letters kept coming, asking for more and more information; and he took days to compose the briefest of replies. And now he was running out of excuses about his failure to visit the Parsonage; firstly, he'd written to her, by way of explanation, that it was closed for the Easter holidays, then that the Brontë Society had tangled everything in red tape and bureaucracy, and was refusing access to anyone who wanted to conduct research in the Parsonage library and archives. But Daphne was relentless, and wrote again, suggesting that he visited the Brotherton Library at Leeds University instead, to get to work on Branwell's manuscripts there, and enclosing a generous cheque for his future expenses, which he cashed, and spent on the mounting household bills.

Symington knew that his presence at the Brotherton Library would be equally unwelcome, might even precipitate another bout of legal action against him. He considered going anonymously – it was twenty years, after all, since he was last seen there; even longer since he worked at the Parsonage – but feared that someone might recognise him, and make an embarrassing scene in public, might even call the police.

And then yet another letter arrived from her this morning in a swift reply to his last note, in which he'd told her that the Brontë Society had not yet responded to his most recent request to have access to the Parsonage library (a request that he had not, in fact, got round to making). 'How maddening for you having so much trouble in getting permission to look at the manuscripts,' wrote Daphne in a swift reply, 'you don't think by any chance that the Brontë Society is afraid you are going to find out something that might show the poor despised Branwell to advantage? (!)'

Symington could see that Daphne had underlined the word 'afraid', very firmly, and he wondered if this might be a message to him. There was nothing for it, he realised now, but to let her have something from his collection of manuscripts, and perhaps some snippets of information about Wise's forgeries, to keep her occupied. At least this should buy him a little more time; not only with Daphne, but also with Beatrice, who warned him that they would lose the house, and much of its contents, if money were not swiftly forthcoming. There were several manuscripts of Branwell's poems that he could sell to Daphne, none of them controversial, for though he had borrowed them from the Brontë Parsonage Museum while he was working there, no one knew of their existence at the time, as far as Symington could tell, and therefore no one mourned their disappearance. In fact, it was the lack of interest shown by anyone at all in these poems that had prompted Symington to remove them from the Parsonage in the first place; they seemed to him to be like unloved, neglected children, whose interests would be best served by providing them with a far more caring home.

It took Symington all morning to locate one of these manuscripts; he had hidden it some time ago, between the leaves of an unrelated book, as a defence against burglary. Once he had found it, he read it – for this was one of Branwell's more legible manuscripts, which was why it pained him to let it go. It contained two sonnets, one written on the upper half of the page, another on the lower half. Both were equally gloomy, reflecting Symington's current state of mind, both were signed 'Northangerland'. It had been some time since Symington had read any of Branwell's writing; he had avoided it, ever since his stay in hospital, almost as if it were a necessary part of his convalescence. But as he read the poems, over and over, speaking them out loud, he felt the old sense of excitement stirring inside him again.

The first was his favourite – 'Peaceful death and happy life'
– and it seemed to Symington to be at least as good as
anything written by Branwell's more famous sisters. These
were lines that should be learnt by heart, thought Symington,
and he set to work, repeating them, until he felt almost as if he
had written the poem himself, and Branwell's voice (the voice
that must be kept out of his head, for no good had ever come
from it) was drowned by his own:

Why dost thou sorrow for the happy dead
    For if their life be lost, their toils are oer
    And woe and want shall trouble them no more,
Nor ever slept they in an earthly bed
So sound as now they sleep while, dreamless, laid
    In the dark chambers of that unknown shore
    Where Night and Silence seal each guarded door:
So, turn from such as these thy drooping head
And mourn the 'dead alive' – whose spirit flies –
    Whose life departs before his death has come –
Who finds no Heaven beyond Life's gloomy skies,
    Who sees no Hope to brighten up that gloom;
Tis HE who feels the worm that never dies –
    The REAL death and darkness of the tomb.

Once he had committed this to heart, Symington discovered
that the second poem, written on the lower half of the page,
was also unexpectedly rousing, when read out loud. The
house was empty, but he imagined an audience before him
as he declaimed the title – 'The Callousness produced by care'
– and then the poem:

Why hold young eyes the fullest fount of tears
        And why do youthful breasts the oftenest sigh
When fancied friends forsake, or lovers fly,
        Or fancied woes and dangers waken fears:
        Ah! He who asks has seen but springtide years,
Or Times rough voice had long since told him why!
Increase of days increases misery,
        And misery brings selfishness, which sears
The hearts first feelings – mid the battles roar
In Deaths dread grasp the soldiers eyes are blind
To other's pains – So he whose hopes are oer
Turns coldly from the suffering of mankind.
A bleeding spirit will delight in gore –
A tortured heart will make a Tyrant mind.

Several hours later, Symington was hoarse, having chanted both the poems over and over again, yet triumphant. And by the time Beatrice had returned home after another of her committee meetings, well into the evening (and too late to cook him a hot dinner), Symington was still feeling strangely exhilarated, despite the fact that he was about to lose the manuscript that had inspired him so much today; for finally, it was sealed up in an envelope, ready for the post.

What remained safe with Symington, however, was a careful copy of the manuscript; perhaps not quite as convincing as one of Wise's forgeries, but a very reasonable attempt, nonetheless, and made entirely his own. Symington was not quite certain what he would do with his version, but the mere fact of its existence was a comfort. It was good to create secrets again.

Newlay Grove,
Horsforth,
Leeds
Telephone: 2615 Horsforth

20th May 1959

Dear Miss du Maurier,

Thank you for the cheque to cover my expenses, and my apologies for the delay in replying to your letters, but I have been deep in research on your behalf. Despite my best efforts, it has not been easy. One runs up against so many annoying regulations at the Parsonage, and then at other libraries one discovers that certain books and manuscripts are missing, which is yet more evidence of the shoddiness of care and lack of proper guardianship.

Nevertheless, I have managed to unearth an interesting manuscript of Branwell's poetry, which I will be sending to you in due course. I am also making plans to visit the Brontë Parsonage over the Whitsun Bank Holiday weekend, when I should have the place to myself.

Now, I know I can rely on your discretion, but I must ask you to destroy this letter after you have read it, because I am going to give you the exact page references from the Shakespeare Head edition that relate to those suspicious signatures of Charlotte Brontë. I personally doubt the genuineness of the signatures that appear on the facsimile manuscripts in the following pages of volume 1 of the Shakespeare Head: 221, 298, 313, 327, 329, 331, 352,

376, 378, 405, 480. And in volume 2, you should
examine Charlotte's signatures on page 51, 54, 65, 69, 93
and 97.

   The subject of the forged signatures was not one that
Wise would discuss with me, and I never had the
opportunity to put the question to Mr Shorter before his
death. Make what you will of this mystery . . .

   I will report back with any further news after my trip to
Haworth next week,

   Yours sincerely,

J. Alex Symington.

CHAPTER TWENTY-ONE

Hampstead, 2 June

I'd given up all hope of seeing Rachel again – I guessed she was back in America – and then the phone rang this morning, quite early, though Paul had already gone, and I picked it up, and a woman's voice asked for him. I knew it was Rachel, before she'd said her name, before I'd even told her that Paul had left for the airport, on his way to an academic conference in Italy. And I did something entirely unexpected, I don't know why, I'd done it before I could stop myself. I said to Rachel that I was Paul's new wife, and that I'd met her a few months ago, in the Reading Room at the British Museum, but I'd been too shy and inept to tell her then. 'I'm so sorry,' I said. 'You must think I'm an idiot.'

'You're the young girl in the Reading Room?' she said, slowly. 'The one who's interested in Daphne du Maurier? I do remember you . . . How very odd . . .'

'I know, it must seem like a peculiar way to behave,' I said, 'inexcusable, really. But I was wondering if we might meet up, when you're in London next?'

'I'm back here already,' she said, 'though it's just for a couple of days, on my way to Yorkshire. That's why I was ringing Paul. I realised I'd left some of my books in the house, and I wanted to come and pick them up, today, if that was OK with him. There's one I need, in particular, for a talk I'm giving up there.'

'He's not back till next week,' I said, 'but you could get your books anyway – whenever you want. I'm here, I don't have any plans for the day.'

She arrived an hour or so afterwards – quickly enough for neither of us to change our minds. And it was extraordinary, of course, yet also surprisingly easy; she made it easy for me, even though it must have been strange for her, because as far as I know, nothing has changed in the house since she left it, nearly two years ago, apart from me moving in.

Anyway, she rang the doorbell, though it occurred to me that she might still have a key, and there was a brief moment of awkwardness in the hallway, when she waited for me to gesture where we should go – downstairs to the kitchen, or to the right, into the living room – and I didn't take her cue, it was as if I was waiting for her to take the lead. I saw her glance at herself in the mirror, and she put her hand up to her hair, very quickly, and swept it away from her face. 'Let me take your coat,' I said, and she took it off, an immaculate cream-coloured trench coat; and as I hung it on the hook in the hall cupboard, I couldn't suppress the thought that if I'd worn it, it would already be covered in streaks of dirt, and how did she keep it so perfectly unmarked? 'Would you like a cup of tea or coffee?' I said, and she said yes, tea would be lovely, so we went down to the kitchen, and I regained just enough composure to go first, though my hands were shaking as I filled the kettle with water, presumably a kettle that she'd already used, thousands of times before, and the cup, too, and we sat down at the table. It was still her kitchen, really, she seemed entirely at home, more at ease than I was; though she kept her eyes on me, rather than looking around the room.

'How's it going?' she said, and for a moment I thought she was asking about Paul, and felt too panic-stricken to say anything, but before I could blurt out an answer, she'd added, 'Have you found out anything new about Daphne du Maurier?'

So I told her about the Symington correspondence, and also about the suggestions contained within the letters that there were forged signatures on Branwell's manuscripts. 'It would be amazing if I could prove that were true,' I said, 'though it's odd that Daphne never went into this in her biography of Branwell, nor anything else she wrote about him, as far as I know. But Symington made it pretty clear to her that he believed Charlotte's signature had been forged on some of Branwell's Angrian manuscripts, though they're all juvenilia, essentially. What would be even more interesting, of course, would be to discover if some of the Brontë sisters' adult manuscripts were, in fact, by Branwell.'

Now, I'm wondering if that was a stupidly incautious thing to do, if I was giving too much away, but at the time, I just wanted Rachel to know everything, and she was so encouraging, such a sympathetic listener. 'What a marvellously intriguing story,' she said, at the end, and reached out to me across the table, touching my hand, very briefly, with hers.

As she did so, my eyes filled with tears, maybe because it was so long since anyone had reached out to me like that. On the rare occasions that Paul brushes against me, it's as if he's done so by accident and then he pulls away, I can feel him trying to maintain the distance between us.

'What's wrong?' said Rachel, taking my hand again, but I couldn't answer, I just shook my head. 'Look, I know this must feel very strange for you,' she said, 'but it's OK, I bear no grudge against you, truly. I was the one who left Paul, after all. You haven't wronged me in any way, you have nothing to feel guilty about.'

'It's not that,' I said, and then I felt a lump in my throat, and I had to choke back sobs; it was hideous, I didn't know where they were coming from, I didn't know how to hide them, but I couldn't break down entirely, not in front of Rachel, and so I struggled, and swallowed hard, and kept silent, apart from the occasional gulp.

Rachel looked at me, quizzically, and then stood up and came round to my side of the table. 'Come on, let's go and find these books,' she said, putting an arm around me, and I could feel the warmth of her skin, bare and tanned where it emerged from her white T-shirt. I wanted to rest my head against her shoulder, and just stay there for a little while, not saying anything, but I managed to pull myself together, and we went upstairs to the living room, which is lined with bookshelves; Rachel leading the way, me following behind her.

'There it is,' she said, pointing to one of the highest shelves to the right of the fireplace, and she went and got a wooden chair that unfolded into a step-ladder, opening it out in a way that I'd never done myself. As she climbed up the steps, I tried not to stare – not at her, though she was an imposing sight, towering above me on the ladder – but at the shelf, where she moved the front row of books aside to reveal another row, hidden behind them, that I'd not even known were there.

Rachel handed a book down to me. 'The Collected Poems of Emily Brontë, with all my scribbles inside.' I opened it, and the pages were covered with her handwritten notes, between the lines and up and down the margins.

'This reminds me of that scene in Wuthering Heights,' I said, 'when Lockwood finds Cathy's old book in the bedroom where he is supposed to be sleeping—'

'—and the book is filled with her scribbled notes,' said Rachel, finishing my sentence, which might have been irritating under other circumstances, but I was grateful to her, because she seemed to understand. 'And this somehow presages her appearance as a ghost later that night, as if the act of reading her handwriting is an unintentional way of summoning up her spirit. I wonder, does that mean that I am a ghost in this house?'

I didn't answer her, and then she said, 'Of course, some people insist it's not Cathy's ghost, in any real sense, it's Lockwood's dream, and her summoning up is a psychological one, rather than anything supernatural.' I knew when she said this that she was talking about Paul, for this was an argument that I'd already had with him, because it enraged me when he dismissed the supernatural in Wuthering Heights as being 'nothing but your own projections.' (His words, not mine.)

'Was there anything else you needed?' I said, giving the book back to Rachel, even though I was longing to study her annotations, particularly those around Brontë's 'Self-Interrogation', which was the most well-thumbed page.

'Well, that's the book I needed most urgently,' she said, 'but there are a few others here of mine. Would you mind if I had a look for them?' I could tell, without her being any more explicit, that she wanted me to leave the room, so I did; it would have seemed rude to have remained there, hovering, as if I didn't trust her. Why trust her? I know that's the obvious question, but I wanted to believe in her, I felt as if I needed to, that it was terribly important to do so, almost as if in trusting her, I might find a compass for the future; something I am badly in need of . . .

I went back downstairs to the kitchen, and left her to it, and after about twenty minutes, she joined me again, balancing a small pile of books in her hands. 'All my missing Brontë books,' she said, with a smile. 'Not really Paul's taste, either, so I'm sure he won't mind me reclaiming them.'

'Where are you going to do your talk?' I said, feeling uncomfortable at the mention of Paul's name, even though it was always going to be there, hanging in the air between us. 'I'd love to hear it . . .'

'Haworth,' said Rachel. 'The Brontë Society has asked me there, as part of its annual get-together at the Parsonage. I'm talking about the literary influence of Emily Brontë on subsequent female poets – Emily Dickinson, Sylvia Plath, and so on. You could come, if you'd like . . . I mean, if it would be helpful to go there, anyway, as part of your research. You could spend a bit more time in the library, or whatever? I'm driving up first thing tomorrow morning – I could give you a lift, if you wanted, if you don't mind leaving early.'

'Yes,' I said, without pausing to think, and she smiled, and said, 'Good, that's settled.'

It's unbelievable, I know, but there you are. Here I am, setting my alarm for 5 a.m. tomorrow morning, because Rachel said she'd be here just before six. I still haven't told Paul; his mobile is switched off, which is a relief, because I don't have to feel guilty about not telling him, though now I've decided to stop worrying about what he might think if he knew where I was going. Because he doesn't need to know, and he isn't here, anyway, and who knows what he is doing in Italy; all I know is that I don't know, that's all that's certain; and that will have to be enough.

CHAPTER TWENTY-TWO

Menabilly, June 1959

Daphne threw down her copy of the *Times Literary Supplement* with such force that it skated off the polished table and on to the floor. 'Well, that's it,' she said, though there was no one in the dining room to hear her. 'I'm done for now.'

The headline that had caused her such distress still glared up at her from the floor. GERIN GOES HEAD TO HEAD WITH DU MAURIER. She was almost as shocked as when she discovered Tommy's affair with the Snow Queen; an affair which she guessed was still continuing, though only in intermittent dribs and drabs, for Tommy seemed too faded, too depressed, to be burning with desire for anyone. And anyway, the affair would doubtless come to an end soon, for Tommy was retiring from Buckingham Palace at last, and returning to Menabilly next month, where he would reside full-time, a prospect which was causing Daphne some apprehension. But worse than that – worse than anything else on the horizon – was this discovery that she had been ambushed by another rival, Winifred Gerin, who according to the *TLS* was engaged upon a new biography of Branwell, which would follow her recently published, critically acclaimed volume on Anne Brontë.

Daphne scanned the piece with the same breathless yet sinking feeling with which she'd read bad reviews in the past, and the sensation was one of a self-inflicted wound, or a humiliation that she must accept as being deserved, which was curious, given that it was entirely out of her control. She had already read Gerin's book about Anne Brontë, and the glowing reviews it had received in the last month; all of the praise twisting like barbs in Daphne's side, for it seemed to her to simply highlight how snide the critics had been about her own writing. 'You never remember the good things,' Tommy said to her, whenever she complained about unkind reviews, 'only the bad. Why can't you concentrate on what people admire in you, instead of picking over unpleasantness?'

And yet despite the part of her that shrivelled up inside upon hearing the news of Gerin's book about Branwell, Daphne was also aware of another, stronger instinct, which was to make contact with her rival — to reach out to her, just as she had done with the Snow Queen. Indeed, she intended to send Miss Gerin a letter; a conciliatory one, wishing her every success, and saying that she was far better placed in every way than Daphne to do a thorough biography of Branwell. For there was no hiding the fact that Daphne had planned her own book, the *TLS* article had already made this abundantly obvious, and the competition between the two of them. But when Daphne sat down to write her letter to Miss Gerin, she tried to sidestep this, brushing aside her own work as 'some sort of study or portrait that need not affect yours'.

What, exactly, her portrait should consist of, remained unclear to Daphne. She knew that she must act quickly – Victor Gollancz had told her that if Miss Gerin's biography came out first, then Daphne's book would be killed. 'Killed': he actually used that word to Daphne, when she telephoned him this morning to discuss the matter, and her throat constricted in panic, but then a surge of adrenalin came racing through her bloodstream, readying her for the fight.

Daphne knew, too, that she must keep Mr Symington on her side; that she must not nag him about why he had not yet accounted for the £100 cheque she'd sent him for expenses, or complain about the interminable delays in posting her the research material and manuscripts that he had already prom- ised her. His latest excuse was that his presence was needed at home, because of his wife's arthritis. But at least he had, finally, spent some time at the Parsonage, much to her relief, over the Whitsun Bank Holiday weekend when it was closed to visitors; apparently having followed up on Daphne's exasperated in- struction to give a generous tip to the museum caretaker, a Mr Mitchell, rather than go through the official channels of the Brontë Society. After this visit, he promised her various copies of Branwell's unpublished manuscripts – he'd borrowed them from the museum, he said, for the time being, and sent them off to a local printers to be copied as facsimiles. But despite the tantalising prospect of these manuscripts, she was still no closer to coming up with the dramatic literary discovery that she needed to give her the edge over Miss Gerin.

It had been an exceptionally dry and sunny summer so far, the kind of blessed weather that Daphne would usually be basking in, swimming in a sea the colour of turquoise, in between the dark rocks or out to the reef, and sunbathing during the long June afternoons, in a private corner of Polridmouth beach, the sand warm against her back, and then walking back to Menabilly, to lie on the newly mown lawn beneath a chestnut tree. But instead, she stayed indoors, shut away in her writing hut for hours at a time, oblivious to the hum of the bumblebees, reading through her notes from the British Museum, puzzling over Branwell. All that she had read so far of his writing suggested that he was not as talented as his sisters, yet she wanted to go on believing in him, for so many of his manuscripts remained lost or missing or indecipherable.

She reminded herself, as she worked, that if his sisters had been judged only on their Gondal and Angrian chronicles, they, too, would have been considered as irrelevant as Branwell; and she still went on hoping for some revelatory Branwell work to appear, a story as astonishing as *Wuthering Heights* or *Jane Eyre*. There was that tantalising reference in one of Branwell's letters to his 'novel in three volumes', which made it all the more frustrating that she had so far failed to decipher several of his manuscripts at the British Museum, and was therefore unable to judge if they formed part – possibly a brilliant part – of his unpublished novel.

But as for the question of the forged signatures on Branwell's manuscripts: she was becoming less hopeful of proving anything there. Yes, Symington had eventually given her specific references of pages that he believed to contain forgeries of Charlotte's signature, all of them reprinted as facsimile manuscripts in his Shakespeare Head edition; but as

Daphne worked her way through these – and she had spent many long days on this Herculean task, using a magnifying glass, studying the illegible pages until she felt the words would blind her – they all turned out to be Angrian juvenilia, childish and rambling and no proof of genius. It was all very well Symington being secretive, demanding that she destroy his letter to her that contained the numbered page references – which she had already done, burning it after marking the pages carefully on her edition of the Shakespeare Head – but in the end, he had provided no real evidence about Branwell's talents as a writer. She was almost certain that these pages were collaborative efforts, anyway, between Branwell and Charlotte, each of them adding to the labyrinthine stories in their microscopic handwriting; a private and secretive endeavour, too coded for the outside world to unravel. What did it matter if T. J. Wise had scribbled Charlotte's signature on to these pages – for Charlotte surely had a hand in many of them, if not quite all, as she and Branwell expanded on their endless, incomprehensible chronicles of Angria?

Meanwhile, Daphne had also paid for several diligent researchers at the British Museum to transcribe two of Branwell's Angrian stories held there in the collection that T. J. Wise had left in a bequest after his death. They were still labouring over the utterly illegible 'A New Year's Story', but were closer to delivering a transcript of the oddly titled 'The Wool is Rising', a hand-sewn pamphlet dated 26 June 1834. This, Daphne noted with some excitement, was Branwell's seventeenth birthday, and she couldn't help but imagine him as a confident, ambitious lad, knowing nothing of the future failures that would blight him. Unlike the elusive Mr Symington, these researchers – Mrs D'Arcy Hart, Mrs St George Saunders, and Miss O'Farrell – provided detailed accounts of their modest expenses (bus fares and the occasional cup of tea), and also of their lengthy endeavours, in regular and conscientious reports that they posted to Menabilly.

The most intriguing of their reports, so far, concerned a passage from 'The Wool is Rising', which appeared to be a brief sketch of a 'colour grinder . . . a fellow of singular aspect'. Miss O'Farrell had thought it interesting enough to send it in advance of the rest of the transcript, and having read it, Daphne felt certain that it might constitute a more realistic self-portrait of Branwell than his romanticised alter ego, Northangerland. 'He was a lad of perhaps seventeen years old,' Branwell had written, 'and his meagre freckled visage and large Roman nose, thatched by a thick mat of red hair, constantly changed and twisted themselves into an endless variety of restive movements. As he spoke, instead of looking his auditor straight in the face he turned his eyes – which were further beautified by a pair of spectacles – away from him, and while one word issued stammering from his mouth it was straight way contradicted or confused by a chaos of strange succeeding jargon.'

'Bravo!' Daphne had written by return of post to Miss O'Farrell, and went on in her letter to express some regret that she was not working alongside these three industrious ladies. 'Unfortunately, my husband needs me at home with him in Cornwall, which keeps me away from the delights of the Reading Room,' she concluded, and then felt guilty about not telling the truth. But she had vowed not to return to the

British Museum, in case it might precipitate another crisis of her own. For she still shuddered at the memory of her encounter there with the Snow Queen, and the subsequent episodes, which she now labelled simply as a prolonged attack of 'the horrors', borrowing her father's phrase for what might, perhaps, be a family affliction; certainly, her cousin Peter had spoken to her, in the most guarded terms, of suffering in a similar way. 'I fear we carry the seeds of madness within us,' he had said to her last month, towards the end of a lunch at the Café Royal, when they had talked about Gerald's bouts of black despair, that were kept hidden from everyone but his family, covered up by stage make-up or stagecraft; the latter as effective a disguise outside the theatre as within it. 'It's what did for poor Michael,' said Peter, 'and you and I must bear the burden of that inheritance, too . . .'

Daphne was aware that Peter was struggling with his own book – an edited edition of an enormous trove of family letters and history. 'The family morgue,' he called it, bitterly, and she found her mind drifting towards her cousin, as the hours passed by in the writing hut, wondering how he was getting on. But Daphne tried to concentrate only on Branwell, who had suffered himself, after all, dogged by misery and brought down further by drink, like Gerald; no, stop now, stop thinking about Gerald, this was not about him . . .

She knew from previous experience that her own horrors must be kept well away from here; held at bay with hard work and strict routine. Sometimes, she thought of telephoning Peter – of asking his advice, of confiding more in him, about Tommy, about the Snow Queen, about everything. But Peter had his own problems; he was constantly worried about money, she knew, though it was an uncomfortable topic of conversation between them, given her own wealth. And she wondered if the real root of his melancholy had less to do with his present circumstances than those of the past, that must have been coming close again as he delved further into the family morgue.

But if Daphne was honest with herself – and she was trying very hard to be, to see more clearly than she might once have done – then the real truth of her recent avoidance of Peter was that his offices were in Great Russell Street, across the road from the British Museum, and the very knowledge of his proximity to the scene of her disgrace (yes, disgrace, there was no other word for it) made her feel increasingly uncomfortable; indeed, it was so troubling that she was struggling to keep it out of her head. And still, she kept returning to it. Might Peter have seen her, meeting the Snow Queen in the forecourt of the British Museum, a little less than two years ago? And did he also see her, running from the scene, pursued by a man in a trilby hat? And if he had been witness to these events, what would he make of them?

The more that Daphne tried not to think about this, the more persistent the thought became, until at last, she buried her face in her hands, closing her eyes to everything, which only made matters worse, for then she could see the scene more vividly, played out on an endless loop in her head. 'There's nothing for it,' she said out loud, 'I'll have to speak to Peter.' And she made her way back to the house, hoping that it would be empty, so that there was no possibility of anyone overhearing her phone call.

Once inside, Daphne went to the long wood-panelled passageway where the telephone squatted on a small table, surrounded by forlorn raincoats hanging on rusty hooks, forgotten boots and a child's bicycle. There was a small mirror hanging above the telephone, but she turned her head away from it, and looked up Peter's telephone number in her address book. 'Museum 3946,' she said, under her breath, forcing herself not to read anything sinister into the random configuration of numbers. She dialled the number, half-hoping that there would be no answer, but a secretary answered, and then Peter was on the line.

'Daphne,' he said, 'how splendid to hear from you.' But he was surprised, she could hear it in his voice; for this was not her usual time to speak to him, it was a break from routine, an unswerving timetable that incorporated telephone calls to family and friends on specific evenings, and never during office hours on a weekday, unless in times of crisis.

'I'm sorry to disturb you at work,' she said, 'but I'm feeling rather doom-laden. I've discovered I'm up against another woman – it turns out I have a rival . . .' Daphne paused, remembering the feeling she had in London last month, at Sloane Square tube station, on her way from the flat, when she'd been standing close to the edge of the platform, and had suddenly thought how easy it would be to jump in front of the next train; how easy it would be not to be; just one last step, and then she could stop trying, stop everything . . . But now, as then, she pulled back from the brink; for she could not imagine how to find the words to tell Peter about her encounter with the Snow Queen, however close it had been to him. 'Have you heard of Winifred Gerin?' she continued.

'Well, it's most unfortunate, but she's my rival for Branwell's affections.'

'I did happen to notice that piece in the *TLS*,' said Peter. 'But try not to worry, your biography will be far better than Miss Gerin's, and anyway, I'm sure there's room for more than one book about Branwell Brontë, given that everyone has ignored him until now.'

'That's not what Victor says,' replied Daphne. 'He informed me, rather unhelpfully, that my efforts to revive Branwell would come to nothing if Miss Gerin gets there first. Poor Branwell, on the verge of being brought back to life, and then killed again . . .'

'Take no notice of Victor,' said Peter. 'And if he doesn't want the book, I do. You know I'd be delighted to publish it.'

'Oh, that would cause a terrible fuss,' said Daphne. 'Victor's terribly possessive – or at least he would be if he discovered that another man was interested in me. I shall just have to get a move on with the writing, and beat my rival to it.'

'That's the spirit,' said Peter. 'Just think of Uncle Jim, turning out his plays, churning out the novels, writing like there was no tomorrow . . .'

They said their goodbyes, and made a date for another lunch in London in September, and a tentative arrangement for Peter to visit Menabilly before the summer was over. Then Daphne returned to the writing hut, determined to be determined. But somehow, Peter's final phrase had lodged itself in her head. What might it mean, wondered Daphne, to write like there was no tomorrow? And where could the lack of a future lead her? Might it be a better place than here?

Menabilly,
Par,
Cornwall

27th June 1959

Dear Mr Symington,

Much gloom down here in Cornwall, despite the sunny weather, after reading the news in the latest edition of the TLS, which doubtless has already come to your attention, though I enclose a copy for you here, just in case you hadn't seen it.

I have written to Miss Gerin, saying that I am sure there is room for both of us in Branwell's life. But to be frank, I am feeling despondent about her forthcoming biography. Her latest book has been very well reviewed across all the papers – a whole page in the Illustrated London News! – and it has been hailed as the definitive life of Anne Brontë. It has received much more notice than the other rival biography of Anne, which was published a month before Miss Gerin's and subsequently sunk without trace. Certainly, Miss Gerin has had a *succès d'estime*, though I would think her book will also sell well.

What is giving me further cause for concern is that I am sure Miss Gerin will get every sort of backing from the Brontë Society, as well as the London critics. She has placed herself on the map as a biographer, and any forthcoming book of hers will be met with interest and sympathy. We have to remember that although my novels are what is known as popular, I am <u>not</u> a critic's favourite. Indeed, I am generally dismissed with a sneer as a best-seller, and either reviewed badly, or not at all. So should our two biographies of Branwell be published at the same time, and appear to rival each other, I would come off second best, I have no illusions about that!

Added to my problems is the fact that Miss Gerin lives in Yorkshire – in Haworth, no less – so she will go over the local ground very thoroughly; indeed, has probably already done so while researching her Anne biography.

What I do have on my side, however, is your expertise, and, hopefully, some original manuscripts not available to Miss Gerin. I am much encouraged to hear that you were able to pay a discreet visit to the Brontë Parsonage Museum over the Bank Holiday weekend, and I trust that you took my advice and tipped the museum caretaker, Mr Mitchell? I am also delighted that you were able to borrow various of Branwell's manuscripts from the Parsonage, and send them off to the printers in Leeds to be copied as facsimiles. Do you know when you might be able to get these to me? As you can imagine, I am awaiting their arrival with more than a little anxiety.

You will understand, I am sure, that now that we are up against a rival, there is no time to lose. I expect Miss G is whizzing around Haworth in a car, making all sorts of enquiries, while I am stuck here at my desk in Menabilly. Still, at least Mr Mitchell appears to be prepared to help us, and it looks as if you will have to turn detective if we are to gather more material and information. By the way, if you have a moment, would you ask Mr Mitchell to let you see the Reverend Brontë's medical textbook, which as far as I know is still kept in the Parsonage? The last time I went to

Haworth, several years ago, I was able to look at it, and the Reverend Brontë had scribbled all sorts of notes on certain of the pages – it is a medical dictionary, and his handwritten notes, as far as I can recall, appeared alongside the entries for nightmares, delirium tremens, and epilepsy. If my memory is correct, then his annotations may turn out to be rather significant. It might also prove my theory that Branwell suffered from the minor form of epilepsy known as petit mal, which could account for why his father did not send him away to school.

So sorry to hear about your wife's arthritis! It is a wretched thing. Perhaps you and your wife are like myself and my husband, in that when one of us is up, the other is down. At the moment I am in good health, but my husband is less robust. However, these things will pass, and I hope to be able to come to Yorkshire before the summer is over.

No more for now. Good hunting!

Yours sincerely,

Daphne du Maurier

CHAPTER TWENTY-THREE

Newlay Grove, July 1959

Symington was overwhelmed this morning; astonished and as close to jubilance as he could remember, having read his name in print in the *Times Literary Supplement* for the first time in a quarter of a century. 'Listen to this, my dear,' he said to Beatrice, waving his copy at her like a victory flag. 'A letter from Daphne du Maurier to the *TLS*, about her Branwell research, with a very kind reference to myself. She says, "I realise that living at Haworth as she does, Miss Gerin is happier placed than I am"—'

'Who is Miss Gerin?' Beatrice said, interrupting him, as she cleared the breakfast crockery from the dining room table.

'Miss Gerin,' he said, still too exhilarated to be irritable, 'you know, that woman in Haworth who is writing biographies of all the Brontës, and it's Branwell's turn now, poor devil, she's got her sights on him. So Daphne and I are up against her in a race to be out first. Hence this letter: "I realise that living at Haworth as she does, Miss Gerin is happier placed than I am, and with one Branwell biography 'under her belt', as the saying goes, it would be foolish of me to attempt to cover identical ground. I am, however, the lucky possessor of the Brontë library of Mr J. Alex Symington, editor and compiler, with the late T. J. Wise, of the incomparable Shakespeare Head edition of the Brontë Works, Lives and Letters, and long correspondence with Mr Symington over the past years has confirmed my opinion that Branwell Brontë and his work – most of it untranscribed – have been too long neglected. I believe that both Miss Gerin and myself can help to remedy this fact, and if we approach our subject in different ways, with possibly our views of Branwell as a boy and young man widely opposed, surely the reading public may be interested enough to buy both our books when they eventually appear? I am sure neither Miss Gerin nor myself is aware of any sense of rivalry; rather we see ourselves as students engaged in the same passionate research." Well, what do you make of that, Beatrice? You are in the presence of an incomparable editor, the catalyst for passionate re-search!'

'Very nice, dear,' Beatrice said, 'but don't overexcite your-self. You don't want another fall, and you're not to start moving those old boxes again.' Then she was gone again, to one of her interminable meetings of the Women's Institute, and as the day wore on, Symington was beginning to feel crestfallen, even cheated. The *Times Literary Supplement* had printed Daphne's letter beneath a headline: LITERARY REDUN-DANCY, and Symington was assailed by a sudden suspicion that this might be a veiled message to himself. For perhaps he had, in a sense, been made redundant by Miss du Maurier and Miss Gerin, who would both be publishing their biographies on

Branwell, while he would not, for he had been reduced to a lowly assistant to Daphne, no more than that, when all was said and done. And the longer that Symington thought about this, the more it struck him as being monstrously unfair. Soon, a black mood had descended upon him, clouding everything, overshadowing his earlier jubilance, and he found himself picking over the memory of his enforced redundancies from the Brontë Parsonage Museum and Leeds University, of the many humiliations heaped upon him, and the disappointments that ensued.

At last, after several hours of wretchedness, Symington decided to write a letter to Miss du Maurier, who had been pestering him for the copies of Branwell's manuscripts that he borrowed from the Brontë Parsonage six or seven weeks ago. No one else knew that he had taken these – not even Mr Mitchell, the museum custodian who had given him access to the library when it was closed to the public on a Sunday, and left him to his own devices. Mitchell wasn't a bad sort; he'd been there since the museum opened in 1928, and respected the fact that Symington was a Freemason, like himself; like Lord Brotherton, and Branwell, come to that. Not that Symington ever got out to lodge meetings these days, but the connections came in useful, nevertheless, at least where Mitchell was concerned. 'Best to stick together, old chap,' he'd said to Mitchell, as he gave the masonic handshake upon arriving at the Parsonage.

As for the matter of the facsimile copies of Branwell's manuscripts: well, he muttered to himself, let Daphne wait a little longer. He would tell her that a printers' strike was causing lengthy delays in the copying process; after all, patience was a virtue (a lesson worth learning for a rich and famous lady novelist). He paused, and then was seized by a stream of ideas that he must set down in a letter to Daphne.

Dear Miss du Maurier,

   Thank you for your kindness in mentioning me in your letter to the Times Literary Supplement, which I read today with great interest. It has set me thinking, because after all, 'Literary Redundancy' is not new. It started with the early scholars of the Greek and Latin Classics, followed from the Continental Universities to Oxford and Cambridge. Then the writers of the Bible, Shakespeare, the early English dramatists, and with the rise of other universities, the concentrated work on English writers followed, until the end of the last century with the Victorians and Pre-Raphaelites, the increase of students and work for them to do – the Brownings, Rossetti, Swinburne, and many other individual writers including the Brontës have been a constant source of redundancy.

He put his pen down, for his head was throbbing, and he was feeling increasingly confused; unsure of what it was he was trying to explain in his letter to Daphne. 'Concentrate, Symington,' he said to himself, but concentration had been difficult, ever since he had slipped on a garden path, three weeks ago, in the twilight, whilst trying to carry a carton of Branwell's manuscripts from the house to his wooden shed beyond the overgrown orchard. Where, exactly, was that box, he wondered now? It contained the borrowed manuscripts from the Parsonage; he had an idea they would be safer in the shed that night, though once in the garden, he had felt uncertain; had stopped, put the carton down again, then tried to lift it, and lost his grip.

He picked up his pen again, and continued with the letter to Daphne.

You will be wondering, Why no news from me during the past two or three weeks? The printers' strike still holds up the replicas of Branwell's manuscripts, whilst my own activities were cut short about three weeks ago. My wife had gone to a meeting of the Old People's Welfare Committee. I sauntered off into the garden, and trying to stoop and pick up a carton on the garden path, fell full-length, receiving a nasty cut over the right eye. Lying there two and a half hours until I was found unconscious at 10.30 p.m. However, I seem to have rallied to action and will be 'on the job' during the next few days!

There had been some embarrassment after the fall, the details of which did not need to be disclosed to Daphne. Beatrice had accused him of falling down dead-drunk, having found an empty whisky bottle in his study, and claimed she could smell the alcohol fumes on his breath. 'You weren't knocked unconscious,' she'd hissed at him, 'you'd drunk yourself into a stupor that evening, while I was out.'

The throbbing in his head was getting worse now, and he longed for a small sip of whisky to dull the pain; but there was none to be had, for Beatrice watched him too carefully while she was in the house, and even when she was out, Symington had no money to go and buy new supplies of drink.

Which reminded him of his predicament. He would have to sell something – not everything – to Daphne. And this thought, at least, cheered him a little; for despite her claims in the *Times Literary Supplement* that she was possessed of his library, he knew better. She had a fraction, just a fraction of it; she pored over the detritus, while he retained the jewels. So who was the literary redundancy, now? 'Not me,' murmured Symington, closing his eyes, for the room was spinning, 'not me . . .'

CHAPTER TWENTY-FOUR

Hampstead, June

Rachel arrived very early this morning, as we'd arranged, and I was already waiting in the hallway, ready to run down the steps from the front door, hoping that the neighbours would still be sleeping. And perhaps she guessed what I was thinking as I slipped into the passenger seat, for she said, 'Don't worry, no one will be witness to our dawn eloping,' and though she laughed as she spoke, I could not stop myself blushing, silently cursing my gauche embarrassment, and my hopeless naïveté, for I had no witty rejoinder or clever repartee.

She was wearing a scarlet silk wrap dress, with smooth bare legs and high-heeled strappy leather sandals that showed off her beautifully painted red toenails. All of which might sound absurd for a trip to Yorkshire, but she looked entirely at ease; somehow more *herself* than anyone else I'd ever met. Sitting beside her, in my faded jeans and navy T-shirt and plimsolls, I felt like a badly dressed schoolgirl, with nothing interesting to say for myself, and I wondered if she was regretting bringing me along for the ride. But she must have taken pity on me, as she drove us out of London in her hired car, very fast, while the sun rose higher in the sky, because she made no more jokes, and took care not to mention Paul. Instead, she asked me to tell her everything I knew about Mr Symington, so I did, glad to be able to unravel the story that had been getting tangled in my head.

'One of the many odd things about Mr Symington,' she said, eventually, as we were getting closer to Haworth, 'is that his papers – everything relating to him, really – are kept in a file closed to researchers at the Brontë Parsonage. I've asked to see them, several times, but always been refused. So it seems even more extraordinary that you, of all people, should have stumbled across his legal correspondence with the Brontë Society. I'd love to take a look at those letters, if you wouldn't mind?' She glanced sideways at me as she spoke, catching my eyes, just for a second, no more than a heartbeat, and then I turned away, feeling as if I had been somehow caught out.

'Well, they're back in London,' I'd said. 'I didn't bring the file here with me . . .'

'Oh, never mind,' she said, lightly. 'I'll just have to go back to Plan A. Breaking and entering into the Parsonage library to get at the Symington papers!' Rachel laughed, and I laughed, too, glad that the moment of tension between us had been broken.

It wasn't until I listened to her deliver her lecture – which took place not in the Brontë Parsonage, but just around the corner, in the local Baptist chapel – that I realised she might not have been joking. Of course, I could have been making too many assumptions about the subtext of her speech – she wasn't explicit about her interest in Mr Symington; indeed, she only mentioned him once. But she did talk about a missing notebook of Emily Brontë's poems – known as the Honresfeld manuscript, Rachel explained, because it was last located in the collection of Sir Alfred Law, a Conservative MP who lived in a Lancashire mansion named Honresfeld. 'Emily's notebook contained thirty-one poems, handwritten over twenty-nine pages, including fifteen of the twenty-one poems she published in her lifetime,' said Rachel to an attentive audience, 'and one of these is "Self-Interrogation", which has been a particular source of inspiration to my own work as a poet.' She paused, smoothing her dress down over her legs, just for a second or two. 'A reproduction in facsimile of this poem, and the rest of the Honresfeld manuscript, was included by a former curator of the Brontë Parsonage Museum, a Mr J. A. Symington, in his Shakespeare Head edition of the poems of the Brontë sisters, published in 1934. After this date, there is no record of the fate of Emily Brontë's notebook. I imagine that I am not the only person in this room who would dearly love to discover what became of what I believe to be the most precious of the missing Brontë manuscripts . . .'

As she spoke, I felt her words were addressed to me, but I kept my eyes down, though there was a bubbling excitement inside me. Part of me wanted to get on the train to London, and get back to my desk as fast as possible, to check those solicitors' letters from the Brontë Society to Mr Symington, and see if they contained any references to the Honresfeld manuscript. But I also knew that this was extremely unlikely, given that Emily's notebook was not part of the Brontë Parsonage collection, but that of Sir Alfred Law. It was not impossible, however, that the local archive of Symington's papers in Leeds might contain some important clue that I'd missed when I went there earlier this year – after all, I'd gone through it so quickly, searching only for papers relating to Branwell and Daphne du Maurier. But I also began to realise that Rachel might be on to something, if she could somehow gain access to the material relating to Symington in the Brontë Parsonage. And if she was going to do that, then I wanted to be in on it, too.

After her talk, Rachel was surrounded by a gaggle of admirers, asking her to sign their books of poetry, so I hovered to one side, watching her writing her name in bold black ink, over and over again, until at last she'd finished. 'Well,' she said to me, raising one of her elegantly shaped eyebrows, 'are you up for a bit of research in the Parsonage library? The librarian is going to be out for a little while, but I've promised we won't touch anything while he's not there . . .'

I couldn't believe that we were actually going to be allowed into the library without supervision – I'm sure it's strictly against the rules – but Rachel had managed to talk her way in, which isn't surprising, because she's got this quietly seductive charm that gets under your skin, and she's beautiful, too, in a way that makes people want her to like them, as if her approval would validate them. 'I'm here for such a short time,' she said to the librarian, as he unlocked the door for us, 'and obviously, I'll follow strict academic protocol at all times, as will my research assistant.'

'Since when was I your research assistant?' I said to Rachel, after the librarian had gone, having first locked us in, with an apologetic explanation that he was obliged to make sure no one else could gain access to the library.

'Do you want to be here or don't you?' she said, and I just nodded, and although it might sound as if we were being short with each other, it wasn't like that at the time; it felt like we were comrades, which was the most exhilarating of sensations.

I'm not sure how she knew where to start looking – I guess she'd done some discreet research, on previous trips to the library, when she was editing a new edition of Emily Brontë's poems for an academic press – but she headed straight for a large filing cabinet, in the furthest corner of the room. 'I reckon we've got half an hour before the librarian comes back,' she said, pulling out a bulging foolscap file from the bottom drawer, 'so let's divide this between us, and start reading.'

'And what if he does come back before then?' I said.

'Don't fret, child,' she said, and put a sheaf of papers in my hands. We sat down on either side of a large mahogany table – as Victorian as everything else in the room, which is in a late nineteenth-century addition to the original Parsonage building – and started reading and making notes. 'We could really do with a photocopier in here,' said Rachel, as she scribbled furiously, but I didn't answer, I was too busy writing out extracts from Symington's letters, dating from the period when he was still curator and librarian at the Parsonage. The papers were scrambled – they weren't filed chronologically, or indexed; in fact, they looked as if they'd been put there decades ago, and then left untouched, if not forgotten – so it was hard to make sense of them, given that we were working separately, having divided them randomly between us. But what did become clear, slowly, was that Symington had spent several years asking for access to Sir Alfred Law's collection at Honresfeld, and was finally granted permission, just a few months before his dismissal from the Brontë Parsonage. By the time he was preparing his Shakespeare Head edition, he had borrowed many of the manuscripts from the Law collection, including the notebook of Emily's poems, which he arranged to have copied as a facsimile reproduction.

I read my way through several letters he wrote to his publishers, concerning the volume of Emily's poems – which was a supplement to the original scheme for the Shakespeare Head edition, and contained the facsimile of her notebook – and then another letter, soon afterwards, referring to the death of Sir Alfred Law. So it seemed to me to be perfectly possible that Symington could have borrowed the notebook of Emily's poems, and seized the opportunity offered by Sir Alfred's death to keep hold of it, rather than returning the Honresfeld manuscript to the estate. 'You know, I really think that Symington was the last known person to have the Honresfeld notebook,' I said to Rachel. 'We're getting closer and closer here—'

It was then that we heard footsteps outside the door, and while I looked up, panic-stricken, as the key rattled in the lock, Rachel swept all the papers off the table into her capacious leather handbag. By the time the librarian was in the room, she was calmly flicking through a copy of the Brontë Society Journals, with the sort of cool you'd expect to see in a film about spies, though not in a respectable academic.

'How are you getting on?' said the librarian.

'Slowly,' said Rachel, with another of her most charming smiles, and as she turned towards him she revealed a crescent of golden-skinned cleavage, 'but I have come across this very useful article in volume 23 of the Brontë Society Journal, in which Daphne du Maurier wrote an epilogue, or what she termed, "Second Thoughts", to her previously published book on Branwell Brontë.'

'I didn't know you were interested in Branwell?' said the librarian.

'Not especially, but my assistant is. Might she take a copy of this?' He nodded, and she passed it over to me. 'I've marked the most relevant passage,' she said, and I started reading it aloud, partly as a way of covering my embarrassment; though once I'd started, I felt rather stupid. 'Both Charlotte and Branwell's appetite for reading was prodigious,' Daphne had written, in an essay I'd never even heard of until now, 'and that Branwell suffered from a surfeit of ill-digested matter is proven from his long manuscript "The Wool is Rising". I had the whole of this manuscript transcribed – the transcription is now in the Parsonage Museum – and I defy any student to read through these interminable unpunctuated pages without suspecting that the young author's verbosity was somehow compulsive; words poured from him without pause and often without meaning, just as they do at times from the insane.'

My voice trailed away, and the librarian rather kindly suggested that I go with him to use the photocopier, so that he could explain to me how to use it. 'It's rather idiosyncratic, you see,' he said, and as I followed him out of the room, I wondered what, exactly, Rachel might do while we were gone.

And that's what I'm thinking about now, at four o'clock in the morning, turning everything over and over in my mind, getting more confused, not less. I didn't get a chance to spend any time alone with Rachel afterwards; first we were with the librarian, and then the curator came to say hello to her, and then she was taken off to have tea with various dignitaries from the Brontë Society. She was staying the night in Haworth in a little bed and breakfast, within sight of the Parsonage, but nowhere had been booked for me, of course, given that I was just an afterthought, so I said it was no trouble, I'd catch the train back to London.

Which leaves me here, alone in Rachel's old bed, while she is there, with her cache of Symington's letters. She hasn't rung, and I can't get in touch with her, because I don't have her mobile number, nor do I even know the name of the place where she's staying; not that I could ring there at 4 a.m., anyway. And everything seems completely mystifying, most of all, Rachel's motives. Why did she include me in her raid on the library, given that she could have done the whole thing herself? What was the point of sharing that secret with me? Yes, I know she wants to see my cache of Symington's letters, but even so, they're not necessarily vital in her hunt for Emily's notebook, especially now that she's got all the Symington papers from the Parsonage.

No, there's something else going on; almost as if she needs me to be complicit with her. Or is that reading too much into it? And how does one read too much into a situation like this? Isn't it all in the reading?

CHAPTER TWENTY-FIVE

Menabilly, July 1959

'Have you any idea how much blood there is, when a person is shot?' said Tommy. 'It spills everywhere – it takes for ever to clean up.'

He was standing by the fireplace in the Long Room, holding his revolver, and then he lifted the gun, and pressed its muzzle against his head. 'I might as well kill myself,' he said to her. 'I can't go on like this any longer.'

Daphne was unable to move, to speak, but Tommy seemed frozen, too, his finger to the trigger, yet motionless, and his voice was flat, his face hard, and then suddenly, his eyes filled with tears, and he was crying, sobbing, his hands shaking, like his shoulders. And Daphne had gone to him, taken the gun from him, as easily as a rattle from a baby; then she walked out of the room, very quickly, locking the door behind her, and phoned the doctor in Fowey, who drove straight to Menabilly.

'It's a cry for help,' the doctor said to her, after he'd spent a little time with Tommy, 'not a serious suicide attempt, he was probably too drunk to know what he was doing.' But Daphne wasn't certain what her husband had intended to do; though it occurred to her that he could have shot her as easily as himself, he was a soldier, unafraid to use a weapon, and yet he looked so desperate, so uncertain.

'It's *Rebecca*, all over again,' she said to Tod, after the doctor had finally left, just before midnight, and Tommy was sedated and sleeping in his bedroom. Tod shushed at her, told her not to be so silly; not that Tod had ever liked Tommy, but she tried to reassure Daphne, like the doctor had done, and sent her to bed at last with a cup of hot milk, as if she were a child again, home at Cannon Hall.

Daphne woke early the next morning, having dreamt of her father. 'It's not fair!' he'd said, tears in his eyes, sitting on the bed beside her, large as life and resurrected, younger than Daphne now. 'It's not fair that you're marrying Tommy. What's to become of me?' Gerald's voice seemed too real to be a dream; and his words were those that he'd used, in reality, twenty-seven years ago, when Daphne had confirmed to him what she'd already written in the letter to her mother, that she and Tommy were to be married, and as soon as possible.

'Daddy,' whispered Daphne, opening her eyes to the watery dawn light in her bedroom. 'It's not fair, Daddy.' She focused on the portrait of Gerald that hung on the wall opposite her bed, and his collection of lucky charms that he'd kept in his theatre dressing room that were now arranged on Daphne's dressing table. Today was her wedding anniversary, but it felt funereal; Tommy in his bedroom, on the other side of the corridor, still sedated after the drama of yesterday evening; too close for comfort, yet also entirely remote from her.

Daphne closed her eyes again, but that was no better; for she could not escape the vision of Tommy with his gun, and the scene played over and over again in her head, like an endlessly repeating reel from a film, one of the old melodramas her father had appeared in towards the end of his career, except sometimes there was a shift in the action, and Tommy pointed the gun at her head, not his own.

'I must be strong,' Daphne said to herself, but she did not feel strong, she did not know how to nurse Tommy through this latest crisis. She wondered whether it would be better if he simply returned to London, to the Snow Queen's flat in Covent Garden; though she half-suspected that his misery might stem from the recent ending of that affair, an ending engineered not by himself, but by the Snow Queen, who could have tired of his mood swings, which were worsening since his retirement from Buckingham Palace.

She thought of her mother, of what she would have done, in Daphne's place, for she was as icy as the Snow Queen at times, yet the perfect wife, or so it seemed; apparently able to turn a blind eye to Gerald's infidelities, except for once, when he had overstepped the mark. 'It's too much!' her mother had shouted at Gerald, one evening, loud enough for Daphne and her sisters to hear through the bedroom walls. 'I saw your car outside Gertie Lawrence's house this afternoon, it was there for hours, and her bedroom curtains were drawn! And don't tell me you were in a private rehearsal with that little slut; don't humiliate me even more, by behaving as if I were stupid, as well as unattractive.' Afterwards, her mother's voice had been muffled, as if Gerald had taken her in his arms, and held her close to him; that's what Daphne had thought at the time, though now she imagined her mother burying her face in a pillow, refusing to look at Gerald, muffling her sobs in the feathers.

'I don't know how to do this,' whispered Daphne into her pillow; not that she was sure what 'this' might be. Last night, once her fear and anger had ebbed away, she was seized by a sudden impulse to laugh – it was so absurd, really, and such a clichéd scene – and then she started feeling guilty again; as if she had betrayed everyone, not just Tommy, but her mother and her father, too, by falling in love with Gertie; for could it be this that was the real root of Tommy's despair?

Today, though, she wasn't certain if she knew the meaning of love, or its consequences; for she felt empty, as if everything had been drained away from her, like a medieval blood-letting, and Gertie meant no more, or no less, than a character in one of her novels. And it was a good plot – more original than the episode with Tommy last night – the married woman who falls in love with her dead father's lover, a story there for the telling. But that doesn't make it true, thought Daphne; even though the stories in her head, both written and unwritten, had felt more true to her, at times, than her so-called real life.

She got out of bed, still in her nightgown, and walked quietly to Tommy's door, listening, but there was no sound from within, and she hoped he was still sleeping; that he would go on sleeping until later this morning, as the doctor had promised he would do. It was still too early for the doctor to call, or for Tod to be about, so she decided she might as well get on with some work at her desk in the alcove of her bedroom. That way, she would hear if Tommy started moving about his room.

When she pulled back the curtains, the sky was overcast, the day looked to be dreary, and she longed to be absorbed in writing a good story again; something to take her out of herself, out of this mess, this insoluble problem of Tommy; to lose herself in someone else's life. But Branwell seemed to be going nowhere – or rather, she was getting no closer to him – and neither was she proving any more successful in her efforts with Mr Symington. What on earth was the man doing, stumbling about in Yorkshire? There was still no sign of the promised manuscripts, or answers to her many questions; and as for her ambitious plan to provide evidence of Wise's forgeries, and uncover a sensationally talented novel by Branwell, and beat Miss Gerin to publication – well, all of this seemed impossible now.

Daphne sighed, wishing she could go back to bed, but she knew that sleep would not be forthcoming. For a moment, she felt close to laughter, and then tears, everything was mixed up; though one thing was certain. She was no better at dealing with Branwell and Symington than she was with Tommy; she was failing with all of them. 'I'm no good with men,' she said, to her father's portrait; and as she looked into his eyes, he seemed to smile at her, his melancholy lifting, just for a little while.

Menabilly,
Par,
Cornwall

19th July 1959

Dear Mr Symington,

Just a brief note – for today is my
wedding anniversary, and I must spend some time with my
husband. I am feeling increasingly anxious about the need to
get ahead with the book, if I am not to be beaten by Miss
Gerin, and it really is most frustrating, hearing no news on
the outcome of the printers' strike. Is there no way of finding
an alternative printing press, or could I perhaps be allowed to
study the original documents, rather than waiting for the
facsimiles?

I am, of course, sorry to hear about your fall. I trust you
are now recovered, and look forward to your next letter.

Yours sincerely,

Daphne du Maurier

CHAPTER TWENTY-SIX

Newlay Grove, August 1959

Symington had, at last, posted the manuscripts of three of Branwell's poems to Daphne, including the two sonnets, 'Peaceful death and happy life' and 'The Callousness produced by care' that had been ready in an envelope to be sent to her for several months. He had finally given up the attempt to make fruitful use of their titles in an accompanying letter to her; a letter that he drafted and redrafted until it made no sense at all, and he could no longer remember what his original point had been in writing it, other than a vague hope that he could prove his scholarship to be of a higher grade than hers. This last endeavour had left him exhausted and frustrated; and he felt increasingly irritable about her continuing demands for further information, and disconsolate that these manuscripts had finally gone from his house, though not from his heart. He had, at least, made copies of all of them, yet it grieved him to have relinquished the originals to Daphne, particularly as some lines from one of the poems had lodged in his head, repeating themselves over and over again, even when Symington felt that he had forgotten everything else; for everything was slipping away from him, just as it had done from Branwell.

'Increase of days increases misery,' he muttered to himself, when Beatrice was out of the room, closing his eyes and seeing the words on the manuscript appear before him, as if being written for the first time, 'And misery brings selfishness . . .'

And it was these lines that Symington quoted to his son, when Douglas telephoned to complain that he was never invited to the house; but Douglas didn't understand, he never had done. 'None of you boys ever understood me,' said Symington.

'It's the poem I don't understand,' said Douglas, 'that, and why you care more about the inconsequential words of Branwell Brontë than you do about your own family.'

'Inconsequential!' said Symington. 'There will be consequences, just you wait and see . . .'

Since then, he had not heard again from Douglas, and his other sons were silent, too, Colin flying the world as a pilot, and Alan down in Wiltshire, while Jim was farming in Norfolk and Donald was all the way over in New Zealand; no time for their father, so what was Douglas complaining about? Always complaining, that one . . . But never mind them, Symington told himself, he had work to do, he was overwhelmed with work, fielding endless queries from Daphne, who appeared to believe that he had nothing better to do than answer her questions about Branwell.

It was this rising sense of injustice – for it was unjust, thought Symington, her expectation that he would do her bidding, just because she was a famous author – along with his pressing need for money, that had prompted him to sell Daphne another of Branwell's poems, entitled 'On Landseer's painting', in the hope that she might take the hint contained within the opening lines:

The beams of Fame dry up Affection's tears,
    And those who rise forget from whom they spring –
Wealth's golden glories – pleasure's glittering wing –
Distinction's pomp and pride, devoid of fears
All that we follow through our chase of years –
    Dim or destroy those holy thoughts which cling
    Round where the form we loved lies slumbering . . .

Indeed, as Symington reread this manuscript just before sealing it into an envelope – a brown paper coffin, he thought gloomily – along with the others for Daphne, it struck him that he had something in common with the subject of Branwell's poem, and that of Landseer's original painting, 'A Dog keeping watch at twilight, over his master's grave'. Even if Daphne was too grand and famous to feel real affection for Branwell, then Symington knew himself to be a true and faithful mourner. Not that he would be able to prevent Daphne from digging up Branwell's bones, which she seemed intent upon doing; picking over the manuscripts at the British Museum, as well as demanding more from Symington.

As for those manuscripts which he had recently borrowed from the Brontë Parsonage: he decided to let her see eight pages from one of them, a notebook from Branwell's time as a clerk at the railway station of Luddenden Foot, though Symington was not permitting Daphne to examine the original notebook, simply the facsimile reproduction that he had arranged to have printed by a local firm that had done similar work for him in the past. It was a strange mixture of notes on railway affairs, fragments of poetry and sketches; Symington had agreed to allow Daphne to have reproductions of the sketches, but the original notebook he would keep for himself, for as long as possible. It might form an interesting comparison with the handwriting in Emily's notebook of poetry; if, that is, he could find her notebook again, for it remained buried somewhere in his boxes and files. Still, not to worry, he reassured himself, for at least it was safe in his care, while he watched over it like the faithful dog in Landseer's painting; keeping his silence, as always.

Newlay Grove,
Horsforth,
Leeds
Telephone: 2615 Horsforth

31st August 1959

Dear Miss du Maurier,

Just a few lines, to let you know that
the printer's dispute is at last settled, and I enclose facsimiles of
eight pages from Branwell's Luddenden notebook – those with
sketches on them, which you may find helpful.

I also enclose manuscripts of three of Branwell's original
poems, which will, I trust, keep you well ahead of Miss Gerin
in the race! These are from my private collection, and really
priceless, as you can imagine, but I hope you will agree that
£100 is a reasonable figure for them. I am sure they will be
helpful to you in a myriad of ways.

Yours sincerely,

J. Alex Symington.

CHAPTER TWENTY-SEVEN

Hampstead, June

Ever since my day in Haworth with Rachel, I've been day-dreaming about similarly daring escapades – climbing over the high brick wall into Cannon Hall, say, and exploring the garden that I can see from my attic window; maybe even slipping into the house itself. Or catching the train down to Cornwall, and trespassing on the Menabilly estate, like Daphne did as a young woman, when the house was still deserted, abandoned and overgrown with ivy. Because that's the only way I'll be able to see either of the places where she once lived – they're both closed to the public, kept private from the outside world, which only adds to their mystery, and to my intense desire to see inside their walls.

I've actually got as far as writing letters to the current occupants of both houses, explaining that I am a graduate student, engaged on further research, and was keen to visit the places where du Maurier wrote, but whoever owns Cannon Hall didn't respond, and the owner of Menabilly sent me a polite reply saying that he and his family lived quietly, and did not wish to be disturbed. I wasn't surprised, not really, because who would want legions of du Maurier fans tramping around, poking their noses into cupboards, hoping for skeletons?

And of course, I haven't stopped thinking about Rachel since our expedition; if anything, I'm even more obsessed than before, because I still don't know if she's now in possession of a letter that definitively proves that Symington stole the notebook of Emily's poems; and if that crucial piece of evidence linking him to the Honresfeld manuscript was in the file of papers that she smuggled out of the Parsonage. If she does have the proof, then she will have beaten me hands down. And I can't help wondering if that's why she hasn't been in touch again, because she doesn't need me any longer (if she ever did), and the next I hear of her will be another laudatory newspaper article, proclaiming her astonishing discovery of a literary scandal. When I really want to torment myself, I imagine that Rachel not only has the evidence to link Symington with the theft of the Honresfeld manuscript, she has also used this to track down the notebook itself of Emily's poems – an achievement which would make her the most famous literary detective in the world, and leave me as the also-ran.

All of which makes it impossible to banish Rachel from this house. Sometimes, her presence here feels more powerful than Paul's or mine; and I find myself wondering whether she gazed into the garden of Cannon Hall, like I do, and if she argued with Paul while they sat in the kitchen, or was it in bed, and did she get up and go into the spare room, just leaving a trace of her amber scent behind?

He's away again this weekend, at another conference – who'd have thought there could be quite so many academic conferences on Henry James? – and this time I didn't even ask him if I could go with him; I didn't want to see the look on his face when he tried to find a plausible reason to say no. And I still haven't told him about Rachel, about her coming here, and taking the books, and our trip to Haworth together. I know I should tell him when he gets home; I shouldn't let Rachel hide in the silence, beckoning to me behind Paul's back.

But the thing is, it's not quite so uncomfortable any more, that silence; we're beginning to grow accustomed to it, and the tension between us seems to be lessening, as if the taut thread that once held us together has slackened. There are still nights when we don't sleep in the same bedroom, because Paul says I keep him awake; but at least he doesn't look at me as if he hates me; the expression of his face is more quizzical these days, though I often wonder if I am as much of a stranger to him as he is to me. That's what is so odd: that we can live together in this house – that we are married, for God's sake – and yet we still know so little about one another.

It's not that he hasn't tried to find out more about me, and I can see it must have been quite annoying last week when I said to him, 'What's to tell?' He'd been asking me about my parents, and as I struggled to find a few facts – because all I really knew was that my parents were librarians who'd met at the British Museum, and that they were both only children, whose parents were dead by the time they got married – I realised that I didn't actually want to tell him anything else. I suppose it was an omission on my mother's part, not to have filled in the factual gaps of our history; but also on mine, not to have made it clear to her that I needed to know more about my father, and my grandparents. Except I don't think that I did feel the need, back then, which probably means I was a very odd child. No wonder I didn't have many close friends at school; no wonder my teachers used to write on my report, 'she lives in a dream world'.

Maybe that's why the most vivid scenes of my early childhood are woven into the pages that I read in my favourite books, or that my mother read to me, at bedtime. I know that some observers might have looked at the two of us and thought we were very alone – no father, no husband, no siblings, no visible web of family – but it never felt that way, because we were surrounded by the people in the books that I loved, and they were as alive to me as the other children in the playground; and often more consoling. Narnia seems almost more real, as a memory, than learning geography at infant school, because when I looked at the map that my teacher pinned to the wall, I was certain I could see the ocean that the *Dawn Treader* voyaged across, or the high mountains that were home to Aslan. *The Wolves of Willoughby Chase* is more indelible in my mind than the classroom in which I read it, though I do remember coming home across the heath in a wintry twilight, and hearing a wolf howling on the other side of the lake, and I turned, wide-eyed, to my mother, and she took my hand in hers, and smiled at me. Was that before, or after, we went to Kensington Gardens, while we were reading *Peter Pan*, and she told me that this was where Peter had lived? I'm not sure, but as I looked around – at the manicured lawns and ferociously neat herbaceous borders – I thought that my mother must be mistaken, that Peter could never have lived here, that maybe he had flown over it, on his way to Hampstead, swooping through the night sky, skimming the tree-tops, over the wolves, but never touching the ground.

Last week, after Paul realised how little I could tell him about the facts of my childhood – and I could see he was shocked, it was as if he couldn't quite believe what he was hearing (or not hearing) – he said to me that maybe I should start seeing a therapist. I laughed, and said I didn't need therapy, my childhood was far too boring for that. And Paul said he didn't think that boring was necessarily the right word to describe it. 'So how would you describe it?' I said.

'Devoid of something, perhaps?' he said. 'And maybe you're trying to fill up that space with the details of someone else's life? Could that be why you're so absorbed in the life of Daphne du Maurier?'

It seemed too glib an analysis, to be honest, a sort of mistranslation, but I was touched that he was trying to understand me. I could have pointed out to Paul that he was equally absorbed in Henry James – not the biographical details, perhaps, but the minutiae of his novels, the subtext of the texts. And I've been thinking about this since then, and I don't know, is being interested in a writer's life an indication of some hidden neurosis? I remember once at college, overhearing an argument in the room next door to mine, and a girl's voice was saying, 'Oh, get a life!' And it stuck in my head. Get a life. Is that what I'm doing? Trying to kidnap Daphne du Maurier's life, when I should be living my own?

Or perhaps that's too trite a reading of the situation. OK, reading is probably the wrong word to use here, given that I'm supposed to be finding ways of living that aren't necessarily to do with reading; at least I think that's Paul's prescription for me. But I feel alive when I think of Daphne du Maurier; I feel that her life contains all kinds of clues and messages that might help me make sense of mine. And if that is evidence that I need to see a therapist, well, I'd rather not. Not yet, anyway.

CHAPTER TWENTY-EIGHT

Menabilly, September 1959

Daphne possessed them, at last: Branwell's poems arrived in the post this morning from Mr Symington; the Brontë ink on the Brontë paper, there before her, laid out on the desk in her writing hut. She'd kept them hidden from Tommy, unwilling to share them with him, or anyone else; waiting until he'd driven off in his car to Fowey, coughing, like the engine, and so wistful looking, when she turned down his offer to take her out to lunch at the Yacht Club. 'Darling, I've got to work today, you know I have,' she said to him, and he had shrugged his shoulders, his mouth down-turned like a reprimanded child, looking just as he did when she reminded him to swallow his pills with a glass of milk every evening, and not to touch a drop of alcohol.

The sunlight slanted in through the window of her writing hut, making the dust motes dance in the rays like tiny fireflies. And the manuscripts themselves seemed almost made of dust, fragile, ashy, like the surviving remnants of an ancient conflagration. Yet all of them were clearly legible, unlike the hieroglyphic texts she'd studied in the British Museum; for these were poems written to be read. But Daphne found it hard to concentrate on the meaning of the words on the manuscripts, rather, it was Branwell's handwriting itself that fascinated her. It was less neat than his sisters' adult copperplate, but full of idiosyncratic flourishes and curlicues, forming an ornate yet slightly inconsistent pattern on the page.

As Daphne studied the handwriting, trying to imagine her path into Branwell's head, she suddenly felt a jolt of recognition, for she was reminded – in the most visceral way – of another morning, soon after her wedding, when she had sat and read a similar-looking ink copperplate. What had possessed her as a young wife to search through Tommy's desk that day, when she was alone in the house, knowing that her husband would not come home to disturb her? Daphne hadn't been entirely sure what she was hunting for then – though she remembered a strange compulsion, and a sense of excitement, as well as foreboding – but when she found the hidden drawer, with its key still in the lock (poor Tommy, never very expert at keeping secrets), she was certain that its contents were there to be read for a reason.

Inside, she discovered a small bundle of love letters to Tommy, written to him by his former fiancée, a beautiful dark-haired, almond-eyed girl called Jan Ricardo. Daphne had known her name and her face from a photograph, though not the details of her story – Tommy simply described her as 'highly strung', but always said it would have been 'ungentlemanly' for him to discuss why his engagement to Jan had been broken off, which made Daphne feel her curiosity to be repellent to him, and therefore something that must be kept secret, if not completely repressed.

What had struck Daphne then – and it had been as forceful as a physical blow – was not the contents of Jan's love letters, for the phrases were the usual conventional ones, but the handwriting itself, which seemed far more powerful than the sentiments expressed. It was confident, markedly individual, and the more Daphne had stared at it, the more it made her own writing seem cramped and halting, childishly unsophisticated, evidence of her lack of a university education. Daphne had never spoken of these letters to Tommy, because she felt it would be too humiliating to confess that she had been searching through his private papers, rifling through his desk like a common thief; but also because she had feared that if she'd admitted to finding the letters, then Jan might become an even more menacing presence in their marriage.

'Very menacing,' Daphne whispered to herself now, in the writing hut, remembering her father's voice. 'Are you menaced?' her father used to say to her, long before Tommy came along, using his idiosyncratic codeword for sexual attraction, trying to find out if Daphne had a new boyfriend, and somehow, the code had stuck, and she used it herself, without ever really thinking why. 'He's fearfully menacing,' she'd said to her sisters, soon after meeting Tommy for the first time; what a little fool she was, then, and what a fool she'd remained . . .

Of course, her anxiety about Jan's letters had worked its way out in the novel – in those pages that Daphne had written, almost without thinking, about Rebecca's handwriting; the second wife as transfixed as Daphne had been by the sight of her predecessor's bold, slanting strokes of ink, with the R of Rebecca standing out, black and strong, dwarfing everything around it, stabbing the white paper, so certain, so entirely self-assured. The second wife had tried to destroy the message to her husband from Rebecca, tearing out the flyleaf of the book of poetry that Rebecca had given Maxim, and then setting fire to it, the heavily inked 'R' the last to go, twisting in the flames. But no one could destroy Rebecca, she rose again, like a phoenix; she would always return, in the end. 'A blessing,' murmured Daphne, 'and a curse . . .'

And if Jan's letters had in some sense proved a blessing to Daphne – sowing the seeds of the book that made her fortune – then were both of them bound together by a subsequent curse? Daphne knew that Jan had gone on to marry someone else in 1937, and died a few years afterwards, towards the end of the war, when she threw herself under a train. Tommy was posted abroad at the time, and the Blitz was overshadowing everything; but still, Daphne had been terribly shocked when she read about Jan's death in a small piece in a newspaper. Yet something within her had also quivered in recognition when she saw the reference to a coroner's report, that gave no reason for why Jan had killed herself, aside from the standard explanation, that the balance of her mind had become disturbed.

Daphne shuddered, and tried to make herself concentrate on Branwell's handwriting, but it was no good, her mind was racing over the past with a terrible sense of dread at all that Jan had summoned up. Worst of all was the frightful court case in America over a decade ago, though now it felt as if it was creeping up on her again, to assail her with new persecutions.

She had been called to the witness box to defend herself against accusations of plagiarism, brought there by another woman, a writer that she had never even heard of. The woman was dead before the case came to court, but her family had pursued the legal action, relentless as a pack of bloodhounds. She'd had to travel all the way to New York to appear in court, sailing there on the *Queen Mary*, feeling horribly sea-sick, and filled with anxiety that she would be bankrupted by the trial, that everything would come crashing down around her, that she would lose Menabilly, and all that she held dear.

It was nonsense, of course. How could she have stolen the story of Rebecca, when it came from deep inside her? It was her story, it had bubbled up like lava, overflowing and dangerous, though she had struggled to contain it. But she'd thought she would break down entirely, if she were to be forced to tell the judge the origins of *Rebecca*, of how she'd discovered Jan's letters to Tommy, and feared that he'd always found Jan more attractive than her; and then Jan's death during the war, that dreadful suicide, it would have been unbearable for this to have come up in court, and if it had got into the papers . . . imagine how they would have feasted on the story, like vultures on rotting corpses, imagine the horror of that?

It hadn't come to that, thank God, and the case against her had been dismissed, after Daphne had produced her original notebook from ten years previously, with its handwritten outline of the plot of *Rebecca*. But what no one knew – what no one must ever know – was that when Daphne had read the news of Jan's death, she said to herself, 'It could have been me . . .'

It could have been me . . . The words ran through her head now, over and over again. She could have killed herself; God knows, she'd thought about it often enough, thought about what Michael must have felt, in those last hours, last minutes, last seconds, letting the water enfold him and his companion. Did they struggle, or was it peaceful, a slow dance to the bottom of the pool? Drowning seemed to Daphne a gentle way to let go; easier to contemplate than the violence of Jan's death . . .

And then Daphne was suddenly struck by an even darker idea. Did she, in fact, have something to do with Jan's death? Tommy's engagement to Jan had been broken off before he fell in love with Daphne, but she never knew which of the two of them had ended it. Jan must have known that he had married Daphne, of course, but then what did she make of the publication of *Rebecca* in 1938, just a year after her own marriage? Did she recognise herself as Daphne's beautiful predecessor, who had died and risen again? And what might she have heard of the echoes of *Jane Eyre* in *Rebecca*, a deranged first wife stalking through the nightmares of the second?

No, she must stop thinking like this, it would get her nowhere, and she had to stay on top of things, especially when Tommy was having bad days, again, when his hands shook and his face looked wan. But today was one of his good days, when the pills seemed to be working, and he was sufficiently robust to go out, so she must seize the moment, if she was to ever get ahead of Miss Gerin. Daphne put her head in her hands, rubbed her temples, which were throbbing, and forced herself to concentrate, to stop this wandering of her mind, which could only lead her to a more dangerous place.

She must drag herself away from thoughts of Jan's handwriting, and return to Branwell's poems, or rather, Northangerland's, for all three were signed with his flourishing signature. Not that there was much flourishing within their lines, she realised, after reading her way through them, for they could not have been more lugubrious, though there was an odd kind of vigour in their morbid examinations of death. Daphne decided that her favourite of the three was 'Peaceful death and happy life', once she'd come to terms with the fact that the title was somewhat misleading, given Branwell's point seemed to be that there was more misery in life than death. 'Why dost thou sorrow for the happy dead,' murmured Daphne, reading his opening lines aloud to herself, 'For if their life be lost, their toils are oer/ And woe and want shall trouble them no more . . .'

She wondered if this might be Branwell's message to her, from beyond the grave, to let him rest in peace. Why not leave him safely entombed within the pages of his manuscripts? But it was impossible to let go of Branwell, now that his handwriting was in her hands; hand in hand, they were together, for better or for worse . . .

Menabilly,
Par,
Cornwall

24th September 1959

Dear Mr Symington,
Forgive my appalling delay in
acknowledging your last letter – I was so delighted to
receive it, and the manuscripts of the three poems. What a
marvellous find of yours! I enclose a cheque for £100,
which seems very reasonable to me for such rarities. The
poem about the dead is my favourite of Branwell's; I am
proud to possess the original manuscript, and I will treasure
the other two poems, as well.

Unfortunately, it seems that I will be forced to postpone
our meeting, yet again. It has been the old trouble, my
husband's ill-health, which keeps me from settling to any
uninterrupted spell of constructive work. I have to be in
constant attendance upon him, whenever he is poorly, and
my longed-for visit to Yorkshire looks further off than ever.
It really is too disheartening for words. I feel rather like
Charlotte Brontë when she was nursing her father, during
his convalescence from an eye operation, and she was
finding it difficult to get on with 'Villette'.

Nevertheless, I will not retire from the race with Miss G,
and am therefore attaching a list of queries that I hope you
will be able to answer for me, either from your existing
files, or from your next trip to Haworth and the Brotherton
Collection. Apologies for the lengthy list – enough to give

you ten headaches, I fear – but I will, of course, reimburse you for your time and expenses.

I do very much look forward to meeting you in due course, despite all the delays, and finally having the opportunity to be able to talk in person about Branwell, the Brontës, and other shared passions!

Yours sincerely,

Daphne du Maurier

CHAPTER TWENTY-NINE

Newlay Grove, September 1959

Another envelope arrived in the morning delivery for Mr
Symington, bearing the now familiar postmark of Par in
Cornwall, and his address written in Daphne's spidery hand.
Inside, along with the letter and a handsome cheque, there
were two more densely typed pages, filled with a list of her
queries; lots of them, he could already tell, by the question
marks that punctuated the lines, some of them punching
through the paper itself, as if Daphne had hit that particular
key with intense urgency. Symington's heart sank at the
prospect of yet more of her impossible demands, though
he took some comfort from the fact that her remarks in the
letter were conciliatory ones, apologising for postponing, once
again, her trip to see him in Yorkshire.

Symington was torn between feelings of disappointment
about the fact that he had still not met Daphne, and relief. He
had imagined, with intense pleasure, a scene in which he
would escort her into the Brontë Parsonage, past a crowd of
sightseers, everyone there admiring him for being her chosen

guide, the scholarly advisor to the famous lady novelist. He would graciously acknowledge Mr Mitchell, his friend the custodian, but sweep past everyone else, all those jumped-up busybodies at the Brontë Society who had shunned him for so long. And it would be as satisfying to visit the Brotherton Collection at Leeds University with Daphne on his arm, showing her where his big octagonal office had been when he was in charge there, and brushing aside the current librarian, explaining to Daphne that it had all been his work, the amassing of Lord Brotherton's collection, showing her the treasures, the original Brontë manuscripts that were the crown jewels of the library.

But then at other times, most often when he was sleeping, these triumphant scenes would turn into nightmares, in which he was humiliated in front of Daphne, turned away with jeers at the doors to the Parsonage and the Brotherton Library. In one of these most vivid nightmares, which woke him before dawn this morning, Daphne's husband had been there, Lieutenant General Sir Frederick Browning, dressed in full military uniform, and he had turned on Symington, barked at him that he was a disgrace. 'You're not only a thief and a scoundrel,' the general said, flourishing a buff-coloured file of papers in his hand, 'but a coward as well. I have your military records here, and they show you were too lily-livered to serve your country in the Great War.'

'But I had poor eyesight, sir,' Symington stammered in his dream, a feverish panic overcoming him.

'A likely story,' Daphne's husband said. 'Call yourself a man? You're a little yellow-eyed rat, not a blind mouse.' And as the general spoke, Symington felt himself shrinking, dwindling while everyone loomed above him, larger and larger as he was reduced to a nonentity on the ground. And as he shrank, his voice became inaudible, but he still kept trying to explain himself, even as he felt the words shrivel inside his mouth, fading into nothingness. 'My eyes were bad from the library work,' he whispered, struggling to speak. 'I was appointed an assistant at the Leeds University Library in 1910, when I was twenty-two, you'll see it in my records, sir, should you care to look . . .' But Daphne's husband had simply ignored him, looked away in contempt.

The news of Browning's ill-health in Daphne's latest letter was, therefore, almost reassuring to Symington; he felt a strange sense of well-being, as he reread this news, though he tried to check this in himself, knew it to be shameful. Her letter, he noted, was dated 24 September; the anniversary of Branwell's death, one hundred and eleven years ago, though she made no mention of this coincidence, presumably it had passed her by, unnoticed, overshadowed by her concerns for her husband's health. Symington felt a pang of sympathy for Branwell, his death-day ignored even by his putative biographer, and also for himself; for all in his life that had gone unnoticed by the outside world.

He tried to imagine what it would be like to talk to Daphne, telling her more about his past, instead of Branwell's; about the momentous events that he had hidden for so long; about his emotions that were as powerful as any expressed in a Brontë novel, as passionate as those in Daphne's own novels, behind his locks and shutters. He would speak to her of his marriage in 1915 to Elsie Flower at Pocklington Parish Church; 'a wedding of meat and books,' his mother had said, straight-faced, referring to the fact that Elsie's father was a local butcher. Afterwards, someone had thrown a handful of white feathers at him, along with all the confetti, as they'd come out of the church. Or was it just an accident? Had the feathers floated down from the sky, or been carried from a bird's nest in a sudden flurry of autumnal wind, on that October wedding day? And then twelve years later, just a couple of days after their wedding anniversary, Elsie had died, unexpectedly, and in great pain. 'Ulcers in the gall bladder,' the doctor said, but it was too late, there was nothing that could be done for her, and there had been another church service, but at a different church this time, for they were living in Newlay Grove by then, in this house; she had died in this house, and gone from here in a coffin, and as Symington had followed after it, a feather had floated before his eyes, not a white one, but pale grey, like the sky, like Elsie Flower's eyes.

How little Daphne knew of him . . . how little anyone knew. Even Beatrice seemed like a stranger at times, even after their thirty years together, for she had never been interested in Branwell, nor had he wanted her to be, not really . . . As for his sons, those five little boys who'd grown up when he wasn't watching, he'd not known what to do with them after Elsie's death, he'd not had a clue where to begin, had buried himself in his work, instead; that was the thing to do, to bury oneself . . . Not that he had been lonely, in those days, for there was work to be done, and he had preferred the conversations of men to the clatter of domesticity at home. He had believed Lord Brotherton and Wise to be his friends then, even though neither of them had appreciated his true worth, nor Branwell's, come to that.

Still, Daphne had proved herself to be different, at least in her persistence. And she was alive, unlike Brotherton and Wise, though sometimes they seemed almost more real to him than the living, and it felt as near as yesterday, the Saturday afternoon that Lord Brotherton had walked into his father's bookshop and Symington had seized the opportunity to introduce himself. Such a fortuitous encounter for a young librarian, and later built upon in lodge meetings at the local Masonic Hall, and so Lord Brotherton had turned to Symington for advice in building up his library; but Wise muscled in, of course, Symington could see that now, though at the time, he had been in such awe of Wise, who was at the height of his fame and authority as a bibliographer, and President of the Brontë Society, as well. How much money had Wise made out of Brotherton, selling him thousands of pounds' worth of manuscripts and rare books for his growing library at Roundhay Hall, and how much had Symington spent, too, on his own private collection? It was so hard to resist Wise, and to resist the little treasures he offered him on the side, particularly when they related to Branwell. Not that Wise could ever leave him feeling fully sated, for the Branwell manuscripts that Symington bought from him seemed always fragmentary; crumbs from a rich man's table, rather than the feast itself.

And now Daphne was filled with the same desire, Symington knew that from her letters, he could feel it, seeping through the paper like an inkblot. Well, let her share another of his meagre crumbs, though she must buy it from him, as he had bought it from Wise. Symington delved into a box beneath his desk, and pulled out a letter written by Branwell to one of his friends, Francis Grundy. 'My Dear Sir,' he had written, on an undated page, though he gave his address as Haworth, 'If I have strength enough for the journey and the weather be tolerable I shall feel happy in calling on you at the Devonshire Hotel on Friday 31st of the month. The sight of a face I have been accustomed to see and like when I was happier and stronger, now proves my best medicine.'

The letter was signed by Branwell, and Symington noticed that his signature was less flamboyant than when he used Northangerland's name, the writing more cramped and subdued; there was a resignation to his words, a tacit acceptance of his fate.

Well, let Branwell's letter be sent on another journey, in an envelope to Menabilly in Cornwall, not far from Penzance, where the Brontë children's mother and aunt had lived, their birthplace by the sea, hundreds of miles away from the inland graveyard where they had been buried. Symington had always wanted to go to Penzance, to see where Branwell's maternal relatives had lived – the Cornish Branwell family, for whom the Brontë boy had been named. He had imagined driving down there with Beatrice, even planned a route on his maps, tracing the roads he would take, all the way down to Bodmin Moor, and beyond, to the very edge of England. But it was too late now, and he was too tired to make that journey, though he would send Branwell to Cornwall, instead.

Newlay Grove,
Horsforth,
Leeds
Telephone: 2615 Horsforth

27th September 1959

Dear Miss du Maurier,
                Thank you for your letter, and the
cheque. I am so sorry that Sir Frederick has been unwell and
unable to enjoy his retirement in Cornwall, and also that your
visit to Yorkshire must be delayed.

However, I will get over to Haworth in a few days to follow up
all the clues that you suggest, and I will have another look at the
medical volume of the Reverend Brontë and copy his notes for you.

Meanwhile, Mitchell will keep me posted on Miss G, have
no fear of that!

I also enclose another original manuscript (the invoice is
attached), for a letter sent from Branwell to his friend Francis
Grundy. I wish I were able to deliver this to you in person at
Menabilly, but will entrust it to the railways instead; a
journey which will have a certain poetic quality, given that
Grundy was a railway engineer, befriended by Branwell
while he was working at the Luddenden Foot station.

I hope that your worries will be over soon,

With kindest regards,

J. Alex Symington.

CHAPTER THIRTY

Cornwall, August

It was my wedding anniversary yesterday – our first anniversary, though Paul and I don't seem sufficiently united to describe anything as 'our'. It's his house, his car, his job, his book. Yes, his new book: he's started writing one about Henry James and George du Maurier. 'I might as well,' he'd said, 'given that you didn't take me up on the suggestion for a PhD. It's a terrific idea, after all . . .'

Anyway, he asked me what I wanted to do to celebrate – though he seemed almost amused when he said this, as if it were a private joke – and I said I wanted to go to Cornwall, to get away from London. 'And get closer to Menabilly?' he said. 'Well, why not . . . Fowey might be as good a place as any, I suppose.'

So he chose a sweet little hotel in Fowey for us to stay in, overlooking the water and the harbour. We drove down here the day before yesterday, in terrible traffic and torrential rain, hardly speaking the whole way, and arrived after dark, and the darkness seemed to seep between us and spread around us, a black cloud of misery. But in the morning we woke up to sunshine, it flooded in and spilled into me, and I felt filled with hopefulness, as unexpected as the high blue sky, and I turned to Paul in bed and kissed him. And he didn't turn away. 'I love you,' I said, and I meant it, as the silvery light from the sea came through the open windows and the ripples were reflected in the mirror opposite the bed, and so were we, the two of us entwined together in the looking glass.

Afterwards, we ate breakfast on an outdoor terrace, and the air was so clear after London, with a gentle breeze, and across the water I could see Ferryside. And my optimism spilled over, because instead of keeping quiet about Daphne, I said to him, 'Do you see that beautiful house on the other side of the estuary? That's Ferryside – Gerald du Maurier bought it for family holidays in the 1920s, and it's where Daphne wrote her first book.'

He nodded his head, thoughtfully, and said, 'Have you been to Fowey before?'

'Only once,' I said, 'when I was a child, too young to remember much, but I've seen pictures of it, and looked at maps . . .'

'And of course you've read du Maurier's books,' he said.

'Yes!' I said, so grateful that we could finally acknowledge this, without him getting angry, 'I've read them over and over again, and the thing about her novels is that you begin to feel you inhabit the places that she describes; she gives so much detail, it's like walking into the landscape of someone else's mind.'

Paul just looked at me and smiled, and that's when I seized the moment and told him that I wanted to walk along the coast from Fowey to Polridmouth beach, on the outskirts of the Menabilly estate.

The sky was still blue, and the wind was behind us as we took the road out of Fowey, down the hill to Readymoney Cove, where Daphne had lived in a little white cottage at the beginning of the Second World War, just before she'd made enough money from *Rebecca* to lease Menabilly from the Rashleigh family. I told Paul all about this as we walked – about how she'd started writing *Rebecca* in Egypt in 1937, while her husband Tommy was stationed there, and then when war broke out she'd come with her children to Fowey, where her two sisters and her mother were living in Ferryside. Her father was dead by then, and Tommy was fighting abroad, so Daphne was alone with her daughters, Tessa and Flavia, and her baby boy, Kits.

'How do you know all of this?' said Paul.

'Reading,' I said, 'though du Maurier's memoirs and autobiographical writing is quite opaque, there's quite a lot of information, especially in some of her essays. But it's like searching for the hidden pieces of a jigsaw puzzle or clues to a treasure hunt.'

'So what's the treasure?' asked Paul.

'I don't know,' I said. 'And that's the point, isn't it? You don't know what you're going to find at the end of a treasure hunt, and you don't even know where you're going, until you've got to the end.'

By then, we'd left the cove, and were climbing the stepped footpath up to the little ruined fort on the other side, St Catherine's Castle. It was steep, and I was feeling dizzy, because I'd run up the first half of the steps, and maybe that made me a bit light-headed. But anyway, when we reached the castle walls, I suddenly remembered being there before as a very small child, or at least, I felt I'd been there, but maybe I was imagining it, because there was something dream-like about the memory. I was holding my mother's hand, and she said, don't go too close to the edge; but I wanted to look over the edge of the castle walls, all the way down to the rocks and the waves below. So we'd stood there together, looking down at the sea, my hand in hers, and she said . . .

'What are you thinking about?' said Paul, interrupting my reverie.

I told him I was trying to remember if I'd been here before with my mother. 'And there was something she said to me, but I can't remember it, even though it feels so close, it feels as if it's just around the corner of my mind.'

'Déjà vu,' said Paul. 'There's a physiological reason for it, apparently. Something to do with a trigger to the optical and neural pathways . . .'

I didn't reply – I couldn't think of anything to say – but I didn't want him to think I was being silent, again, so I just took his hand and kissed it. 'Sweet girl,' he said, and then we started walking again, hand in hand, along the coastal path, towards Menabilly, while the swifts soared high above us, in a display of aerial acrobatics.

'I'm not sure if this is the way Daphne came, from Ferryside, when she first saw Menabilly,' I said. 'There was an old driveway in those days, at a crossroads just outside Fowey, that led to the house, so she might have come along that. But I don't think you can go that way now, and anyway, we'd be trespassing . . .'

Paul laughed, and said he thought that that was the plan – to do as Daphne had done, and creep through the overgrown woods to get to the main house. 'How do you know about that?' I said, surprised, because I hadn't told him the full story about the first time Daphne had discovered Menabilly, when it was deserted and half-choked by ivy, and she'd had to get up very early one morning as dawn was breaking and walk for miles through the abandoned estate, where the undergrowth was running wild, an orgy of wilderness, just as she described it in *Rebecca*.

Paul looked embarrassed, briefly, and then said, 'Rachel told me. She was always passionate about Daphne du Maurier.'

'So have you been here before?' I said, suddenly gripped by the thought that they'd come this way together, and he'd never told me, even though he'd seen it all before, and heard it all before, everything that I said to him today, on our wedding anniversary; Rachel had already told him everything, they had already shared our day, and why had I not realised that, why had I blinded myself to the obvious?

He turned his head away from me, but I couldn't let this pass, I had to know, I told him, I had to know. He paused, and looked out to sea, and then he said, very fast, 'Yes, we went to Menabilly, to a cottage in the woods. Rachel wanted to stay there for a few days while she was working on some poetry. It was an old gamekeeper's cottage that you can rent for holidays, though it's not widely advertised. Rachel found out about it – she was very persistent. Apparently, it's the only way you can see Menabilly, by renting this spooky little cottage in the grounds. She loved it there, but I thought it was rather sinister . . .'

'I can't believe you've never told me this before now,' I said. 'Why would you not tell me?'

'I don't know,' said Paul. 'I mean, I do know – there are all sorts of good reasons not to tell you. I didn't want to talk to you about Rachel, and I especially didn't want to talk about that holiday. It was the last one we'd had together, just before we split up. In fact, it was then that she told me she'd accepted a job in America, which seemed like the beginning of the end for us; I felt like she was abandoning me. And then, when you started obsessing about Daphne du Maurier, I thought, Jesus, it's happening all over again, it's like a nightmare, like history repeating itself, how could I have not realised what I was doing, when I married you.'

'But I'm not leaving you,' I said.

'Not yet,' he said.

'What's that supposed to mean?' I said. 'You've got everything the wrong way round – it's you that's been abandoning me.'

We hadn't stopped walking – actually, we'd been walking faster than before, as if we were trying to get ahead of ourselves, or maybe run away from each other. The sky clouded over, the swifts disappeared and as it began to rain, I felt like crying; I couldn't believe it, everything seemed to have gone so wrong, and I didn't understand why. By the time we reached the path down to Polridmouth beach, it was raining hard, a torrent driven into our faces from the glowering sky, and the rocks were slippery, and I wished Paul would reach out and help me, but he was in front of me, not looking back. I called out to him, but he didn't hear, he was too far in the distance. So I followed, quite slowly, and when I got to the beach, I went down to the edge of the sea, because the tide was a long way out, and there was this mass of litter that had been washed up on to the sand, left there by the last high tide, plastic bottles and broken glass and odd trainers, mixed with greying, decaying seaweed; it was all so depressing, really, in the rain.

And even when I realised I could see the remnants of the shipwrecked boat that had inspired *Rebecca*, it didn't seem romantic or mysterious, just like a dead animal's rotting bones. I can't imagine there was so much litter when Daphne lived in Menabilly and walked here every day, and I didn't like to think of this rubbish-strewn beach as being Rebecca's sanctuary, either, even though this was where Daphne imagined her, a place of freedom and escape, until she was shot dead by Maxim in the old boathouse just above the shoreline. The house is still there, but it's obviously been smartened up, it looks like a bijou holiday cottage, with ruffled chintz curtains at the modern aluminium windows, though outside, beyond the terraced patios and neat flower-beds, the lake remains the same, with swans and ducks gliding across its dark surface in the rain.

That's where Paul was standing, staring at the water, on a little bridge across the stream that runs from the lake to the sea. I looked at him and thought, how does it all go wrong? He loved me this morning, and now he doesn't; he loved me when he met me in Cambridge, and then he didn't. And I just didn't know how to make sense of it.

Eventually, I started walking in his direction, and he came down to meet me on the sand, and I didn't say anything, I just buried my face in his chest; it was so miserable in the pouring rain, like being drenched in the cold water from a sluice, and I wanted him to put his arms around me. 'I'm sorry,' he said, and sort of patted me on the back.

I should have told him then about how I'd met Rachel – I know I should have said sorry, too – but I felt too weary to say anything, really; and too confused. I couldn't see the point of talking, so I just stayed where I was, closing my eyes against the rain, shutting out everything, shutting out the grey sky and the grey sand, the scattered litter and the waves, churning against the shingle. Eventually, Paul suggested that we head back to Fowey, and when I didn't move, he tried to lift my head up, so that he could see my face. 'Come on,' he said, 'you'll feel better after a hot bath.'

'I don't want to go yet,' I said. 'I want to see Menabilly . . .'

He frowned, and sighed, then shrugged his shoulders and said, 'Well, I suppose we could walk up the path for a bit, into the woods, and at least get out of the rain. I don't suppose anyone will be out looking for trespassers today, not in this weather. But for God's sake, if we do come across a gamekeeper or whoever, let me do the talking. I'll say I've rented the cottage before now, and just wanted to take another look at it, for old times' sake.'

And it was as simple as that, really. He remembered where the path was, into the Menabilly estate, through a padlocked gate marked 'Private'. We climbed over the gate, and then we were in the woods almost immediately, the trees forming a canopy, high, high above our heads, like a green cathedral. The rain still dripped down, but not as heavily as before, and there was a sort of sighing sound all around us; I couldn't tell whether it was the wind in the leaves, or the waves breaking on the beach, but muffled now by the dense undergrowth. On either side of the path were rhododendrons, but not like any I'd seen before; these were huge giants, over fifty feet tall; some had toppled over and their pale roots were exposed, looking somehow indecent, and there was a sort of sour smell to them, if you got too close. Neither of us spoke, until the path forked, and Paul said, 'Menabilly is up there, to the left, and the cottage is to the right.' He'd stopped walking by then, and we were standing beside a pool that was covered in emerald algae, though not entirely, so you could see the black water between the islands of green. The pool looked very deep, and dangerous, but maybe that was illusory, because of all the shadows cast over the water from a strange giant-leaved plant, too exotic to be growing in an English woodland. I took a few steps along the right-hand turning, just far enough to be able to see the cottage, which was like a witch's house in a Brothers Grimm fairy tale, except it was built out of granite, rather than gingerbread, and the trees were all around it, pressing in, making a circle with those dense, dark banks of sinister rhododendrons.

'Come on,' said Paul, 'we'd better turn back.'

'But I want to see Menabilly,' I said, again, even though I knew I must be sounding like a whiny, irrational child.

'It's private property,' he said, irritated. 'It's not part of some du Maurier heritage trail, for God's sake, with a tearoom attached, and a shop selling Rebecca's azalea-scented handkerchiefs. Just leave it alone now, we've come far enough.'

'OK, you go back to Fowey,' I said, 'I don't care, you don't want to be with me anyway.'

'Don't be so adolescent,' he said.

'Go on,' I said, suddenly furious. 'Tell me to grow up! That's what you want, isn't it?' And I came back down the right-hand path, to the fork where he was waiting for me, but I wasn't going to go back to the beach with him, I was heading in the other direction, for Menabilly. He called after me, but I didn't turn around, not until it was too late, and he had gone, and I was alone on the path, walking up a slope, my footsteps muffled by fallen leaves. I was still furious – I wanted to shout out loud, to stamp my feet and shriek, to ask why Paul had brought me back to the same place where his first marriage had ended. It seemed like a monstrous thing to do, and I found myself muttering the word to myself, 'monstrous, monstrous', like it was a mantra or something. And then suddenly, I turned a corner and saw grey stone walls rising out of a clearing, and gracefully symmetrical windows, looking out on to the trees . . . and there she was: Menabilly.

I gasped, and stood still, holding my breath, as if even the softest of sounds would alert the inhabitants of the house to my presence, or the house itself, which seemed to be breathing, too. Everything was quiet and still, until something came crashing out of the trees, and I ran from the path, heart pounding, to hide myself in the undergrowth. The crashing had lasted for only a few seconds, and then I saw what had been making all the noise, it was just a pair of pheasants, running down the path together, looking as startled as me. For a moment, I thought I should run after them, and catch up with Paul and try to make everything right between us. But I didn't, I just sat down in a small gap between the rhododendrons, waiting for something, I don't know what. But there was nothing, just the silent house, and the sighing in the trees, and after a while, that was enough, that was all I needed.

CHAPTER THIRTY-ONE

Menabilly, October 1959

Daphne woke with a sense of rising anxiety, curdling her stomach, coming up into her throat, sour and corrosive. She forced herself to get out of bed, to stick to her routine, a quick breakfast, and then straight to her desk in the writing hut, until lunch. But when she sat there, surrounded by the mounting piles of paper – the newly prepared transcripts of Branwell's manuscripts from her diligent researchers at the British Museum; the opaque letters from Mr Symington – she felt even more panicky. She knew she must start writing her book – she must win the race and publish ahead of Miss Gerin – but she felt overwhelmed by her research, and Branwell seemed even more elusive than before, slipping out of her fingers in these disordered piles of paper.

She had taken an extra sleeping pill last night – she felt she must sleep, she would go mad if she lay awake, night after night – but even so, she was plagued by nightmares, in which the Brontë manuscripts crumbled away in her hands. And as they fell to pieces, dissolving into dust and ashes, the Snow Queen watched her, and laughed. 'You don't have the right touch,' she said to Daphne, and her face was cold, even as she smiled. 'You never did. Does the phrase "deathly prose" mean anything to you? You know what I am referring to, don't you?'

'Tommy doesn't love you any more,' whispered Daphne in the dream, but her voice was barely audible and she could feel the Snow Queen's icy breath, making her hands freeze, her mind grind to a halt; and she could not write, she could not think straight, she was like the boy in the fairy tale, caught in the Snow Queen's grip, imprisoned inside an ice palace, trying to solve an impossible problem, a Chinese puzzle with no solution.

In the daytime, the dream receded a little, but not enough; and she felt furious with Tommy, though not openly, for the doctors had reiterated that he must be in a calm environment if he was to recover from his breakdowns. Daphne tried to smile at him, tried to sound soothing, like a mother nursing a sick child. But when she was alone – when she escaped to her writing hut, between mealtimes – she seethed, knowing that he was still drinking, hiding his bottles from her in the cupboard of a disused bathroom, on the far side of the house; hiding everything, his letters from the Snow Queen, and his treacherous love for her. And it was in these moments, too, that Daphne's rage mingled with fear, when she was tormented by the suspicion that the Snow Queen had got the best of Tommy – his charming urbanity, his wit and intelligence – while Daphne was left with the dregs, the broken bits and pieces of himself that he brought home to be put back together again. Except Daphne did not know how to make her broken husband whole, he was as insoluble a problem as

Branwell; and when they sat together at lunch today, she felt a kind of icy contempt for him, or a numb emptiness, as if she was beyond caring, as if in his weakness, he could no longer touch her.

'I'm thinking of taking the boat out this afternoon, if the weather holds,' he said to her, when the maid cleared away the dishes. 'I don't suppose you'd care to join me?'

She looked at him – dabbing his mouth with a napkin, fastidious in his habits, as usual, yet furtive, somehow, almost dog-like – and wanted to say, 'Why would I want to join you, when I know you'll be desperate for a drink, and your hands won't be steady on the tiller until you have one, and then you'll be tipsy and belligerent.' But she simply smiled and said, 'That sounds lovely, darling, but I'm still trying to make headway with the book . . .'

As for Branwell: well, what a fool he was, like Tommy, drinking too much and thrashing around in life, lurching from crisis to crisis, weeping like a little boy when it all got too much for him. Daphne had just about given up on him as a writer of unrecognised genius, at least when it came to his juvenilia, so it didn't matter whether or not Symington was right in his allegations that Charlotte's signature had been forged on Branwell's Angrian manuscripts. The question was inconsequential, surely, because the stories were far too childish for anyone to really care about who wrote them. And the transcripts of Branwell's prose manuscripts at the British Museum had turned out to be equally useless, hardly worth quoting from in a biography, because they would do nothing but befuddle and bore a reader.

So why bother with Branwell, she asked herself, at the beginning of every day in the writing hut? It was too late to turn back, she replied, writing down the words as a message to herself in her notebook. She must not give way to her rival, Winifred Gerin; it would be too humiliating, and anyway, there might still be secrets to unearth. So she forced herself onwards, drawing up a chronology of Branwell's life, sending letters to anyone who might have a scrap of information about him.

But all too often, she was thwarted by the news that Miss Gerin had got there first, visiting the descendants of Branwell's friends, or researching in the archives of the Brontë Parsonage, while Daphne was stuck at home in Cornwall as Tommy's nursemaid. In her darkest hours, and there were many of these, Daphne imagined that Miss Gerin had already beaten her by getting the best of Branwell and tracking down a previously undiscovered manuscript, that revealed him to have written an unpublished masterpiece, to rival *Wuthering Heights* or *Jane Eyre*. When she tormented herself with this scenario, she imagined Gerin hailed as a great literary detective, as well as a consummate writer, while Daphne was pushed to one side, forgotten.

But she could not give up, she must keep going, for the idea of abadoning her book was even worse than the prospect of writing it. To step aside now would be a final admission of defeat, and then what would she do with herself? So there was nothing for it but to strain every nerve, to dig deeper into her reserves of determination and ambition, and hope that Branwell's story would emerge from the papers that surrounded her in the hut, the white drifts of them, rustling in the draughts from the window.

'Don't look out of the window,' Daphne told herself, but she could not help it, her eyes returning always to the view, almost hidden by the trees, of the sea; the silvery expanse of it beyond the headland, darkening toward the horizon, a thin grey line with a distant sailing boat against it, and then the water merging with the sky.

This was Rebecca's place, of course – the woods and the sea, the blurring lines of leaves and sand and water – but one afternoon, as the autumn mist turned into dusk, and Daphne's eyes were aching from the manuscripts, she looked out of the window, and saw not Rebecca, but another girl, a younger one, almost hidden in the undergrowth. Daphne stared intently, rubbing at the obscuring condensation on the window, trying to identify the trespasser, but then the shadowy figure was gone, disappeared as if she had never existed. Daphne wondered if she had imagined the girl, or perhaps she was another ghost, mingling with all the others that flitted around Menabilly, before disappearing again, like migrant birds.

But Rebecca's ghost was going nowhere; she remained right here, sighing into Daphne's ears, or tapping her fingers on the windows of the hut, and she seemed to bring others with her, nameless presences, lost causes, hopeless cases.

'*Go away*,' said Daphne, as she attempted to write, trying to drown out Rebecca's tapping fingers with her own at the typewriter, 'leave me alone.'

But Rebecca just laughed. 'Leave you alone?' she whispered. 'Why, that would be leaving myself.'

Menabilly,
Par,
Cornwall

10th November 1959

Dear Mr Symington,

Here is a cheque for your expenses at Haworth. Thank you so much for your note. I do hope you feel better soon. There's nothing like being out of sorts for getting one down.

I have just checked up on Mrs Gaskell's statement that Branwell's pockets were found stuffed with letters from Mrs Robinson after he died. This is completely refuted by Leyland, through the testimony of the servant at the Parsonage, Martha Brown, who said 'there were a number of letters found, but all from a gentleman of Branwell's acquaintance who happened to be living near the place of his former employment with the Robinsons.'

Now, if only we could track down this gentleman! Though not a word to Miss G! Annoyingly, I have to report that she is ahead of us with the Robinsons. I wrote off for the second time last week, trying to trace the present members of the family, and got a reply two days ago, a bit stiff, from a Canon Cuthbert, one of the descendants, telling me that Miss Gerin had visited them a month ago! Infuriating. If my poor husband had not been so unwell all summer, I should have been there in September. How funny if Miss G and I had clashed on the doorstep! However, I will write a very polite letter back to his

Reverence, but whether I get any information out of him is doubtful. He has no doubt spilt it all to Miss G.

Nevertheless, I have got one coup. Having slowly – but steadily – worked my way through the old Brontë Society Journals, I came across an interesting article about the curate at Haworth, who was there between 1837 and 1839 and lodged in a haunted house in Haworth. He knew the Brontë family very well, of course, but was a particular friend of Branwell's, and persuaded B. to stay a night with him in his room to experience the ghostly presence. Branwell had previously scoffed at the story, but after sleeping in the old-fashioned bed, which heaved up and down in the night, he was convinced of the ghost's activities. No doubt he told the story the next day to his sisters, with graphic descriptions – and what a seed of an idea for Mr Lockwood's haunting when he spent the night in Cathy's old room at Wuthering Heights!

Which brings me to my much-delayed visit to Haworth – because at long last, I think that I will be able to come to Yorkshire at the end of November or very early December. I plan to spend some time at the Brotherton Collection in Leeds, and if it is convenient for you, I also hope to call on you at your house, and see the wonders of your library. And perhaps you could come and lunch with me in Leeds, as well? Then I will go over to Haworth to meet Mr Mitchell, and study Branwell's manuscripts at the Parsonage. I am quite sure that there are many fascinating manuscripts of his tucked away there, which no one has shown the slightest bit of interest in (apart from ourselves, of course). An old mitten worn by Charlotte has always been considered of greater value to the public interest than half a dozen sketches or notes by Branwell.

Now, very much <u>entre nous</u>, but when I get up to Haworth, where do you think is the best place to stay? Is it possible to stay at the Black Bull? Last time I went, several years ago, I stayed at the Brontë Guest House, and though very pleasant, it was rather confined, and a bit chilly, with a tiny sitting room where one sat with the other guests rather on top of each other. It is possible that one would feel a bit less confined at the Black Bull, and it does have those colourful connections with Branwell as the scene for his drinking sessions. On the other hand, the people were extremely kind at the Guest House, and did not intrude in any way, whereas when I went for a drink at the Black Bull on my last visit, it got round almost at once that I was there, and the attention, though kindly meant, was a bit of an embarrassment. The thing is, when I am working, I like to feel quite anonymous, like any student, and just be left to get quietly on with what I am doing.

Perhaps Mr Mitchell might be able to advise on these matters? If you see or write to him, could you tell him that you know I will make it worth his while if he can show me certain items in the museum which may not be on view?

Yours sincerely,

Daphne du Maurier

CHAPTER THIRTY-TWO

Newlay Grove, November 1959

Symington was feeling increasingly besieged, though he was torn between wanting to be left alone, and craving contact with those whose advances he had so far rejected. Several letters had arrived this month from Daphne, confirming that she was, at last, coming to Yorkshire at the beginning of December, and was keen to meet him at his house, where she would doubtless bombard him with more unanswerable questions. The thought of such an encounter exhausted Symington – it was as tiring a prospect as a visit from one of his sons or grandchildren, all of whom he had been keeping at a distance. But Daphne was unstoppable; she was rather like Beatrice, he had come to believe – at least as indomitable, once she had a fixed idea in her head.

And then there was the young American graduate, a Mr Mattheisen, currently studying in Leeds and pursuing what he delicately referred to as 'the remainder of your collection', on behalf of Rutgers University. Mr Mattheisen was always courteous when he telephoned, but also persistent, though

Symington had believed (until this morning, anyway) that he retained the upper hand over the young American. Mattheisen had come to the house twice in the last month, but Symington would not allow him to examine his collection; simply withdrawing the most tantalising-looking manuscripts contained in the forty unlabelled boxes that lined one wall of his study, and showing them briefly to Mattheisen, before putting them safely back again.

But last week, however, the American had suddenly become impatient. Either Symington sold him the collection for £750, he said, or the deal was off; especially given that Rutgers had already paid Symington $10,000 in 1948, for what they had believed was his entire collection. 'Well, young man,' Symington replied, 'that just goes to show how a clever bibliophile such as myself can build a new collection, full of treasures, in a decade.'

In the end, though, Beatrice intervened. 'You've got to get rid of those boxes before we move house in the new year,' she said, 'and Lord knows, if someone will pay you good money for them, then take it. It's bad enough having to leave this house because we can't pay the bills, but at least we'll have a little extra to tide us over, and anyway, there'll be no room for your boxes in a smaller house.' Symington found it hard to believe that she would actually force him to sell the house – his house; his castle; she had no right to make him leave this enclave – but he hoped that striking a profitable deal with Rutgers might keep Beatrice quiet, at least for a while. Not that he had any intention of selling everything; Emily's notebook of poems, for example, could not possibly go to Rutgers, there would be far too many questions asked about its provenance, and where he had acquired it. But there was no harm in letting the Americans buy the minor material – the pamphlets and newsprint, and a few less important manuscripts that had nothing to do with the Brontës. Everything else – Branwell's manuscripts, Emily's poems – was safely hidden away in the recesses of the attic.

And so Mr Mattheisen had arrived at the house this morning, along with another young man from Leeds University, a student, who was to help with the loading of the boxes into his car. Symington watched as the pair took the cartons from his shelves in the study, piling them in the hallway, ready to be ferried to the car; and suddenly, he felt overcome with panic. Could he have been mistaken, and allowed any of Branwell's manuscripts into one of these boxes? How could he be completely certain of their contents? Even though he had gone through them last week, perhaps his checks had not been sufficiently thorough, for the briefest loss of concentration might have proved catastrophic. Could he, in fact, trust himself?

'Just wait a moment,' he said to Mattheisen, opening up one of the boxes, trying to keep his voice and hands steady. 'I think there may be nothing but duplicates or photostats in this carton. I might as well keep them, given that they can be of no use or value to you.'

Mattheisen stepped forward to stop him, tried to take the box out of Symington's hands, and an unseemly tussle ensued, Symington feeling the heat rising in his face, as he struggled with the younger man. 'This is completely absurd,' said Mattheisen after a minute or so, looking suddenly disgusted, pulling away and raising his hands, as if in defeat. 'Do you want to sell the collection or not? And is it even yours to sell? Your reputation at the Brotherton Library seems somewhat blemished, from what I hear in the university common room.'

'How dare you!' Symington said, and ordered the two men out of his house, so angry that he would have pushed them to the door, were it not for the fact that his arms were still firmly clasped around the box. As they left, embarrassed and empty-handed, Symington felt triumphant, as if he had defended his house from marauders. But this afternoon, waiting for Beatrice's imminent return home from her Woman's Institute meeting, he was becoming more and more uncertain about how to explain the events of the morning. The piles of boxes remained in the hall – he felt too weak to move them – and the cheque for £750 that should have been in his hands by now was still in Mattheisen's pocket. Beatrice's rage, he feared, would be immense, if she discovered the details of what had happened today.

And so, as he sat in his study, listening for her key in the front door, he was desperately trying to come up with a story that would satisfy Beatrice. He considered telling her that Mattheisen had never turned up, but what if one of the neighbours spied the unfamiliar car parked outside this morning, and the arrival of the two young men? Perhaps it would be better to stick to the truth: that Mattheisen had been insulting, and Symington had told him to leave. He ran through the conversations over and over in his mind – the one that he had already had with Mattheisen, and the one that he would have with Beatrice. After a time (how long? The cursed day seemed to be going on for ever) he began to feel confused about who had said what, and to whom, and his confusion was mingled with rage and regret; until at last, sitting in the twilight, the lights out, the fire turned to cold ashes in the grate, Symington found himself weeping. He was unable to understand quite why; he had not cried for as long as he could remember; even when Elsie died, he did not shed a tear, he had felt too frozen and numb with shock, and rage, too, at the unfairness of it all. Suddenly Symington heard his dead mother's voice in his head, sharp and cold as it had been in her lifetime. 'You're a good for nothing, Alex,' she said, 'and a whiner, and a cheat.'

He looked up, startled, almost expecting to see her in the shadowy corner of his study. 'You didn't complain when I invited you to the opening of the Brotherton Library at the university,' he muttered. 'You said how proud you were of me that day, when the Archbishop was there, and the Princess Royal and the Duchess of Devonshire, and all the other fine ladies.'

His mother's voice did not respond; though in the silence – in death, as in life – he sensed her continuing, disapproving presence. He reached out to a photograph in a silver frame on his desk; there they stood, the three of them, their arms linked, himself in the centre with his mother and Beatrice on either side of him. The date and place was handwritten in the corner of the picture: October 1936, at the official opening of the Brotherton Library. But Symington needed no reminder that this was the high point of his career, when he was announced as Keeper of the Brotherton Collection, and interviewed by the *Daily Express*; and they had been so proud of him then, Beatrice and his mother, satisfied at last. The

Archbishop of Canterbury made a speech, and afterwards it was broadcast on the BBC, and Symington had copied down a phrase that had struck him at the time, and that he remembered still. 'The treasures of the Brotherton Collection,' said the Archbishop, 'are an abiding reminder that there are things whose value cannot be measured by their practical utility – the imponderable things of truth and beauty.'

The imponderable things of truth and beauty: Symington said the words to himself again now, like a prayer. But they had not kept him safe all those years ago; he had been fired just a few months after the opening, the locks to the doors were changed overnight, and he arrived for work to discover the library bolted against him, its very creator, barred from the things of truth and beauty that he had so painstakingly gathered. After that, door after door had closed to him: he'd applied for dozens of jobs as a librarian, but had been turned down by everyone, rejected without so much as an interview, until at last he had stopped trying; tried to stop thinking about the dwindling of beauty and truth.

Then the war came, and he'd felt useful, for a little while, helping out at a regional office of the Ministry of Food, but that had come to nothing, too, and he had found himself spending more and more time at home, while Beatrice busied herself with her charities and committees. Whenever anyone asked what he was working on, which was seldom, he would explain that he was writing a book about Branwell Brontë; though when he had suggested this to Blackwell's, the publishers of his Shakespeare Head editions of the Brontës, they sent him a dispiriting rejection letter, saying that they could see no market for what they termed 'the most marginal of writers', and Symington had been stricken by this phrase, wondering whether it was referring to him or Branwell, or both of them?

'You always thought you were too good to go into the family business,' said his mother; and this time her voice seemed to come not from inside his head, but whispering into his right ear, which was hurting now, as painful as when she had seized it and shaken him when he was a child.

'I am a writer of books, not a seller of them,' he said, into the darkness.

'Your books never sold,' said his mother's voice. 'No one wanted to buy them. And who can blame them? Who would want to read the story of a wastrel's life, written by another wastrel?'

'If you're referring to Branwell Brontë,' he said, 'my biography of him remains unwritten.'

His mother was silent, but Symington imagined her scorn. She had wanted him to take over the family bookselling business after his father had died in 1934, but he'd been dismissive at the time, saying he was far too busy to run the shop, he was still working on his edition of the collected works of the Brontës. 'That'll not pay your bills,' she had snapped. 'You need to be selling books, not spending your days with your nose stuck in all those old papers and wearing your eyes out, too. What makes you think you were born to write books, anyway? My father was a printer, and your father was a bookseller – both of them honest men doing honest jobs, not too big for their boots, like you . . .'

Symington swallowed hard, choking back a sob, and reached for the flask of whisky in the top right-hand drawer of his desk. He was cold, chilled to the bone and shivering. He sipped the drink, but it did not still the trembling in his hands, and there was a pain in his chest, his heart was hurting. 'Is my heart broken?' he whispered, but no one answered, and no one heard his words.

CHAPTER THIRTY-THREE

Menabilly, August

I don't know how long I sat in the Menabilly woods; it could have been hours, but it was hard to tell, everything seemed like a dream in there, like an enchanted forest, though the smell was real: damp moss and earth and bark. The rain stopped, and a white mist descended, reaching out to me through the trees, which was reassuring. I felt that I was safely hidden, not that anyone seemed to be in the house or the gardens or the woods, it was just the birds and me. After a while, I realised that I was sitting to one side of the house, well away from the drive that led through the parkland from the West Lodge, curving towards Menabilly. The curtains were not drawn at any of the windows, but the house had a closed look, and I began to think that the windows were like blank, unblinking eyes; not blind to me, just impassive.

I tried to imagine what it would have been like the first winter that Daphne spent here with her three young children, when the war was still being fought, and Daphne was fighting her own war, to stop Menabilly falling into ruin. It was the beginning of 1944, the year that Tommy was appointed the Allied Commander of the Airborne Division, preparing his troops for the terrible battle of Arnhem. I remembered that from watching *A Bridge Too Far* on the television when I was about fourteen, and my mother had explained to me that Dirk Bogarde was playing Daphne's husband, Boy Browning – she knew I'd be interested, because I was already obsessed by Daphne's novels. And then I started wondering what my mother would say to me, if she could see me now, crouching behind a rhododendron bush, looking for ghosts in the mist around Menabilly. I didn't see any ghosts, as it happens. I didn't see Daphne or Tommy or Rebecca, though I wondered if they could see me.

Eventually, I decided that I'd have to start moving again if I was to find my way out of the woods and back along the cliff-top path before it became too dark to see anything. The mist was beginning to darken in the dusk, and bats were flying between the house and the trees; and I realised then that I'd always lived in a city, that London was what I understood, however alone I felt there, and that this place was absolutely not mine, that I was a trespasser here. I didn't like the thought of being among all those flitting, quivering bats – I felt blinder than they were, as I started walking back along the path that I thought had brought me here. But it was difficult to be sure, because all the trees looked the same in the twilight, and the rhododendrons seemed even bigger than I'd remembered them – too large for life, somehow; too big to be true. I was half-running by now, but the path wasn't going downhill, like it should have been, back towards the sea, and though I thought I could hear the waves in the distance, it might have been the sound of the wind in the highest branches of the trees. Eventually, I knew I must have taken the wrong path, because there was no sign of the witch's cottage that Paul had shown me earlier today, and I seemed to be going slightly uphill again, away from the sea, though it was hard to tell in the mist, I was losing all sense of direction. And then suddenly I came to a clearing, and I could see that five paths led to it, including the one I had taken, like the spokes of a wheel, and that one of them must lead to the sea. I was just about to run across the clearing to the other side, when I realised that the ground gave way to a dark pool, larger than the one I'd seen by the path to the cottage, black and still . . . just like Daphne's short story. And I remembered a line from that story, almost as if someone had spoken it out loud to me: 'To show fear was to show misunderstanding. The woods were merciless.'

I began to wonder if I was dreaming – because it was beginning to seem as if the whole day had been a nightmarish dream, and that if I could only force my eyes open, I'd wake up in the bedroom in Hampstead, but my eyes were wide open, I was looking all around me, not sure of which way to go. The girl in the story heard a voice saying, 'This isn't a dream. And it isn't death, either. It's the secret world.' And then she'd seen a child by the pool – a little blind girl, only two years old, trying to find her way. And pity had seized her and she had gone to the child, and bent down and put her hands on the child's eyes, and as they opened, the girl in the story had realised that she was looking at herself, her younger self, at two years old, when her mother had died.

But I couldn't see anybody, just the dark trees and the dark water. There didn't seem to be any meaning to me stumbling to the edge of this pool. I had not found myself like the girl in Daphne's story, I was lost and alone and I didn't know what I was doing here. I couldn't even see my reflection in the water, it was too dank and opaque. And then I started panicking, not about finding my way out of the woods (though there didn't seem to be an end to them), but about why I had come here, and what I thought I would find. It seemed like such a crazy thing to have done; to be looking for my reflection here, to have hoped to find meaning in this place. And it wasn't just coming here that was crazy, but everything leading up to it – the search for Daphne's letters, and for Symington's, the adventure in Haworth with Rachel, wanting to be Rachel's friend, because I was so lonely. And as for marrying Rachel's husband – because that's what he still seemed to me to be, when it came down to it – well, what on earth had possessed me? How could I have thought that it was ever going to work out between us, when we couldn't even talk to each other? He'd kept his secrets from me, and I had from him; because I still hadn't told him about Rachel coming back to the house, let alone our trip to Haworth together. So I had behaved just as badly – as irrationally – as him.

It was then, thinking about Paul, that the panic began to subside, and I just started feeling incredibly tired, and I began to wonder if I should sleep here for a while, like the girl in Daphne's story. Not that I felt like that girl – she had been filled with wonder and a sense of oneness with the woods and the sky and the world around her, and I just felt exhausted, too tired to walk. It would be so peaceful, really, if I could get over being scared of the dark and the bats. 'I wouldn't stay here, if I were you,' murmured a voice in my head, soft, like my mother's voice, and I tried to keep my eyes open, tried not to give in to the longing to lie down. But it was impossible, like trying to keep your eyes open on a motorway, when someone else is driving, and you can't stay awake . . .

So I suppose I fell asleep, though I don't remember it happening, I don't remember that moment of lying down. But I must have been dreaming when I saw a woman by the pool, a cloud of dark hair around her face, not blonde like Daphne, and she was smiling at me. 'The one who got away,' she said to me.

'But I'm here,' I said. 'I haven't gone away.'

'You will,' she said. 'You must.'

'I want to stay here,' I said. 'I haven't got anywhere else to go.'

'You must find a place of your own,' she said.

And then there was a screaming, but it wasn't her that was screaming, and it wasn't me, either; I was awake again, the scream had woken me, and it was high and unearthly, coming from somewhere in the woods. 'It's an animal,' I said to myself, out loud, to make sure I wasn't still dreaming, and as I spoke, I made myself get up from the ground. The moon had risen – not a full moon, but a crescent bright enough in a cloudless sky for me to be able to see my way to the path that would lead me back to the beach. Once I was walking along it, towards the sound of the waves, it seemed easier not to get lost again; it was just a question of staying calm, that was what I told myself as I kept walking, eyes ahead, not looking into the shadows between the trees and the uprooted rhododendrons. Eventually, the path joined another, wider one, and the waves were getting louder and louder, and at last I could see the beach again, high tide now, the moon shining on the water, and the surf churning up the shingle.

There were lights on in the cottage, and I hesitated, wondering whether I could face the walk back to Fowey, four miles along the cliff top; but I couldn't decide if that was a slightly less daunting prospect than knocking on the cottage door, and asking for a stranger's help. It occurred to me that if I was in a novel by Charlotte Brontë – something like *Jane Eyre* – then knocking on the door would produce some startling turn of events; a previously unknown relative of mine would come forward, a cousin who would later be the means by which I discovered the secret of my childhood. Which was a tempting prospect, of course, but unlikely, and anyway, it seemed to me that it was time to stop imagining myself into other people's stories. There had been no reflection of myself in the pool at Menabilly – no ghostly, phantom-green face, with hair like a shroud; just pondweed – and my time in the woods had not revealed anything of myself to me, except an inept sense of direction.

But at least the path to Fowey looked clear enough in the moonlight, well worn by all those people who had been here before me, so I set off again, back up the slippery steps that I'd come down earlier today, and then out in the open, the sea to my right, the fields to my left, and a huge starry sky above me. Suddenly, I felt braver, almost exhilarated. I was on my own, and I didn't know where I was going – well, I knew I was walking back to the hotel, but I didn't know whether Paul would be waiting there for me. And it didn't seem to matter. I was suspended in time, inconsequential, and therefore free; and I started running, down a slope with the wind behind me, in the warm air of an August night, my feet steady, my legs strong, but feeling so light, as if I might lift off from the ground, wings unfurling, up and over the cliff tops, flying high into the darkness above the ocean.

CHAPTER THIRTY-FOUR

Newlay Grove, December 1959

Daphne arrived, as arranged, at three o'clock, having taken a taxi from the station, and stood on the doorstep, feeling as shy and nervous as a sixteen-year-old girl; which was absurd, of course, but the meeting with Mr Symington had been a long time in the coming, after nearly two and a half years of correspondence. The house was a substantial one – a redbrick Victorian villa, with a large garden surrounding it, all rather tangled and overgrown, unlike its more manicured neighbours. Ivy climbed up the front, the tendrils reaching into the roof, and entangled with a Virginia creeper, its fallen leaves still lying unswept in the drive, sodden and slippery, and the house looked as chilled as Daphne, on this grey wintry day, sunk in the early dusk of dark enveloping clouds.

It took a few minutes for anyone to answer her knock on the door, though she was aware of the sounds of movement within, the shutting of doors, and a creaking that might indicate footsteps. She tried ringing the bell, but it seemed to be broken, so she knocked again, harder, feeling her

337

knuckles against the peeling black paint. And at last the front door opened, to reveal a man that Daphne assumed must be Mr Symington: bespectacled, greying, though still with a thick head of hair. 'Ah, Lady Browning, how good of you to come,' he said, holding out his hand, which emerged from a frayed shirt cuff and the threadbare sleeve of an ancient brown suit.

'Mr Symington—' said Daphne, but the man stopped her by shaking his head. 'Unfortunately, Mr Symington could not be here today,' he said.

'How very odd,' said Daphne. 'We had arranged to meet at three o'clock – he wrote to me last week, confirming this.'

'Yes, most unfortunate,' said the man, stepping back, yet at the same time seeming to shrink into himself, like a tortoise.

Daphne felt annoyed and confused and embarrassed. She very much wanted to see inside the house, and to see Mr Symington. Indeed, it occurred to her that the grey-haired, tortoise-like gentleman might be Symington, yet why on earth would he pretend not to be? She asked the man on the doorstep if she could leave a message for Mr Symington, and then, overcome with a sudden irritation, asked him his name.

'I am Mr Symington's assistant,' said the man. 'He has been called away on important business regarding a rather precious manuscript.'

'And your name is?'

'Mr Morrison.'

He said it with such finality that it seemed to mark the end of their conversation, at least as far as he was concerned, but Daphne was not giving up so easily, not after travelling 400 miles from Cornwall to Yorkshire. She asked the man if she might come inside to write a note for Symington, and to ring for another taxi to take her back to the station; a request he agreed to, with some reluctance, but it was beginning to sleet by now, and he could hardly send her back to Leeds station by foot. Daphne followed him into the hall, before he could change his mind, and removed her coat, in an attempt to take charge of this curious situation. 'May I wash my hands?' she said, and the man flushed, slightly, and pointed her to a door at the end of the dimly lit hall.

The cloakroom was clean – it smelt of disinfectant, like the hallway – but it was terribly cold and damp, as if it had been unheated for a very long time. Daphne glanced at her face in the mirror; a greenish-grey reflection gazed back, with a frowning down-turned mouth and slightly puzzled eyes, as if the woman in the looking glass did not recognise Daphne. 'What on earth are we doing here?' she murmured to herself.

When she returned to the hallway, the man had gone, but she heard his voice in another room, and followed it through an open doorway, into a large study, overlooking the garden, yet filled with so many cardboard boxes and wooden packing cases that very little light came in from the windows. The man was sitting at a mahogany desk, speaking on the telephone to what Daphne presumed must be a taxi company. 'No, that's far too long to wait,' he was saying. 'I'll need a driver within the next half an hour, as a matter of some urgency.' He put the telephone down with a sigh, but remained seated, so Daphne sat down too, in a sagging armchair beside the unlit fire.

'What a great many books,' she said, gesturing to the shelves that lined the walls of the study, from floor to ceiling.

'As you know, Mr Symington is a leading bibliophile,' said the man. 'And his collection has been described as the Bodleian of the North.'

'I thought that was the term applied to Lord Brotherton's collection?' said Daphne, who had visited the Brotherton Library at Leeds University the previous day to examine some of Branwell's manuscripts held there.

'I think you'll find that it was Mr Symington who assembled Lord Brotherton's collection in the first place,' said the man, with a sniff. 'And of course, Mr Symington has a great many treasures of his own.'

'Might I see them?' said Daphne.

The man regarded her from behind his spectacles.

'I have come a very long way,' she continued. 'As you may know, I have travelled here from Cornwall, which is quite an expedition to undertake.'

'Yes,' said the man, 'Mr Symington was most upset not to meet you today.' He stood up, walked over to one of the packing cases, and proceeded to rummage through its contents, while coughing into the box with such violence that Daphne feared he might vomit. At last, he pulled out a small, mildewed leather notebook, and passed it to Daphne with a shaking hand.

She took it, with some hesitation – not because of its obvious fragility, but because of her distaste at touching the visible evidence of the man's coughing fit that was left on the book. Such was her disgust at his coughed-up phlegm that it took her a little while to read the name written on the first page of the notebook. 'Emily Brontë?' she said, hardly able to believe what she saw before her. 'This is Emily Brontë's notebook?'

'Yes,' said the man, with some pride. 'Hence my description of Mr Symington's library as the Bodleian of the North.'

Daphne carefully turned the pages, counting them to herself. Twenty-nine pages, thirty-one poems. 'What an extraordinarily precious document,' she said to the man. He reached out to take it back from her, but she said, quickly, 'Might I just see if one of my favourite of Emily Brontë's poems is here? There was one in particular that inspired me to write my first novel . . .'

The man nodded, and she turned the pages again, her hands trembling, as his had done, until she reached the fifteenth poem, about halfway through the notebook. 'It's here,' she said, ' "Self-Interrogation",' and she scanned the verses until she reached the seventh stanza – so familiar that she could have read it easily, even if Emily's handwriting were as illegible as Branwell's, which it was not – and read the lines aloud:

> Alas! The countless links are strong
> That bind us to our clay;
> The loving spirit lingers long,
> And would not pass away!

When she came to the end of the verse, the man took the notebook from her hand, and wrapped it up in a damp and grubby brown-paper shroud. 'Should this not go to the British Museum for further study?' asked Daphne.

'And leave it to the mercy of thieves and scoundrels?' said the man. 'You are aware, perhaps, that precious manuscripts such as these have been mutilated, both in the Reading Room of the British Museum and elsewhere? The security in these places is abysmal, and the curators are shoddy.'

Daphne felt uncertain of how to proceed with this conversation; for she did not want to offend the man by pointing out that it was Mr Symington's former colleague, T. J. Wise, who had been rumoured to have stolen pages by surreptitiously tearing them out of manuscripts and rare books at the British Museum. 'I do see your point,' she said, carefully. 'But surely a museum would be able to conserve such a precious manuscript in more suitable conditions than a packing case?'

'That, dear lady, is where you are entirely mistaken,' said the man. 'I can assure you that Mr Symington's knowledge of conservation techniques is second to none. Indeed, Miss Brontë's notebook will be far safer here than it would be, say, at the Brontë Parsonage Museum, where there is a flagrant disregard for proper procedure. And I must ask you, of course, to keep this matter confidential.'

'What matter?' said Daphne, more confused than ever.

'The little notebook that you have just seen. Or not seen,' said the man, tapping the side of his nose. 'Now, if I am not mistaken, I hear the sound of your taxi outside.'

Daphne heard nothing; the house was silent, save for the distant banging of a door in the wind. She turned her head, as if listening, and then shrugged. 'Surely the taxi driver will ring let us know when he arrives?' she said.

'Oh no, I think not,' said the man, but Daphne remained seated.

'I must write a note to Mr Symington,' she said, reaching into her handbag for a pen.

'If you have any message for Mr Symington,' said the man, 'you may give it to me in person. There are no secrets between Mr Symington and myself. We work as one together.'

'Well, then tell him that I am most disappointed not to meet him today,' said Daphne. 'And tell him, also, that I would like to buy any Brontë manuscripts in his collection, if they are available.'

'I am authorised to act on Mr Symington's behalf in commercial transactions, as well as literary matters,' said the man.

'Is the notebook of Emily Brontë's poems for sale, then?' said Daphne.

'I think not,' said the man, sadly, pressing his fingertips together in a steeple. 'But Mr Symington did leave a package that he thought you might be interested in purchasing.' He opened one of the desk drawers, and pulled out another small brown-paper parcel, which he passed over to Daphne. She unwrapped it, heart racing, hoping for something even more extraordinary than the last discovery, the original manuscript of *Wuthering Heights*, perhaps, with Branwell's signature on it, alongside Emily's; but she was quickly disappointed. Inside was a bound schoolbook, a Latin primer by the look of it. 'Branwell's schoolbook,' said the man, 'with his drawings inside, on the opening frontispiece.' He gestured to Daphne to open the book, and she did so, to discover a couple of roughly drawn sketches of a pugilist.

'Yours for thirty-five pounds,' said the man, briskly. Daphne shook her head, and handed it back to him, and he looked suddenly stricken, even paler than before, yet with beads of sweat breaking out on his forehead. He returned to the packing case, and pulled out another parcel, wrapped in brown paper, and Daphne stifled a laugh, for it was absurd, like a tombola at a village fete; yet at the same time she wanted to cry, for there was something so dreadfully sad about the man. 'Perhaps you might be interested in taking Branwell's schoolbook, if I also included another manuscript of his poetry?' he'd said. 'Together, they offer an insight into his extraordinary intellect, at a very reasonable combined price of seventy-five pounds.'

He unwrapped the manuscript, and placed it in her hands, as tenderly as if it were a baby bird. There were four pages, entitled 'Morley Hall', written in what Daphne recognised as Branwell's legible adult handwriting, rather than the microscopic childhood print of the Angrian chronicles. As before, she read the opening lines aloud:

> When lifes youth, overcast by gathering clouds
> Of cares, that come like funeral-following crowds,
> Weary of that which is, and cannot see
> A sunbeam burst upon futurity,
> It tries to cast away the woes that are
> And borrow brighter joys from times afar.

As she spoke, the man had nodded, as if in agreement with Branwell's melancholic poetry. 'Too true, too true,' he said, and then began to cough again. Daphne, alarmed and yet also feeling herself sinking into depression, put down the manuscript, and told the man that she would pay the seventy-five pounds; though her purchase did not fill her with much enthusiasm. She felt, as she wrote out the cheque, that Symington had trapped her into tacit complicity, so that she was party to this ridiculous pretence that he was not the man in the study with her; yet at the same time, she retained a sliver of hope that the man might be telling the truth when he said his name was Morrison.

By the time the taxi had arrived to take Daphne back to the station, she was relieved to be escaping from the house. The man's cough was worsening, and he looked feverish, which made Daphne anxious that he might be infectious with a horrible, consumptive disease, as virulent as that which had killed Branwell, then Emily and Anne, within a few months of each other. But it wasn't just a fear of physical infection taking hold of her, in that dim, cold study; she was beginning to think that his failure would be contagious. For it seemed to Daphne that a smell of failure lingered around him, and the house, a kind of mouldering dampness, against which his fever fought in vain. When he had shaken her hand in farewell, his palm felt clammy, and Daphne wiped her hand with a handkerchief once she was safely in the taxi, but his clasp remained with her tonight, his breath seemed to have stayed with her, even after she had bathed and changed her clothes.

It was now past midnight, but Daphne lay awake and restless in her single bed at the Brontë Guest House, the frost creeping in through the crack in the window. She got up, shivering, and pulled back the curtain, so that she could see the view of the Parsonage, its stone outlines still visible in the starlight. Daphne was trying to imagine the events of the last century – Branwell staggering back to the Parsonage after an evening at the Black Bull, past the graves of his mother and aunt, buried far away from their Cornish birthplace; and were they restless, still, waiting to return to the sea, but caught here, as loving, lingering spirits?

Branwell would be drunk, but not so much so that he did not think of his dead mother; nor was he immune to the disapproval of his sisters and father, waiting at home for him. Daphne stared into the darkness, hoping to summon up a wild-eyed, red-headed ghost, weaving his way through the graveyard, but there was no sign of him, nor any other creature, dead or alive. As for those purchases of Branwell's schoolbook and poem that now sat on the spindly bedside table: she could find nothing within the pages that redeemed either Branwell or Symington's faith in him. The boy who had doodled over his Latin primer turned into the fourth-rate writer of 'Morley Hall', an introductory fragment of a presumably unfinished epic, all lamely rhyming couplets and drearily interminable, even in these initial pages.

And yet . . . she had not given up on Branwell, or Symington, or her book. If these were hopeless causes, she would be cutting short her trip, and leaving for London early tomorrow morning, then catching the night-train home to Cornwall. But instead, she was staying in Yorkshire for another two days, as planned, determined to make use of the library at the Parsonage, and to walk in the footsteps of the Brontës, along the cobbled streets of Haworth, and up across the moors behind their home. She'd fantasised about meeting her rival biographer on the doorstep of the Parsonage – looking directly into Winifred Gerin's eyes, and telling her that Branwell was hers, and hers alone. But there had been no sightings so far of Miss Gerin, and Daphne wondered whether the woman was avoiding her.

The church bells chimed once, and Daphne shivered, and climbed back into bed. Nothing would be gained if she caught cold; she must be practical and level-headed if she was to edge ahead of Miss Gerin. Tomorrow morning, she had an appointment with Mr Mitchell, the custodian of the Parsonage, and the opportunity to study more of Branwell's manuscripts. She'd already had one encounter with Mr Mitchell, soon after arriving at Haworth, three days ago – he had spent a great deal of time telling her about his difficulties with the workmen who were building his new quarters at the Parsonage, and how his wife did not want the stove where they had put it. Daphne had felt like crying with frustration, thinking of the manuscripts waiting for her, but not wanting to offend Mr Mitchell, who was their guardian. She had hoped that Mitchell could tell her some interesting stories about the Brontës, given that he was born and bred in Haworth. But when she had tried to steer his conversation away from the builders and towards John Brown, the sexton who had been Branwell's friend and fellow Freemason, Mitchell started talking about one of Brown's descendants, a great-grandson who went to Australia and had three children out there.

Daphne was struck, suddenly, by the idea of a putative biographer coming to Fowey in a hundred years' time, to seek out information about herself ... The biographer would doubtless end up talking to the great-nephew of a long-dead housemaid at Menabilly, who'd say something about Lady Browning writing in a hut in the woods, and then it would get all confused, the biographer would think this referred to the cottage in the woods, the one where the old ladies had lived – a pair of spiritualists, according to the housemaids, Miss

Phillips and her companion, Miss Wilcox, in their witch's cottage down the hill from Menabilly. And then the story would get round that Daphne had called up the spirits, and got them to write her books, while she was in a trance or something.

She laughed to herself, as she huddled under the eider-down, and switched out the bedside light. But in the darkness, she wished that she could call up the spirits, out of all those dried-up manuscripts. If only Branwell's ghost could appear to her now, and Emily and Charlotte and Anne. She would not be frightened of them, however wraith-like and consumptive their appearance; she would greet them as they stepped out of the shadows. But the Parsonage had just been redecorated with new wallpaper and fresh paint, and Daphne feared that the Brontës had fled from the workmen and the tourists and the endless intrusions. So be it. She could wait for them, at least for a little while longer . . . And perhaps they were lying in wait for her, still.

CHAPTER THIRTY-FIVE

Newlay Grove, January 1960

Symington felt that he was burning up with anxiety, and his throat was constricted, his stomach twisted. He still could not understand why he pretended to be someone else when Daphne came to visit him last month; it was inexplicable, given how much he had been looking forward to meeting her. And yet, perhaps he had never believed that the meeting would actually happen; for why else had he kept it a secret from Beatrice? Why else had he ensured that Beatrice was out of the house when Daphne arrived, for he had been intent that the two women should not meet.

He could not remember when he took the decision to say that he was Morrison, a name that he had plucked out of the air, like a passing feather, though it was his mother's maiden name, of course, now that he came to think of it, and the name of her father's printing firm. But the more that he thought of the moment when Daphne arrived at his front door, the more it seemed to him that his assumption of another identity was not a decision; the words had simply floated out of his mouth, before he could stop them and stuff them back down his throat again.

She had looked so fine, standing there on his doorstep, in her grey flannel trousers and glossy blonde hair; so *expensive*, with that silk scarf knotted at her neck, and the pearl earrings, and a big diamond ring on her wedding finger. And he had felt shabby and provincial and inconsequential, when he had wanted to appear before her as a lofty scholar, authoritative and urbane, like a professor giving a tutorial to a naïve young girl.

'Lady Browning . . .' As soon as the words were out of his mouth, he had forgotten himself, forgotten everything. She was Lady Browning, the wife of a war hero, and he was an impoverished, unemployed librarian. Worse, he was disgraced. He was a disgrace. He had nothing, and she had everything.

Except Emily's notebook: he had that, but Daphne had not known he had it. That was what had made him behave so foolishly: he wanted her to know that he possessed something of such value. It was priceless, and it was his. But now he was filled with panicky dread: for in showing her Emily's notebook, he had given away his secret. Had Daphne realised that the notebook was not his to show? Had her research been thorough enough – had she delved deep enough – to know that this was the notebook that had gone missing from Sir Alfred Law's collection at Honresfeld, and that modest Mr Symington, a man as quiet as a mouse, was the last person to have it in his possession?

But he had never intended to steal the Honresfeld notebook; just as he had never meant to keep the fragments of poetry bound together in green morocco leather, that little volume he had taken from the Brontë Parsonage nearly thirty years ago, in an attempt to prove that the handwriting was Branwell's rather than Emily's. It was Wise's fault, not Symington's, for attributing Branwell's verse to Emily in order to sell it to the highest bidder; and sold it was, to a rich man foolish enough to accept Wise's authentication, when anyone with an ounce of sense could see that it was Branwell's handwriting, not Emily's; and Branwell, therefore, who had written 'The Heart which cannot know another'.

That is what he had wanted to tell Daphne; and to show her Branwell's poem, alongside Emily's verses, so that together they could compare the handwriting, becoming collaborators in their endeavours. But when it came to it, he had made a mess of the meeting. 'Just like you make a mess of everything,' hissed his mother's voice into his right ear, which was hurting, like the rest of his feverish, aching body.

And now Daphne was back in Cornwall, silent and distant, no letters sent between the two of them since the meeting last month, as though a veil had been drawn over it, to cover up their mutual embarrassment. Unless, of course, she'd fallen for his cover as Morrison, but that would mean she had never seen a photograph of him, and she must have come across a picture somewhere, in an old magazine article about the Brontë Society, perhaps . . . just as she must have encountered a reference to the missing Honresfeld notebook of Emily's poetry.

As his thoughts spiralled in upon themselves, Symington's head felt as if it would crack open; something had to give, for the tension was intolerable, it felt as if there was a boiling steam inside him. 'You have always been full of hot air,' whispered his mother.

Meanwhile, Beatrice was grumbling and nagging him about their debts, insisting that they must sell the house; her demands that he pay attention to her growing ever more shrill, but she would have to wait, he would not move, he could not move from his chair in the study. 'Go to bed, Alex,' she was saying to him. 'Go to bed, and I will ring for the doctor.'

'There is nothing a doctor can do for me,' said Symington, but he did not know if she could hear him; his voice was drowned out by his coughing, and he was burning up, everything was burning, everything consumed at last . . .

CHAPTER THIRTY-SIX

Hampstead, 1 September

I've spent so many years in education that September always seems like a beginning, but I know it's an ending, as well. This year, there's no fresh start of a term, though I've found a new job, at a local bookshop. I've got to earn some money – I've got to start supporting myself, instead of relying on Paul – and I'm about to move out of his house, and start paying the rent on a room of my own. It was his suggestion that I go, but he was right; I can't go on living with him, like a sleepwalker. That was his description for our marriage – 'sleepwalking' – and at first, I didn't understand what he meant, but now I do, and I can see it was a bit like dreaming, though not in a good way; it was like one of those dreams when you're watching yourself, as if you have no control over the narrative, and things just happen . . .

Everything unravelled between us after I came back from Menabilly. Paul was in the hotel, waiting for me, white-faced and angry. He said he had been worried, that he was just about to call the police and report me as missing. 'We can't go on like this,' he said, and I thought, what a cliché, but it was true. I was too tired to cry, or to argue with him; I just nodded my head, and had a shower, and got into bed. He put his arms around me, and said he was sorry, that he shouldn't have got involved with me so soon after Rachel leaving him, and he was too old for me, anyway. 'What you mean is I'm too young for you,' I said, and he said, 'It doesn't matter which way you phrase it, we're just not meant to be together.'

'Did you ever love me?' I said to him, resting my head against his shoulder.

'I thought I did,' he said. 'But I was still in a mess over Rachel, and I couldn't think straight. I thought I was falling in love with a girl who was completely different to Rachel – you were so young and guileless, such an innocent. And then after we got married, and you came to live with me, I wondered if I'd fallen in love with a young Rachel, as if you were what she had once been, before it all went wrong.'

'But I'm not like Rachel,' I said. 'You must be able to see that?'

'I don't know whether I'm seeing anything clearly,' said Paul. 'I'm too confused to trust myself, or anyone else, including you.'

Everything felt so broken that night – even the words we said to each other, all of it broken-down and impossible to fix; even when we were making love, and he was as passionate as the first time, but I knew it was the last. Afterwards, in the darkness, I said, 'I've got something to tell you.'

'I already know what it is,' he said. 'I've already spoken to Rachel. I rang her tonight, because I couldn't think of anyone else to talk to.'

'Rachel told you we'd met?' I said.

'She told me that she had come to the house, to collect her books and that you went with her to Haworth.' His voice sounded flat, not angry, just exhausted. I wanted to say, 'Is there anyone else?' But of course there was, it was pointless asking; I knew that Rachel was on his mind, that he'd not yet had a chance to work out what he felt about her, because he'd thought that by convincing himself he was in love with me, that would obliterate all of his misery and uncertainty about Rachel. It didn't work, and how could it? I was just a red herring, a wrong turning on his map. I was a forged signature, and Rachel was the real thing.

And I got everything mixed up when I was with Paul – getting obsessed with the relationship between Daphne and Symington, when I should have been paying more attention to what was going on between Paul and me; or maybe between Paul and Rachel. I still don't understand the state of their relationship; when I think about it now, it seems like a nation state, and I'm an illegal immigrant who somehow stumbled across their borders.

I'm mixing up my metaphors, aren't I? And I know I'm probably still not thinking straight, and although there's a certain liberation in that, I don't want to let my thoughts twist in on themselves. That's why my first instinct was to start working as a librarian, after Paul told me I needed to get a job and find somewhere else to live, and, by implication, someone else to love. I thought it would be soothing, to spend my days putting books in alphabetical order; that indexing and filing would be a useful way to smooth out my problems. But when it came to it, I decided I didn't want to fall into following my parents, not without trying something else first. I can see that working in a bookshop might not seem the boldest of alternatives to librarianship, but it's a start. And unlike libraries, you have to talk in a bookshop, and that's been good for me, though it's a struggle sometimes. Customers come in and ask for advice on what they should buy as a birthday present for a melancholy teenage daughter, or an irritable great-uncle, and I do my best to be helpful, to make useful suggestions.

This morning, a woman said to me that she was looking for something to read when she went into hospital for an operation. 'I need a book to save my life,' she said, half-smiling. 'And I don't mean the Bible, or any religious tract.'

I looked at her and I said, 'What about *Jane Eyre*?'

'What about it?' she said.

'Well, it's about being a survivor, isn't it?' I said.

She laughed, and shook her head. 'I want something slightly more cheerful.'

'So that rules out *Wuthering Heights*,' I said. 'And probably *Rebecca* and *My Cousin Rachel*, as well.'

'Daphne du Maurier?' she said. 'That's not a bad idea. I could do with a bit of romantic escapism.'

I thought about telling her that Daphne du Maurier wasn't necessarily escapist, nor was her writing particularly romantic – it's much too menacing for that – and that actually, *Jane Eyre* has a very happy ending, which most people found cheering in some way. But I stopped myself, and went off to the far corner of the shop to find a copy of *Frenchman's Creek*, du Maurier's most straightforwardly romantic novel, and when I came back, the woman said, 'Thank you, my dear, that looks just what the doctor ordered.'

So I was feeling reasonably pleased with myself and wondering if I might turn out to be quite a competent bookseller, after all. And then I saw Rachel walk into the shop. I don't think she had expected to find me there – because she looked as surprised as I did; her cheeks flushed red, and she put her hand to her forehead, almost as if she were taking her own temperature, to see if she was feverish. And as I looked at her, looking at me, I suddenly guessed that she'd come from Paul's house – their house – and they had been talking about me. Perhaps that was just me being childishly self-centred; they might have had better things to talk about, or maybe she hadn't been with him, and the entire episode was coincidental. But anyway, once the thought had lodged itself in my head, it wouldn't go away.

'Hello,' I said to Rachel, because it wasn't a big enough shop for us to pretend that we hadn't seen each other. 'Can I help you?'

She raised an eyebrow, as if trying to regain her usual composure and self-possession. 'I don't know,' she said. 'Can you?'

Suddenly, I found her incredibly annoying. 'Rachel, don't be arch with me,' I said, 'and please stop manipulating me.' Which struck me as one of the bravest and boldest things I've ever said to anyone; pathetic, I know, but you have to start somewhere. 'I suppose you've already heard that Paul and I are separating. It wouldn't surprise me if you've just come from his house, and the two of you have been discussing me. I must seem like a problem that needs to be got rid of.'

'It's not like that,' she said.

'Like what?' I said, and folded my arms, to stop them from trembling.

'Look, do you want to talk?' she said, and I said no, I was at work, and it wasn't appropriate. 'Inappropriate because you're at work, or because my ex-husband is now your ex-husband?' she said, and smiled at me.

There was something about that smile that was so beguiling and seductive that I wanted to laugh and to be seduced again, even though I'd hated her a minute ago. But I stopped myself, because I knew that if I fell for Rachel's charm, I'd be back where I started again; which would be hopeless – it would be like falling into someone else's scheme of things, instead of my own. Not that I have a scheme, but even so . . .

'Well?' said Rachel, reaching out to touch my cheek.

'I just don't get you,' I said, which wasn't a very elegant turn of phrase, but I was feeling flustered. 'I don't see why you dragged me into your burglary of the Symington papers from the Brontë Parsonage.'

'I thought you'd be interested,' she said, letting her hand drop again, by her side.

'Well, of course I'm interested,' I said, 'but then you disappeared. So I'm an accessory to your crime, but with none of the proceeds.'

'I'm surprised at you,' she said, 'I thought you'd be more enterprising, and come after me.'

'I don't want to come after you,' I said. 'That's the point. It's been bad enough coming after you with Paul. I'm not going to chase you over some old manuscripts. Did you find what you were looking for, anyway? The notebook of Emily Brontë's poems?'

'The Honresfeld notebook,' she said, and a wistful look passed over her face. 'There are some very interesting references to it in those papers that I borrowed from the Brontë Parsonage.'

'*Borrowed*?' I said. 'I imagine that's how Symington would have explained his thefts. "Borrowed in the interests of academic research . . ."'

'Don't be such a boring child,' said Rachel. 'And I returned the Symington file on the same day that we were there, as it happens, before anyone had noticed that it had gone. Anyway, aren't you interested to know that Symington was the last person to have the Honresfeld notebook? He borrowed it from the Law collection, supposedly in order to have it copied as a facsimile for his Shakespeare Head edition. He mentioned it in several letters in the 1930s, and then it disappears from sight. Sir Alfred Law died childless in 1939, and no one knows what became of his collection – whether it was sold and dispersed to other private collectors, or whether it was passed down to another branch of the family. But wherever the Law collection went, Emily's notebook never turned up again, and I'm desperate to find out what Symington did with it. As far as I can see, he didn't return it to the Law collection at any point . . .'

As she talked, I was finding myself getting interested, despite my vow not to be sucked in again. 'I already knew that Symington had taken the notebook,' I said, not wanting Rachel to think that she'd discovered something new to me. 'But I wonder if Symington sold it to Daphne du Maurier, along with the other Brontë manuscripts that she bought from him?'

'That's what I've been wondering,' said Rachel, 'so it's a shame you didn't tell me you were going to be making an expedition to Menabilly. We could have gone together, and done a bit more research . . .'

When she said that, I felt angry again, thinking of how Paul had told her that we'd been to Cornwall last month; and that they *had* been talking about me. And yes, I know that sounds childish, because I should have been the one who told Paul about my encounters with Rachel; I shouldn't have let him discover that from her, rather than me. 'Rachel,' I said, trying to keep my voice steady, 'you can't possibly believe that we would find a lost Brontë manuscript in Menabilly. Daphne moved out of the house in 1969.'

Rachel clicked her tongue, impatiently, and said, 'I *know* she left Menabilly, but she moved down the road to Kilmarth, and there might be someone who remembered what became of her library. Did she leave it to her family, or sell it, or what?'

'Apparently she had a huge bonfire of papers when she was forced to leave Menabilly,' I said, slowly. 'I've always thought it sounded a bit like a re-enactment of the end of *Rebecca*, like Mrs Danvers setting the house on fire, or Mrs Rochester in *Jane Eyre* . . .'

'Surely you're not suggesting that Daphne du Maurier burnt a priceless Brontë manuscript?' said Rachel.

'No, I'm not,' I said, 'but I wouldn't be surprised if a few of the letters she had from Symington are missing, and I've sometimes wondered if she burnt those.'

'Why?' said Rachel. 'It doesn't make sense, when she kept the other letters from him. Which I'd still very much like to read, by the way.'

'I bet you would,' I said. 'I suppose you need them for a new book.'

'As a matter of fact, I do,' she said. 'I was going to dedicate it to you.'

'Why would you do that?' I said.

'I love the idea of the scandal it would cause in academia,' she said. 'And it seems fitting, as well. You know how interested I am in exploring the idea of literary influences – of what has been passed from the Brontës to du Maurier, and of what passes between women.'

'I don't think I do know,' I said.

'Oh yes you do,' she said. 'You just haven't realised it yet.'

And then she scribbled down her phone number on a bit of paper – a London number, I noticed, not American. 'Keep in touch,' she said, over her shoulder, as she walked out of the shop, 'and don't forget to tell me your new address.'

I didn't say anything – I couldn't fit the words together in my head, let alone my mouth. But now, I'm thinking of all the things I should have said to Rachel. What did she want from me, apart from Symington and Daphne's letters to one other? Why had she involved me in her relationship with Paul? Was it some sort of strategic move, which formed part of a larger plan that would bring them together again? Or had they ever really given up on each other? Was I just a temporary interloper?

As for talking to Paul about all of this: well, I want to, but he hasn't come home yet, and it's late, past midnight. I imagine he's with Rachel, wherever she might be; her dark glossy hair swinging over her face, over the curves of her lips and cheekbones, so that I can't see her properly, even in my mind's eye. It's probably just as well, though, that Paul isn't here to answer my questions. If I started talking to him about Rachel, I'd be part of her triangle again, and I know that it would be better to stay out of it. Actually, I'm probably still in it, but edging my way to a different place; slowly, slowly, but I'll get there, eventually.

CHAPTER THIRTY-SEVEN

Menabilly, January 1960

A new year, a new decade, but Daphne felt caught in the past, not just Branwell's, but her own. She was working on the book for long hours every day, determined to finish it before Winifred Gerin completed her biography, forcing herself into the writing hut every morning, whatever the weather, wrapped up in a blanket in front of her typewriter, while the wind rattled the windows. Sometimes, in the dark evenings, she longed to see a child's face at the window, like Cathy's ghost in *Wuthering Heights*, or to feel its ice-cold hand reaching out to hers; to hear its voice saying, 'Let me in – let me in', and she would welcome it in, she would welcome the ghost of the young Branwell if he came back to his Cornish motherland. But it was not Branwell that she glimpsed one night at the window of her writing hut, but herself as a child, a frightened child who did not realise that she was seeing herself in the future; a child aghast at the grey-haired woman working in her shabby hut, an old-looking woman surrounded by the dark woods, lost in the wilderness of her thoughts.

But no, this will not do, Daphne told herself, to dwell on the child she once was. 'Children do not see into the future,' she wrote, in her notebook. 'Remember the Brontës, who wrote their youthful diary papers, knowing nothing of their deaths to come; early deaths, yet whose shadows do not fall across their present, which is long past now.' Yet still her thoughts circled around her, filling the hut in eddying currents of anxiety. Branwell had been troubled by nightmares of phantoms as a child, just like her cousins Peter and Michael, who had seen ghosts coming into their windows at night, the shadow of Peter Pan, or was it their dead father they had seen, or another phantom conjured up by Uncle Jim?

But Branwell had nothing to do with Peter or with Michael, she must not let these boys get muddled in her head; Branwell's Angria was not the same as Neverland, and she must concentrate on mapping out his world, the infernal world that would provide the title to her biography of him. Her eyes ached, like her head, when she tried to assemble the Angrian manuscripts into order, for though some had been transcribed by her researchers at the British Museum, others remained unreadable. But as far as she could tell, Branwell's history of the kingdom of Angria was told in nine parts, including many poems, covering dozens of sheets of manuscripts, all of them written in microscopic handwriting, and now scattered between various collections: the British Museum, the Brontë Parsonage, the Brotherton Collection, and elsewhere, sold to an unknown number of private collectors by that scoundrel, T. J. Wise, with Charlotte's name forged on the pages, if necessary. It was a gigantic fantasy, this imaginary colony of Angria, founded by Branwell's soldiers and adventurers when he was eleven or twelve years old, split into kingdoms and then united into an empire; Branwell the chief architect of its constitution and the commander of its army, the boy who noted every detail of the Angrian geography and population. He drew its maps, recorded its military and political history, and the life stories of the individual Angrian leaders, describing in minute detail their personal appearances, their hopes and fears and failings and triumphs.

And yet it had all come to nothing, for even as Branwell's alter ego, Northangerland, had journeyed through the world, Branwell had declined at home in Haworth, burnt up with thwarted hopes and frustrations, while Angria was always just out of reach, a promised land that remained beyond his horizon; a forgotten kingdom now, locked away in airless library vaults and museum cabinets. But would anyone else care about Branwell and Angria? Daphne knew she could not prove his literary worth to the world – his writing was naïve and undisciplined, and what did it matter that Wise had forged Charlotte's signature on some of Branwell's Angrian chronicles, for those pages were no more finely written than any of the others; they were all a rambling childish fantasy. Poor Branwell, whose early talent had never unfurled itself into a novel to equal *Jane Eyre* or *Wuthering Heights*; poor Branwell, whose only champion was an ageing novelist in a draughty hut in Cornwall; a woman out of time with the outside world, trying to rescue a boy who never came into his own.

Nor did Branwell's love-life amount to anything, for Daphne was now certain that he imagined the entire affair with Mrs Robinson, the mother of the boy he had tutored, before losing his job for some unspecified act of gross misconduct. As for what that act might have been: Daphne had no proof – for there was nothing but hearsay and gossip about the supposed affair, nor any detail about the circumstances of his dismissal – but she could not help wondering if Branwell had perhaps tried to lead his young charge astray, had made tentative sexual advances towards the thirteen-year-old Edmund Robinson? Something had gone badly wrong for Edmund; he never married, and drowned before he grew old . . . Just like Michael, but what was she to make of that? What was she to make of anything?

Back in the big house, Tommy was writing a little book of his own, a short history of the Queen's life when she was Princess Elizabeth, covering the period while Tommy had been Comptroller of the Royal household. He seemed calm enough, and as far as Daphne could tell, the Snow Queen had removed herself entirely from his life, from their lives; Daphne must have rescued him from her icy grip, without even realising. Yet sometimes, Daphne found herself wondering if a sliver of glass has remained lodged in his eye, and hers; if perhaps they were both deluding themselves now; and her cousin Peter, too, who was engaged on what appeared to be a never-ending task of editing his family history. 'How goes the Family Morgue?' she said to him on the telephone, in their weekly conversation.

'Rotten,' said Peter, 'sometimes I can't see the point of going on with it all . . .'

'I do feel for you, darling,' she said, 'I truly do. The middle of a book is always the hardest to write, and now that I'm halfway through this hideous marathon of Branwell's biography, I can't imagine making it to the end.'

'Ah, but you will finish it,' he said. 'You are a natural survivor, Daph, even though you don't necessarily realise it. You'll always make it through to the end.'

Then Peter sighed, so deeply that she felt his unhappiness seeping out of the phone line, into the receiver she held to her ear; and she imagined the two of them in a sepulchre, picking over the bones of corpses, making notes as they sat there, surrounded by the skeletons and skulls.

But she must not give in; she must bring the dead alive again, like Rebecca, whose body was washed up from the sea, who was buried in a family crypt, yet who walked again. 'Walks again,' whispered Rebecca's voice in Daphne's ear. 'Present tense, and still waiting for you . . . I made you rich, but Branwell will make you nothing, his story will never be read and remembered like mine. Forget him, forget Michael, forget Edmund, forget all of those lost boys . . .'

Occasionally, on her afternoon walk through the woods (a brief respite from the writing hut, snatched in the short hours of daylight), Daphne came across the two elderly ladies, one of them blind, who lived in what used to be a gamekeeper's cottage, halfway between Menabilly and the sea. She was not sure if they were sisters or friends – she wondered if they were once lovers; if they looked at her, and recognised her as one of their own – but the Menabilly housemaids said that that the blind one was a psychic medium, who summoned up the voices of the dead at weekly seances in the cottage. It remained unclear whether or not the maids' gossip was entirely true, but Daphne longed to know; and a part of her hoped to be invited by the pair into the cottage, though she also felt repelled by them for reasons she did not quite understand, by their grey tweed skirts and masculine shirts, by their direct gazes. Even the blind one stared straight at Daphne, but what did she see? Did she see Daphne with Gertie Lawrence? Did she see their kisses, or something more than that?

She wondered if Branwell might make his presence felt at a seance, and what would he say, if he did? Would he still be a hopeless reprobate, asking for a sovereign to spend on gin and laudanum, or would his spirit have been purified? Daphne had even considered taking a dose of laudanum herself, to share the same sensations as Branwell. Indeed, she had got as far as procuring a phial from a helpful local chemist; 'purely in the interests of research', she'd explained to him. But when it came to swallowing the drug, she could not do it – she felt suddenly terrified of what she might see or hear whilst under its influence – and poured it down the basin of the downstairs lavatory. Afterwards, she washed her hands, and then returned to her hut, feeling shaky and yet also inspired, and wrote a scene for the biography, as if through the eyes of Branwell, when his pain and misery were blotted out by laudanum, but just before oblivion descended upon him, he saw visions of his dead mother and sister, the two Marias, mother and daughter, their shining faces merging into one.

Daphne had read the stories about Branwell's laudanum-induced debauchery – the upset candles, burning bedclothes, concealed carving knives – but somehow, when she came to write them herself, she could not see Branwell in her mind, but Hindley Earnshaw in *Wuthering Heights*, and even that figure was unclear, his face in shadow. And at night, half-dreaming, half-awake and fretting about her book, she dozed and saw Tommy's face instead of Hindley's, drugged and weeping, like he was in the nursing home; but he was not being cared for by nurses, he'd escaped and come back to Menabilly, a carving knife hidden beneath his navy flannel dressing gown, making his way to her bedroom, carrying a candle in his shaking hand. In the dream, her husband was menacing, yet also pathetic, and she felt a sudden wave of sympathy for him, at the same time as fear. When she woke − lying there alone in her bed, in the dark − she wondered if Tommy was sleeping in the bedroom along the corridor.

And where was Branwell in all of this? A lost boy, still, along with all the others, though his face was not at the window, and his fingers did not tap at the glass.

CHAPTER THIRTY-EIGHT

Newlay Grove, March 1960

Symington would not move, he could not move, he had taken to his bed. Beatrice would have to put the bed in a removal van and shift him along with the rest of the furniture, if she was to have her way, and sell the house. 'This place is crumbling around us,' she said, despairingly, 'and there's no money to fix the roof, the rain has been pouring into the attic all winter, and now it's running down the walls, into your study, Alex, the damp is getting everywhere. *Alex*, are you listening to me?'

He opened his eyes and regarded her, briefly, and then closed them again. He knew about the leaking roof and the rising damp; he knew that the mildew had crept through his boxes and files and cartons, like a curse. A fortnight ago, while he was still able to get up and down the stairs, he had examined his most precious manuscripts, and found them covered in green mould. The pages of Emily's notebook of poems were damp and clammy, like his hands, and his fingers were trembling while he tried to rub the mildew from the paper, and the ink had come away beneath his touch, disappearing into the mould. Emily's words were becoming invisible, and so were Branwell's; but then so much of Branwell's writing had always been as good as invisible; still impossible to make sense of, even after all these years of living with it, of tracing his fingers over Branwell's words.

Symington had felt the mildew rise from the pages and into his mouth, and now it was mouldering in his lungs, he knew it was taking a hold of him there, colonising his body, its tentacles spreading steadily, like they had done through the house. Beatrice had sent for the doctor, who said he was suffering from pneumonia, and must be moved to hospital, but Symington refused to go. 'I am not going anywhere,' he said.

He was not writing, either. His last letter to Daphne was posted several weeks ago, when he had felt compelled to tell her that Lord Brotherton had never even seen or handled the Brontë manuscripts in his collection. 'I had everything to do with the whole collection,' he had written to Daphne, in a sudden fit of irritation. 'Lord Brotherton just financed my activities.' And yesterday, finally, a letter had arrived from Daphne, brought up by Beatrice to his bedroom, along with a cup of weak tea. 'Shall I read it aloud to you?' she asked; and he said no, he would do so himself, and Beatrice had looked annoyed, and clicked her tongue.

'Dear Mr Symington,' he read. 'I have left you without news for too long, but I am happy to report that at long last I am close to completing the book about Branwell. I must tell you, however, that I have been very disappointed in the manuscripts I had transcribed for me at the British Museum. I had hoped that they would at last show us something that would put Branwell on a level with Charlotte and Emily, or at least with Anne, but alas, the writing is very immature, even for a young man, and the stories make tedious reading, very verbose and difficult to follow, and after ploughing through them for all this time, I have reluctantly come to the conclusion that his writing talent was not equal to his sisters', and he was chiefly remarkable for working out the conception of Angria, and its history, politics, geography, etc. It is disappointing, because I had hoped to quote large extracts from all the manuscripts, but frankly, apart from a page or two, I shall not bother to do so. In other words, Branwell turns out not to be the man I had hoped him to be . . .'

Symington felt a terrible misery descend upon him as he read, and he wanted to stop reading, wanted to throw her letter to the floor, or tear it up into tiny pieces, obliterate her words, but he could not, he had to reach the end. 'Nevertheless,' continued Daphne's brisk typescript, 'I think I have followed Branwell's career from childhood and boyhood through to manhood and decline in a clear, straightforward fashion, quoting extracts from prose and poems where necessary (the ordinary reader is going to be a bit fuddled by Angria but it can't be helped, there is scarcely anything of Branwell's that is *not* Angrian) and I have taken the line that there was *not* anything in the Robinson affair, I am more than ever certain that Branwell imagined the whole thing . . .'

He put the letter down, and stopped reading. So, Daphne had given up on Branwell, too; and for all her early promises of championing him, she had joined his detractors, and marked him down as a deluded fantasist, an untalented writer who had imagined the unhappy love affair that had been the cause of his decline and death. Well, so be it.

'You have made your own bed, and now you can lie in it,' murmured his mother's voice in his ear.

'That's no help,' he muttered, 'but when were you ever a help to me?'

'I've always helped you, Alex,' said Beatrice, 'I've always done my best by you and your boys.'

The boys, thought Symington, and his lips made a shape of the words. The boys. They were all scattered now, over the oceans and across the waves, gone far from home, and they were lost to him, lost like Emily's words.

'Shall I ask Douglas to come and visit you?' said Beatrice.

But Symington was deep in the darkness that seeped through his head, and he did not hear her. 'Branwell,' he whispered, his lips barely moving.

'Burn what?' said Beatrice. 'I can't understand what you're trying to tell me, Alex. You'll have to try to say it more clearly . . .'

'Branwell Brontë,' murmured Symington, but he did not speak again.

CHAPTER THIRTY-NINE

Hampstead, September

I am sitting in my room – a room of my own – at the top of the house, a little attic with a view of the rooftops and chimney pots, and if I lean out of the window, I can see the heath, and the rooks circling over the trees in the evenings. I've rented it from a couple who need a bit of extra help with childcare, and I can hear their boys playing football outside in the garden; there's three of them, all under ten, and the deal is that I do a couple of nights' babysitting each week. I don't mind – I like the children, I even like their noise, the way their voices fill the house, and they seem to like me, as well. I play endless games of Monopoly and snap with them, and it means my rent is less than it would be, so I can afford to live quite close to the bookshop, and still walk to work. I think Paul would have preferred it if I'd moved further away, to the other side of London, but I don't see why I should. It's not him that's keeping me here in Hampstead, and it's not anything to do with staying near to Daphne's childhood home, not really, though it's a familiar part of my landscape. This is where I grew up, and I happen to like it round here, whether or not I bump into Paul again.

As it happens, I haven't seen Paul, nor Rachel either, not since she came into the bookshop earlier this month, but I rang her a couple of days ago, and got her address, which wasn't far away, just on the other side of the heath in Highgate. 'Are you coming to visit me?' she'd said, and I said no, but I was sending her a set of copies of the Symington and du Maurier letters in the post.

'That's very generous of you,' she said; but I didn't feel like I was being self-sacrificing. It made me feel good, actually, to let go of those letters. I mean, I still have my own set of copies, but I've put them in a file at the bottom of a drawer in my desk. I don't need to do anything with them – not just yet, anyway. I'm not going to do a PhD on du Maurier and the Brontës; I'm not going back to college again. I'm not sure what I will do, actually, but I'm happy at the moment. I feel as free as I've ever been, the same feeling as when I was running along the cliffs from Menabilly last month, though without the undercurrent of fear. I can't really explain why – though I suppose it's got something to do with leaving Paul, at last, and earning my own living, and I've just got back in touch with my friend Jess, and she said it was so good to hear from me again, and that I should come out to America to visit her this winter.

But there's something liberating, also, in not knowing what's going to happen next. I think that's why I don't want to write a dissertation – I don't want to try to marshal my feelings about Daphne du Maurier into a neat academic theory, though admittedly, I still find myself wondering about her, from time to time, and trying to work out what she means to me. But I don't believe that her stories define me any more; I don't feel like I'm living in some echoing version of *Rebecca* or *My Cousin Rachel*. I don't look in the mirror and see anyone but me.

'Don't look back . . .' That's what Paul said to me, when we said goodbye. I'm not sure whether he meant it literally – that he didn't want me to turn round and wave as I walked down the street. Or am I supposed to be moving on, and not dwelling on the past? If that's what he meant to suggest, then of course, it's not possible. I went back to my parents' flat the other day – I just wanted to look at the outside of the house, and then I noticed the elderly couple who'd lived in the flat below ours, and they recognised me, and waved from the front door. They'd been out shopping, and invited me to come in for a cup of tea, so I did, and we ended up talking about my parents, because this couple had owned their flat for years, even before my parents had married, when my father was living there alone. I can't understand why I hadn't asked them about my father before now, it would have been so easy, but I suppose I had a sort of tunnel vision; as if no one else could know anything about my father, just because I didn't know him.

Anyway, it turns out that my father and the man in the flat below, Mr Miller, had a shared interest in local history, and apparently my father had been researching the life of a bookish Victorian, Sir William Robertson Nicoll, who had owned Bay Tree Lodge, the house that was later converted into the flats where we lived. 'As I recall, your father was rather disappointed than no one shared our interest in Nicoll,' said Mr Miller. 'He'd approached several publishing companies about writing a biography, but they all told him that his subject was far too obscure to sell. Such are the demands of the modern marketplace . . .'

Frankly, Nicoll sounded pretty obscure to me, as well, but his name was familiar, for some reason – maybe because my mother had mentioned it to me as a child, though I couldn't remember her doing so. And then all of a sudden, it clicked. 'That's extraordinary,' I said, nearly knocking over my teacup in my excitement. 'Sir Robertson Nicoll was a former president of the Brontë Society, wasn't he? I bought his biography in a second-hand book shop in Haworth earlier this year.'

The Millers seemed less surprised by this coincidence than I was – they just sort of took it in their stride, and carried on chatting about how Robertson Nicoll had been a great friend of J. M. Barrie, and that my parents had taken me to see *Peter Pan* when I was a very little girl, and I'd been frightened, and couldn't sleep that night, in case Peter came to get me, and carried me away out of the window. 'You were still too young, I suppose, for the theatre,' said Mrs Miller. 'You can't have been much more than three – just a baby, really.'

'I only dimly remember it,' I said. 'I don't really remember the theatre, except for the little light that danced in the darkness, which was Tinkerbell, and everyone had to shout out that they believed in fairies, so that she didn't die. And then afterwards, being scared in my bedroom, that's got sort of merged into a different memory, from when I was older, and I'd been reading *Wuthering Heights*, and my mother was already asleep, and I thought I could hear Cathy's ghost at the window, but then it turned out to be a strand of ivy, brushing against the glass.'

'You were such a sweet, serious child,' said Mrs Miller, 'always with your head in a book.'

'No bad thing, that,' said her husband. 'Out of children's books come the eerie landscapes of imagination. Just look at *Peter Pan.*'

'It's quite odd,' I said, 'because I've been doing some research into Daphne du Maurier, and it seems that her father was also great friends with Barrie – Gerald was the first Captain Hook and Mr Darling in the stage version of *Peter Pan.*'

'Ah yes, the doubling,' said Mr Miller. 'The good father and the bad one. The shadow side that every child fears . . .'

'You can tell that he did his degree in psychology, can't you?' said Mrs Miller, and they both started laughing in a comfortable way, and I looked at them, and realised how happy they were together, and a bit of me wished that I was part of their family – that they could be my grandparents – but it was just a pang, not a terrible heartache; and I reminded myself of my new vow, which is to make friends, but not try to attach myself to people too soon; not to repeat the mistakes I made with Paul and Rachel.

I said I ought to be getting home – it was my evening for babysitting – but as I was leaving, they asked me round to dinner next week, and they said they'd introduce me to their nephew, which was nice of them; he's my age, apparently, and has just moved to London. On the way back, I went along Church Row, as the late afternoon sunlight was slanting over the graveyard where Daphne's relatives are buried – all those du Maurier headstones, crowded together as if in a family gathering, her grandparents, George and Emma, and her parents, Gerald and Muriel, and Gerald's sister Sylvia, who died young, like her husband, Arthur, and their children, the five lost boys who Barrie had adopted. And I wondered if my father had thought about them, too, as he walked this way, along the pavement where the du Mauriers walked, my feet following in his footsteps, and theirs.

Or was he just interested in Robertson Nicoll? And did he ever make the connection between Nicoll and J. M. Barrie, who must have come to visit him here? Did he think of them as he walked along Church Row, or in the hidden lanes just to the north of the graveyard, where there is a beautiful little chapel that still seems as remote from the city as it must have done when my father first came to Hampstead, and long before that, too, when Nicoll and Barrie strolled together through these peaceful streets, talking of Charlotte Brontë. I wanted it all to make sense – to fall into place, like the missing pieces of a jigsaw puzzle – but it didn't, not really. I wanted it to be meaningful, but to be honest, it seemed a bit random, though there were those oddly chiming resonances: me buying the book about Nicoll in Haworth, not realising that I had grown up in his house; not knowing anything of my father's interest in him, and bringing the book home to Hampstead, but never reading it, because I was more obsessed by Symington.

When I got back to my room, I found the biography of Nicoll, and examined it more carefully. There was the in-scription I remembered on the frontispiece – Christmas 1925, To J. A. Symington. But what I hadn't noticed before was the signature beneath, in rusty-coloured ink, so faded that it had nearly disappeared: 'from T. J. W.'. So it had to be from Wise, it just had to be, and I was holding in my hands a book that Wise had held in his; a book whose pages had been turned by Symington. I went through the chapters, more carefully than I'd done before, and came across some photographs – of Bay Tree Lodge at the end of the nineteenth century, and the book-lined library inside – and I wondered if my father had studied the same photographs, if he had longed to be able to go back in time as I had done, to slip into an old photograph, or between the printed lines of a page; to become a bystander in the past, to see it as it really was, rather than as it has been seen in retrospect.

Since then, I've tried to read Nicoll's biography, but to be honest, it's quite boring. Yes, he knew some interesting people – Barrie, and George du Maurier, and Robert Louis Stevenson – and he founded and edited a successful journal, the *British Weekly*, as well as writing a series of volumes called *Literary Anecdotes of the Nineteenth Century*, in which he collaborated with T. J. Wise, of all people, though I suppose at that point Wise was still highly regarded as a bibliophile, and not yet disgraced for his forgeries and thefts. Apparently Volume II, which appeared in 1895, included a fairy tale said to have been written by Charlotte Brontë at the age of fourteen, which came from Wise's collection of manuscripts; and I've also come across a story that has Nicoll travelling to Ireland with his friend Wise, in search of more of the Brontë manuscripts and relics taken there by Charlotte's widower. So I can understand why my father was interested in Nicoll, but I can also see why very few other people are. Surely it would have made far more sense to have written a biography of Wise – who turns out to have lived just round the corner from

Robertson Nicoll, in Heath Drive – given that my father's work at the British Museum would have presumably given him access to some of the details of Wise's scandalous forgeries and thefts? But other people's obsessions and passions must remain incomprehensible, I suppose.

I've also dug out my father's leather-bound notebooks, and tried to decipher his writing, now that I know he was researching Nicoll. There's a quotation that I've only just discovered is from a J. M. Barrie novel, that my father copied out on the opening page in professionally neat copperplate: 'The life of every man is a diary in which he means to write one story, and writes another; and his humblest hour is when he compares the volume as it is with what he vowed to make it.' Aside from those lines, I can recognise a few names in the rest of the notebooks – J. M. Barrie, Clement Shorter, T. J. Wise – and the occasional address, like Heath Drive or Bay Tree Lodge, but it's still almost entirely illegible, it seems to be mostly written in a sort of coded shorthand of his own devising, or maybe it's not, maybe I just can't make out the tiny scratchy marks of his pen. I know I could drive myself mad, trying to understand the hieroglyphics, using a magnifying glass or whatever, but I'm not going to. I've got my father's notebooks, and that will have to be enough. Although actually, today I bought a black notebook that looks almost exactly like his, and I've written my name on the inside cover, and when I start filling the empty pages in my own handwriting, I think it will be legible.

There's one good thing that emerged out of my father's notebooks. I was looking at them just now, before I put them away into a drawer of my desk, and for some reason, as I glanced out of the window, out across the rooftops and up into the sky, which seems so high and clear tonight, I thought of that day in Fowey with my mother, standing on the cliffs by St Catherine's Castle, and I remembered what she said, finally; it just came into my head, without me trying, without me searching for it.

I was holding my mother's hand, and she said, don't go too close to the edge; but I wanted to see the waves crashing on the rocks below. So we were standing there together, my hand in hers, and she said, 'Don't keep looking down, sweetheart. Look out to sea – it goes all the way to the sky. Just look how far you can see, Jane . . . You can see forever today.'

CHAPTER FORTY

Menabilly, April 1960

The phone call, very early in the morning, woke Daphne from sleep. At first, she was confused, thinking that the ringing was the bell on Cannis Rock, out beyond the headland, being tolled by the swell of the sea, in warning to boats that might run aground on the reef, and she was struggling to reach it, to surface from a dream; but then she realised it was the telephone in her bedroom, the one she kept there for emergencies.

'Hello?' she said, her voice still thick and heavy with sleep.

'Daphne,' said a woman's voice, 'I'm so sorry to wake you, but I have very bad news.' She paused, as if choking back a sob, and for an awful moment Daphne thought that it was the Snow Queen, ringing to tell her that Tommy had shot himself in London, for he had been there for the last few days.

'It's Margaret,' said the woman, and then Daphne recognised her voice, Peter's wife; what the hell was she ringing about, at six thirty in the morning? 'I had to call you, before you saw the papers,' she said. 'I didn't want you to find out the news that way. Peter killed himself last night, and it's going to be everywhere this morning, the reporters were on to it from the start.'

'That's impossible,' said Daphne. 'I can't believe it . . .'

'Well, I'm afraid it's happened,' said Margaret. 'He threw himself under a tube train at Sloane Square yesterday evening. I can't talk now, Daphne, but I'd appreciate it if you could tell your sisters, before they see some hideous headline this morning.'

'Of course,' said Daphne, 'but Margaret, this is terrible, there must be something else I can do? Please tell me if there's anything I can do to help.'

'I fear it's too late for that,' said Margaret, and then there was nothing, just the click of the receiver, and silence.

Daphne felt breathless, there was no air in the room; she lay down on her bed, but that was worse, she couldn't breathe, so she sat up again and put her head between her knees, then went to the window, and opened it wide. It had rained in the night, but the sky was clearing, and there were gleaming ribbons of light streaming down across the sea. 'The Spirit moving on the Waters,' Tommy used to say, whenever they'd seen the same light, that often appeared to be shining over the sea after heavy rain or a stormy day. 'Oh God,' said Daphne, quietly. 'I have failed in every way.'

She had finished her book, less than a week before, and had sent Peter a copy of the final draft. Indeed, she had rung him three days ago, to tell him to expect it in the post, and to share her sense of triumph at getting it to her publishers long before Winifred Gerin had completed her biography. Now, she found it hard to remember why she had cared so much about Branwell Brontë, or what had made her so determined to win her race to outdo a rival author; but she forced herself to remember the details of the final telephone conversation she'd had with him. What had she said to Peter, and how could she not have realised that he was suicidal? It was so brief, that was the trouble; and she had made it brief, she had not given Peter sufficient time to talk about himself, or to share his troubles with her. She told him that she had delivered her biography, at last, and that it was to be titled, *The Infernal World of Branwell Brontë*, and dedicated to the mysterious Mr Symington. 'Not that I'll say "mysterious",' she said to Peter. 'I shall keep it concise, something along the lines of, "To J. A. Symington, editor of The Shakespeare Head Brontë, whose life-long interest in Branwell Brontë stimulated my own." That should keep him happy, don't you think?'

But Peter had said very little in response, just that he was 'sinking under the weight of the Family Morgue'; those were his words, 'I am sinking . . .' Yet she had not taken them seriously, just brushed them aside, instead of reading between the lines. 'I must let you get on,' she'd said, her cue to him that she had other things to do and was ending the conversation. Afterwards, she'd sent him a copy of her final draft of the book, and a note, saying, 'I am imbued with consumption, schizophrenia, epilepsy, sleep-walking, split personality, alcoholism – the (Brontë) Works. Hopefully, you will delight in it.'

And now she felt wretched and worthless, knowing that he would have received the package on the morning of his suicide. She did not know whether he'd started reading the book – Daphne hoped not – but when she rang Peter's younger brother, Nico, before breakfast, to try to discover more about the circumstances of Peter's death, he mentioned to her that it had arrived in the first post, at the office he shared with Peter in Great Russell Street; that Peter had even commented on the manuscript to him. 'He said something about the Brontë family history being slightly less oppressive than our own,' Nico told her.

'And what else?' said Daphne.

'Well, there's much I can tell you,' he said. 'Peter was still in the office at five o'clock, and that's when I headed off home. He told me he had an appointment with an author, but apparently he just went to the bar of the Royal Court hotel, spent some time alone there, drinking, before crossing the road to Sloane Square tube station, where he threw himself under the first passing train.'

The papers had been full of it, of course, just as Margaret had warned her; the headlines were everywhere, and they stuck in Daphne's head, like a foolish song from a West End musical or a jaunty nursery rhyme. PETER PAN'S DEATH LEAP. THE BOY WHO NEVER GREW UP IS DEAD. THE FINAL FLIGHT OF PETER PAN.

The headlines were bad enough, but what was even more tormenting was her imagined enactment of the scene; for however hard Daphne tried to concentrate on something else, *anything* else, she could not escape returning to Peter's suicide . . . It was a Tuesday evening, 5 April, just yesterday, but it was a lifetime ago. There had been a spring breeze in Menabilly, and even the city streets might have seemed fresher than before, if you were young and hopeful, but Peter did not feel the warmth in the air, nor the blossom budding on the trees, he felt nothing but the darkness around him as he hurried to the tube station, and down the steps, the same steps that Daphne took every time she went to and from their flat in London. Then he was out on to the platform, not stopping to look at anyone, just gripped by tunnel vision, looking into the tunnel, readying himself to step over the edge, leaping in front of the first incoming train. And Daphne saw him, then, caught by the headlights, just for a split second, flying in a swan dive . . .

But what was Peter thinking? Daphne could not imagine what was going through his head before he smashed it to pieces; even though she was trying to, as she typed a letter to Nico, now the only surviving one of her cousins. He would dismiss her as absurdly sentimental, perhaps, because she was writing to him that she believed that Peter would make his way out of the impasse of Purgatory, having finally had it out with Uncle Jim. 'It may be, that in creating Peter Pan, Uncle Jim planted the seeds of the real Peter's destruction,' she wrote to Nico. 'But I can see Peter shaking hands with Uncle Jim, everything settled in the end, and rushing into Sylvia's arms, his mother's arms at last, because really, it was about time he did, having longed for her for about fifty years.' She typed on and on, the typewriter keys making their comfortingly familiar click-clack, describing her lunches with Peter at the Café Royal. 'We talked of grandpapa George, who as you know lived for a time just a few doors along from your offices in Great Russell Street, before moving the family to Hampstead. We talked of the past, sometimes with weeping nostalgia (after the second Dubonnet) and later with uproarious and irreverent hilarity (after the third).'

Daphne paused, overcome with remorse again, knowing that Peter would not see the unveiling of the plaque commemorating their grandfather's former house on Great Russell Street – a ceremony which had been planned for the end of March, but which she, Daphne, had delayed, in order to finish her wretched book about Branwell, even though it was Peter who had gone to the trouble of editing their grandfather's letters. And now the ceremony was to take place next week, which was too late for Peter. Poor Peter . . .

'I believe so tremendously in an after-life,' she continued in her letter, 'and indeed, it was one of our regular topics of conversation at the Café Royal, and Peter *then* seemed to be undecided about it. My insistence that our grandparents, along with Gerald and Sylvia, were delighted to see us lunching together, would bring a dubious nod of his head. "You're probably right," he would say, eventually. So, dearest Nico, one knows that all is well.'

But she did not know that all was well, and what would Peter think of her now; if indeed he was still thinking? Daphne started typing again, tears running down her face, though she did not pause to wipe them away. 'What angers me, and makes me question myself, is that possibly if I had sent Peter a very jolly letter just beforehand (intended, and never written, you know how it is), it might have tipped the scales for him, from frustrated despair to at least a momentary chuckle.' But she had not sent him a jolly letter, just a manuscript of her depressing book about an alcoholic failure, and that stupid note, that Peter might have taken as a reference to his own depression and drinking, and his sense that he had never really come to anything, for his publishing company was winding down, and he was being forced to leave the offices in Great Russell Street, they were too expensive for him, he'd admitted as much to Daphne on the telephone when they'd spoken last month, the time before the last time, and yet another occasion when she had failed him.

'You're the only true success amongst us,' he'd said to Daphne, and she'd said no, don't be so silly; but she should have said more, she should have said that she had admired him, that he never published anything cheap or tawdry or sensational, that his edition of their grandfather's letters represented everything that was true and good about the family; that she was the one who had let everyone down, not him.

Daphne sighed, and returned to her letter to Nico. 'Being myself, constantly, and for no earthly reason, a potential suicide, I don't think one does it from despair, but from anger – it's a hit out at THE OTHERS – The Others being, to the potential suicide, everything that ONE is not. The violent feelings rising within can only be assuaged by greater violence, hence Peter's decision to kill himself beneath the wheels of the train. The off-balance Self says to the mythical Others, "If this is what you are doing to me – Right, Here We Go." ' She stopped, appalled by her own words on the page before her. What if everything she was writing was meaningless? What if it all meant nothing, in the end? What then?

Newlay Grove,
Horsforth,
Leeds
Telephone: 2615 Horsforth

5th May 1960

Dear Miss du Maurier,
> *I am sure you will be sorry to hear that my dear husband has passed away. His funeral took place a fortnight ago. I am sorry not to have written sooner, but the shock has been terrible, and I am packing up our house, which has had to be sold, and I am to move to a very much smaller house, quite close to this one.*

Sadly, my husband died just a few days before the typescript of your book reached him in the post, so he did not have a chance to read it, nor did he see your kind dedication of the book to him. He would have so appreciated it, and to have known that it was his life-long interest in Branwell Brontë that stimulated your own, and encouraged you to undertake your recent biography of Branwell.

While I was going through my husband's study, I came across this package, which he had addressed to you, but not yet posted. I am therefore sending it on to you, and hope you will find the contents interesting,

Yours very sincerely,
Beatrice Symington

THE YORKSHIRE POST
PO Box No. 168
Leeds 1

Telephone: 32701 (22 lines)

1st June 1960

Dear Miss du Maurier,

Thank you very much for your letter, and for sending me a draft copy of your forthcoming book, *The Infernal World of Branwell Brontë*.

I have just finished reading it, and find it uncommonly good. The suggestion that Branwell had to leave Thorp Green because he had a bad influence on the boy has never appeared in print before, so far as I remember, but this possibility that the tutor was thought to be a dangerous influence on the child's mind and morals had long ago occurred to both Mrs Weir (my colleague at the *Yorkshire Post* and the Brontë Society) and myself. These are dark depths, and we cannot be sure of ever throwing strong light at what happened at Thorp Green and other places in Branwell Brontë's story.

Now to the other matter that you raised in your letter, a memorial fund for the late Mr Symington. I can understand your distress on receiving Mrs Symington's letter, and appreciate your sympathetic thoughts, as well as your observations about Mr Symington's considerable contribution to Brontë scholarship. But there is clearly much that you do not know about Mr Symington and his former relations with the Brontë Society and the University of Leeds. It is a sad and disturbing story, which is best kept confidential. I can rely on your discretion, I am sure, but you should be aware that in view of the trouble we had in our dealings with Mr Symington, it is most improbable that members of the Brontë Society would wish to contribute to the memorial fund you have in mind. At one time the Society was faced by the very disagreeable prospect of taking legal proceedings against Mr Symington. You will realise from this that the trouble was very serious. The less said about it the better, but Mr Symington was far from trustworthy in his dealings.

I notice from the bibliography of your excellent book that you purchased a number of Brontë manuscripts from Mr Symington. It is, I am sorry to say, entirely possible that the items sold to you by him may have come from the Parsonage Museum or the Brotherton Collection. He was forced to leave his post as librarian and curator to the Parsonage after various key items were found to be missing from the collection. Mr Symington subsequently left the Leeds University Library staff after it had been discovered that he took some of the manuscripts that the University considered its own. His explanation was that Lord Brotherton had told him that he could help himself to anything he wanted from the contents of the Brotherton Library, but he never produced any documentary support of this claim.

A very brief notice of Mr Symington's death was reported in the *Yorkshire Post* but there were evidently no tributes from the University or any members of the Brontë Society.

Yours sincerely
Linton Andrews

CHAPTER FORTY-ONE

Menabilly, June 1960

The darkness was dwindling now, the days lengthening toward midsummer, and Daphne listened to her grandchildren's voices calling out to each other across the lawn in front of Menabilly, where the long grass had just been mown. A blackbird sang in the chestnut tree, and the light was clear; the dust washed away by last night's rain. Tommy was outside with the grandchildren, rounding them up for a game of cricket; his face was less haggard, his hands less shaky than earlier this year. As Daphne looked out at him, through the open windows of the Long Room, she felt a rush of tenderness, seeing him take his granddaughter's hand, then limping slightly while he walked alongside her. She remembered the long-ago days when he had played on the lawn with their children, before the years had overtaken them; yet on a June morning such as this one, the past seemed to offer some promise of hope to the future.

When Daphne came out of the house, and walked across the grass, she called out to Tommy, saying that she would join them soon, as a wicket-keeper, but first she must spend a little while in her writing hut. 'I won't be long,' she said, 'I'm nearly finished.' In her hands were a brown-paper parcel and two letters that she laid out on her desk in the hut: the first a letter from Mrs Symington, that had accompanied the parcel, the second, which had only just been delivered today, from Sir Linton Andrews, the chairman of the Brontë Society, and editor of the *Yorkshire Post*.

Daphne had already replied to Beatrice Symington's letter, as soon as she received it last month, sending her heartfelt condolences, and expressing her admiration for Mr Symington, her sorrow that he had not lived to see the book that she had dedicated to him, and her thanks for the contents of the parcel. Immediately afterwards, she had written to Sir Linton Andrews, suggesting that a memorial of some kind be made in honour of Symington's unflagging work on behalf of Branwell Brontë. But Sir Linton's response was profoundly disturbing, as she read it through for the first time at her desk now. Of course, she noted his initial description of her biography as 'uncommonly good', which was encouraging, and went some way to allay her creeping fears that rather than resuscitating Branwell, she had killed him off, somehow smothering him within the pages of her biography; though she had not spoken of her anxiety about the forthcoming publication to anyone, feeling it to be dishonourable and selfish in the wake of Peter's death, which must take precedence over her own, more trivial worries about reviews and sales.

And at first, she thought Sir Linton was being particularly complimentary about her theory concerning Branwell's dismissal as tutor from the Robinson household; but a few seconds afterwards, on re-reading the relevant passage in his letter, she wondered if he might in fact be quietly reminding her that she was no closer to reaching the real truth about Branwell than anyone else had been.

His comments on Mr Symington, however, were forthright and to the point, and as soon as she reached this part of his letter, Daphne began to feel alarmed and angry and foolish and ashamed. How could she not have realised that Symington was quite such a slippery character? It wasn't just that odd encounter when she'd visited his house last winter, but also his evasiveness about spending time in the Parsonage library on her behalf. In fact, realised Daphne with a sinking heart, it might very well have been on his eventual trips to the Parsonage last year that he had pilfered more manuscripts, spurred on by her demands for fresh material.

And yet, she could not bring herself to condemn him altogether, for he had certainly not made himself rich on the proceeds of his obsessive collecting. When she had telephoned Symington's widow last month, soon after receiving the news of his death from pneumonia, it had become abundantly clear that the poor woman was left penniless; hence the sale of the house, and the brief report in the local paper that Mr Symington's estate had amounted to just over £400.

Still, it was also becoming evident to Daphne – even without Sir Linton's delicately phrased hints – that the manuscripts she had bought from Symington must now be donated to the Brontë Parsonage Museum, along with the two items sent to her in the parcel last month by Mrs Symington, which she picked up again now, and turned over in her hands. Daphne would be sad to lose these: the first a slim morocco leather-bound volume, containing the fragmentary drafts of a poem that T. J. Wise had attributed to Emily Brontë, and presumably sold as such, and yet which was clearly in Branwell's handwriting. Daphne liked the poem, even though it was obviously unfinished, and had copied it out in her own handwriting, and pinned it to the wall of her writing hut, where she glanced at the first stanza again:

> The Heart which cannot know another
> Which owns no lover friend or brother
> In whom those names without reply
> Unechoed and unheeded die.

She was also admiring of Mr Symington's perspicacity in recognising the handwriting as Branwell's – which he had pointed out to her in one of two notes tucked into the package posted by his widow (albeit written in the shakiest hand himself) – and also in identifying the poem as having been written on the back of Branwell's torn-up draft of a letter of application to study art at the Royal Academy. That Branwell had never become an art student – indeed, might never have posted his letter of application – seemed to Daphne to be a failure that was reflected again in Mr Symington's own failings. He had never written his book about Branwell Brontë; he had never proved that T. J. Wise had forged Charlotte Brontë's signature on Branwell's child-hood chronicles of Angria, or Emily's signature on Branwell's poetry; he had not even posted this letter, or the accompanying package, to Daphne; perhaps he had thought better of giving her either a gift of the manuscripts, or the insights in his letter. It had been left to his widow to do so, but that had been a matter of chance; she might very well have overlooked the package, in the stress of moving and sorting through his ramshackle library and study.

And whatever Mr Symington's intentions, his motives were difficult to fathom in the second handwritten note, which seemed to be less immediately relevant to the morocco leather-bound volume, or indeed to the question of Branwell Brontë. Daphne picked up this note, and looked at it again. On it, Mr Symington had written, '"Self-Interrogation": do with this what you will.' Presumably, his message concerned the other item in the parcel from Mrs Symington: a small, mildewed leather notebook, whose contents had been destroyed by rampant damp and mould. Daphne had, at first, intended to include this enigmatic note, and the ravaged notebook, in her package to the Brontë Parsonage Museum, with the morocco volume and the manuscripts of Branwell's poems and letters that she had previously purchased from Mr Symington.

At the last minute, however, she took out the little notebook, and Symington's one-line note to her. There could be no harm in keeping this back, when everything else was being returned to the Parsonage, to be examined and catalogued and exhibited to the world. But this: this belonged with Daphne, here in Menabilly; a wordless book in the wordless woods. Let it rest safely here with her, along with the others, the secrets and the ghosts.

Daphne stood up, put her head back, and stretched her arms, so that her fingertips reached the ceiling. Then she walked out of the writing hut, out of its shadows and into the sunlight, and the day was so bright, her eyes were dazzled, and as she stepped forward, she could not yet see what lay before her.

DAPHNE DU MAURIER FAMILY TREE

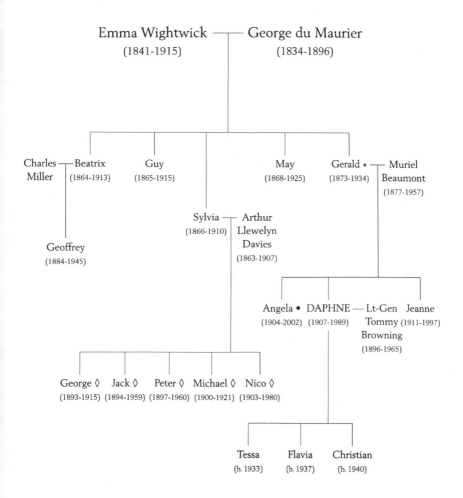

* Gerald du Maurier was friends with J.M. Barrie and played Captain Hook and Mr Darling in the first and subsequent productions of *Peter Pan*.

• Angela du Maurier, Daphne's older sister, played Wendy in a later production of *Peter Pan*.

◊ When the five Llewelyn Davies brothers – the inspiration for *Peter Pan* – were orphaned in 1910, they were adopted by J.M. Barrie.

ACKNOWLEDGEMENTS

Although this book is fiction, it is based on a true story. Like the contemporary narrator of my novel, I became utterly possessed by the story, and obsessed by the paper trail of Brontë manuscripts and what passed between Daphne du Maurier and John Alexander Symington; like her, I burrowed through the catacombs of library archives and second-hand bookshops to discover lost or forgotten letters; like her, I was born in Bay Tree Lodge in Hampstead, around the corner from the du Maurier and Llewelyn Davies family graves in Church Row, and Daphne's childhood home in Cannon Hall.

But unlike my narrator, I was fortunate enough to receive a great deal of help from the du Maurier family in researching this novel. I am grateful to Daphne's son and daughter-in-law, Christian and Hacker Browning, for their patience and good humour in the face of my questions, for their generosity in allowing me to see Ferryside and their hospitality whenever I came to Fowey. Daphne du Maurier's daughters, Lady Tessa Montgomery and Lady Flavia Leng, were similarly helpful, and provided a huge amount of insight and information, as did her grandson, Rupert Tower. I am also indebted to Henrietta Llewelyn Davies, greatgranddaughter of Sylvia Llewelyn Davies and great niece of Peter Llewelyn Davies, for her wise and perceptive advice.

Further insights into Daphne's story came from her friends, Oriel Malet and Maureen Baker-Munton (formerly Tommy Browning's secretary). Daphne's oldest friend, Mary Fox, who knew her from childhood, was kind enough to share her memories with me, as did Mary's sister, Pam Michael, and their nephew, Robert Fox, who visited Menabilly as a child.

Symington's grandson, Charles Symington, provided a great deal of background to his family history and the book trade. (He now runs an excellent bookbinders in York.) Juliet Barker, a former curator and librarian of the Brontë Parsonage Museum, was the first person to draw my attention to that most enigmatic of her predecessors, J. A. Symington, and her expertise has been invaluable; while her kindness extended to letting me stay with her in Yorkshire. I have also drawn on the definitive scholarship contained within her book, *The Brontës*.

Ann Dinsdale, Collections Manager at the Brontë Parsonage Museum, has been unfailingly helpful and knowledgeable in her responses to my queries, as has Andrew McCarthy, deputy director of the Brontë Parsonage Museum, along with the rest of the staff there. I would also like to thank the Brontë Society, in particular its president, Rebecca Fraser.

Uncovering the relevant letters and papers that I have drawn on in this novel would have been impossible without the help of Dr Jessica Gardner, Head of Special Collections at the University of Exeter, which holds the du Maurier family archive; Chris Sheppard, Head of Special Collections at the Brotherton Library at the University of Leeds; and John Smurthwaite, at the University of Leeds library, who is the author of *The Life of John Alexander Symington*.

I am also indebted to the following authors and books: Margaret Forster, *Daphne du Maurier*; Flavia Leng, *Daphne du Maurier: A Daughter's Memoir*; Angela du Maurier, *It's Only the Sister*; Oriel Malet, *Letters from Menabilly*; Andrew Birkin, *J. M. Barrie and the Lost Boys* and, of course, du Maurier's own autobiographical books, *Myself When Young*, *The Rebecca Notebook* and *Gerald*. These and hundreds more books (some of them very rare indeed) can be found at a wonderful bookshop, Bookends of Fowey (www.bookendsoffowey.com) which is run by Ann Willmore, a literary sleuth who not only helped me in my quest to untangle various du Maurier mysteries, but also – along with her husband, David – looked after me in Fowey.

The numbered page references in Symington's letter concerning his suspicions about forged Brontë signatures are accurate, and I have included them in this novel so that anyone who wishes to investigate further can check these against the facsimiles contained within the Shakespeare Head edition. The lines from Emily Brontë's poem, 'Self-Interrogation', are from the missing Honresfeld manuscript, which has not yet been found. As for the quotations I have used from Branwell Brontë's poetry: these come from manuscripts held at the Brontë Parsonage Museum, donated by Daphne du Maurier to the Parsonage, and originally sold to her by Symington. I have also consulted *The Works of Patrick Branwell Brontë*, edited by Victor A. Neufeldt, and *Emily Jane Brontë: The Complete Poems*, edited by Janet Gezari. Both of these professors were generous in sharing their time and knowledge with me, as were Professor Helen Taylor, Sally Beauman and Andrew Birkin.

Finally, thanks are due to my rigorous yet patient editors, Alexandra Pringle and Gillian Stern; my agent Ed Victor, along with his colleagues, Grainne Fox and Linda Van; Polly Samson, Ol Parker and Maggie O'Farrell, for their suggestions and incisive comments; my sons Jamie and Tom, who braved the Cornish winter and Menabilly ghosts with me; my husband, Neill MacColl, whose encouragement and support was entirely unlike the narrator's husband, even when I was at my most obsessive; and my mother, Hilary Britten, who kept me from giving up or going under.

A NOTE ON THE AUTHOR

Justine Picardie is the author of *If the Spirit Moves You: Life and Love After Death*, the novel *Wish I May* and, most recently, *My Mother's Wedding Dress*. She is also the co-writer or editor of several other books. She was formerly the features editor of British *Vogue* and is now a columnist for the *Sunday Telegraph Magazine* and also writes for *Harper's Bazaar*. She lives in London with her husband and two sons.

A NOTE ON THE TYPE

The text of this book is set in Berling roman. A modern face designed by K. E. Forsberg between 1951–58. In spite of its youth it does carry the characteristics of an old face. The serifs are inclined and blunt, and the g has a straight ear.